No plumber or me[illegible]ng an unskilled appre[illegible] if he did, expensive [illegible]e, and the customer [illegible]e-force, the equival[illegible]ns and backfiring ca[illegible]is-handling of incide[illegible]n-dous consequences for the 'customer', and which might never be rectified – once the legal process had closed in on and claimed a victim, it was virtually impossible to prise open its jaws. MacHale was aware that it was the public in those streets out there, as well as himself, who were vulnerable . . .

By the same author

The Animal Letter

ROD MILLER

The Commissioner's Cowboys

GRAFTON BOOKS

A Division of the Collins Publishing Group

LONDON GLASGOW

TORONTO SYDNEY AUCKLAND

Grafton Books
A Division of the Collins Publishing Group
8 Grafton Street, London W1X 3LA

A Grafton Paperback Original 1987

ISBN 0-586-06924-0

Printed and bound in Great Britain by
Collins, Glasgow

Set in Times

Contents

To 'Crazy Horse': a good street-cop who at least shared *some* compassion; and to the three Rs: Indians among the Cowboys, and Chiefs among the Indians.

PART ONE
Cowboys
1985

1

Three A.M.

The street . . . dark, deserted, eerie . . . blocks of minatory shadows, impenetrable to the eye . . .

A full, radiant moon; stars pulsating in the midnight-blue sky, charging the bitter cold; a translucent film of spangling, brittle frost . . . everywhere: clinging to the surface of the road, the roofs of parked cars, the pavements, the bare trees and withered gardens, the tiles of serried lines of semi-detached houses . . .

And a potent, unnatural stillness, intumescent with evil vibrations.

Suddenly, a shrill scream . . . terrifying, cracking through the frozen air, echoing . . . fading away . . . Then silence once again, but far more menacing than hitherto.

His body tensed and his senses bristled; no longer did he feel the burning cold, the hunger and the fatigue, which had threatened to overwhelm him only a moment ago; adrenaline ripped through his veins, touching-off an implosion of terror in his gut, and loosening his bowels; but he ran towards that which every vital part of him had commanded he must flee in the interests of self-preservation.

Relentlessly he pressed on, his boots slipping and sliding over the pavement, his left elbow clamping his helmet to his side, his right fist punching the air, his gaping mouth spurting plumes of vapour, high into the night sky. Yet he had the overwhelmingly frustrating notion that he was getting nowhere . . .

But now, as if by magic, he found himself outside

the house, his body steaming, his chest heaving, deeply distressed by an amorphous fear of . . . Death?

The house was in total darkness, but the front door was ajar, a wreath of holly affixed to it; and on the step, an enormous black cat with brilliant emerald eyes.

The cat rose to greet him, drawing him on . . . then brushed against his legs, buzzing with pleasure, saliva oozing from the corners of its mouth. Hands outstretched, he squatted, and moved to pick up the cat, wanting to caress it, to caress his own face with its warm, silken fur; but it retreated, its back arched, its fangs exposed, spitting and hissing; then it sprang at him, drawing its claws down the backs of his hands, ripping his flesh.

Curiously, he felt no pain as the blood flowed from his wounds and dripped steadily onto the frozen path . . . red blobs of ink on a pure-white blotter. He just stared at the cat, his mind empty, while the cat stared back at him.

Then it was gone. And the overpowering dread of Death returned.

Strange, therefore, that he should now find himself moving inexorably towards the half-open door . . . then past it, inside the house.

The room was wide, long, and bare. And freezing cold. Glittering cobwebs, weaved from gossamer-fine threads of ice, hung from wall-to-wall. He shivered, put on his helmet, and turned-up the collar of his mac. But he was sweating profusely, and a voice was cautioning him: 'Get out! Get out of here! Before it's too late!'

He turned to run, filled with panic, but was trapped. It was already too late.

The door slammed shut, and a searing hot wind rushed through the room, completely transforming it before his burning eyes: he now found himself surrounded by heavy, black, antique furniture; behind him, an open coal-fire was fiercely alight, its flames casting writhing shadows on the red-velvet-papered walls.

Without warning the door creaked slowly open, and a long, deep shadow fell across the floor. He gasped, bracing himself, but was nevertheless jolted by the demoniac scream which preceded her entrance.

She was . . . horrible! . . . evil! . . . lank, shoulderlength grey-hair, a gaunt, dirt-ingrained face with sharp, hooked nose, and wild, staring eyes that were dark pools of fermenting venom; blood dripped from her lower lip onto the front of her emaciated and naked body; in her right hand she held a long knife, its serrated blade glistening with a red wetness; her left hand held a glass tumbler, half full with the same, red wetness . . . Blood!

She giggled dementedly, stabbing the knife before herself, motioning him to look over his right shoulder.

He was shaking with fear. Slowly, reluctantly, he half-turned his head. Lying on a rug before the roaring fire was the most shocking thing he'd ever seen, or was ever likely to see; yet he was unable to stop himself turning fully to face it; it was as if he were mesmerized by it when it ought to have repelled him.

The corpse was that of an elderly lady; obese, wrinkled, blood-spattered . . . and horribly mutilated.

Her head, sparsely covered by wisps of fine, white hair, had been severed at the shoulders, then placed – eyes popping, mouth gaping, tongue protruding – face up, between her left arm and sagged breast. She'd been eviscerated, too, and the entrails were scattered along the hearth. Finally, a broom-handle had been rammed into her vagina, splitting her wide apart.

Sickeningly ritualistic.

The insane cackling forced him to disengage his eyes and turn back to face . . . The old lady's daughter?

'Yes!' she shrieked. 'Mother! . . . Who never loved father . . . And father! . . . Who never loved mother.'

Raising the glass tumbler to her lips, she took a mouthful of the viscous blood, chewing it voraciously. Then she began gnashing her broken, yellow teeth, and muttering obscenities . . . finally, screaming, 'He loved me! Not her!' as she jabbed the knife in the direction of the hearth.

What's the matter with her? he inwardly shouted. Can't she see I'm a police-officer?

He found himself moving towards her, holding forth his right hand, and, in a low voice, shot with fear, saying, 'Give it to me. Give me the knife.'

Her eyes refocused, and she prodded the knife at his chest. He hesitated, withdrew his hand, and she lunged at him, hurling into his face the contents of the glass tumbler.

His helmet fell to the floor as his hands clawed at his eyes; he tasted the tepid, sticky liquid, and felt nauseous. Then she was on him, and he felt the blade thudding deep into his gut, knocking every ounce of breath from his ruptured lungs. He doubled up, ripping open his mac and tunic, clutching his intestines as they burst forth from within him.

She was dancing all around him, the knife poised for a second strike, while he futilely groped at his side, trying to hook his thumb into the truncheon strap that dangled from his right, trouser pocket . . .

The knife flashed downward through an arc, its blade glinting in the firelight, and was embedded deep in his back. He fell to his knees, groaning; blood gushed up from within him, flooding his mouth and nostrils, his eye sockets, his ears; he was helplessly aware of the knife being twisted, and ripped free of him . . . then a sickening squelching sound as once more the blade hurtled into his back, knocking him onto his face . . .

He knew he was dying. But he wasn't in the least afraid. There was a pure, gently-rippling whiteness before his eyes . . . His last conscious thought was that he'd conquered Death.

2

As he hurtled back to reality, the brilliant whiteness became a haze . . . clearing . . . lingering in the preconscious state, where fantasy and reality fought for supremacy . . . his torso jolting upright, his left hand throwing back the bedclothes, his right hand twisting around and up towards the centre of his back, fingers groping wildly for the handle of the knife, his feet swinging down to touch the floor . . . running away . . . his eyes, jet black, wide in panic, frantically scanning for some familiar and reassuringly-benign object to lock-on to . . . his mind at last regaining its balance and bursting through to a stark awareness.

He came to an abrupt halt, his trembling hands moving up to cover his perspiring face . . . hagridden, on the verge of tears, breathless, his nerves snapping and twanging; the wet, dusky flesh of his taut body, glistening and rippling in the near darkness of the tiny bedroom.

But the tears just wouldn't come, no matter how hard he tried to force them up from his aching chest; maybe he was trying too hard; then again, maybe he wasn't trying hard enough . . .

Thank God he *hadn't* cried. Because . . . He shrugged . . . Well, just imagine it: a cop, *crying*! Jesus Christ!

What sort of a blood-'n'-guts, hell-raising, macho – above *all*, macho – cop would even *contemplate* shedding tears?

The idea of a cop with tears in his eyes was as untenable as the idea of a cop sucking his thumb . . . or a cop cuddling a teddy bear in bed . . . or a cop suffering a nervous breakdown because he could no longer cope with the vagaries of the job: the unexpected, *every* day, which filled him with a terrifyingly-real anxiety that something unspeakably dreadful *was* going to happen to him.

Maybe the Fear wasn't irrational, though? Dreadful things *did* happen to cops on the streets of the metropolis . . . all too often. Something dreadful had happened to MacHale himself, only eight weeks ago, and he'd just relived every wicked moment of it.

He turned on the light, his eyes squinting at the brightness, and sat, hunched over the edge of the bed, trying, once and for all, to rid himself of the horror.

He was twenty, a raw, inexperienced probationer, only months out of training, and almost recklessly eager and willing to . . . well, to do anything, anything which would, ultimately, earn him the approbation of his supervisors and colleagues at the nick. Jesus, how he'd love someone like Tasty Tom, or Punchy Paterson – or even Old Crikey – to say to him, 'John, you're one hell of a good copper, my son.' But he doubted that anyone whose opinion counted would *ever* say that to him.

His survival as a PC in The Job, depended almost exclusively on the number of offenders he was able to detect and bring to book. The training school had made him almost totally offence-orientated – or so it seemed – with all its instruction and advice on definitions of offences, procedures, powers of arrest and detention, suspects' rights, the rules of evidence . . . and so on . . . *ad infinitum*, it had seemed; *ad nauseam*, it actually was.

Of course, there'd also been the Human Awareness – or Policing Skills – Training, integrated with the instruction on police duties – and forming a major part of the course – when the class had received lessons on subjects such as body language, attitudes, perception, stereotypes, and race-and-prejudice, all of which was designed to make the recruit a more humane enforcer of law.

The problem was that the veterans, the street-hardened

cops of ten-to-thirty-years' service, had had little or none of this training; and they'd not had any training in the theory and practice of law since completing their induction courses, and, over the years, they'd forgotten the finer points of law and procedure, and tended to be guided by their experiences and by 'instinct and commonsense'.

Instinct and commonsense forbade them to trust anyone because people were bad: thieves, drunks and liars, and potentially violent. Forewarned was forearmed, and bitter prejudices, together with a catalogue of learnt stereotypes, were significant parts of that armoury.

So it was that Tubby Tompkins, on hearing of this new Human-Awareness Training at the school, had raged, 'Fuck me blind! What're they tryin to *do*? They wanna turn us all into a buncha fuckin nigger-lovin social-workers!' Then, florid faced, he'd stormed out onto the streets, looking for a black man to claim and bang-up in the cells – what *for*, didn't matter.

What chance, then, did the training school stand? The police-station environment was destined to be by far the more influential because that was where MacHale would spend the remainder of his service, learning from his veteran colleagues, and, ultimately, either conforming to their way of things or throwing it all up and resigning.

It seemed, then, that community policing and enforcement policing were, in practice, mutually exclusive concepts. Besides, MacHale, being a probationer, had to justify his existence to the supervisors, and was regularly reported on.

If, when asked for his monthly return of arrests, and reports of offences, he were to say, 'Sorry, Sarge, Inspector, I haven't nicked *any* bodies, this month, and I haven't done any Process, either; but I *have* made friends with a couple of black kids on my beat, thereby promoting police-public relations,' how would Sergeant Barker or Old Crikey – the Relief's Inspector – react to *that*?

Thinking about it made MacHale shiver. He swung his feet up on the bed and lay back on the damp undersheet, staring at the yellowed ceiling.

It was a rhetorical question – he'd be found unlikely to make a good and efficient Constable, and then be dismissed.

Results were what counted. He'd been told so on the very first day of his attachment to the District and the Division.

With the crime-rate as high as it is and the clear-up rate as low as it is, the law-abiding public's deep concern will never be assuaged by an assurance that police-community relations are, on the whole, harmonious. The public wants Results, too. The Law just hasn't got time to be nice to nice people . . . Anyway, who are these nice people? – Old Crikey's philosophy.

But, sir, MacHale had thought. If police-community relations *were* harmonious, surely there wouldn't *be* a high crime-rate and a low clear-up rate? The public would be assisting us to the best of its ability, and giving us help and information to arrest offenders. He hadn't dared give voice to his opinion, though. After all, something else the training school had taught him was that authority was never to be questioned from beneath. *Never*.

So, the member of the public was simply not to be trusted: he was to be viewed with the utmost suspicion, particularly if he should attempt to become familiar with the Constable on his beat; in such circumstances he was undoubtedly guilty of a crime and was attempting to *disarm* the officer. Turn him over then and have a look in his pockets; either claim him or kick his arse out of it. It's *Us* versus *Them*, when it comes down to it.

Results!

And therein lay MacHale's biggest problem: he just couldn't get *sufficient* Results.

Process was easy enough: all you had to do was loiter

by the kerb, pull any car that looked like a banger, and sooner or later you'd come up with a defective exhaust, maybe; or a bald tyre; or defective wipers; or . . . hell, there were a thousand-and-one con-'n'-use offences that a motorist *could* commit.

All easy, run-of-the-mill stuff. So easy, in fact, that Process didn't really count for much in the Results tables, although every prob' had to do his fair share of it, if only to prove that he was *capable* of doing it.

And in that way, countless thousands of otherwise law-abiding people were antagonized by figure-hungry probationers, chased by figure-hungry supervisors.

Harder to obtain, though – and, accordingly, most highly prized – was a *real* Result: a body, for crime; any crime. Except shoplifting, possibly, because the store detective had done the detecting and detaining. All in all, they were a right friggin nuisance, shoplifters, and every experienced cop detested them.

More often than not, they turn out to be neurotic females, high on tranquillizers and anti-depressants, who're cryin out for help. But when ya give 'em that help, nickin their bodies and chargin 'em with theft, whadda they do? They turn y'over, go bent on ya: plead Not Guilty and elect to go up the steps. Next thing ya know, you're at the Crown Court for a couplea days, all for a quid's-wortha fuckin' cheese or somethin'. – Tasty Tom's cynical philosophy.

No prob' could duck them, though, and MacHale had been obliged to claim more than a few of them.

What he desperately needed, however, was the body of a good-class villain . . . for a burglary, maybe, or a mugging . . . or a TDA . . . a drug-pusher would make Old Crikey sit up and take some notice, as well, and his next written-report on MacHale would be *commendatory*.

He began to wonder if he'd *ever* make it through the two probationary years of his service. Should he kick The Job, before it kicked him? he asked himself. Go back to being a senior shop-assistant in a men's-wear store in Southend, where you could actually *help* people who were sincerely grateful, and be nice to them, take an interest in them. And there was no stress . . . no *nightmares*.

It was impossible, though. He'd burned his bridges. When he'd left school, aged sixteen, with seven GCE O-Level passes, he'd had mountainous hopes, even though he'd had no idea at all of the career he wanted to chase; but it was all immaterial, anyway, and if he'd studied the job-market, beforehand, he'd quickly have discovered that there were *no* really worthwhile jobs for inexperienced school-leavers, whatever their qualifications.

So, rather than suffer the ignominy of the dole queue, he accepted – no, *clamoured, competed* for, and *won* – the position of junior shop-assistant, and was promoted after eighteen months.

But then his father showed him an advertisement for the police . . . in one of the daily tabloids. 'You'll never be put out of work in the police,' Dad had said. 'Villains, there'll always be. And the pay's not bad, either.'

He thought about it. The recession was biting deep into the clothing industry; redundancy was a real threat. It'd be a big step, though . . . how big he couldn't conceive. But the pay *was* good, and there was free accommodation, or, in lieu, a rent allowance; there'd be excitement, too, the thrill of the unknown, and it was this aspect which most attracted him. Overall, a *glamorous* way of life.

So he did it. And here he now was, a young, probationer PC, far from home, lying on an unyielding mattress in a small room on the second floor of a police section-house, worried, fed-up, with an acute suspicion that he was despised by the world.

If *only* he could gain the full acceptance of his colleagues and supervisors, and *earn* their respect. If he hadn't felt so hard-pressed to demonstrate that he *could* do the job, on his own initiative, he'd never have set foot inside that house; at least not before first having got on the PR and asked for back-up. But when the shout was put on offer, he'd jumped at it.

A PC couldn't usually reckon to claim a body from a disturbance shout, but you just never knew. For instance, marital disputes – or Punch-'n'-Judy shows, as the cops called them – did sometimes escalate from verbal abuse to physical violence and damage to property. The distraught wife might then pour boiling chip-pan fat all over the old man's head – a nice case of GBH, thanks very much. Or the old man might give his old lady a nice smacking . . . a fractured arm, maybe – a Section Forty-Seven assault, known in the trade as ABH. Of course, if an implement had been used to cause injury, or to threaten injury, there was then the possibility of a knock-off for Offensive Weapon, under the Vagrancy Act if the offence took place on private property, or under the Prevention of Crime Act if it were in a public place, the disturbance having spilled onto the street.

But, MacHale now thought, he could never, ever have anticipated what actually *was* in store for him at Twenty-Four Bury Street. If the shout had come over as a *serious* disturbance, or as, *female screaming*, then maybe he'd have been just a little bit more wary.

As it was, he should still have held back when he'd seen that the front door was half open and the house was encased in a still darkness; there might have been an armed burglar in there . . . there were many possibilities of danger for an unaccompanied cop armed with no more than a thin stick of wood.

But if there were a body to be claimed inside that house, then MacHale had wanted to ensure that it would be *he* who did the claiming, not someone who'd turned up because he'd shouted for assistance.

In MacHale had gone, then, the house in complete darkness . . . just as the bad dream portrayed it. But much of the rest of that dream was weirdly distorted, and he just couldn't figure out why.

It *was* a freezing cold night, but there was no ice, least of all inside the house, hanging as frosty cobwebs. And there'd been no cat, either; nor a wreath affixed to the front door . . . What the hell was his mind playing at?

The old lady, though, *was* lying before the fire, decapitated and horribly mutilated; and her daughter *was* responsible, having, it turned out, been mentally unstable for many years. But the daughter certainly *hadn't* stabbed MacHale; she'd entered the room, naked, wielding the knife, and had *threatened* to attack him when she'd seen him unclip from the lapel of his mac, his PR's transceiver, and press his right index-finger on the Transmit button. Back at the nick, they'd heard every word that was spoken inside the house, recognizing MacHale's voice as he talked gently to the daughter, asking her a series of Whys? – Why did you chop off your mother's head? Why did you slash her belly? . . . And so forth.

They knew where he was, of course, because they'd sent him to the shout and had recorded details of it on the message-pad. So the next thing MacHale knew was that half the MPD – or so it had seemed – came crashing into the room, wielding truncheons, iron bars, dustbin lids, and other improvised weapons of defence and attack.

Three cheers for the Commissioner's Cowboys! MacHale had thought.

But that was the last he ever saw of his body. And *what* a body! For murder, no less.

So it was that while the SPG pulled her this way, the DSU crew pulled her that way, each unit claiming ownership of her body. Eventually, the dispute was settled outside in the street, by a Skipper from an adjoining Division, who pulled rank and claimed the body for *himself* and three of *his* PCs.

All MacHale got for his troubles was a dose of diarrhoea and a severe bollocking from Old Crikey. And, two months later, a horrible, distorted dream which had grown arms and legs, as it were . . . Why?

The heavy frost? . . . He couldn't interpret it. And the cat, which had lulled him into a false sense of security before turning on him with razor-sharp claws? . . . Unconsciously, he withdrew his right hand from behind his head and inspected the back of it . . . Nothing, of course – no scratches, no scars. Maybe that cat had been a warning symbol . . . Don't enter the house!

He slowly shook his head, and sniffed. Whatever these symbols really meant – *if* they meant anything, that was – the real problem with his mind, his unconscious, had arisen because he'd striven to suppress the horror of the experience inside that house. Oh, sure, he'd related it to those of his young, section-house colleagues who'd been interested, and had been happy to *revel* in the gore of it when he'd seen the effect it was having on them: it made him feel like a real, macho cop. Hey, listen to what I've been through; and I'm still in one piece – *Supercop!*

What he hadn't confessed, though, was that he'd felt fear; raw, unadulterated fear, the like of which he'd never before known.

So it was the *fear* he'd suppressed.

But while he'd succeeded in banishing it from his conscious state, it eventually rose and burst when he was most susceptible and vulnerable: during sleep.

Now, hopefully, that nightmare would prove to have acted as a catharsis.

He rose from the bed, stretching, yawning, the tiredness shuddering from his limbs, then opened the door of the built-in wardrobe, bending inside the cubicle to pick up his alarm clock from the floor. It was now six o'clock in the evening. He'd set it for three o'clock this afternoon, and it had gone off, too, but he'd been so deeply asleep, its vibrant ringing hadn't so much as stirred him; it never did.

He felt uneasy about lying all day in his pit, off night-duty. It was . . . unnatural, a waste of an afternoon. Maybe he should try again placing the clock beside his bed? Its ringing would be louder and more penetrating. But that incessant, tick-tick-tick was penetrating, too, and he'd have the same old problem trying to concentrate on relaxation and sleep when he climbed between the sheets.

He put the clock back in the wardrobe and shut the door, then walked over to the window, leaning across the room's small desk in order to draw aside the faded-green curtains . . .

Darkness. Again.

He hadn't seen daylight for three days, now. Not since Monday afternoon. In the winter months, as now, he finished a nightly shift in darkness – at six-thirty A.M. – and when he awoke from a day's sleep – usually at about six or seven P.M. – it was *still* dark; had there ever *been* daylight?

Opposite his window, lights were blazing in the nick; he could hear the drunks, kicking their cell doors, shouting for their freedom; below, in the yard, a stray dog, yelping and barking, leaped up and forward, stretching the chain that was clipped to its collar; noisy PCs were coming and going, their PRs crackling messages; now an area-car streaked from the yard, its beacon flashing, its tyres squealing as it turned, leaving the precincts of the nick . . . whip-tones on . . . wow-wow-wow . . . the noise becoming fainter and fainter . . . then inaudible.

It might have been any time of the day or night. The scene below never changed. He felt a quiver of excitement in his gut. *That* was what The Job was all about. The thrill of the chase, the unknown and the unexpected. How many civvies, in passing, had told him that they wouldn't have his job for all the tea in China? Lots of them. Because they were *incapable* of doing his job; they were frightened, of crime and criminals. But he wasn't afraid. Fear was something you crushed and stacked away.

To hell with bad dreams; those he could cope with; he was young, fit, resilient; he *needed* stimulation. And with experience would come hardness of character and mind; he *needed* to be hard.

On waking, he'd felt tired and strained, but his reverie had now given him strength, renewing his determination to succeed.

He let the curtains fall together, then moved to the small washbasin which was mounted on the wall opposite his bed, on the same side as the wardrobe. As he fixed the plug and ran hot water, he caught his reflection in the mirror of the small wall cabinet in front of him.

'Hmmm,' he murmured, frowning, studying his features from all angles . . . Maybe his mother was right. Maybe he *was* looking pale; but he was unable to see that his smooth face wasn't as chubby as it had been, some seven or eight months ago. Now he combed his fingers through his black, curly hair, examined them and nodded relievedly at the lack of strays; they said that wearing a cap or helmet was bad for your scalp, suffocated it, loosened the hair follicles, made you prematurely bald.

He bent over the sink and splashed the tepid water on his face. As he dried his face and began combing his hair, he became aware of sounds from outside the room. Always there were sounds, ringing around the interior of the building, at every hour of the day and night. Two or three PCs, walking noisily along the corridor . . . a radio blaring . . . the rattle of cups and saucers and plates, echoing up from the canteen on the ground floor . . . And . . . not *Harrison* at it *again*, surely? . . .

MacHale threw his towel onto the bed and pressed his

ear against the wall, listening, holding his breath . . . Yep! Harrison *was* at it again, the randy bastard. No wonder he was so skinny, the long streaka piss.

The first time MacHale had heard Harrison at it in the room next-door to his own, it had sounded quite alarming . . . like a cat, being slowly strangled on a bed with rusty springs. Who *is* this bird that Harrison's giving the horizontal treatment to? he'd wondered, his chest heaving as he listened and imagined and *envied*.

Well, the very next day he happened to see her with Harrison, in the canteen. And she was absolutely gorgeous . . . *the-ee* business. MacHale had just sat there, opposite her table, surreptitiously ogling her, mentally drooling, jealous as hell, thinking about old Harrison giving her one. The *lucky*, randy bastard!

MacHale wondered if he himself would ever make such a score. Not much chance, though, he decided. It was work, work, work, with little or no social life. On early-turn you couldn't really afford to go out in the evenings because you had to be up for duty at six-thirty in the morning. On late-turn you didn't finish duty until ten-thirty in the evening, and the pubs closed at eleven; *if* you had the energy, you could, of course, go clubbing up the West End, but you didn't *know* anyone, while everyone knew *you, and* what you were, and steered well clear – it was the eyes, usually, which gave you away: making everyone, slotting them into stereotypes, *frisking* them with your eyes. Night duty spoke for itself: you were working, while everyone else was out on the town, enjoying themselves . . . You *jammy*, lucky, randy bastard, Harrison!

Harrison was a nine-to-fiver, working – *working?* Idling, more like – in the nick's Admin Unit, recycling pieces of paper, in-between drinking tea in the canteen and playing snooker in the games' room. So he had no such problems with his social life. Or his love life. You *star-spangled*, jammy, lucky, randy bastard, Harrison!

MacHale pulled away from the wall, and now his eyes caught sight of the IB, lying, closed, on top of the table beneath the window. That was another impediment to normal living.

The Instruction Book was the PC's manual of guidance and instruction on law and procedure – more procedure than law – and the probationer's Bible. During each month of his two years' probationary period of service, he was required to attend the Continuation Training Centre for two consecutive days, when he'd then be examined, orally and in writing, by the instructors, on his knowledge of the IB. There were periods of classroom instruction, too; and 'practicals', when the instructors would act-out incidents of police duty, and the probs' would be called on to resolve them.

Of course, in order to pass the written examinations at CTC, a PC had to study the IB throughout the month prior to his attendance; and that studying had to be done in his off-duty periods – they never told you *that* in the ads for police recruitment. So more than a few probs left all their studying until the evening before . . . with a predictable outcome: they failed the examination. Then followed caustic bollockings, and adverse written-reports to their Chief Superintendents and Commanders.

MacHale's results had been good, though. He was a conscientious worker, and one who found it relatively easy to assimilate theory. In addition, he had spread the workload over the whole month, committing it piece by piece to memory.

But, as he'd discovered, a good book-man didn't necessarily make a good street-man. There was a *real* secret to be unlocked, there.

Suddenly, he was startled by a light knocking at the door. Then a voice, calling, 'Juan? Are you in?'

His stomach somersaulted again as he recognized the voice – Hercules.

'Just a minute,' he shouted, and quickly took a bath-towel from the rail below the sink, wrapping it around his midriff; no way was he going to let Hercules see him naked. He walked the few paces to the door and pulled back the catch, unlocking it; on night duty, you were wise to lock yourself in, otherwise you'd have the cleaner coming and going all morning. Curious, MacHale had thought, on first occupying the room: there was a catch on the inside of the door, enabling you to lock yourself *in*, but when you vacated the room, there was no means of locking yourself, or anyone else, *out*. He'd been told by a colleague that at one time, section-house rooms had had *no* locks whatever; then, after an Inspector was caught, in the middle of the night, entering young PCs' rooms, armed with a bottle of chloroform and a jar of Vaseline – not to mention a bestial intent – catches were fitted to the insides of the doors. 'So,' the PC had advised, 'if you don't wanna wake up with a sore head, a throbbing arse and a John Wayne walk, *always* lock yourself in before you go to bed.'

MacHale opened the door. 'Oh, hello,' – it came out flat; no welcome.

Hercules smiled; his hair was wet, slicked back over his head, looking glossy black when it was actually a dark, matt brown; he, too, had a bath-towel wrapped around his waist, and his bony, hairless chest, and that long fleshless face of his, with its sunken cheeks, were glowing a hot, clean shade of pink. He was about twenty-six, MacHale believed, tall and thin – fragile-looking, but actually quite sinewy, and deceptively strong; although, because of his permanently-rounded shoulders and slight, forward stoop, he looked to be no more than of average height, say, five nine, ten, and weakly. Every time

MacHale laid eyes on him he was reminded of Charles Dickens' Uriah Heep.

'I was wondering,' Hercules began, eyebrows hopefully raised, 'if you fancied a pint . . . across the road, before night duty?' All the while, his big brown eyes were exploring MacHale's physique: the well-defined shoulders and biceps and pectorals, the latter muscles covered by a sprinkling of short, curly black hair, which also ran, in a wide, straight line, down the centre of his flat belly, disappearing beneath the fold of towelling around his waist.

MacHale felt acutely uncomfortable. He was certain that Hercules was gay, although the man had no obviously-effeminate mannerisms. His voice, which was fairly deep, complemented the – albeit ironical – sobriquet, Hercules, which his colleagues had long ago given him, and which he, good-naturedly, had accepted. No, it was just that . . . well, it was the way he *looked* at you, plus the fact that he was always getting himself involved with homosexual prisoners, either by way of nicking them himself, or by making it his business to talk to them in the charge-room. And for any cop who *was* gay, and who, therefore, had to repress the proclivity, this might well be the only way in which he *could* make some socially acceptable – in the eyes of his colleagues – form of contact with a fellow gay.

Everyone at the nick was certain that Hercules was a ginger beer – although no one could adduce any real evidence in support of the conviction.

MacHale briefly considered Hercules' invitation to go out for a drink, before night duty. Then he said, 'No, sorry. I'm late getting up, today, and by the time I've had a shower, my dinner, and done a bit of studying for CTC, it'll be too late.' He was somehow afraid to say that he didn't *believe* in drinking alcohol before parading for duty . . . how he just didn't feel it right that a uniformed cop should be breathing Scotch or beer all over a member of the public . . . because if his colleagues were to discover that he'd merely *thought* such things, they'd say *he* was queer, too . . . a puritan or something.

'You sure?' Hercules asked, disappointed.

'Mm-hm,' MacHale nodded. 'I'm certain. Maybe some other time.' He began to feel even more uncomfortable, and couldn't hold Hercules' gaze; if he were fully clothed, or unrestricted in his movements, he'd have felt stronger.

Hercules' narrow, bony shoulders rose and fell. 'Oh, well. I'll see you later, then, Juan. 'Bye.' And he turned to walk away along the corridor, leaving wet footprints on the highly-polished, green-marble-patterned lino.

MacHale relaxed and closed the door, then sat on the edge of his bed. *Juan!* he thought. The prat will keep on calling me *Juan*.

He now wished he'd never told Hercules anything of his background: '*No*, he *wasn't* a Paki'; his darks looks were donated by his mother, who was of Spanish extraction; she called him *Juan*, pronouncing it, *Whon*; he didn't like it, but tolerated it, and often wished that the recessive genes of his father's Irish ancestry had been more dominant . . .

Then he began to feel a twinge of pity for Hercules. The man didn't appear to have any close friends, and none of his fellow officers cared much for him; he was probably very lonely. Trouble was, if he were to sense a change in MacHale's disposition towards him, he might misinterpret it.

He rose from the bed, breaking away from his reverie, collected a sachet of shampoo and a bar of soap from the wall-cabinet above the sink, and went out to the bathroom.

When he appeared on parade, he'd be clean and smart, and smelling of perfume; but if he didn't nick a body off the streets, Old Crikey would probably say that he smelled lousy.

3

Ten thirty-five P.M.

The Collator's office, on the first floor of the three-storey, red-brick Victorian building: a long, narrow room, containing desks and chairs, filing cabinets, typewriters and beat-crime books; brightly lit by neon strips that hung from the mottled white tiles of the lowered, acoustic ceiling; at one end of the room, a bank of tall windows, black and shiny, reflecting the interior; all around, affixed to pale-green walls, notice-boards, bearing Collator's bulletins, mugshots of particularly active villains who were considered long overdue for a nicking, and maps; maps with pins that had round, glossy plastic heads of many different colours; *lots* of such pins, each one representing a crime, a victim.

The Relief, its silent members seated in a line abreast, awaiting the arrival of the Duty Officer, Old Crikey, had been posted to beats and patrols. The Collator's daily-bulletin sheet had been read, as had the parade book, but only MacHale had bothered to write down the registration number of the lost-or-stolen artic' that contained a load of Scotch; only he had recorded the description of the missing, fifteen-year-old girl; only he was interested, it seemed. But he *had* to be interested; he was a prob'. The others had proved themselves. Or so they believed. In the main they were men with steel-hard shells, but their underbellies were pink and tender. What had made them hard had also made them soft, anxious, vulnerable, and, above all, cynical and bitter – life had served them up a double portion of everything that was bad.

Bob Barker – fifty, slim, wavy grey hair, dull, tired

blue eyes – was tonight's Section Sergeant, while his opposite number, Harry Tanner, was Station Officer. Tomorrow night they'd swap duties, and go on alternating like that until Ray Schriber had finished his posting to Vice; then, *he* could take *his* turn at being banged-up in that front office for eight hours at a time, with screaming, shouting, spitting bodies flying head-first through the charge-room door every five fuckin minutes, the telephone ringing every other fuckin minute, and a caller at the counter, every *half* a fuckin minute. Jesus, it was *bedlam*, down there.

Which reminded Barker of Derek Palmer, the Relief's fourth Skipper. If Palmer hadn't decided to throw a wobbly and have a nervous breakdown, he'd've been taking *his* turn at SO, too, and the workload would've been spread that much further. The selfish prick!

Actually, it was hilarious, Barker thought: Palmer, at four in the morning, wandering around St James's Park, dressed in pyjamas, a twelve-bore under his arm, a ten-gallon stetson on his head; and when that Hobby-Bobby-Wally from the Park Constabulary had asked, 'What're you doin in here at this hour of the mornin, guv, dressed like *that*?' old Palmer stuck the twelve-bore up his hooter, narrowed his crazy eyes, Clint-Eastwood-style, and drawled, 'Ooh, jist out shootin me some rats, Marshal . . . You *seen* any rats . . . ?'

Now, Palmer was banged-up in a mental hospital, somewhere out in the sticks, and they'd probably never again see him back at the nick.

As Barker's weary eyes came back into focus, he looked along the line of PCs who were seated before his desk. Any one of them could go the same way as Palmer, he considered – Miss Coles, the *W*PC, too . . . why not? – and no one would give a shit. Any copper who allowed – yes, *allowed* – himself to become afflicted by a nervous illness was immediately considered to be weak, spineless, a miserable failure, a *nutter*. They'd all *said* that Palmer was now a nutter, and had had a bloody good laugh, too, doing their Nutty Palmer impersonations in the canteen.

Little wonder, then, that any copper who felt himself becoming stressed to an intolerable degree was *afraid* to report himself sick with such a symptom: he'd be branded a nutter, by his own colleagues. His affliction would only ever come to light, therefore, if it led to his going completely over the top, and, like Palmer had, committing either a criminal or disciplinary offence, or both. By then, of course, The Job wasn't interested in treating him as a sick man, only in prosecuting him.

The Job still wanted to know where Palmer had obtained his shotgun; he certainly didn't have a shotgun certificate, authorizing his possession of it.

Well, Barker wasn't going to put *himself* on offer to a nervous breakdown. No way. After twenty-five years he was entitled to take things a little easy whenever he could.

He frowned, glancing over his shoulder, up at the wall-clock – ten-forty. Talking of nutters, he thought, where the fuck's Old Crikey got to?

At that moment, Old Crikey Crawford came rushing in through the door, looking, as usual, as if a swarm of wasps were on his tail, and carrying a sheaf of papers and a PR. He stepped aside to allow the door to swing shut behind him, then just stood there for a moment, his brow ploughed, the merest trace of a wince producing slight muscular-twitches at the corners of his mouth and eyes.

A Scotsman in self-imposed exile, he spoke in earnest tones, with only a trace of his native accent. He was forty-seven, bald, with just a fringe of white hair around the back and sides of his large head: a twenty-eight-year man, anxiously awaiting his thirty, so that he might retire unscathed, before these Cowboys who were seated in a line before him, succeeded in dropping him *right* in it, up to his bushy grey eyebrows. What sort of trouble might they get him into, tonight? he wondered. And the facial twitches became more pronounced.

He was a bit of an old woman, Old Crikey, sometimes pedantic, but always worried; and it showed in his pale, haggard face and blue-grey eyes. Anyone meeting him for the first time, however, would undoubtedly have been most struck by his mouth: always mobile, lower jaw sliding from side-to-side and clicking up and down; his tongue, sucking on a digestif, a white film of congealed mucus ever present on his colourless thin lips. Remarkable, too, was the fact that he never swore. 'Oh, *crikey*!' was the closest he ever came to profanity, even when all hell threatened to break loose – hence his nickname.

He looked quickly away from the Relief, to his right, at Barker, drawing the back of his left hand across his mouth.

Barker was already on his feet. 'All correct, sir,' he said. 'Everyone's accounted for and posted.' He gave him the duty board. Old Crikey was favourite to be the next one who cracked up, Barker believed.

All correct? Old Crikey agitatedly thought. All *corrupt*, more like. He glanced up and down the list of numbers and postings on the duty board, then returned it to Barker. 'Thanks, Skip.' He turned to face the Relief, now shuffling his papers, reading from them when they were sorted to his satisfaction. 'Just a couple of SOEs, tonight: *The Prince of Wales*, Green Street, an engagement celebration, until midnight; and the *Goat in Boots*, Lester Place, a wedding-anniversary celebration, until twelve-thirty. I don't anticipate trouble at either of these functions.' Oh, how he *hoped* there wouldn't be trouble.

'Guv?' – it was Vindscreen, a young, long-haired PC who seemed to believe he was an American Swat-Squad cop; they called him *Vindscreen* because his surname was Vipas. *Vindscreen Vipas!*

Old Crikey sighed and tut-tutted. '*Yes*, Vipas?' he snapped. 'What is it?' He just *knew* it would be something contentious; it always *was* where Vipas was concerned.

'Well, guv,' Vindscreen began, 'I *was* gonna try for a drug bust, in the Prince . . . tonight. I mean, I've had some info' from a snout, so I thought I'd – '

'You keep *out* of there!' Old Crikey shouted, panic-stricken by the idea of Vindscreen turning-over an engagement party. 'Give it to the CID . . .' His left hand swept sideways through the air, batting away the drug bust. 'If you go in there, there'll be *hell* to pay: there'll be an almighty punch-up, the celebration cake'll end up sliding down the wall, *and* there'll be a complaint against police.' His eyes were wild, and his lower jaw was cracking as it slid back and forth.

Vindscreen shrugged. 'Okay, guv. I'll leave it.'

That settled, Old Crikey's jaw was set firm, and he nodded defiantly. Then, to the Relief: 'Now I'll see your appointments, please.'

The members of the Relief came to their feet, shuffling about and bumping into one another as they fished in the capacious pockets of their uniforms, producing truncheons, report-book wallets, pens, whistles and chains – which had no practical use whatever, these days – and torches.

Then there was complete silence again as they stood erect, eyes front, holding at arms' length their appointments, awaiting Old Crikey's inspection.

Old Crikey narrowed his eyes, moved forward and to the left, and stood a couple of feet in front of the first man in line. Barker remained where he was, and sat at his desk, a wry expression on his face. Few of the nick's other Duty Officers ever bothered to demand the production of appointments; fewer still actually bothered to inspect them. It was a wonder Old Crikey wasn't still requiring the Relief to produce marking materials – pieces of chalk and thread. The nitpickin ol' fucker.

Little did Barker know, though, that MacHale, if asked, *could* have produced a piece of chalk and a small reel of thread; such materials still did have a practical use on night duty.

First in line was Punchy Paterson, a heavily-built man whose face was like scuffed brown leather – full of scar tissue and bony ridges, with a broad, flat nose which had been broken more times than either he or the staff at the local hospital were able to remember. Now, at forty-one, his muscles were loosening and sagging, his speech thick and deliberate, full of nasal vibes. He'd been an outstanding boxer in his time, though: ex-heavyweight champion, Lafone Cup, ABA and European Police. Nowadays, nicking bodies and sticking motorists in the book didn't much appeal to him, although he would stir himself if such work came unavoidably his way. Most of the time, though, he'd be reflecting on his past, contrasting it with the present, feeling sad and depressed; then he'd turn to drink, and feel even more sad and depressed.

Old Crikey looked him up and down. He wasn't as smart as he ought to have been; his trousers hadn't been pressed for God knew how long, and his boots needed cleaning and polishing. He *smelled* of *Scotch*, too. Old Crikey shuddered. The last time Punchy Paterson had taken to drinking Scotch, he'd gone completely overboard; thought he was Superman again. He'd pulled a young black kid, down the High Street, and questioned him regarding his possession of a pedal-cycle; during the interrogation, the kid had started nervously flicking the cycle's bell . . . Then he'd given it a couple of real hard flicks: *ding-ding!* At which point, Punchy Paterson's brain had scrambled itself, and he was back in the ring, at the start of the final round, the crowd shouting and cheering him on, demanding blood. So, Punchy gave 'em what they wanted: he punched the black kid *right* up in the air.

Fortunately it was four A.M. and the street was deserted; even more fortunately, the kid *had* stolen the bike, and when his head cleared he found himself in the factory, going on the sheet for Take Conveyance; his sore chin and throbbing brain, he put down to experience.

Without a word of reproval for Paterson's untidy appearance, Old Crikey moved on to the next man; no way was *he* going to chance ringing a bell in Paterson's head.

Tasty Tom Reynolds. Evil. A monster of a misanthrope who probably hated himself as much as anyone else. A big, powerful man, too – bigger than Punchy Paterson – with a gruff voice, huge brown eyes that reflected mayhem, and brush-cut grey hair over a big-boned *ugly* face. He rarely smiled or laughed, but when he did it was usually at someone else's misfortune and was more of a tight sneer.

It was Tasty Tom's ambition to kill someone. Preferably a Chelsea Football-Club supporter . . . one of those skinny little slimeballs with shaven head, bleached denims and jungle boots, who believed himself to be the man that Tasty Tom actually *was*. Failing that, one of those left-wing, bearded, four-eyed social-workers would do quite nicely. Or a Labour Party supporter. Arthur Scargill, too; most *definitely*, Arthur Scargill . . .

Along to Pat Coles. A WPC. A squaw among the Cowboys, and treated as one, too. Sometimes, their practical jokes and sexist jibes, moved her to tears; although not in their presence – she'd never give them that satisfaction. When she'd first joined A-Relief, some four years ago, now, they'd bundled her along the cell passageway, pulled down her drawers and smacked the station stamp on her left buttock; it had taken her several days of sore, intermittent scrubbing with a nailbrush and soap, too, before all traces of that violet ink were removed. Another time, they'd wrapped clingfilm over the pan in the ladies' toilet, then lowered the lid of the seat over it, so that, at a cursory glance, the stretched film was invisible; in went Pat Coles, and got herself a wet bum, much to the delight of the members of the Relief, who were keeping obbo from around the corner.

Ooh, they could be *bastards*! Well, most of them, anyway. Snatch was *always* nice to her, and John MacHale was *very* nice. Now, if John MacHale had wanted to rip-off her drawers . . . well . . . Little did she know that MacHale had *had* such a fantasy, but had dismissed it; he didn't believe it was really on with her.

Miss Coles was the one member of the Relief whom Old Crikey actually *liked* looking at. She was cuddly, affable and tolerant, and her plump face, jovial, with its amused, hazel eyes and full red lips, did things to him which he was ashamed of.

He noted her smart turnout – highly-polished shoes, unwrinkled skirt, sharp creases in the sleeves of her tunic – and nodded his approval. As he moved away, past her, he offered, 'Well-done, Miss Coles,' and, out of the corner of his eye, saw her face, filling out, beaming. *God*, how he wished his Relief were entirely made up of women officers.

A sneer made the face of Tasty Tom. What's the matter with the silly old fart? he asked himself. Doesn't he *know*? She's a bull dike.

Next to Pat Coles: Vindscreen Vipas.

You're a *lout*, a damn hooligan, Old Crikey told himself.

Old Crikey wasn't a bad judge, either. Dominant, energetic, impetuous, Vipas had the reputation of being a flash little git whose brains were distributed fairly evenly between his mouth and his wedding gear. In his mid-twenties, he walked with a spring in his feet, bouncing along, oozing confidence, his smug expression saying, Look at *me*! I'm *hot* shit, man! The others said he ought to have been born black.

Old Crikey paid particular attention to Vindscreen, noting his mousy hair, which was growing down an inch over his ears . . . That right ear, with a puncture mark on its lobe! What the hell sort of man *is* it that wears a *ring* in his ear? Just let him try wearing it *on* duty, that's all.

'Vipas!' he snapped. 'I thought I told you, last night, to get that hair of yours trimmed.' His eyes narrowed and his lower jaw cracked back and forth, making his teeth grate.

'Sorry, guv. I was at Process court, this afternoon, and didn't have time.' – a lie.

'Tomorrow, then,' Old Crikey ordered. 'Without fail.' And he was away to the next man on parade.

Vindscreen emitted a controlled sigh of relief. Had Old Crikey pulled up either of his trouser-legs, he'd have seen that the hooligan was wearing orange glow-socks. *Orange bloody glow-socks!*

Filthy Phil Smith; another late-service PC, with twenty-three years under his belt, he was just *about* five feet eight-inches tall – the minimum height-requirement for entry to the service – well-built and, unlike most of his colleagues, healthy-looking, with a rustic, unlined face, dark, sparkling eyes, and well-oiled black hair.

Filthy Phil regarded The Job as a sinecure, doing little or nothing in the way of official duty, and maybe this was why he exuded such a salubrious air – he was almost totally unstressed. The bastard had even conned the CMO into certifying him unfit for duty on the RT-car, perhaps the one posting which made inevitable a fair amount of involvement in policework, because it was the RT-car that took all of the hotshot Emercalls from IR.

It was rumoured that Filthy Phil was at present working on a thesis which would persuade the CMO that the radio waves emitted by his PR were a health hazard – radiation sickness would be the prognosis, he hoped, so that the CMO would certify him exempt from having to *carry* a PR. In the meantime, he just ensured that he always selected a run-down or defective battery to clip into his set, or, if that were impossible, that it somehow detached itself from the set, while in his pocket, and thereby took him off the air.

However, the 'bad back' which precluded Filthy Phil's posting to the RT-car, didn't appear to affect his ability to ride a bicycle, and he was often to be seen pedalling hell-for-leather through the manor, en route to his next hidey-hole.

He was a voyeur – hence the nickname, *Filthy* – who spent practically the whole tour of night-duty perching on back-garden walls and climbing trees that overlooked private homes; all in the hope of spotting a naked, female form and thereby fulfilling some perverted sexual-fantasy. No one on the Relief had actually *seen* him in action, and MacHale, on being told, by Tasty Tom, of Filthy Phil's nocturnal activities, had gone so far as to dismiss the stories. Tasty Tom had taken offence: no one should doubt his word, he'd felt, and he'd dragged MacHale off to the locker-room, posted Punchy Paterson on the door, and then proceeded to screw Filthy Phil's locker. As the grey-metal door sprang open, guided by a heavy-duty screwdriver, MacHale's jaw dropped, his eyes widened, and his uncertainty vanished. On the floor of the locker there was an assortment of ladies' underwear; and out of the pockets of Filthy Phil's spare tunic and mac, Tasty fetched a large selection of pornographic photographs and a bundle of semen-stained handkerchiefs.

'*Now* d'you believe it?' growled Tasty Tom.

On day duties, Filthy Phil often posted himself outside an underground station, during rush-hour periods, so that he could ogle all of the young, female office-workers as they travelled to and from their places of work; and what the hell he got up to when he was *off* duty . . . well, that was anybody's guess, but most of his colleagues reckoned he either went flashing on the common, or shopping in large stores, with a mirror glued to the toecap of his right shoe. He was a married man, too, with a couple of kids in their early teens, and those members of the Relief who'd seen his wife, reported her to be an attractive woman; it was also reported, though, that Filthy Phil was over the side with a divorcee who lived on the manor, although no one claimed to have seen *her*, or have knowledge of her exact address.

As Old Crikey paused in front of Filthy Phil, looking at the man's bulging mac pockets – which contained dirty pictures, women's drawers and damp, soiled handkerchiefs, no doubt – he felt acutely anxious. If Filthy Phil ever *did* get himself captured by an irate husband or boyfriend who'd caught him peeping in through a bedroom window while he made love to his wife or girlfriend, there was a terrible danger that the hierarchy, seeking to absolve themselves from all responsibility, would look for a sacrificial lamb, and stick-on Old Crikey, for lack of supervision.

Oh, *crikey*! What to *do*? . . . Nothing . . . Do *nothing*, he told himself, fighting his rising panic; Filthy Phil was as keen as he himself was to do thirty and get the hell out of it, unscathed. But if anything ever *should* happen, before then, well . . . he'd just tell the Commander that Smith *wasn't* a Peeping Tom, at all. He'd probably laugh as he said it, too, and spread his hands and shrug his shoulders, just for effect, just to intimate how totally preposterous the very idea was . . . *Smith*, a *voyeur*? *Ridiculous!* Then he'd probably say something like, 'No, sir. Impossible.' Maybe laugh again, more nonchalantly, before adding, '*Smith* is a conscientious cop, sir . . . always on the look-out for suspects on private property;

that's why he was prowling around like he was . . . softlee, softlee catchee monkey, sir.' And then he'd relax over tea with the Commander, before being thanked and dismissed.

He moved away from Filthy Phil, on to Norman Mathieson. Mathieson, twenty-eight, thin as a stick, with rheumy green eyes, hollow-cheeked, melancholy face, and an unruly mop of fair hair, was an incipient lush whose breath always smelt of liquor. Not since finishing his probationary period of service, some seven years ago, had he put hand to collar or pen to paper; he was completely uninterested in police duty, spending the early part of night-duties and the latter part of late-turns, in the private room of one or other of the local pubs whose licensees were pro-police – most licensees *were* pro-police, because the uniformed branch was responsible for enforcing the Licensing Laws, and a free glass of ale for the beat PC would undoubtedly induce him to overlook, say, a little after-hours' drinking, now and then. Of course, if the pub in question were a regular resort of off-duty police-officers, then it would probably be *they* who were *doing* the after-hours' drinking.

Mathieson had two basic problems, really; and they were mutually parasitic: depression and drinking. When he was depressed, he drank; and when he drank, he became even more depressed – eventually. Maybe he was a *confirmed* alcoholic, who just couldn't *stop* drinking without some kind of psychiatric help: help which it didn't seem likely he'd ever seek out for himself.

Four years ago, his marriage had broken up, childless, but whether any of that had either caused or aggravated his problems, no one seemed to know – he was remembered as having *always* been a morose loner who drank heavily. No one seemed to *care*, either, that was the real difficulty, because it only needed one person – a colleague or a supervisor – to report Mathieson's state to the Chief

Superintendent, in order to oblige *him* to act, by placing Mathieson sick, and ensuring that he sought treatment.

The Skippers certainly didn't care; they just wanted an easy life, and popularity – luxuries which the best of supervisors had to forfeit. And as for Old Crikey, well, he was frightened to act. Supposing he did report Mathieson, and Mathieson was subsequently cast as medically unfit? What would his fellow PCs say about that? They'd accuse Old Crikey of having *ratted* on the bloke, of having deprived him of his livelihood.

No. It was by far easier to tolerate the worry and stress that such men caused you, and hope. Hope that they didn't drop either themselves or you, or *both* of you, head-first in the bog.

On to Hercules. A taciturn man, all sideways glances and deep thought. What *was* he forever thinking about as he covertly eyed people? Still, *he* wasn't likely to drop Old Crikey in it . . . Well, not unless he got himself captured, *on* duty, having a cross-hand boogey in the *Gay-Trade Centre*, down on the sleazy part of the manor. They all *reckoned* he was fruit.

And MacHale . . . Hercules standing next to him on parade. As *usual*.

Old Crikey began to wonder if the pair of them were having an affair. Oh, *crikey*! Imagine the headlines that'd give rise to in the tabloids, if it were to get out. And MacHale not even twenty-one! That made it a *criminal offence!*

What a Relief to get fitted-up with. Those that aren't lunatics are alcoholics, and the other two are queers! And *you*, Barker, he told himself as he about-turned and walked to Barker's desk; don't think I'm unaware that *you're* swinging the lead, too. I *know* what you and the night-duty telephonist are up to. I've *seen* the pair of you making for the hay loft in the stables!

'Who's on comms?' he asked Barker.

'Dave Hall, of course, sir.' – *of course*, because Hall was on permanent light-duties after an operation to remove a stomach tumour, and had volunteered for shiftwork comms on A-Relief.

'And the VDU?'

'Blinky, sir. But he's also doubling as gaoler-cum-ASO. We're *still* supplying the DSUs, the Beat-Crime office and the District Crime-Squad with three PCs and a WPC.'

'Hmm,' Old Crikey murmured. As soon as a discernable pattern of crime emerged or threatened to emerge, the cry went up, *Form a Squad!* And the Reliefs were often severely depleted. 'Can Blinky manage, d'you think?'

'If not,' Barker said, 'I'll pull in Miss Coles. She's a VDU operator.' He glanced at Pat Coles, and she nodded affirmatively.

'Yes, good,' Old Crikey muttered. As long as Barker, never, *ever* again allowed Vipas near that Visual Display Unit, Old Crikey didn't care *who* operated it.

Last night-duty, he'd caught the hooligan with the back off the set, its intestines hanging out all over the comms-room floor, trying to convert it to *Space Invaders. Bloody Space Invaders!* And half the Relief was out there on the streets, unable to get processes on name-checks, vehicle checks, disqual' and misper checks.

Old Crikey was almost certain, too, that it was Vindscreen who'd fed the computer with the registration number of the Commander's private car, recording it lost-or-stolen. Just imagine it: the Commander, thrice removed from God, getting himself nicked for thieving his *own motor*; and the arresting officer, on hearing the Commander's protestation that he *was*, indeed, a senior policeman, not a criminal, grabbing him by the scruff of the neck and the seat of his pants, and shouting, 'Oh, yeah? And I'm the fuckin Commissioner, sunshine,' before lobbing him, head first, into the meat-wagon.

Old Crikey felt himself shudder. 'And who's on the van and the RT-car, tonight?' he wanted to know.

'No van, sir,' Barker told him. 'It's got a Fifty-Four stuck on its screen. Defective brakes, apparently. So, we'll have to get someone else's van to cover. As for the RT-car, Tubby Tompkins is driving, and Snatch is riding shotgun. They're out at the moment, though, dealing with a shout.'

'Right,' Old Crikey said, and turned to face the Relief. 'That's all, thank you.'

The members of the Relief replaced their appointments, turned away, and began making for the door. First, they'd go down to the front office, on the ground floor, where they'd draw their PRs and batteries, before reassembling in the canteen, which was located in the basement; there, Blinky should, by now, have made tea for the Relief. Come eleven o'clock, Old Crikey would probably poke his bald head around the canteen door, and expect to see the place deserted, with all officers out on patrol; if any officer were still there, though, Old Crikey would just glare at him – or her – gnash his teeth, retract his head, then disappear himself; that tacit admonishment would usually be sufficient, too, to dislodge anyone who'd lingered longer than was approved of.

The older cops never lingered, however; if they wanted to sit around, gossiping and drinking tea, then they knew of more than enough hidey-holes on their beats, where they could do it without fear of interruption by the Duty Officer.

As for Filthy Phil, he was most careful *never* to go to the canteen, after parade. Hang around on police premises, and someone with an urgent look on his face and a message-pad in his hand was likely to spot you, raise his eyebrows, extend that piece of paper, and say, 'Good! *You* can deal with that.'

MacHale was the last officer to reach the door of the Collator's office, and as he was halfway through it, he heard Old Crikey call out his name. He paused, turned, and reentered the room, his heart sinking.

4

'Yes, sir?' MacHale asked, bracing himself.

'I've got a progress report to complete in respect of you,' Old Crikey told him, frowning, compressing his lips.

'Yes, sir,' MacHale agreed, and felt even more disheartened.

'Well, it's got to be in within the next few weeks . . .' He paused, his eyes sweeping up and down MacHale, from the silver-coloured rose on top of his helmet, to the bulled toecaps of his boots . . . now settling on MacHale's eyes. 'And it won't be very complimentary, unless, between now and then, you can prove to me that you've got what it takes to be a copper.' He glanced at Barker, still at his side.

'The guv'nor's right, MacHale,' Barker put in. 'There's no complaint about your demeanour, nor your appearance, and, well, you've done a few Process, right enough. But what's the primary objective of an efficient police-force?'

'The prevention of crime, Sarge.' – no hesitation: the Primary Objects was the first report that each newly-inducted recruit was required to commit indelibly to his memory.

'And what's the next objective?' Barker continued.

'That of the detection and punishment of offenders, Sarge.'

'Right.' Old Crikey took over the conversation's direction. 'And that's the problem with you, MacHale: you're not detecting offenders; offenders who've committed crime, that is. Now, get out there . . .' He jabbed a finger in the direction of the windows. '. . . on the streets, and *show* me you can do it!' With that, he walked past MacHale, Barker following him.

When the door had closed and he was alone in the office, MacHale felt distressed. All that Old Crikey and Barker could do was moan at him, and press him for Results. Why, though, couldn't they *take* him out on the streets, and show him *how* to do the job they were demanding of him? Probationers, after all, were mere apprentices, learning their trade. No plumber or mechanic would even contemplate setting an unskilled apprentice to work, unsupervised; because if he did, expensive mistakes would inevitably be made, and the customer would refuse to pay.

In the police-force, the equivalents of leaking central-heating systems and backfiring cars, were wrongful arrests and the mishandling of incidents: mistakes which might have horrendous consequences for the 'customer', and which might never be rectified – once the legal process had closed in on and claimed a victim, it was virtually impossible, thereafter, to prise open its jaws.

MacHale was aware that it was the public in those streets out there, as well as himself, who were vulnerable, and at risk. True, he wasn't as lacking in confidence as he had been during the first few weeks of duty by himself, when he'd been almost overwhelmed by the fear that something would suddenly happen and he wouldn't be able to unconsciously flick through the pages of the IB and locate a paragraph that would accommodate. The 'something' hadn't happened, fortunately. But it *could*, yet. And what then? He believed that the end result would be either an unlawful arrest or an escaped offender – he'd either overreact or underreact, through fear and panic.

It is wrong! he told himself – so forcefully that his head hurt and he felt the need to sit. They *shouldn't* be chasing him out there with a nebulous brief to deprive criminals of their liberty. It was motivation by fear, with its implied threat of dismissal if he didn't succeed. They ought to have been out there with him, guiding him, showing him by their own example.

As soon as MacHale had completed his four weeks' Street-Duties' Course – during which time he was taught the boundaries of the beats, shown the problem areas of the ground and some of its criminal residents, as well as the basic workings of the nick – he was on his own.

Crime and criminals, though, were altogether different from Process. Unless you actually caught a villain, bang to rights – that is, in the act, more or less, of committing a crime – you didn't know where the hell you were, as a young, inexperienced probationer. You might have the body there, right in front of you, but you hadn't a clue what he'd done wrong, or, indeed, if he *had* done anything wrong. It might have been something *in*tangible which had caused you to pull him. Maybe he'd crossed the street when he'd spotted your approach; maybe you just hadn't liked the look of him, and had been aroused by an intuitive feeling of suspicion; or maybe he'd got possession of something which it hadn't seemed right that his 'type' should have . . . All hazy, subjective stuff that didn't even begin to constitute the *reasonable* suspicion which the relevant Statute declared you must have, before you even *thought* about pulling anyone and asking him what was what.

How to proceed, then?

The others wouldn't have hesitated – those of them who were interested in policework, that is – to go in, guns blazing, and give chummy a pull; but these experienced cops had the wherewithal to survive: if they wanted to stop any person and turn him upside-down, they'd *do* it; *then* they'd find the reasonable suspicion which had indicated that their body was up to no good; whether or not such suspicion *really* existed was immaterial. It wasn't too difficult to see symptoms of drug abuse in the eyes of a man you wanted to search for controlled narcotics; neither was it too difficult to imagine that a sober man who'd had a drink, and who'd refused to tell you who he was and where he lived – because he knew he didn't *have* to tell you – was drunk and disorderly. And so forth. The cop's imagination, when need dictated, could outmanouevre and accommodate any Jack-the-Lad of the streets. Every time.

But if you were a prob' . . . Well . . . you had no experience. And even if you were prepared to bend things a little, you just didn't know how *much* bending you could get away with. But say you did give this vaguely 'suspicious'-looking body a pull, without really knowing why you were doing it? And say he didn't lose his bottle? Say he wouldn't let you turn him over and have a look in his pockets or the boot of his car? Supposing he started thinking that *he'd* got charge of the situation, having sensed, maybe, that you were a mere prob' who didn't really know his arse from his elbow when it came to *real* policework?

What then? Did you lose face and let him walk all over you? Or did you nick him, *hoping* that you had a power of arrest, and *hoping* that when you got him to the factory, there *would* be something incriminating in his pockets, or that a name-check *would* turn him up as *Wanted*?

But what sort of supervising officer *would* tutor and guide a prob, when he could far less effortlessly laze around the station building or streets in *avoidance* of policework? Only a conscientious supervisor who was proud; and they were a rare breed, indeed.

Another factor was that supervisors, in too many cases, didn't know *how* to do The Job. At least not in accordance with official practice and procedure. Sure, they were the ones with the experience, acting instinctively, and it was that experience which they drew from when confronted by most incidents. They just *knew*, for instance, that you *always* arrested a man who'd committed theft; and they knew what theft *was*; but scarcely any of them – and this was equally true of the older PCs – would be able to tell you the precise *wording* of the power of arrest, or define for you the *essence* of the offence of theft, as laid down by the Theft Act.

An awareness of this had come, bit by bit, to MacHale, and was reinforced when he'd looked at *Police Orders*, one day, and seen the results of the yearly promotion examinations for PCs and Sergeants. Most of those who'd sat the exams, had failed. Yet the set questions were exclusively about *policework*! On top of that, the pass mark was only sixty per cent, which meant, or so MacHale had concluded, that The Job found acceptable a man whose knowledge of his duties was defective or deficient by as much as forty per cent.

Christ, they didn't even know what the official training-school teaching on charging and report-writing was. Barker had actually ordered him to rewrite a Process report, once, just because *he* couldn't follow it, saying, '*Forget* that crap they taught you at TS. On District, it's *different*.'

And whereas the training school taught you that you *always* must make notes of arrest, immediately on arrival at the nick, then read them out in the presence of the prisoner and the Station Officer, so that the prisoner might comment and the Station Officer might determine what if any charge is to be preferred, on District, the PCs, especially the older ones, just dumped their bodies in the charge-room, left another PC to stand guard, then, hands in pockets, slouched into the front office and said something like, 'Got one in for TDA, Skip. I'll start taking his dabs, while you type-out the sheet.'

MacHale began to suspect that you *had* to be a Cowboy in order to get Results. Certainly, if you were ducking and diving and short-circuiting procedures, not to mention the law, then those Results could be easier to come by.

Couldn't they?

Maybe . . . Take again the business of stops in the street. If you did allow your actions in this sphere to be limited by reasonable suspicion, how many villains would go undetected? Not all drug-abusers, for instance, wore long hair, beards and scruffy clothes; but they were the ones, the stereotypes, who always got pulled and turned over; the cute ones, smartly dressed, well manicured, got away because the law didn't bother them. Why *not*, then, just turn over *anyone* who gave you a buzz? . . .

The line of thought began to worry him. Where would it end? It confused him, too, and he was unable to answer the questions he'd posed himself. It actually *frightened* him that he should find himself contemplating whether or not it might – might *just* – be acceptable, in certain circumstances, to break the law as a means of enforcing it.

What he really wanted was to be a successful, professional, but, above all, *honest* cop.

He got up and left the office, muttering, 'To *hell* with those Cowboys.'

He wanted to go his *own* way.

5

The way he saw it, he was responsible for millions – maybe billions – of pounds'-worth of private, residential and business property, not to mention the priceless mental and physical security of law-abiding people.

Then there were the vehicles. Everywhere he went, lining the kerbs in every street, nose to tail. They had to be worth millions, too.

Of course, gone were the days when a beat PC would be woken from his sleep off night-duty to account for not having detected a break-in that had occurred on his patch, during his tour. But, nonetheless, a conscientious and professional officer still felt a sense of personal victimization when a villain committed a crime on his beat, and got away with it.

You could only prevent so much, though. Indeed, MacHale had wondered if you could actually prevent *any* of it.

MacHale, though, believed that he himself would *never* give up. He was replete with ideals of his own. He shook hands with almost every shop's doorknob on his beat, and, occasionally, tugged at a car's door-handle as he passed it by on the street. You just never knew: there *might* be a body inside the shop whose door hadn't been locked; or the car whose door was open, *might* prove to have been stolen, so that a covert obbo could reveal that it hadn't yet been abandoned by the thief.

Then there were other, more traditional and subtle methods.

All of the parade's lock-up shops were vulnerable, but the jeweller's shop was *particularly* vulnerable. It contained thousands of pounds'-worth of stock in its night safe, and any would-be burglar who made his way along a narrow alley near the end of the parade, would have access to a grass-and-mud pathway which ran along the back of the shops, at the top of a railway embankment. Then, if he scaled the seven-feet-high brick wall that ran parallel to the path, he could drop down into any of the shops' small yards, and work undisturbed and out of sight.

Most of the shops had occupied, private flats above them, but the flat above the jeweller's was used as an office, and was empty during the night; so it wasn't just the value of its stock which made this shop vulnerable to attack. A burglar could climb the fire escape from the jeweller's yard, force an entry to the office, then tunnel down through the ceiling. Alarms and iron window-bars were no deterrents to professional burglars.

It wasn't a would-be burglar, though, who was squatting atop the wall, now, at one-thirty this morning, silhouetted against the night sky, breathing heavily after his exertions, trying to compose himself before dropping down into the jeweller's yard. And he wasn't armed with a would-be burglar's tools, either. He was MacHale, armed with nothing more innocuous than a piece of chalk and a reel of thread.

Kneeling on top of the narrow wall, he cautiously turned, his back now facing the shop, and began lowering his feet down into the yard. When his body was completely over the side, he hung there, by his fingertips, then dropped, bending his knees to absorb the impact as his boots hit the concrete yard. Now he paused, straightening his helmet, holding his breath, intently listening, afraid that someone in one of the adjacent flats, above him, to his left and right, may have heard a noise and been stirred from sleep . . .

Nothing, though. Only the thumping of his own heart

as it drummed his ribcage . . . Then the sound of a car, cruising along the street at the front of the parade . . . A train, rattling past on the other side of the wall, its wheels clicking along the metal track . . . Now, the sound of cats, wailing in the near distance as they squared up over disputed territory . . . Then, complete silence again.

He began breathing normally, and went quickly to work. First, he climbed the fire escape and arrived at the door which led into the office above the shop. Kneeling, he took out his reel of thread, snapped off a length, then moistened it with spittle before sticking one end of it to the bottom of the door, and the other end to the jamb. As he stood, looking at his work, he nodded his satisfaction. If anyone went through that door, tonight, the piece of thread must be dislodged, and MacHale would know for certain that the office had been entered – you didn't *always* find signs of a screwing on the jambs of doors that had been forced, so this method, MacHale felt, was not only worthwhile, it was infallible.

Next, he began to descend the metal treads of the escape, pausing at every third one to rub his chalk across the centre of its upper surface. If anyone else climbed those stairs, tonight, his shoes would almost certainly erase *part* of MacHale's chalkmarks.

Back in the yard below the office, he returned to the wall, poised himself, cat-like, then sprang, his fingers pressing flat against the wall's ridge, his boots scrabbling for grip on the brickwork, pushing him upward. Now he was atop the wall, once more . . . now dropping down onto the grass-and-mud path.

At regular intervals throughout the night, he'd return and inspect his marks, hoping like hell that he'd find them disturbed, *and* a body or two inside the jeweller's.

As he turned right, leaving the path and entering the alley, he suddenly jolted to a halt, startled. At the far end of the alley, there was a bulky, dark form . . . a man, leaning against the wall. A *big* man.

MacHale's eyes stung as he strained them through the darkness, and he began moving slowly forward, towards the silhouette . . .

Halfway there, he relaxed, and cursed himself for his skittishness. It was only Tasty Tom, helmet in hand, smoking a roll-up. As MacHale drew closer, sniffing, coughing, so as to give Tasty some advance warning of his approach, he noted a pool of wetness, still steaming, on the black-tarmac surface of the alley, immediately behind Tasty.

Tasty spun round on hearing MacHale's approach, then, after identifying the prob', turned back to face the street.

'All right?' MacHale tried, on reaching Tasty's side – he had to say *something*.

Tasty sniffed, jerked back his head, and hawked. Then he spat a wad of phlegm, out onto the pavement in front of him. Turning his head, he licked his lips, sniffed again, swallowed hard, looked up and down MacHale, and said: 'What the fuck're you doin, creepin around the back of the shops?'

'Oh, just checking premises.' *He* might have asked what Tasty was doing on *his* beat, when he was supposed to be on Six Beat, a couple of miles away. If he'd *dared*. Really, though, MacHale didn't care – what was it to *do* with MacHale? Nothing.

Tasty emitted a disdainful grunt, and sucked on his roll-up, spitting out smoke with a strand of tobacco. 'Wasta fuckin time.'

MacHale shrugged, and began brushing brick-dust from the front of his tunic and the knees of his trousers. 'Well, anyway,' he said, uncomfortably, embarrassedly . . . most of all, *inadequately*, he felt. 'I'll be away, then.' And he went to move out the alley.

Without warning, Tasty's huge right arm shot out from his side and locked itself horizontally across MacHale's chest, barring his way. But the rest of his body was motionless, alert, tense, and his eyes were trained intently, obliquely, across to the far side of the street, all the while his fearsome expression growing harder.

'Well, fuck a duck an bugger a bat,' he growled. 'Look who it ain't! Fuckin *Super*-yob!' Now his right arm arced upward, and his hand moved flat across the top of his grey brush-cut, its erect bristles of hair popping up and back into position as the hand passed over them. Then his left hand placed his helmet on top of his head, and he was away, striding menacingly across the road.

MacHale stayed where he was, looking to his right, his eyes on Tasty's target: a young kid, about eighteen, MacHale judged; a *skinhead*, in fact, who wore a pair of black Dr-Marten's, a pair of faded blue, skintight denims that were streaked white with bleach burns, and a quilted, green bomber-jacket, elasticated at the cuffs and waist, about two sizes too big for him, making him seem powerfully built when he was merely slim; his skinny legs, and thin, pale face, covered in red blotches, suggested he might be a junkie.

What he certainly was, though, was stoned, weaving along as if his huge boots were following a serpentine channel that was gouged out of the pavement, his head jolting around, his eyes downcast, his hands stuck deep into his jeans' pockets, his shoulders drooping forward. Occasionally, he stumbled, jarred forward, stopped, faltered sideways, lolled his chin on his chest, then thrust forward with his midriff to get himself going again – it might all have been choreographed, the actions and facial expressions were always in the same, sequential order. He was oblivious of Tasty's advance, but he wouldn't be oblivious for much longer, because Tasty was fast bearing down on him, murder in his eyes, *praying* that Super-yob was a Chelsea Football-Club supporter. By *Christ*, was he gonna get some stick!

MacHale winced, and momentarily closed his eyes. Tasty had just walked straight *through* the yob, knocking him backwards onto his arse. Now, sitting on the pavement, the yob was slowly shaking his head, staring, disbelievingly, up at the huge mountain of cop who'd stepped back and was looming over him, snarling.

'Why don'tcha watch where ya goin?' demanded Tasty. 'Ya sacka dog's crap!'

The yob was now on his knees, his eyes shut tight, spluttering, 'Sheee-*it! Tell* me it ain't real!' But when he opened his eyes and looked again, he saw that it *was* real. 'I . . . I never *saw* ya,' he protested, his speech thick and sloppy.

'Never *saw* me!' exploded Tasty, his coarse voice reverberating around the empty street. 'What am I? The Invisible-fuckin-Man or somethin? *Didn't see me*. Huh!' He cocked aside his head, and his expression took on a leering, challenging facet. '*You're* lookin for a punch-up, ain'tcha ya slag?'

The yob thrust forward and up with the palm of his right hand. He swallowed hard '*No!* Honest! *I'm* goin *home*. I've just been to a party, an I'm goin *home* . . . officer.'

'*Party!*' spat Tasty. '*I'll* give ya a *party*. At *my* place. Ya skinny little hard-faced little fucker, ya.'

'No, no! I *wanna* go home . . . *please* . . . officer.' Now he was climbing up Tasty's legs.

'Officer, my *arse*!' mocked Tasty. 'If you was at a Saturday football-match, now, with all ya slaggy mates behind ya, *you'd* be takin the piss outa me, behind my back . . . loudmouthin it up, fuckin-'n'-blindin, letting everyone know how hard y'are, just *dyin* for a bit of aggravation with an old-age pensioner, so's y'could put some claret on the toecapsa them bootsa yourn. Well, now's ya chance. *I'll* give y'all the aggravation ya want. An *then* some. See just how hard ya *really* are.'

'No, no!' wailed the yob, panic on his numbed face. 'Leave it *out*! *I* ain't hard. Not *me-ee*! I just wanna – '

The rest of his protest came out as a strangled squeal, because Tasty, having bent down, had grabbed him by the scruff of the neck and was hauling him to his feet. Then, left hand gripping the yob's gizzard, pushing hard upward so that he was teetering on the tips of his boots, gasping for air, Tasty began slapping him around, muttering, 'You *bastard*! . . . You *bastard*! . . .'

Smack! Smack! Smack! counterpointed by a series of grunts and groans, and shrieks, echoed all around the street.

MacHale, fearing that the whole episode was being witnessed by someone who lived in one of the flats above the shops, decided to go on the trot and leave Tasty to it. The last he heard of it was Tasty telling the yob that he was nicked for threatening behaviour.

Chelsea, nil; Metropolitan Police, *wipeout*!

Suck back! thought MacHale. If *anyone* had been guilty of using threatening behaviour, it was Tasty Tom.

At three-thirty, MacHale, having had his refreshment break, was back at the parade of shops, holed-up in the recessed doorway of a mini-supermarket, thinking that a worthwhile stop might come by him. Why *couldn't* some slag appear from nowhere and lob a brick through the window of the electrical shop, opposite? They were *always* doing the shops along the parade – smash-'n'-grabs and screwings – but rarely were they caught in the act . . . or even subsequently, come to think of it.

Only last week, when MacHale was early-turn, he'd been called on to report a screwing at one of the shoe shops, where they'd gone over the wall at the back, forced a sash window, then unscrewed the iron bars that were fixed to the inside of the window's frame, and climbed inside. Then they'd shut the window, screwed the bars back into place, and closed the curtains.

When the manager arrived, at eight-thirty the next morning, there wasn't a shoe left in the shop – apart from those that were in the window display, out front; just a mountain of empty cardboard boxes.

MacHale peered around the supermarket's recessed doorway, to his left . . . nothing, just darkness, saturated by the foggy orange light of the tall street-lamps . . . to his right . . . a black figure, cycling up the road, towards him . . . some way off, yet, but pedalling like there was a gale-force wind behind him . . . Maybe he'd nicked the bike? . . .

MacHale moved out of the doorway and stood by the kerb, ready to pull the cyclist and Q-'n'-A him re. his possession of the machine. But as the cyclist drew nearer, MacHale changed his mind and moved quickly back across the pavement and into his hidey-hole. It was Filthy Phil, pedalling hell-for-leather towards him, his head down, his legs going like pistons, his body and the cycle jerking from side-to-side, the bottoms of his mac, flapping in the air.

Is he on a shout? MacHale wondered . . . No, he couldn't be. *No* shouts had come *out* on the PR. And, anyway, Filthy Phil never *accepted* shouts. So what the hell *was* he up to?

At that moment, a shout *did* crackle out over the PR: *Any offers? Teachers' Training College, Branston Road, suspect disturbed in grounds; believed a Peeping Tom.* Branston Road? MacHale thought . . . That's just a quarter of a mile away; Filthy Phil must just have cycled *past* the college . . . *No; from* the college.

MacHale had his answer: Filthy Phil had been bogging female trainee teachers as they slept in their hostel in the college grounds, and someone had spotted him.

The RT-car took the shout, and Filthy Phil began pedalling even more furiously; he swept past MacHale, head still down, the cycle's dynamo emitting a high-pitched whining noise.

A couple of seconds later, the RT-car, swathed in a revolving, opalescent blue-light, flashed by in the opposite direction; but MacHale knew that Snatch and Tubby Tompkins were on a blow-out: the 'suspect' was well gone.

When the air had settled, MacHale's thoughts moved on: time to go and check the jeweller's, he decided, and left the doorway, walking along the pavement towards the alley.

As he reached the entrance to the alley, his senses were alerted, and he came to an abrupt halt. That puddle of urine of Tasty Tom's was still there; and leading away from it, down the alley, towards the path that ran alongside the rear of the shops, were *wet footprints*.

Silently, his heart pounding, his mouth drying out, he moved with a feline stealth along the pitch-black alley, peering, helmet in hand, around the corner of the end shop's brick wall . . . nothing, no one . . . But *wait* a minute! Halfway along the mud-and-grass track, leaning against the wall of the jeweller's-shop yard, there was a small, square, black shape.

What was it? He closed his eyes, shook his head, and looked again, straining his eyes, frowning . . . A sack? . . . A box . . . full of jewellery? . . . Now his breaths were coming in short, deep spurts, while his heart began to *ache*, it was throbbing so fast and powerfully.

Calm down! he inwardly shouted, and decided, No, it's too premature to put up a shout for assistance . . . First, go and have a closer look.

When he reached the object that was leaning against the wall, he saw that it was a dark blue, moulded-plastic milk crate . . . just like the ones that were stacked, full of empty bottles, outside the mini-supermarket. Someone had brought that crate around here, to stand on and climb up and over the wall! He – *they* – *someone* . . . screwing the *jeweller's*!

Oh, my *God*, what to do? he wondered, and his thoughts then scrambled: Bodies! For crime! . . . Danger! Excitement! . . . Glory! A commendation!

Then conditioning took precedence, and he recalled the passage from the IB which set out a course of action to be followed if suspects were believed to be on premises. He knew, then, that he should now be creeping away from here, putting up a shout for urgent assistance, observing the jeweller's – from a distance – ready to capture any bodies who tried to leg it before that assistance arrived.

But supposing he were wrong? Supposing it were a courting couple, say, over the other side of that wall, doing what came naturally? . . . Or a vagrant, kipping down for the night? Unlikely, but . . . Jesus, his name'd be mud if he called for urgent assistance and there was found to be nothing in it. Cops didn't like breaking their necks to get to *blow-outs*, and they liked even less the idiots who'd sent for them.

No, he told himself. I've gotta be certain.

He stood there, then, listening, but couldn't hear a thing from the other side of the wall. So maybe they were already *in* the jeweller's . . . ? There was only one way to be certain: go over and inspect the chalkmarks and thread.

Some of the chalkmarks on the fire escape's metal treads, *were* scuffed . . . and the piece of thread across the bottom of the door, was *missing* . . . more than that, there was a cigarette butt on the top tread of the escape, in *front* of the door.

Oh, Christ, he thought, and was straightaway on a high. He glided quickly and silently back down the escape, slid noiselessly up and over the wall, dropped onto the path, and then went like a bat out of hell to the top end of the alley, out on to the street.

Now, his chest heaving, air rasping in and out of his burning windpipe, sweat trickling down his face, he unclipped his PR and put up the shout: *Urgent assistance; suspects on!*

In the distance, the noise of whip-tones, growing ever louder – stupid pricks! Didn't they know how *far* that noise carried? Then the sounds of powerful engines . . . racing . . . surging up through gears . . . braking . . . cornering, tyres screaming . . . the street filled with a rotating, blue luminescence; doors opening and slamming; RT-sets crackling; boots pounding the footway . . . hands moving to sticks . . .

Now he was *surrounded* by uniforms; others were already at the far end of the alley, disappearing around the corner of the wall, while even more were standing outside the front of the jeweller's shop, doing what all cops do on such occasions: asking one another what the strength of the shout was, slouching up and down, hatless, hands in pockets, and just waiting for a development.

'What's the strength of it, then, shag?' asked an old PC, taking stock of MacHale's flushed, wet face and dust-streaked uniform.

'They're in the jeweller's,' MacHale said. 'They've screwed the back door.' His voice was shot with emotion

The old PC was utterly unmoved by the revelation. 'Oh yeah? How'd'ya know that, then, shag?'

'Me *marks*,' MacHale said. 'They've been disturbed.' Why wasn't this old fart taking him seriously?

'Oh yeah? What marks is these, then, shag?'

'Well . . . *chalk*-marks . . . and a piece of thread.' What was the *matter* with this *scruffy* old fart? Didn't he *believe* MacHale? Apparently not. Most of the PCs who'd initially surrounded MacHale, had now lost interest in the shout and were shuffling away, to wait idly at the front of the premises.

The old boy smiled sardonically and slowly shook his head. '*Oh! Chalkmarks*, eh? I see.' And he, too, walked away.

MacHale just stood there, bewildered. Then he saw his own nick's RT-car cruise up to the shout; but it had no noise on, and its blue lamp wasn't rotating.

Tubby Tompkins swung his huge bulk out of the driver's seat, and waddled over to the pavement in front of the jeweller's, his jowls quivering as he smiled a puzzling smile, his little piggy eyes, with their ginger lashes, glinting in the available light; he glanced contemptuously at MacHale, sniffed, took off his hat, ran a podgy-fingered hand over the top of his wavy, ginger hair, and slowly shook his head. Then he was joined by Snatch, his RT-operator, an elderly, anodyne-featured PC with silver hair, who had the physique of a toffee-apple on two sticks, and the mind of a tarantula spider; the pair of them stood together, chuckling and swapping whispers.

They were joined by the old PC who'd just left MacHale, and for a while the three of them engaged in conversation, the old PC occasionally jabbing his right thumb over his shoulder, in MacHale's direction.

And now, MacHale saw Tasty Tom climbing out of the back seat of the area-car that Tubby had just driven up in; he joined Tubby and Snatch and the old PC, and within a few seconds the whole group was falling about, shaking with laughter at something the leering Tasty had said. Then the old PC left the group and walked to his colleagues who were standing by, further along the road, sniffing back his mirth as he did so, and casting a knowing glance at MacHale.

'It's all right, lads,' the old PC told his colleagues. 'There's nothing in it. It's a blow-out.' Then he lowered his voice, drew his colleagues closer to him, and spoke in hushed, conspiratorial tones which MacHale couldn't interpret. This group then deputed one of its number to go down the alley and fetch back the PCs who were still at the rear of the jeweller's, while the rest, most of them laughing like drains, climbed back into their area-cars and vans, and shot away.

What was he *on* about? MacHale asked himself. *Of course* there's something *in* the shout. There're suspects on *premises*, here. And he was just about to make his way around to the rear of the jeweller's, to see what was going on there, when the last of those officers who'd responded to his shout, began to walk back. Some of them, too, were laughing. But others were clearly annoyed. As they brushed past MacHale, one stopped in front of him, seething with anger, and shouted, 'You *cunt*! *I* could've broken my *neck*, racin here to your bogus-fuckin-shout! . . . And look at my fuckin strides!'

MacHale looked at the PC's trousers: covered in dirt and brick-dust, with a triangular tear in the right knee. 'But . . . I don't understand what . . .' They were all gone, though, and MacHale was even more bewildered.

Until, that is, his eyes relocated Tasty Tom, who was *still* laughing – well, sneering, with his lips parted, exposing those huge yellow teeth of his – and muttering, 'Fuck a duck an bugger a bat . . . What a gutbuster!'

Then MacHale fell in. *Now* he understood.

That bastard, Tasty, *knew* that he, MacHale, had been inspecting premises at the rear of the shops, and he'd obviously guessed that MacHale had left some marks. After getting that yob put on the sheet, for threatening behaviour, he'd come back here, found the marks, and interfered with them, knowing full well that MacHale would be returning to check on them. And just to lure him on, Tasty had also left his wet footprints in the alley and that milk crate against the wall.

The *evil* bastard.

MacHale was well choked. He felt so *inept*. They all believed him to be an idiot. But he'd make damn sure that nothing like it ever happened again. He took out his reel of thread and his piece of chalk, and threw them away.

Tubby Tompkins and Tasty Tom were now making their way back to the RT-car, but Snatch came walking over to MacHale.

He patted MacHale's right shoulder, and chuckled, but not maliciously, MacHale felt. 'Never mind, dear boy,' he said. 'You'll get over it. No harm's been done, so try'n see the funny side of it. A good copper's gotta have a sense of humour, ya know.' And he looked askance at MacHale, his eyebrows hopefully raised.

MacHale studied Snatch's paternal countenance. He was reckoned to be a good cop, old Snatch, an example both to his older colleagues and to younger ones, like MacHale. Ever diligent, always in search of bodies, and always finding them, too. That's why they *called* him *Snatch*. Give him an offence, the body to go with it, and the smallest amount of evidence with which to substantiate it, and he'd snatch that body off the street and sit him down in the charge-room. And the old boy was so genial, so seemingly honest and sincere, he could've blagged the Pope into pleading to a trumped-up rape charge. So it was said.

'Yeah, you're right, I s'pose,' MacHale wearily told Snatch. And he managed to force a smile.

'That's the spirit, dear boy,' Snatch enthused, as he turned around and walked away to the RT-car.

Now, MacHale was again alone. Suddenly, he felt drained of energy, if bloated with frustration. Just how much of it could your body take? he wondered. Throughout a tour of duty, you'd put yourself on full alert, God knew how many times; and your heart would begin thundering like crazy, while adrenaline surged through your veins, straining every muscle to the point of snapping . . .

MacHale took out his handkerchief and wiped sweat from his face and eyes. He brushed down his trousers, settled his helmet on his head, and walked away into the night.

6

MacHale decided that the man who was some two-hundred yards ahead, on the same side of the road, was probably a vagie.

What *other* class of citizen would be breakfasting at a road-side litter bin at six o'clock on a cold, dark morning? Or at *any* time of the day or night?

The man's hands were almost a blur, working overtime as he sorted through the previous day's accumulation of rubbish; and soft-drink cans, rolled-up newspapers, cigarette packets and take-away food cartons were among the many items that were minutely examined before being rejected and lobbed over his right shoulder, onto the pavement. Occasionally, though, he'd pause, and his right hand would move up and pop a decomposing morsel into his salivating mouth; then the sifting of rubbish would momentarily cease while he took a break to look about himself and chomp on whatever it was that had tempted his appetite.

The approach of a uniformed cop didn't concern him, either, and, having seen that MacHale was closing in on him, he once again bent over the litter bin and began scavenging for his next course.

'The cheeky sod,' MacHale muttered, as a crumpled beer-can came clattering towards him along the pavement; and his mind began processing offences and powers of arrest . . .

Traffic was now building up in the three lanes of the High Street's one-way system, and the vibrant noise of exhausts and engines was distracting, but within a couple of seconds, MacHale had decided his course of action: do the vagie for depositing litter.

The vagie glanced up as MacHale arrived at his side, and stood his ground, ankle-deep in rubbish, piling a handful of soggy, crinkle-cut chips into his mouth; obviously, they were stone cold, and most of them were covered by a grey-black fur of cigarette ash.

MacHale grimaced, and felt his gut tightening and rippling. Then he nodded, and bid the vagie a good morning.

The vagie nodded, as well, and smiled, showing bony, toothless gums and fragments of masticated chips; and as he swallowed hard, cocking aside his head, the tip of his chin – glistening with a film of grease and saliva – almost touched the point of his nose. Then he went back in search of more food.

MacHale looked at him. Aged about fifty, he thought, with his head shaved around the back and sides, leaving just a tufty white outcrop on top, ironically a haircut which was the height of fashion among certain of the young, cult groups. The creased-up suit he wore was a dark colour . . . grey probably, but more like black, now, with its patina of shiny dirt; beneath the jacket, he had on a filthy, collarless white shirt, and his sockless feet – caked black around the ankles – were encased in a pair of battered, brown brogues that were scuffed white along the sides and on the toecaps: Oxfam's autumn collection, MacHale mused. And by Christ, didn't the vagie hum? In the summer, MacHale thought, there'd be more flies on him than on a camel's . . . well, than on *any* part of a camel's anatomy.

Now the vagie was sucking on a spare-rib, and that, too, when he'd finished with it, went flying over his shoulder.

MacHale tapped him on the forearm. 'Oi, I've been watching you,' he began, 'and I've seen you chuck all this rubbish over the pavement. Don't you know it's an offence to deposit litter?'

The vagie stopped rummaging, turned to face MacHale, and smiled gormlessly, touching his forelock. 'All right, guv'nor. No trouble . . .' He paused to give a flurry of regal waves to the occupants of passing cars.

He's barmy, MacHale thought . . . Humour him; his sort can turn. 'Look,' he said, in a patronizing tone. 'Tell you what: if you pick up all this rubbish, and chuck it back in the bin, we'll forget about it. Okay?'

'Oooh!' the vagie said, his eyes popping. 'All right, guv'nor . . . But what about the murder?' And he arched his eyebrows and looked enigmatically at MacHale.

'*Murder?*' MacHale said. '*What* murder?'

'*Rape*-'n'-murder!' the vagie roared, stamping his feet and waving his arms. '*I'm* the most wanted man in the *world*!' He turned his head to look at a couple of elderly charladies who'd just passed by, on their way to work, then bellowed, 'Get yer drawers off! Let's have a gang-bang!' And he folded up, screaming with laughter.

The two old dears had a quick look back over their shoulders, and then carried on their way, giggling.

That is *it*, MacHale thought, and moved forward to claim the vagie . . . Insulting behaviour would do, he thought.

'Leave him alone.' – the weary voice came from behind MacHale.

He spun round. It was Vindscreen.

'Don't waste ya time nickin *him*,' Vindscreen said. 'He *wants* to get nicked, all right, but he won't plead to anythin. He's a regular. All he really wants is weekly remands to Brixton, for as long as possible, so's he can enjoy their free bed-'n'-breakfast facilities.' He looked at the vagie. 'Ain't that right, George?'

George grinned and nodded, touching his forelock. 'That's right, guv'nor. Free bed-'n'-breakfast. *Lovely*!'

And he licked his lips and smacked his chops, and rubbed his hands, waiting to be claimed.

'Well what *are* we gonna do with him, then?' MacHale wanted to know. 'We can't just *leave* him here, throwing crap all over the pavement, and shouting the odds at people . . . Can we?'

Vindscreen smiled mischievously, and tapped the tip of his right index-finger on the side of his nose. 'Leave it to me, son.' Then, to George: 'First, pick up all this rubbish, George, and then we'll sort somethin out for ya. Okay, mate?'

'Ooh, lovely,' George said, his mad eyes twinkling, and he squatted down on his haunches and began collecting up the litter, dropping it all back in the bin.

'Right,' Vindscreen said. 'Now we'll see to it that you get what you want. Only, it'll have to be the early Relief, probably, who'll accommodate you, 'cause we're going off-duty in about fifteen minutes.' Vindscreen took him by the arm and guided him across the pavement, into a shop doorway, where he whispered something in his ear. George vigorously nodded his head and began giggling excitedly; then he was off, scurrying up the Street and disappearing, left, into a side road.

Vindscreen rejoined MacHale. 'That takes carea that,' he said. 'Come on. Let's go and check-in our PRs.'

MacHale shrugged. 'Okay. But what did you tell him . . . George? I mean, wha's going on? Where's he gone . . . ?'

'You'll see. You'll see, my son.' Vindscreen smiled, and winked, and began walking away towards the nick.

MacHale again shrugged, and fell in at Vindscreen's side.

Old Crikey entered the Inspectors' office on the ground floor of the nick, switched on the light, and made his way over to the desk, where he pulled out a chair, sat, took off his cap, and opened the OB.

Leaning forward and resting his elbows on the desk-top, he sighed, closed his eyes, and pulled his fingers down over his sore lids. Thank *God*, he thought. Another night over and done with . . . Then, opening the OB, he began writing.

A minute later, the early-turn Reserve knocked at the door and entered. 'G'mornin, sir. Here's that cuppa tea you asked for.' He put the white cup and saucer on the desk, by Old Crikey's right elbow.

'Thanks . . .' Old Crikey mumbled, not bothering to even look up.

The Reserve politely coughed.

Now Old Crikey looked up, and frowned; then he glanced down at his tea, saw that the saucer was brimming with the milky white liquid, and frowned even more deeply. Lastly, he tut-tutted, leaned over sideways in his chair, put his right hand in his trouser pocket, and brought out some loose change. 'Here,' he begrudgingly muttered. 'Take it out of that.'

'Thanks, sir.' The Reserve took six-P, about-turned and left the office, closing the door behind himself. Then he faced the door, aggressively contorted his face, and jabbed a couple of V-signs up in the air. 'Gitcha own tea, in future, ya snotgobblin Scots prat!'

Inside the office, Old Crikey took a small sip of the luke-warm, sickly-sweet tea, scowled, almost spat, then popped a digestif in his mouth and carried on writing.

Along the corridor, in the comms room, the night Relief was waiting for the wall-clock's hands to hit six-thirty A.M. Some of the PCs were seated, lolling sideways or backwards, while others were standing, leaning against the wall.

Jean the civilian night-duty telephonist, hadn't yet

been relieved, and was seated at her desk, before the miniaturized switchboard – no bigger than a loaf of bread – fast asleep, her chin resting on her chest, her arms dangling limply down at her sides, her heavy breaths rasping in and out of her nose and throat.

Filthy Phil, his tunic and trousers covered in dirt and brick-dust, was seated across from her left side, his bleary, red-rimmed eyes covertly studying her legs; he began frowning, compressing his lips. Behind her back, he reminded himself, the cops called her Foxtrot Lima, the letters representing the words, *Farter Lil*, which was the nickname they'd bestowed upon her because she was always passing wind. She always smelt unclean, too, of the sweet, pungent odour of stale sweat; he sniffed the air, now, shuddered and wrinkled his nose, then ceased to wonder what it'd be like.

At that moment, in came the crew of the RT-car – Snatch and Tubby Tompkins. One or two of the PCs glanced up, lapsed back into apathy, then did double takes. In his left hand, Tubby was holding an empty glass tumbler, while his right hand held a glass tumbler that was full of water; and Snatch was carrying one of the cleaners' red-plastic buckets; both men were having difficulty containing their amusement.

All except Mathieson – still slumbering in one corner of the room, full of Scotch and beer – were totally captivated. What the hell were Snatch and Tubby about to do?

Snatch placed a finger over his lips, and quietly shushed the Relief. Then he tiptoed over to Foxtrot Lima, bent down, and slid the bucket under her desk, placing it between her outstretched, wide-apart legs.

Now the PCs were leaning forward in their seats, and those who'd been standing, shouldering the wall, were completely upright, straining their necks and their eyes in the direction of Foxtrot Lima's desk.

'Right,' Snatch whispered to the PCs. 'Five gets ya twenny-five that she has a slash in the bucket when Tubby pours water from one glass into the other . . . Any takers?'

Tasty Tom yawned – or silently brayed, baring his horse teeth – then sneered, and looked highly sceptical. MacHale looked somewhat bewildered, and shook his head. Filthy Phil smirked, pulled at the tip of his chin, and thought about the odds. Mathieson slept on. Hercules just sat there, his hands washing an invisible bar of soap, softly giggling, darting his eyes at the others. Punchy Paterson stroked the length of his flattened, broken nose. Blinky, the VDU operator, and Dave Hall, the Reserve, were still away in the canteen, tidying up and locking away the tea-club's brewing equipment, while Pat Coles was in her office, writing a report. So that left Vindscreen, who stood, produced a fiver from his hip pocket, and said, 'You're on, Snatch, my son. This Wellington says she *don't* have a slash in the bucket.'

Snatch took Vindscreen's money, then nodded at Tubby. Tubby's little piggy blue-eyes were sparkling with glee, and his jowls and huge, seventeen-stone bulk were quivering as he held his breath and crept closer to Foxtrot Lima's right ear. She stirred, frowned, *moaned*, settled her lips, drew-in a deep breath, which was expired as a contented, nasal sigh, then slumbered on, undisturbed, while Tubby steadied himself and proceeded with the experiment.

First, he extended his left hand and held the empty glass about six inches away from Foxtrot Lima's ear; then his right hand moved up to just above his head, tipping over the full glass . . . slowly, carefully . . . sending a long dribble of water down into the empty glass. As the empty glass began to fill, the noise of sploshing water produced muffled giggles and sniggers from the audience who were now gathered in a half circle before Foxtrot Lima's desk.

Then it sounded as if someone had sat down on a whoopee cushion, as Foxtrot Lima grimaced, groaned, and lived-up to her nickname – more giggling and sniggering.

But now, *all* of the water had passed down from the full glass into the empty glass, and yet there was still no sign of Foxtrot Lima passing any of her *own* water into the bucket.

'One more try,' whispered Tubby, and after reversing the positions of the glasses, he once again began the water-sploshing process.

''Ere, that ain't *fair*!' Vindscreen protested to Snatch. 'You never said nothin about him havin *two* goes at it. I want my – '

But Vindscreen was cut off in mid-sentence by a tremendous crashing noise and the sound of breaking glass, which were immediately followed by a heart-stopping scream.

All eyes – save those of Mathieson and Foxtrot Lima, which were as firmly shut as before – swivelled towards the closed door.

Punchy Paterson said: 'What the fuck was *that*?'

Then they all dashed for the door – which was flung open by MacHale – bunched through it and hurried along the corridor.

Halfway down the corridor, MacHale, leading, stopped dead and caused a pile-up of bodies which almost knocked him on his face, onto the floor. Now, they all stood there, staring in wonder at the sight that was before them.

It was Old Crikey, staggering out of his office, his right hand, stretched out before him, groping the way, his left hand clamped tightly down over the top of his bald head. He was ashen with shock, and his face and tunic were dripping milky-white tea, and were glinting with flecks of broken glass.

'Ooh, *crikey*!' he wailed. 'What . . . what happened? . . . What ha . . . ?' But he didn't finish: his eyes rolled up towards the ceiling and he crumpled-up and hit the floor, where he remained, gently moaning.

While MacHale stepped over Old Crikey's body and had a look inside the office, Punchy Paterson and Tasty Tom placed Old Crikey in the three-quarters-prone position, loosening his tie and unbuttoning his collar.

Inside the office, MacHale saw a jagged hole in the window, and broken glass, lying everywhere. On top of the desk, a brickbat was awash in a pool of tea, amid shards of glass and white crockery.

MacHale could guess what had occurred: the half-brick had come crashing in through the window, landing flat on the rim of the saucer; the cup had gone spinning skyward, drenching Old Crikey in tea, and had then bounced down off his nut, before breaking on top of the desk. But *who* . . .?

MacHale turned and left the office, jostling his way through the crowd of officers who'd gathered in the corridor, before making his way out through the front entrance of the nick.

And there, standing on the pavement, several yards to the left of what remained of Old Crikey's office window, was George, the vagie nutter, nodding to himself and smiling that toothless, gormless smile of his.

You're *mine*, MacHale told himself, and he walked on down to George, claiming him for criminal damage and ABH.

'Ooh, *lovely*,' said George, on hearing that he was under arrest. Then, he fed his left arm to MacHale, and added, 'What's for breakfast then?'

But MacHale didn't realize the *full* extent of what had occurred; at least not until he'd reached the charge-room and sat George down on the bench to await processing by the early-turn Skipper. *Then*, Vindscreen appeared, almost beside himself with glee, and congratulated George, telling him what a good shot he was. Now MacHale realized what their whispered conversation in the shop doorway had been about.

Poor Old Crikey. The last anyone saw of him, that morning, was when he was stretchered out to an ambulance, looking like death warmed-up. 'Skip . . . Skip . . .' he feebly mumbled, raising his head and reaching out for Barker's arm.

'Yes, guv'nor? What is it?' Barker replied, leaning forward over the stretcher.

Old Crikey gripped Barker's wrist, and held on to it. 'The . . . the Relief,' he whispered, his voice weak and emotional. 'Don't let them get away with *anything*!' – now he was almost shouting, and as he was carried on down the steps, towards the waiting ambulance, he bellowed, 'And make sure Vipas gets his *hair* cut!'

At first, he'd been thankful. Well, it was an arrest for crime, and badly needed, too. But now he wasn't so sure. In fact, he was worried. The arrest had been greatly diminished by the nature of Vindscreen's involvement in the events leading up to it, and, when it came down to it, Vindscreen had himself committed a criminal offence by *inciting* nutty George to smash Old Crikey's office window.

Supposing George told the *court*? Supposing he were to say he'd only broken the window because the officer had *told* him to do it? What the hell would the Magistrate make of *that*? He might order George's release on bail, and then ask that an official inquiry be instituted. And MacHale didn't think he'd be able to withstand a CIB interrogation. He'd heard all about the tactics those CIB men employed. First, they sent for you, and when you arrived at the Big House, they banged you up in a tiny office and went away for an hour or so, leaving you there to roast in your own guilt; and, of course, they also seized every piece of official correspondence that was connected with your case, and went through it with a fine toothcomb, until they found an incorrect or an incomplete record: so that if you kept shtum on the matter under inquiry, and thereby precluded their sticking you on for that, they could then hit you with some *venial*, disciplinary offences . . . like failing to book out a PR, or something. There was no doubt about it: if *they'd* made up their minds that you were guilty, you were on a hiding to nothing, and nobody would ever row you out of it. And why *were* the bastards so cannibalistic, when half of them were themselves as bent as clockwork oranges? Well, Tubby Tompkins had put it this way: 'Let's take an analogy: if you were a closet gay, not wanting any of your friends or colleagues to realize or suspect, how would you go about throwing them?' MacHale had considered the question, and could only come up with one answer: 'I s'pose I'd denigrate gays, whenever a conversation settled on the subject of homosexuality; and go out of my way to nick gays for indecency offences. That way, everyone'd believe I was straight.' Tubby had nodded his head as he said, '*Exactly*.'

Now, MacHale began to wonder about the notes of arrest he'd made in his IRB. They were as complete as they could be, *he* believed, but the Station Officer who'd accepted the charges, hadn't bothered to check or countersign them. It was the same old story, though: about the apathy of supervisors, their neglect and incompetence.

Christ, an officer above the rank of Inspector was never, ever seen on parade, and the only time the senior ranks were to be seen on the streets, was when they were accompanying a demo', or supervising some other kind of public-order event. Little wonder, then, that blokes like Vindscreen were able to take so much piss, and get away with it. No one in authority ever knew exactly what the Cowboys were doing, until such time as they went right over the top and committed some serious, disciplinary offence that *couldn't* be squared up. Then, that same, incompetent and apathetic hierarchy claimed credit for having detected and rooted out a 'bad apple', when, in reality, *it* was culpable for not having *prevented* the defaulter's demise.

MacHale sighed. MacHale was the one who'd be punished. It was he who'd lose half a day's sleep, and it was he who'd do all of the worrying in case the job went bent on him.

He looked at nutty George's list of previous: seventeen, in all; petty stuff, too, mostly; like theft – of pints of milk, and bread and pies, from early-morning deliveries to the outsides of shops and supermarkets – and criminal damage – to shop windows, usually, when he'd been desperate for bed-'n'-breakfast, and had wanted to get himself claimed.

That was of some comfort, actually, MacHale realized: if old George did go bent on him, and put Vindscreen in the frame, for incitement, then his eleven previous for smashing the windows of shops, would tend to discredit his allegation; lobbing bricks through glass *was* his favourite MO, and it didn't *need* anyone to put him up to it . . . Well, not usually, anyway.

MacHale yawned, leaned against the wall, and glanced at his wristwatch – eleven-forty A.M. His mouth was dry and sour, his limbs ached, and his eyes were throbbing sore for want of sleep. How much longer? he wondered. In front of him there was a long line of officers and defendants, all waiting their turns for a hearing . . . and these were only the overnight charges, the custody cases; the court had already worked its way through a score or more of remands, since ten-fifteen. And in other parts of the building, three more courts were engaged in identical business. Out in the foyer, there was a seething mass of bodies: defendants who'd been bailed, and civilian as well as police witness. The civvies were usually appalled by their treatment, too. They were doing their public-spirited duty, coming along here to assist the police in obtaining convictions and justice, but when they arrived, they were placed among thieves, beggars, winos, prostitutes, ponces and junkies – *every* kind of human excrement. The demeanour and the language of these slags was frightening, too, for any respectable person who'd been cast among them, and most witnesses resolved never again to become involved in this tedious, coldly impersonal, horrifying process of . . . no, not of justice, but of law.

At twelve noon, they were on. The gaoler appeared at the head of the passage, holding open the court-room door to allow the exit of an officer and prisoner, and consulted his clipboard. His head then turned, and he faced into the court-room, looking up. 'Charge number thirty-four, Your Worship: George Scott.' Then he swivelled his head and looked at MacHale. 'This way, please.'

MacHale prodded George, and they moved forward and into the court. George was guided into the dock, and MacHale made his way over to the witness box, standing at ease as he awaited the reading of the charges. He certainly didn't *feel* at ease, though. As soon as a witness entered a court-room, all eyes were upon him.

To MacHale's right, at the back of the dark-wood-panelled room, was the public enclosure, packed to capacity. While to his left, the Magistrate sat high up on a carved-wood throne, before a long desk which bore a line of hefty, legal tomes, a decanter and glass, paper-work, and the daily register of cases. This morning, the Magistrate was Claud Harris, a stipendiary; he was a hoary old boy of about seventy, who wore a blue, chalkstripe suit, a white shirt with Brigade of Guards' tie, a monocle over his left eye, and a caustic expression on his sagging face. When listening to evidence, he usually tilted aside his head and cupped a hand over his right ear – as he was deaf in his left – while half-closing his left eye; so that his right eye, a huge, shiny, blue-glass one – which replaced the real one he'd had shot out during the last World War – seemed to be preying on the defendant, below him in the dock.

Also to MacHale's right, in front of the public enclosure, was the dock, with George, enclosed by its panelled wood, leaning forward over the handrail, looking well pleased with himself, occasionally glancing to his right and nodding smiles and winks at the rows of tiered benches which accommodated a brief of solicitors and a wig of barristers, all very serious and erudite-looking men and women.

MacHale glanced sideways at nutty George. Now he was standing with his *back* to the Bench, smiling and waving at the public enclosure. The gaoler hurried to his side, grabbed his arm, and spun him round the right way. Then the clerk of the court, who was seated at a small table immediately beneath the Magistrate, began the proceedings by asking the defendant if his name was, in fact, George Scott.

Nutty George smiled that gummy smile of his, touched his forelock, and shouted. 'Yes, Ya Majesty. Tha's me, all right.'

Titters bubbled up from the public enclosure, and Claud Harris himself almost smiled. 'Mister Scott,' he said, most genially. '*I* am the one who is enthroned.'

More titters from the public enclosure.

Nutty George again touched his forelock, and, bowing obsequiously, said, 'Yes, Ya Majesty. Sorry about that.'

'Your *Worship*,' said the clerk, addressing nutty George.

Nutty George dismissively spread his left hand. 'Oh, well, ta very much for your indulgence,' he said. 'But you can call me George, if y'like.'

Loud laughter, this time, from the public.

'Silence!' commanded Claud Harris, his face reddening.

And so it went on for a further ten minutes. Nutty George, playing to his audience; the clerk, tut-tutting and sighing, on the verge of apoplexy, attempting to elicit whether nutty George wished to have his case dealt with here or at the higher court, and explaining the implications of each course; and the Magistrate, straining his good ear and contorting his good eye, occasionally intervening to admonish the public spectators when their ripples of amusement threatened seriously to impinge upon the sanctity of the venue and its business.

Eventually, nutty George put up his hands, and pleaded to both charges; much to the relief of MacHale, who then proceeded to relate the brief facts of the case. After this, and following on nutty George's refusal to comment on the evidence against himself, MacHale read out the last three of nutty George's seventeen previous, each one a conviction for criminal damage to shop windows.

Had the Bench been composed of Justices of the Peace – unpaid, unprofessional, lay Magistrates, who generally sat as pairs or trios to determine cases, never alone – then this job might have occupied the whole of the day. The cops didn't like Justices, because they dithered and dallied, relying too much upon the legal training and experience of their clerks.

Claud Harris, though, was a professional, and no sooner had he heard the last of George's previous, than he said, 'Remanded in custody.'

'Ooh, lovely!' shouted nutty George, on hearing that –

or, more appositely, on *mis*hearing that, for he added, 'Bananas and custard! My favourite!'

Nutty George would now have a week's lay-down at Brixton, for a nut-'n'-gut report, and on the remand date he'd probably be committed under the Mental Health Act.

On his way back to the section-house, MacHale stopped off at a pub, where he bought himself a ploughman's lunch and a pint of lager, lodging himself in a quiet corner, to eat and drink. His stomach full, he felt almost overwhelmed by fatigue, and could scarcely keep open his eyes; he'd now been up for almost nineteen hours. What he'd like to have done was stay there in the pub and drink himself into oblivion; the alcohol relaxed him, and thoughts seemed easier to process, and then, after a few more drinks, thoughts just didn't *matter* any more, because you'd escaped reality. Maybe that was why Mathieson had become dependent upon drink? Maybe *he* had to escape reality in order to survive?

MacHale forced himself to his feet and left the pub, squinting his sore eyes against the light, which wasn't at all bright on this dull, overcast afternoon. He looked pale, washed out, half asleep, like some nocturnal creature, and it seemed strange to him that the streets should be so full of noise and people and traffic, when all week they'd been so empty and dark and silent.

It had been a long, long night, and in less than ten hours he'd be back on duty, walking alone into . . . Who *knew* what?

7

So far, it had been a busy night. Suspects, disturbances, break-ins, a couple of chases over the RT. And fights. Plenty of fights.

The pubs had chucked out, and people who'd set off earlier in the evening, shiny-faced, well-dressed and smelling of perfume, intent on having a good time at a disco' or a pub or club, had finished up in tatters, rolling along the gutter, knocking seven kinds of crap out of one another.

And what *for*?

No one seemed to know. And the law wasn't really interested, so long as no one was seriously hurt and the combatants desisted on request, going quietly away to nurse their cuts, bruises and grievances, and, come tomorrow morning, their hangovers.

Of course, there were those who'd refused to desist, who'd turned their aggression on the law, and who'd then found themselves banged-up for the night, with an early-morning appointment for arraignment at the house of correction, when they'd be castigated by the Magistrate, and then fined for having committed offences such as threatening behaviour and drunk-'n'-dis'.

There were those, too, who *couldn't* go away, and the casualty department at the hospital was packed full with stabbings, cuts, fractures, loosened teeth, concussions, and grievously-wounded prides. Maybe someone would die, before the night was over, and then there'd be *another* Murder Inquiry.

But while there may have been doubts about what caused all of this public disorder, there was *no* doubt that an excess of alcohol, along with the misuse of controlled drugs, was almost always the trigger. The city was crawling with inadequates, with introverts who became psychopathic extroverts as soon as they got wiped out on whatever dope it was which turned them loose: *extremely* dangerous people when intoxicated and unrestrained. Of course, as was the case with all offenders, the courts only ever saw these people when they were stone-cold sober, well after the event, when they'd be back in their shells, meek and mild, pained and repentant; and how *could* the arresting officer, in unemotionally relating the facts of the case, ever hope to recreate the evil and the danger which these crazy people had oozed from their every pore?

Young cops like MacHale found danger, and the prospect of it, very stimulating . . . *exciting*. They knew – or *thought* they knew – exactly what *they'd* do if one of those crazy, freaked-out junkies – or anybody else – came at *them*, looking for a work-out; they'd stick him half to death . . . or . . . whatever, they'd *always win*, just like they did when they'd practised their *hammer, lock-and-bar* holds on passive classmates at the training school. But didn't they *realize*? On the streets, it was for *real*; and crazy, freaked-out junkies who wanted cop's liver for lunch, *weren't* passive.

Older cops – like Filthy Phil and Mathieson – realized, though. Only too well. The prospect – threat, actually – of danger and excitement, *frightened* them, and they went to great lengths to avoid it.

On many occasions, MacHale had felt the need to be afraid, but had succeeded in convincing himself that he'd completely overcome it, and was emotionally hard. The elite of the force belonged to a 'club'; they were members of an all-male preserve, and proved themselves by consistently making valuable arrests, and by downing vast quantities of alcohol while recounting tales of violent conflict and physical prowess. They were *never* afraid.

Or were they? Maybe all this ego preening which they practised while drinking themselves under the table, constituted an *outlet* for fear?

Of course, *their* lids blew off, too, now and then, and the gobby prisoner might then learn the difference between a citizen's arrest and a cop's arrest – in the case of a citizen's arrest, the prisoner *didn't* have that terrible, searing pain in his bollocks.

MacHale was well aware that all sorts of rules were broken by all sorts of coppers. Many of them didn't appear to know what a lot of the rules *were*. He'd seen and heard a lot of things, such as bodies getting a strapping – a euphemism for verbal or physical assault – along the cell passage.

Which reminded MacHale . . . about how Tasty had given that yob a severe talking to – another cop euphemism for assault – only last night. Tasty was well out of order, there; the yob had been minding his own business, and hadn't in the least deserved what he'd got. On top of that, though, Tasty had fitted the yob, for threatening behaviour. And *that* couldn't be dismissed as mere rule-bending: *that* was worth a five stretch in the hate factory up on Wandsworth Common; for *any* cop.

Something else MacHale had learned, however, was that the force was a close-knit family, bonded by an intense loyalty – born of the inevitable, social isolation which cops believed they experienced because of what they were. If a cop came unstuck, it was a real pity. But if a cop came unstuck because he'd been put in it by another cop, then it was a fuckin outrage. No one liked quislings, no matter how well-intentioned they were, or believed themselves to be. A cop had to remember the maxims of the *Three Wise Monkeys*.

He moved out of the darkened shop-doorway where he'd been holed up, thinking things over, and began slowly walking along the road, occasionally pausing to shine his torch into the blackness of a recessed entrance, or along a shadowed alley. Vagies and junkies were often found dead or asleep in such places, during the early hours of the morning; but, if alive and coherent, they were usually worth chatting to, and you could always put them in as stops if name-checks hadn't turned them up as Wanted.

Traffic was very light, now, while the pavements were deserted; it was very lonely, out here, tonight; a thought-provoking loneliness. He felt the chilly breeze casting drizzle onto his face, and glanced upward: no stars or moon, just heavy clouds, drifting south-east across the marginally lighter blackness of the sky . . .

Now a man was approaching him, several hundred yards ahead, on the opposite side of the road, so MacHale came to a halt, moving to the kerb, waiting for the man to come nearer . . .

Aged twenty-five, twenty-six, MacHale thought. Respectable-looking, dressed in a dark trenchcoat, collar up, head bowed into the drizzle and the breeze, walking quickly, hands thrust deep in his coat pockets, sober, apparently not in possession of anything out of the ordinary. Office worker? . . . Salesman? . . . Some sort of fairly well-to-do man, with an aura which declared him honest. Yet he *could* be a rapist or burglar. He might even have a quarter of Moroccan Gold in his pocket, or a gramme of coke. But he wasn't giving MacHale *any* cues . . . didn't even see the uniform as he passed-by and turned right into a residential side-street.

That's the way it was, though. You locked onto a person because he was a suspect – *everyone* was a suspect, until cleared – and frisked him with your eyes, waiting for a cue . . . a certain look, a facial intimation, a change in pace or direction, even a disarming approach to yourself, a style of clothing that didn't seem to match the person wearing it, or the area he was in . . . *something, anything* which tacitly told you that *here* was a villain.

At TS, they told you not to use a stereotype index; but you had to, even if only to eliminate a suspect: *Respectable, looks honest, a professional person* . . . There was *nothing* else to work with. And all of this mental processing and scanning of the stereotype index took no more than seconds, while the *most* experienced cops did it unconsciously.

Intuition. A gut feeling. An indefinable sensation. Or maybe it was no more than a cue from your mental file of past, distilled experiences.

Whatever it was, a cop couldn't for the life of him switch it off when he wasn't on duty, nor even when he was retired, for he'd been permanently conditioned by his training and experiences to seek-out wrongdoers. MacHale's thinking had already been almost wholly transformed; whenever he walked a street, his eyes were highly mobile, picking out people and categorizing them; and he couldn't prevent himself looking at the index numbers of all the cars he passed, either; even checking the numbers on excise licences against the cars' plates, making sure they matched.

When he'd returned home on leave, his mother had remarked on how inquisitive he'd now become; and on how pedantic he could be during conversation, when he'd persistently cross-question her in order to elicit *exact* interpretations of things she'd said.

At TS they taught you to preface a question with one of the Six Ws or an H: Why? Who? Where? Which? When? What? How? So you never said to a man whom you were reporting for an offence, 'Can I have your name, please?' because you'd thereby afford him the opportunity of replying, 'No. I want it for myself.' You simply said, '*What is* your name?' This at least didn't invite a *smartarse* reply.

MacHale smiled and continued on his way along the street. He'd just reminded himself of the black man who'd been nicked for drunken driving and who'd told the arresting officer – Punchy Paterson – that his name was Wilbert Wizard.

'It's true! It's true!' old Wilbert shrieked, as his arse went skidding across the charge-room floor . . .

And so it was, as his driving licence substantiated when it was found in his jacket pocket.

At that moment, the harsh noise of a car's gears, grating and grinding, shattered MacHale's reverie. Approaching him, slowly, and without obligatory lights, was a silver Jaguar XJ6. Now he turned fully around and quickly sidestepped his way across to the centre of the road, torch lit, ready to raise his right arm and cause the vehicle to stop. There was a nightclub, half a mile down the road from the direction the car had come, so maybe this driver was drunk?

The driver accelerated towards MacHale. MacHale raised his right hand, palm outward, and began flashing his torch, signalling the driver to stop. The driver flicked the car's headlamps on to mainbeam, then kicked down with his right toe . . . he wasn't about to stop.

As the car surged towards him, its tyres slipping and squealing on the shiny wet tarmac, its rear-end fishtailing, MacHale lunged aside and let fly with the torch . . . which bounced off the metal ridge around the car's screen, and then shattered in the roadway. 'Stop! You . . . *bastard*!' he shouted. He was angry, scared . . . he might've been wiped up . . .

For a moment he just stood there, rooted to the spot, staring after the fast-disappearing Jaguar. He knew of no precedent. So there could be no, unthinking, conditioned response; never before had a vehicle failed to stop at his signal. Then he ran, belting along the road, one hand flat on top of his helmet, clamping it to his head, the other hand unclipping, from his mac's lapel, the transceiver of his PR . . . bringing it up to his mouth . . . in-between gasps for air, shouting, '*Preston Street! . . . Silver XJ6 . . . Failed to* stop Going west! . . . *West!* . . .'

The cold wet air was rushing over his face and ears as he ran, burning his eyes and skin, freezing his nostrils and throat. His heart was crashing around in his ribcage, thudding in his inner ear and at his temples, so that the intense, snappy back-traffic over the PR was indecipherable to him. But they were coming . . . they *were* coming . . .

Ahead, he saw the Jag's brake-lights glow red . . . heard the shrieks of its rear tyres as they locked and skidded through an arc, trailing smoke . . . winced as he saw the whole vehicle begin recklessly to swing right into Queen's Gardens . . . the rear, nearside wheel striking, then bouncing back off, the west kerb . . .

As the Jag disappeared from view, MacHale once again brought the PR's transceiver to his mouth: '*Queen's Gardens! . . . North in Queen's Gardens! . . .*'

As he himself turned into Queen's Gardens, a dark, deserted, residential side-street with neat, semi-detached houses and well-tended gardens, he saw the Jag, thirty-odd yards ahead of him, stationary in the middle of the road, its engine simmering, plumes of grey smoke being puffed from its dual exhaust system; its driver's door was hanging open, and its interior light was illuminated.

Before he reached the Jag, he knew it was empty, and his eyes began scanning the long, straight Gardens, in search of the driver – although, he suddenly realized, he hadn't a clue what the driver looked like; everything had happened so quickly. But maybe he lives in Queen's Gardens? MacHale thought. And is now tucked up inside his house, pouring double brandies down his throat. *Wherever* he lived, an RO check on the Jag's plates would tell MacHale, and then MacHale, with a bit of back-up, could go and claim him for . . . well, something'd be revealed . . . Drunk in charge, most likely.

As he reached the Jag, he leaned inside, turned the ignition key, and cut the engine; then he began fiddling with the dashboard switches and steering-column stalks, until he'd found the lights-and-wipers' controls, switching off the wipers and cutting the headlamps to sidelights; after that, he closed the driver's door and waited for the back-up to arrive, having scarcely noticed that a pair of black-leather driving gloves was lying on the passenger seat . . . just tossed there, apparently.

In the near distance, he could now hear the sound of whip-tones . . . a horn being blasted . . . engines racing.

And then, out of nowhere, there was a man walking towards him along the east pavement, making for the junction of Queen's Gardens and Preston Street.

Where the hell did *he* spring from? MacHale wondered, his eyes locking-on to the man.

As the man drew abreast of him, MacHale walked over to the pavement and gave him a pull. ''Scuse me,' he said. 'But where have you just come from?'

The man, late thirties/early forties, heavily built, with straight, black hair, no neck, and a tiny scar at the side of his left eye, came to a halt, and looked at MacHale, a what-the-fuck's-it-gotta-do-with-you-pal? expression on his face.

He's gonna punch me *right* up in the air, MacHale thought. Then he felt a little relief. The man's hands were moving into the trouser pockets of his light grey, three-piece suit, but not before MacHale had noted that the thick, rough fingers were tattooed: L-O-V-E above the knuckles of the left hand, H-A-T-E above the knuckles of the right hand; and on the webbed triangle of skin between the forefinger and thumb of each hand, there was a tattoo of a blue swallow. So it was a racing certainty that here was an ex-Borstal boy, a man with more form than Shergar. He knew he wasn't obliged to say *anything* in answer to a cop's questions.

'I just wondered,' MacHale said, 'if you'd seen anyone running up the road, as you were walking down. You live along here, do you?' Now he noted that the man's suit was only slightly damp – pinheads of moisture glistening on the shoulders of his jacket and on his black hair; yet it had been drizzling for some fifteen, twenty minutes, now.

The man's piercing, dark-brown eyes moved right, taking stock of the Jaguar, then panned back to engage MacHale's eyes. He noncommittally shook his head.

What *now*, then? MacHale wondered. Since he couldn't've been out for long in this drizzle, he could've been the driver of that Jag, which, it now occurred to MacHale, was probably a lost-or-stolen.

Either he had to claim this geezer, or tell him he was free to go. And while he was wondering which it was to be, the RT-car came clogging along the gardens, its headlamps blazing, its blue-lamp flashing, closely followed by an unmarked, red Vauxhall Cavalier.

The RT-car pulled up in front of the Jag, and Tubby Tompkins and Snatch climbed out, hatless, hands thrust in trouser pockets. Slovenly pricks, MacHale thought. The Cavalier, which had pulled in behind the RT-car, was the Duty Officer's vehicle, and although Old Crikey had appeared on parade at the beginning of tonight's tour, a plaster covering a small bump and graze on his bald head, he had obviously decided – notwithstanding his nasty experience in the early hours of yesterday morning – that it was still less dangerous inside than out, and had loaned his car to Punchy Paterson and Tasty Tom.

Tubby halted in front of MacHale, hitching up his baggy, badly-creased trousers. 'What's the strength of it, then, Sabu?' – he often called MacHale, *Sabu*, because he'd decided that the dark-skinned young kiddy-cop looked exactly like a little Indian elephant boy. Tasty, Snatch and Punchy were loitering near at hand, trying to sus the man that MacHale had pulled, and their eyes were roving all over him.

MacHale stepped aside and drew Tubby with him, explaining the events which had led up to his presence here with the Jag and the suspect. Then, Tubby bombarded MacHale with questions; none of which he was able to answer:

'Who owns the motor? . . . *Is* it nicked? . . . Where's this toerag live, then? . . . *Was* he the driver? . . . What's he *doin*, here, at this time of the mornin, anyway? . . . Fuck me, Sabu! Haven't you asked him *anything*?'

Finally, his fat face glowing with rage, Tubby told MacHale to stand watch over the man, while he filled-in Tasty, Punchy and Snatch. Still the man hadn't uttered a word, and he appeared to be very self-confident, content to let the filth play their little games and decide what to do with him; eventually, they'd have to let him go, he believed.

Punchy Paterson, having heard out Tubby, returned to the Cavalier, picked up the mainset's transmitter, switched the set to channel six, and began processing 'both checks' on the Jag. He *could* have done them on the PR, but if he had, his colleagues here would have to have unclipped the batteries from their own PRs, so that the suspect would not hear the back traffic.

While Punchy was doing the checks, Tubby, Tasty and Snatch walked over to front the suspect.

'Right, shag,' Tasty snarled. 'Wha's ya name?'

The man just stared defiantly at him.

'Where d'ya live?' Snatch demanded.

Again, no verbal response.

'We're fuckin *talkin* to you, mister!' Tubby snapped, hands on hips, head jutting forward; his jowls were trembling, and his little piggy eyes were just slits.

Still, no comment; but the suspect's eyes flashed Tubby a message: *I could go straight through you, you fat git! No problem*. MacHale read it, but didn't think Tubby had.

'Okay, wiseguy,' Tasty sneered, and his eyes began slowly panning, left . . . then right . . . scanning the darkened windows of the houses which were opposite and behind the suspect . . . Then, his body moved slowly back to the left, and he began turning again through a half circle, his eyes now seeking out any movement there might be at the nearby houses' windows . . . Just before he'd completed the movement, his body whipped round, and his right arm was a blur as it steamed forward, and up, embedding its fist in the suspect's gut.

The suspect folded, air gushing from his parted lips, pain contorting his face, his knees hitting the shiny wet pavement. He groaned, and bit his lower lip, while his huge hands clutched at his midriff. 'You *bastards*!' he hissed.

'Well fuck a duck an bugger a bat,' Tasty leered. 'We *ain't* got ourselves a deaf mute, here, after all.'

Jesus Christ! MacHale thought, his brain panicking. What's going *on*, here?

Tubby Tompkins bent forward as far as he dared without putting his bulk in danger of toppling over. 'Let's start again, shall we, ace?' He paused, regaining his breath, then wheezed, '*Name?*'

The suspect continued massaging his belly; his face was now clear of pain; but he still wouldn't answer. Then his eyes moved down, left, towards the feet of the four cops who stood before him, and he anticipated the boot.

He might well have got it, too, had not Punchy Paterson returned from the Cavalier. He thumbed over his shoulder, towards the Jag. 'It's a ringer, would ya believe? The plates *are* issued to a silver Jag, but it *should* be a Four-point-Two, *not* a Three-point-Eight, like that one is. And, what's more, the tax disc on this one is a snide: it's been altered . . . bleached and rewritten. Like it?'

'*Like* it?' Snatch enthused, his eyes shining with excitement. 'I *love* it!' And his hands moved beneath his tunic, to his right side, where his handcuffs' pouch was attached to the belt of his trousers.

At the same time, Tasty moved in behind the suspect, raised his right foot and kicked down, sideways, catching the suspect on the back of his neck and knocking him flat on his face. Then, Snatch was kneeling astride him, pulling his hands back and up onto the lower part of his spine . . . snapping on the cuffs. The suspect was totally submissive.

What're they doing? screamed MacHale's brain. *I* don't even know if he *was* the driver! He turned to Tubby Tompkins, his face reflecting the alarm he felt within himself. 'Tubby,' he said, a pleading look in his eyes. 'What's he being *nicked* for? . . . I mean, *I* can't say if it *was* him?'

'It was fuckin *him*, all right,' seethed the irascible Tubby. 'Whaddaya *think* he was doin up here at this time of the mornin? . . . Fuckin sleepwalkin, or what?'

'He's a villain, all right,' Punchy put in, nodding his head. 'A pro' blagger, by the looks of him, too.' He suddenly turned on MacHale. 'And don't *you* go and fuck up on this job, y'hear?'

What's he on about? MacHale wondered, and he now felt like running away and leaving them all to it.

Now, Tasty got on the Cavalier's mainset and requested a van – their own nick's van was still out of commission. As well as transporting the body into the factory, the van could supply them with a clamp-on steering wheel, which would enable Snatch to drive away the Jag, without spoiling any prints that might be on its own wheel.

While they awaited the arrival of the van, Snatch took MacHale to one side. 'Now then, dear boy,' he began, fixing MacHale with a benign, utterly sincere look. 'Think about what your evidence is gonna be, when we get down the factory. Okay?' And he patted MacHale on the shoulder.

Evidence? MacHale thought. I haven't *got* any bloody evidence!

8

The charge-room was in one hell of a mess.

Its parquet floor was dirty, scuffed with huge swirls of black, rubber-heel marks, littered with cigarette butts, and dotted with balls of screwed-up paper. Two of the room's three desks bore untidy stacks of used paper cups and plates. In one corner, there was a long row of rough-cider bottles, some empty, others part full, which had been confiscated from drunken vagrants, but not entered on their lists of personal property. In the morning, if he were feeling charitable, the early-turn ASO might take one of these part-filled bottles along the cell passageway, and watch as the dehydrated vagies fought over turns to dance it to their cracked lips and guzzle greedily on the life-giving liquid; if the ASO were feeling uncharitable, though, he might *still* take a bottle along the cell passageway – but not before first having urinated in it.

In another corner of the charge-room, someone had vomited, and someone else had covered over the mess with a few pages of a daily tabloid.

Needless to say, no cop went a bundle on a drunken vagie who did a technicolour cough on the charge-room floor; therefore, while the canteen wasn't into cooking exotic dishes for breakfast – and most certainly not for prisoners – *one* prisoner, the night-duty SO would inform the early-turn SO *which* one, would find himself being served ratatouille on toast. His *own* ratatouille.

The long, wooden bench, bolted to the wall below the high, barred window, seated three bodies: a drunk who was insisting that he was sober; a flasher who was noncommittal; and a real hard-looking slag wearing a grey suit whose front was wet and dirty.

Barker, a piece of yellow straw clinging to his swept-back grey hair, was hunched, bleary-eyed, over a charge-sheet, writing out details of the drunkenness arrest. In the front office, Harry Tanner, tonight's Section Skipper, was preparing the bail section of the flasher's charge-sheet. Tanner was in a filthy mood, too, probably because he hadn't yet had a chance to set foot outside the nick; the bodies had come in thick and fast, and Barker had been overwhelmed – although he'd still managed to find time for a game of Lego, with that old scrubber, Foxtrot Lima, up in the hay loft of the stables. Of course, if the Duty Officer had weighed in, things would've been a whole lot sweeter for both him and Barker. But there was Old Crikey Crawford, banged-up inside his office, massagin his fuckin nut and grindin his teeth, one eye on the OB, the other eye on the boarded-up window. The useless prick!

MacHale was standing by the man in the wet grey suit, who still hadn't told them a thing. Tubby Tompkins, Snatch, Tasty Tom and Punchy Paterson, had all by now retired to the canteen, for grub and a game of three-card brag, telling MacHale to give them a Bell when the SO was ready to deal with their knock-off. MacHale was dreading the SO's investigation of the arrest, too, unable to fathom just how the hell they were going to justify it.

His thoughts were now claimed, though, by the drunk's insistent shouting: 'I *demand* to see a doctor!' he bellowed. 'I'm perfectly *sober*!' And he stood, wobbled sideways, then fell back down on the bench.

He looked like a . . . bank manager, MacHale decided: portly, early fifties, well-spoken; wearing a blue, pinstripe suit, a white-collared grey shirt, a navy-blue tie with a gold-coloured coat-of-arms motif, horn-rimmed glasses, and grey hair that was thinning and neatly trimmed.

The charge-room door now opened and in walked a

man of about thirty-eight, who was dressed in a brown-tweed sports jacket and grey slacks; he was thin, had greasy black hair that was combed back, a small quiff falling over his brow, and didn't look all that sober himself, oozing a post-prandial contentment – although he seemed to be *walking* quite normally. He stood before the drunk, looking him up and down as he pulled up his trousers, tucked his shirt tightly inside the waistband, and rocked gently back and forth on his heels; then he said, 'Good morning. Mister Todd? . . . I'm Doctor Hales, the Police Doctor.'

The drunk's face took on a greatly relieved expression, and he staggered to his feet, clutching the doctor's right shoulder. 'Thank *God* you've arrived, doctor!' he urgently said, his speech wet and slurred. 'These . . . these . . .' He glanced, pie-eyed, at Barker. 'These *Gestapo* have *arrested* me! For being *drunk*, if you don't mind! As *you* can see, though, doctor, I'm *sober* as a *judge*!'

The doctor frowned. 'Hmm. Well, let's examine you, shall we?' And he took the drunk's right elbow and led him slowly, carefully, across the charge area, into the District Surgeon's office.

The PC who'd been guarding the drunk – an officer from the DSU carrier that was parked in the yard – shook his head and laughed softly. *He* was aware that the doctor *wasn't* a doctor, at all. No, he was *DS* Hales, one of the night-duty CID officers who were on call, and who'd come in to give the flasher a strapping. He'd heard the drunk's protestations of innocence and had decided to square him up, good and proper.

Through the half-open door of the Surgeon's office, MacHale could hear the DS saying, '. . . that's it . . . stand to attention, close your eyes . . . feet together, head erect, hands locked at sides . . . Yes, good. Now walk towards me . . . careful . . . Watch it, *watch it!* . . .' And then a *tremendous* crash as the drunk careened sideways, went arse over head, and fell to the floor, pulling down with him a metal cabinet. Hales didn't bother with the subtraction test or the finger-to-the-nose test; he picked up the drunk, assisted him back to the charge-room bench, and gravely informed him that he was ratarsed and had better duck his nut when he got to court.

'*Well!*' gasped the shaken drunk. 'If *you* say so, doctor . . . If *you* say so.'

The flasher didn't *look* like a flasher, MacHale considered. But then what was a flasher *supposed* to look like? They didn't *all* wear dirty raincoats. This one was so young – about twenty-five, MacHale guessed – and good-looking . . . dark-skinned, like himself. A Greek, probably; or, as most cops would have said, a Bubble-'n'-Squeak. So why did such a clean, attractive-looking, decent sort of bloke like this, resort to flashing?

The Greek's arresting officer, a young, crime-squad PC in plainclothes – well, in pink jeans, a brown-leather jacket and a yellow T-shirt – finished completing his Six-Eleven, and, turning to his prisoner, said, 'Y'know, Kris, one of these days, when you run in that fish-'n'-chip shop, throw open your coat, shout, "Yoo-Hooo!" and then wave ya joint at that tart behind the jump, you're gonna get it battered. How many times *is* this, now?'

The Greek shrugged and coyly smiled. 'I dunno. Maybe . . .' He hunched his shoulders, rocked from side-to-side, and gesticulated with his hands. 'Twice, maybe.'

'Twice this week, you mean,' scoffed the PC. The Greek arched his mouth and his eyebrows, and smiled again.

Old Crikey ventured into the charge-room, looked at the prisoners, frowned, and passed on through to the front office. He was chewing on a crust of bread, and crumbs were clinging to the corners of his white-lipped mouth and the front of his tunic; in his left hand he held a screwed-up paper bag. He paused by the Station Officer's desk, dropped the bag into a waste-paper bin, and said to Tanner, 'Give me an update, please, Sarge.'

Tanner continued with his writing, not bothering to glance up. 'Things're quietening, guv . . . *Now*,' he said. 'I'm just about to bail the flasher, and Bob Barker's dealing with a drunk. Then, maybe *we'll* be able to get *our* grub.'

Old Crikey, having finished chewing his crust, popped a digestif into his mouth, and, with the flat of his right hand, began brushing down the front of his tunic. 'What's MacHale got, out there?'

Tanner shrugged. 'Haven't asked, guv. He came in with the crew of the RT-car. Somethin to do with a motor . . . A Jag, I think it is.'

Old Crikey's frown deepened. 'Would you . . . er . . . like me to deal with it, Sarge?' he unenthusiastically offered.

'Yes, please,' Tanner flatly said. He knew, of course, that he was *supposed* to decline Old Crikey's offer. 'Oh,' Old Crikey said, surprised, his lower jaw sliding back and forth as he turned and left the front office, his back teeth now crunching the digestif.

'MacHale!' he snapped, and flicked aside his head, directing MacHale to join him by the entrance to the fingerprint-and-photograph room, where they'd be out of the hearing of the man in the wet grey suit.

'Yes, sir?' MacHale was before Old Crikey, looking and feeling apprehensive.

Old Crikey, hands on hips, nodded at the man in the wet grey suit. 'What've you arrested him for, MacHale?'

'I . . . Well, I don't *know*, sir.' There, he'd said it.

'Don't *know*?' Old Crikey seethed; his hands had left his hips, and were bunched at his sides, their fingers springing in and out. 'What d'you mean, "*Don't know,*"?'

MacHale's innards were squirming. 'What I *mean*, sir, is that I *haven't* arrested him.'

'*Haven't* arrested him?' Old Crikey snapped, and spittle flew from his white-encrusted lips. 'What's he doing, sitting here in the *charge*-room, then?'

'Well, he is *under* arrest,' MacHale tried. 'By . . . Well, Snatch, I *s'pose*. It was Snatch who 'cuffed him, anyway, sir. You see, *I* was only – '

'Where is he, where is he?' Old Crikey cut in, his voice whining with exasperation, and his left hand flew aside, as if he were scattering seed. 'If it's *his* body, then *he* should be here, *guarding* him.'

'He's having his grub, sir, and he told me to – '

'Get him, get him, get him *down* here straight away!' More seed-scattering, as Old Crikey tut-tutted and shook his head and marched off back to the front office.

MacHale quickly went into the comms room to use a phone.

Dave Hall answered the canteen extension, and said he'd send up Snatch. As MacHale was about to make his own way back to the charge-room, Blinky called him over to the VDU, spun round in his swivel chair, and read from a message-pad he'd been scribbling on.

'That Jag you've got in the yard, John. It is a ringer. It's lost-or-stolen from LM-Section, which is Clapham, since the beginning of last month.' He looked up, his eyelids blinking furiously.

'Well that's good news, anyway,' MacHale said.

Blinky frowned, and the blinking intensified. 'This body that's in for it, John. It is *down* to him, isn't it? I mean, you can say you saw him at the wheel of the Jag?'

MacHale stepped towards Blinky, spreading his hands. 'I *can't*!' he earnestly said. 'I just never got a chance to see *who* was at the wheel.'

Blinky twitched his eyebrows, and his eyes pulsated.

Then he shrugged, spun back round in his seat, and began clearing the VDU.

As MacHale reentered the charge-room, Snatch and Tubby Tompkins walked in.

'Over here, dear boy,' Snatch said, and motioned MacHale to follow himself and Tubby Tompkins into the Surgeon's office.

When MacHale was inside the room, Snatch closed the door.

'Look, dear boy,' he said, his voice low, his eyes searching MacHale's face. 'What we've got, here, is a ringer and a professional villain, and it's up to – '

'Well, yeah,' MacHale interjected, uneased by the conspiratorial atmosphere. 'The motor *is* a ringer, for certain. Blinky's just told me it's lost-or-stolen from Clapham. But we don't know anything about *him*, out there in the charge-room.'

'He's a villain, all right,' Tubby Tompkins assured, and he hopped up backwards onto the doctor's couch, where he sat, his fat legs dangling over the side, wriggling his toes inside his black, lace-up shoes. 'It's written all over him. And we're gonna fit him for ringin that fuckin motor.'

'But *I* never saw *who* was driving the Jag,' MacHale pleaded.

'Fuckin suck back!' Tubby Tompkins muttered, looking aside. Then he jumped down off the couch, stuck his hands in his trouser pockets, and began pacing the small room, grimacing and shaking his head.

'Look, dear boy,' Snatch gently and patiently said. 'Just consider the evidence. First, the Jag fails to stop for you, then turns off, a little way along the road. Right?'

'Right.'

'You run after it, find it abandoned, and there's no one in sight. The driver's gone . . . Yeah?'

'Yeah.'

'Okay. Then, while you're waitin for us to show, chummy out there comes walkin along the street, dry as a bone, even though it's pissin down with rain . . . Agreed?'

'Yeah, that's what happened.'

'So where d'you s'pose he'd *been*, dear boy? What had he been *doin*? . . .'

'And why wasn't he *wet*?' Tubby Tompkins put in, now halting, and facing MacHale.

'How should *I* know?' MacHale said. 'He hasn't *said* anything, yet.'

'And nor *will* he,' Tubby Tompkins spat. 'Because he knows he doesn't *have* to.'

'The circumstantial evidence couldn't be stronger, though,' Snatch suggested.

MacHale considered it for a couple of seconds, then said: 'Well, yes, I agree it's *fairly* strong . . . especially if it turns out that the body doesn't *live* somewhere near where the Jag was dumped . . . and he can't put up an alibi for his whereabouts, this evening.'

'But,' Snatch said, jabbing his right index-finger at MacHale's chest. 'If he goes on the sheet, with *just* that evidence, we'll *never* get him down. By the time he gets up the steps, he'll *have* an alibi. *We'll* be the ones who're portrayed as villains, and the job'll get slung. Stand on me, dear boy, I've seen it all before.'

'There's fingerprints, though,' MacHale pointed out. 'In the motor . . . On the wheel, the interior mirror . . . On the insides of the false plates.'

Snatch and Tubby Tompkins just stood there, staring at MacHale, bemused, shaking their heads in disbelief of his naïvety.

'He's a *pro*'!' Snatch impatiently said. '*You* saw the *gloves* inside the motor. There won't *be* any dabs . . . At least, none to match-up with his, anyway.'

'Look,' said Tubby Tompkins, his tone unequivocal. 'It's gonna need you to say *positively* that the body out there is the *same* one you saw drivin the Jag, just before it failed to stop. Either you *say* that, or you can stick the job up your arse, an I'll have no more to do with it.'

'Tubby's right, dear boy,' agreed Snatch. 'It's gotta be all or nothin, really.' He looked hopefully at MacHale.

'How *can* I say I saw him driving, when I *didn't*?' MacHale pleaded. 'I can't tell *lies*, can I?'

'That's it!' shouted Tubby, and he yanked open the door and barged off out, his gut colliding with MacHale's right side, knocking MacHale off balance.

'Sorry, dear boy. Looks like it's down to you, then,' said Snatch. And he, too, walked out.

For a moment, MacHale just stood there . . . hot, unbelieving, sweating. They'd wanted him to become part of a conspiracy to pervert the course of justice.

Didn't they *realize*, though, that it would be perjury? That they could each get seven years for it, if it were discovered? Even if they got *away* with it, how could they live with the knowledge that they might – just *might* – have convicted an innocent man?

MacHale was certain that *he* couldn't live with such knowledge. Sure, he believed that the body out there was *probably* guilty of ringing the Jag. The circumstantial evidence *was* fairly powerful. And, feeling somewhat personally aggrieved, the Jag having almost run him down, it would have been all too easy to feel vengeful as well, and maybe convince himself that the body out there was the driver.

It worried him now, however, that he might be setting free a hardened criminal. But *No*, he decided. I *won't* do it . . . I *can't* do it!

'*MacHale!*' It was Old Crikey's voice, echoing around, outside in the charge-room.

He jolted back to a full awareness of his immediate surroundings, and left the Surgeon's office. 'Sir?'

Old Crikey was standing in the entrance to the front

office, arms akimbo, head and shoulders projected forward, his face angry. 'What's this prisoner doing sitting here unguarded?' he shouted, nodding at the man in the wet grey suit.

The flasher had been bailed, and the drunk had been charged and banged-up for the night, so the charge-room was now empty; even Barker had gone.

'Sorry, sir,' MacHale mumbled. 'I thought Sergeant Barker was still out here.'

'Well, he *isn't*!' Old Crikey said. 'And if the prisoner had done a runner, it'd've cost you two days' pay, MacHale.'

The man in the wet grey suit permitted himself a wry smile. He was being too passive, too tolerant, MacHale thought. Why the hell wasn't he reacting like a normal prisoner, shouting and screaming, demanding his brief, protesting his innocence, threatening to sue the Commissioner's arse, and to complain to the CIB . . .? He just had to be a pro'.

'Now then,' Old Crikey went on, walking to the desk that Barker had earlier vacated. 'I'll hear the evidence in this case.' – *Oh, Christ*, thought MacHale – He pulled out the chair, and sat, elbows on the desk-top, knuckles pressing into his grey cheeks, staring at MacHale; he appeared to have forgotten, now, that Snatch ought to be here, as arresting officer.

MacHale stood before the desk, and began relating the facts of the case to Old Crikey, in the presence and hearing of the prisoner. Just as it had occurred, out there on the street; except he omitted to say that he'd witnessed the prisoner being worked over by Tasty Tom.

And still the prisoner made no comment; although he seemed somewhat surprised, as if something he'd expected to hear had been omitted, and maybe was about to be said, now – belatedly.

'And where's the lost-or-stolen?' Old Crikey wanted to know.

'The Jag, sir? It's out in the yard, immobilized . . . I think Sergeant Tanner put its rotor arm in the safe; he's got the keys, too, and the false plates.'

Old Crikey nodded his satisfaction at that. Then he began looking about himself. 'By the way, where's Snatch? You said *he* was the arresting officer.'

MacHale shrugged. 'So he was, sir. But he's told me the job's now down to me.'

Old Crikey frowned and compressed his lips. Then he picked up the desk telephone, dialled the canteen extension, and asked to talk to Snatch.

When Snatch came on the line, Old Crikey asked him what he thought he was playing at. But as he listened to Snatch's explanation, his expression lost much of its aggression.

'*Did* he?' he said, and glanced at MacHale. When he put down the receiver, he just sat there for a couple of seconds, deep in thought . . .

At length, he refocused his eyes, looked squarely at MacHale, and said, 'MacHale, I'm going to ask you to think carefully, and then tell me if this man sitting here is the man who was driving the Jaguar when it failed to stop for you.'

MacHale was unhesitant in his reply: 'I can't say, sir. I wasn't expecting the vehicle to accelerate and carry on, and, when it did, I was so taken aback, I only had time to think about getting clear. I had no chance of seeing who the driver was. The vehicle's screen was reflecting the streetlights, and the wipers were in motion. I may have seen the vague outline of an upper body, at the wheel, but that's about all.'

The man in the wet grey suit was now openly surprised. What he'd expected to hear, hadn't been said, and, clearly, wasn't *going* to be said. His facial muscles relaxed, his fists uncurled, and his shoulders dropped.

'Very well, then,' Old Crikey said, his eyebrows raised. He looked away from MacHale, and pointed at the prisoner. 'You . . . Come up here and turn-out your pockets.'

The prisoner stood, walked over to the desk, and began turning-out his property . . . loose change, house keys, correspondence, comb, several bank-notes, and a driver's licence. MacHale checked his pockets . . . Nothing else.

Old Crikey picked up the licence and examined it, reading the details of the name and address. He glanced up at the prisoner. 'What's your full name?'

The prisoner was standing there like a con' who was before the prison governor, toeing the line: his hands clasped behind his back, his neck straight, shoulders square, jaw forward, staring into infinity. 'Frederick Arthur Schofield,' he replied, his deep voice Cockney accented. 'Two-Four-One Allander Avenue, Brixton, South-West Two.'

Old Crikey grunted, and nodded, satisfied that the particulars just given corresponded with those printed on the licence. Then he opened the top, right-hand drawer of the desk, took out a large plastic bag, a yellow-cardboard tag, and a racheted strip of plastic with a numbered box attached to one end of it, which was a securiseal for the property bag. 'Bag-up the property,' he told MacHale. 'But don't seal it.' And while MacHale was doing as he'd been told, Old Crikey went away to the front office and returned with the Person-At-Station Book. As he sat back down at the desk, he pulled open the top, left-hand drawer and removed a PAS sheet, with copy. 'Right,' he began, addressing MacHale. 'While I'm putting chummy in the PAS Book, you can write down his pars, and go and have a name-check done on the VDU.'

Accommodatingly, the prisoner said, 'Born at Bethnal Green, on five-eleven forty-three . . . Height, six foot.' He'd *definitely* been inside, before now.

When MacHale returned from the comms room, some five minutes later, he felt sick.

There was no real doubt at all, now, that the prisoner and the man who'd been driving the Jag were one and the same person. Yet the prisoner was about to be set free.

The name-check had revealed that Schofield was Known but Not Wanted, and that he was *Of Interest*, to DCI Bruno of the Central Robbery Squad. A phone call to the Reserve at LD, for a Collator's check, had then disclosed that Schofield had a string of previous, going back for many years to when he was a juvenile. His favourite, these days, apparently, was an armed bank-blag or cash-in-transit snatch. Most interestingly of all, though, was the fact that he regularly associated with a team of heavies who frequented the *La Caer Club* – the very nightclub which was situated just along the road from where MacHale had first spotted the Jag, when it was being driven without obligatory lights.

MacHale handed the message-pad form to Old Crikey, who muttered, 'Oh, *crikey*! We'd better get the night-duty CID to have a word with chummy.' And he got to his feet, went into the front office, dialled IR, and asked them to put up a shout for DS Hales.

Meanwhile, Schofield was binned-up in the detention room, and MacHale was left sitting in the charge-room.

When Hales and his DC arrived, they were first briefed by Old Crikey before going to Schofield. As they passed-by MacHale in the charge-room, they shot him with disparaging glances from the corners of their eyes. He felt as if someone had just told him he'd got cancer.

It didn't take Hales and his DC long, either, to determine that they'd never crack Schofield. Five minutes, in fact. It'd been futile telling a geezer like Schofield that he was bang to rights and had better throw his hands in the air before he got himself bounced off every wall en route to the cell block. He didn't want to trade, either, so it'd been a waste of time attempting to cajole him into pleading to a charge of handling, in relation to the ringed Jag, with a promise that the charge of theft would be dropped out. He just didn't want to know about *anything* – other than his release from custody.

The DC went out to the yard, to sit in the CID car, while DS Hales, red-faced and tight-lipped, reported back to Old Crikey. Then, Hales came out of the front office and approached MacHale.

'He's not having it. Not any of it,' he told MacHale. 'You sure it wasn't him at the wheel of that motor?'

MacHale sighed. This was wearying him, and the smell of stale drink – Scotch, he thought – on the DS's breath, made him feel queasy. 'I've thought about it and thought about it, Sarge,' he said, 'and all I can say is, I don't know *who* was driving the Jag.'

'All right, cock,' Hales indifferently said, patting MacHale's left shoulder. 'Don't worry about it.' But then his face took on a mocking countenance, as he added, '*Unless*, that is, chummy goes out on a blag, next week sometime – when he ought by rights to be banged-up over the wall on a ringin charge – and murders some poor fuckin security guard or bank clerk.' Then he turned on his heel, opened the door that exited to the yard, and disappeared.

Within half an hour, Schofield was set free, on an undertaking to return to the nick, if and when required. In effect, as far as Schofield was concerned, that was that: the end of the affair. But MacHale's ordeal was only just beginning. He knew he'd never be able to repress the inevitable feelings of guilt if he were to verbal Schofield and thereby put him on the sheet; he *couldn't* do it; *hadn't* done it, *wouldn't* do it. But now, having *decided* to do what was right, he *still* felt guilty . . . for *not* having sold himself out. It was the others . . . Snatch, Tubby Tompkins, the DS . . . they'd *made* him feel morally culpable for not having stitched-up Schofield. It was as if he'd betrayed them and the system.

Which, of course, he *had*.

PART TWO
Verbals

9

The public bar of *The Mitre* was a noisy, smoke-filled, spit-'n'-sawdust den of iniquity, brightly lit, poorly decorated, and packed solid with an unsavoury and raucous collection of human garbage: yobs, CRO-men, toms, ponces, junkies and winos.

The saloon bar, though, was altogether different. Situated at the back of the pub, it was reached via a dark alley and a dimly-lit door, and sought to attract a far better class of clientele.

Its floor was fitted with a thickly-piled, deep-red Axminster; its walls were panelled in a dark wood that was decorated with antique plates and Victorian watercolours; and in the centre of the high ceiling there was an enormous chandelier which cascaded down to form a wide circle of crystal teardrops that glittered white and fiery blue amid an arrangement of eight candle-shaped bulbs, covered by gold-silk shades whose bottoms had delicate blue-tassels.

The chairs and well-padded bench seats were upholstered in a dark red, deep-buttoned imitation leather, and the highly-polished tables had elegantly-carved legs. The bar, horse-shoe shaped, had its front upholstered to match the chairs, and above it there hung a wrought-iron canopy, with glass shelves, that was twinkling with a string of multi-coloured fairy-lights. The room had a Christmassy atmosphere about it; all it needed was a log fire to replace the central heating, and tapes of jingle bells instead of orchestral music.

The dart-board, to the left of the door as one entered

the bar, was also incongruous in these genteel surroundings. But that was down to the cops; they'd pestered the licensee, Mulligan, for months and months, until eventually he'd given in and installed the dart-board because he valued their custom and friendship. It was gratifying for other reasons, as well, to know your back bar was full of off-duty cops in half blues; if a running fight erupted in the public bar, they were on the spot.

Tonight, though, things were fairly quiet.

MacHale was sitting alone in one corner of the back bar, watching the others as he sipped at his pint of cold lager.

Filthy Phil was leaning on the counter, his hands cupping a pint of bitter, winking lecherously at Queenie, the twenty-six-year-old blonde barmaid from New Zealand, who wore a turquoise boob-tube and a pair of tight-fitting designer jeans. 'Fancy a gamea Lego, Queenie?' said Filthy Phil, winking some more, and smirking. She dismissed him with a benign smile, but as she bent down in front of him, reaching beneath the counter for a bottle of tonic, he leaned further across and sucked in air through pouted lips as his eyes got belted by her cleavage.

Further along the bar, Mathieson was mumbling something about the good ol' days, when cops were *cops*, and how, single-handedly, he'd taken on a gang of teddy boys and had whipped 'em good. No one was listening, though.

MacHale pulled up the left cuff of his anorak and glanced at his wristwatch – ten-forty. They'd only been in the pub for some ten minutes, having finished late-turn duty at half-past the hour, and yet here was Mathieson, steaming. Why didn't someone in authority give him some help? MacHale wondered. The poor bloke was in a pitiful state, and sooner or later – sooner, probably – he was going to drop right in it.

Tubby Tompkins and Snatch were over by the door, playing darts. Tubby Tompkins was about a ton in front, this game. But then old Snatch's eyesight wasn't so hot, these days. MacHale wondered if *he* would still be in The Job at fifty-five, hanging on.

It'd been almost five weeks, now, since the incident with Schofield. It just wouldn't die a natural in MacHale's mind. Three times he'd had that dream. So far. He'd jolted awake, breathless, wet-hot, his head throbbing; and always the Jag had hit him . . . and it *was* Schofield's face behind the windscreen, too . . . smiling, taunting. It *was* Schofield.

He took a long swallow of his lager and looked at his colleagues. Tasty Tom, Punchy Paterson, and Vindscreen Vipas were seated around a table, playing three-card brag with Mulligan, who, as usual, was half out of his mind on neat vodka. Tasty Tom folded and threw-in his hand. Punchy Paterson, his three cards pressed close to his shattered, simian nose, grimaced, shook his head, and then followed suit. Vindscreen, looking *too* confident, lobbed another three quid into the pot, and, still blind, said to Mulligan, 'It'll cost ya six more, Paddy, if ya wanna stay wi me.'

Mulligan concentrated his dilated eyes on his three cards, his flushed rubbery face expressionless. Now he began toying with six, one-pound notes, rubbing the paper between the forefinger and thumb of his left hand, before saying, 'Ah, what the hell.' His six notes then went into the pot.

Mulligan had unnerved Vindscreen. 'Okay, Paddy,' he said. 'I'll have a look.' And having counted out three pounds from the pile of silver that was before him on the table top, he slid it across into the kitty.

Now, Mulligan smiled confidently. 'Acker-Boo, I'm afraid.' He placed down his cards, face upward, one at a time . . . tantalizingly slowly: Ace of Hearts . . . King of Spades . . . Queen of Diamonds.

Vindscreen bit his lower lip and began revealing his

own cards. First card over was the Five of Diamonds . . . second, the Seven of Diamonds . . . lastly, the Six of Diamonds. '*Wheey!*' Vindscreen roared triumphantly, his backside jumping off his stool, his right fist punching upward through the air. 'Five, six, seven, *on* the *trot*!'

'Well fuck a duck an bugger a bat,' Tasty Tom mumbled.

'An he was *blind*!' Mulligan said. '*Blind*!'

'Seen nothin like it,' Punchy Paterson added.

And Vindscreen, his face split with glee, began scooping-in the pot – about forty quid, all told.

Mulligan stood, swaying, looking in the direction of the bar, snapping a forefinger and thumb. 'Oi!' he shouted at Queenie, who was now sitting on a high stool behind the bar, reading tonight's paper. 'Gimme a rounda drinks, ya big-titted drongo.'

'I'll pay, I'll pay,' Vindscreen generously offered, as he counted up his winnings, folding notes and piling up tall columns of silver and bronze.

'Make it doubles, in that case,' shouted Mulligan, and he fell back down in his seat.

Tasty Tom was stacking the cards, ready to deal a new hand.

An elderly couple – the only civvies in the bar, save for Mulligan and Queenie – got up and left, the lady casting a reproving glance at Mulligan; neither she nor her husband would be back – *ever*.

Why *does* Mulligan talk that way to his staff? MacHale wondered. And why do *they stand* for it? – they all did. He looked at Queenie. She was dispensing the drinks, carelessly humming in tune with the taped music – *Love Letters* had come on, a moment ago.

He finished his pint and went up to the bar, for a refill, standing next to Filthy Phil.

'*Look* at em,' rasped Filthy Phil, jabbing his left elbow into MacHale's side as he nodded at Queenie's chest.

'Couldn't get manya *them* in a bucket, could ya? . . . *Nipples* like fuckin *bullets*!'

'Muck-'n'-bullets . . . *muck*-'n'-bullets!' shouted Mathieson, lurching away from the bar and waving his right hand in the air. '*I* remember when – '

'Anyway,' Filthy Phil was saying, prefacing a change of subject. 'You done your chores, today?'

MacHale frowned. 'What chores?'

Filthy Phil smiled. 'Well, that's very decent of ya, son. I'll have a nice gin-'n'-tonic, then, as you've asked.'

MacHale groaned. He'd been had over yet *again* by that routine. Last time it was Hercules who'd rooked him.

Where *is* Hercules, tonight, anyway? he now wondered, and asked Filthy Phil.

Filthy Phil shrugged. 'Down the *Gay-Trade Centre*, I shouldn't wonder . . . havin a cross-hand boogey in the back stalls of the video room.'

'What about Pat Coles?'

'Yeah, her as well . . . a fuckin Amazon.'

'No,' MacHale said. 'I mean, where *is* she, tonight?'

'At home, I s'pose . . . strappin on a rubber cock. She is a feminist, y'know,' Filthy Phil accusingly went on, by way of justifying his allegation.

'So what?' MacHale responded. 'They only want equal rights . . . the things men enjoy as a matter of course.'

'Yeah, and they'll probably get 'em, too,' Filthy Phil said, most bitterly. 'But what they'll *never* have is what they *most* want . . . big hairy cocks danglin down between their legs.'

MacHale just shook his head and smiled a wry smile.

'Yes, love?' – it was Queenie, back from serving Mulligan's round.

MacHale now smiled more warmly. 'A pint of lager and a gin-'n'-tonic, please.'

And while Queenie was squatting on her haunches,

reaching for a tonic bottle, Filthy Phil was again leaning over the counter, peering down the top of her boob-tube.

Back in his seat, in the corner, MacHale wondered what he'd got in common with his colleagues . . .? Nothing, he decided, apart from the nature of his job. They were older than he, and most of them were of a different generation, as well.

Schofield then floated back across his mind. Perhaps because he, MacHale, had an idea that if he *had* verballed Schofield, and fitted him with the ringed Jag, Snatch and Tubby Tompkins would now have been patting him on the shoulder and buying him pints, instead of proscribing him, as they had. It seemed to him as if his life were fast becoming one huge sigh, recharged by bad experiences and weird dreams.

He sighed, now, before swallowing the last dregs of his lager. Then he walked to the bar, left his empty glass on the counter, and made to leave. It was almost eleven o'clock.

'Oi!' shouted Mulligan. 'Come back here and have one for the road.'

MacHale paused by the door, and turned. 'No thanks, guv'nor. I'm tired.' Then, he was out of the door and away along the road to the section-house, before Mulligan could protest.

The rest of them, though, would remain in the pub until two or three A.M., drinking and gambling, and thereby breaking the licensing laws.

Everywhere there were double standards. Cops like Punchy Paterson and Tasty Tom owed allegiance both to Mulligan and to The Job; it'd be by far easier, then, if a raid on Mulligan's pub were to be planned, for one of them to blow it apart by making a forewarning telephone call.

At Christmas, the licensees of most of the ground's pubs would call at the nick and hand over bottles of spirits and beers, saying, 'Here, this is for the lads.' Most of it would be claimed – or *stolen*, really – by Admin staff, too, and the lads would *never* see it. Regardless of the donors' motives, how *could* this be right and proper, when the police were responsible for monitoring the applications and grants of licences to licensees, and for enforcing the licensing laws?

What of the cafe proprietor, too, who fed and watered the officer on his beat, again, free of charge? When called to a disturbance at such premises, would the officer *always* find, regardless of the facts, that the customer *was* wrong?

Then, in every police station, there were notices displayed, advising officers of where they should shop for goods and services which had been discounted, exclusively for police. Innocuous enough, apparently; but would an officer prosecute a shop-keeper for an offence, when that shopkeeper had at one time afforded him a pecuniary advantage? Probably not, MacHale believed, if the breach could be dealt with in any other way, or altogether ignored.

Maybe that was why Shadrack, the man who owned an electrical-goods' shop down the High Street, had *never* received a summons in respect of any of the parking offences for which MacHale had stuck him in the book. In fact, the last time MacHale had stopped to report Shadrack's delivery van, Shadrack had run from the shop, complaining bitterly, saying, 'Just wait till *you* want something discounted in my shop.' When MacHale had left the scene, Shadrack had probably got straight on to the Admin Unit's CI and arranged for him to square-up the report. Shadrack was certainly never sent to court.

All of these instances, MacHale considered, were the spores of hard-core corruption. But into what they might grow, he couldn't yet fully imagine. Although, he was aware that on a higher plateau, widespread fraud – in relation to the false claiming of official expenses – was totally condoned. A detective, for instance, who went to, say, Pekin, to collect a prisoner who'd absconded abroad, was odds on, if he entered a local bar, to spot one of his own informants, for whom he could then 'purchase' a meal and drinks, the expense to be later recovered from official funds. *Wherever* a detective went, on duty, he'd be certain to pop into a bar and be confronted by a parched and emaciated snout. If the amount of money which it cost to sustain the phantom snouts of detectives were to be correlated with crime statistics and the clear-up rate, the figures would hardly match.

No wonder they said that Book Eighty-Seven – the expenses' book – was a work of fiction: officers claimed refreshment and travelling expenses which had never been incurred. An officer was never required to produce a receipt or ticket so it was easy to claim the *full* refreshment allowance even when he'd bought only a sandwich, and to claim the cost of a tube journey even when he'd travelled in a colleague's car.

But – and incredibly, MacHale felt – no one seemed to realize or care that these were *criminal* offences which were being committed, or that they were either facilitated or tacitly condoned by supervisors.

Trouble was – because it had all been going on for so long, and because it was so widely accepted as routine – it became very easy for a young, inexperienced officer to debase himself. *Too* damn easy. All that a straight young officer could hope for was that he'd be left alone to go his own way.

And if he were, he'd then be pressurized by his own feelings of insecurity. Like when he left a pub at closing time, so as not to be drawn into abetting breaches of the licensing laws.

MacHale knew the others would comment on his early departures from the pub; they'd probably told each other he was faint-hearted, afraid of getting himself into trouble; maybe they'd decided, too, that he was one to be watched for the sake of their own security?

And if they *had* decided that, then it wouldn't be too long before they set about making his life as uncomfortable as possible. All he could do was hope, and try to suppress his fears.

As he walked through the glass-panelled doors and entered the section-house, he saw Sid Broadbent, the night-duty warden, standing by the office door, hands behind his back. At least here was a friendly face. Broadbent usually took up this position, near the entrance, because he wanted to see who was smuggling-in crumpet; not that the PCs *needed* to smuggle-in crumpet, for they were permitted visitors, provided they entered details in the visitors' book. But some PCs had reputations which declared they'd throw a leg over anything wearing a skirt, and if you were one of those types, and you'd scored yourself an ogre – or was it *ogress*? – then you were *wise* to smuggle her in, or at least try and get her unnoticed past the front entrance. Because if you were spotted, groping a Miss Piggy clone, on your way in, or on your way out, your mates would *never* let you live it down; and neither would Sid Broadbent, if it were he who'd spotted you.

'All right, Sid?' MacHale said, smiling at Broadbent.

'Not too bad, John,' responded Broadbent, returning the smile, and he rose up and down on the balls of his feet.

He was a smart bloke, Old Sid. His pure-white hair, thinning, was always neatly trimmed, and his navy uniform, a gold-coloured crown on each of its lapels, was always sharply creased in the right places. He did have his weaknesses, though: gambling, and, most notably, drinking.

He could be amusing, too, when he was drunk. By

about one A.M., he'd be out of his mind, slumped at his desk, his head lying sideways on top of it, his arms dangling limply down to his ankles. Then, every so often, he'd stir, wiggle his backside in the seat, and shout, 'Fuck 'em! . . . *Fuck* 'em!' in that brash, Cockney accent of his. But to whom he was referring, or why, no one seemed to know – not even Sid himself when he was later asked.

MacHale put in a call for nine-thirty A.M. and then turned left and made his way along the corridor to the TV room.

It was an education, that TV room. The section-house dances were held there, for it was a long, wide room with a polished, parquet floor, but ordinarily it was where the off-duty PCs gathered to watch the colour TV, occupying easy chairs that were arranged in rows at one end of the room, by the carved-stone fireplace. This, too, was where anyone who was curious to know what cops were *really* like, should have come.

They lounged in their chairs, swearing and cursing at one another over the choice of programme to be watched, and occasionally a fight would break out, especially if it were late at night, after licensing hours, when more than a few of them would be the worse for drink. Part-eaten curries, in foil trays, would often be lobbed through the air, into the fireplace, as were cigarette butts and fish-'n'-chip papers; and all over the floor there were piles of plates, cups and saucers which had been brought in from the canteen and then just left there for the cleaners to attend to in the morning. Week-ends were particularly bad, because the cleaners were off-duty on Saturdays and Sundays.

Tonight, all of the seats were occupied, and MacHale was obliged to stand at the back of the room. It looked like a good film, too . . . Yes, it was *Magnum Force* . . . Clint Eastword as *Dirty Harry* . . . *A black pimp is driving a pink Cadillac on a highway* . . . A shout from one of the audience: 'Ya black-enamelled bastard! I'd like to cut ya balls off!' Loud cheering from the others.

Later on, there'd be more than a few of those cops practising their *Dirty Harry* countenances before the mirrors on their bedroom walls. And tomorrow, a lot of *Dirty Harry* clones would be patrolling the city's streets, wishing like hell that *they* had shooters at their sides, so that *they*, too, might have a chance of blowing-out some black pimp's brains.

Suddenly, a part-eaten vindaloo in foil tray came sailing through the air . . . and landed, *splat*, in the fireplace, scattering rice and gravy over the feet of a young fair-haired cop who was sitting nearby, legs outstretched. Up he jumped, a bellicose expression on his face, his narrowed eyes probing the darkness to his right. 'Who the fuck did that?' he demanded.

'Shuddup, ya lamebrained prick!' came a loud response. 'An siddown!'

The PC moved in the direction of the voice, identified its owner and stood before him, fists clenched, saying, '*What* did you just call me? . . . Ya slag!'

Then, anarchy in the TV room as the two adversaries squared-up to each other; to add to the verbal chaos, someone then ran over to the TV-set and turned up the sound, full blast . . .

MacHale walked out and left them to it, shaking his head. The public just wouldn't *believe it*; there were more hooligans, there, in that TV-room, than were out on the *streets*.

When he reached his room, he changed out of his uniform, putting on a pair of denims, a wine-coloured sweater and a pair of trainers. Then he went downstairs in the lift, to the basement, where he washed a shirt and pressed the trousers of his uniform, hanging them to dry in the laundry room, which was windowless and equipped with a hot-air blower. It was at times such as this, when you'd spent eight hours pounding the streets and getting aches in places that you hadn't thought existed, that you wished you were married; so that there'd be a wife who'd attend to your washing and ironing and uniform-pressing . . . and a few other things, as well, that were essential to a man's well-being.

MacHale wondered if he'd ever find the time to capture himself a decent woman with whom he might contemplate settling down. She'd have to be someone a bit special, though, he believed. *Every* cop's wife had to be a bit special, though. How *did* they cope with the shiftwork, sitting alone, or lying alone in bed, when their husbands were working unsocial hours, or, too often, performing duty on cancelled-leave days, or, even *more* often, were staying out till all hours, womanizing and getting themselves drunk?

Most of them *didn't* cope, he supposed, and it wasn't right to expect that they *should* cope with husbands who eventually became deceitful, near-alcoholic, untruthful paramour-seekers. That was why cops had the highest divorce rate of all professions

Still, when a cop finished a shift, his nerves jumping and his brain spinning, he'd rather go out on the town, and work off that hypertension, with drink and lively company, than sit at home, pensive and edgy, with a woman who just couldn't understand his moods.

Going up in the lift, MacHale chuckled. He'd just thought of Vindscreen and his woman – his common-law wife. She was a natural blonde with a terrific figure and an effervescent personality, who, according to Vindscreen, made Linda Lovelace seem like Mother Theresa of Calcutta when it came to bedtime. She had her drawbacks, though; naturally. She had the intellect of a guppy, and she couldn't cook.

'What's the difference between my bird and a rural jog?' Vindscreen had once asked. No one had known, though. 'Well,' Vindscreen explained, 'a rural jog is a pant in the country, and my bird is a . . .' But he was drowned out by the laughter.

Then there was the business of Vindscreen's police-issue white shirts. She'd thrown them in the washing machine, along with all of the other soiled laundry, and when Vindscreen arrived home, that afternoon, there she was, standing by the sink, *still* in her diaphanous negligee, holding up one of the shirts, staring at it, a deep frown on her lovely face. The once-white shirts were now an insipid shade of purple: dyed by Vindscreen's navy-blue socks and denims, which had seeped colour in the ultra-hot wash.

Vindscreen, when he'd recovered his composure, had driven over to the section-house, made his way down to the laundry room, and there swapped his shirts for some *pure* white – well, almost – ones that'd been washed, and hung up to dry, by several of the residents. That's why MacHale's shirts, and those of all other once-bitten section-house PCs, now had their owners' District and warrant numbers printed in indelible ink on their tails.

The public just wouldn't believe *that*, either, MacHale considered: thieving – by police – was commonplace in police stations.

Everything you owned had to be indelibly marked if you wanted to ensure your continued ownership . . . truncheons, helmets, report-book wallets, and so on; and no PC would ever be so reckless as to leave unattended cash or valuables in his section-house room. It was as if criminality were a highly contagious disease which you were bound to contract after several years' exposure to it in charge-rooms, in courts, and on the streets.

He arrived back at his room, closed the door, and went to sit at the table. Could you be immunized? he wondered. Anyway, what *was* immunization from disease? Surely, it meant treating like with like? So did that mean, then, if you were to beat, or keep on top of, criminality, you had to be imbued with a certain amount of it?

But then . . . *he* couldn't be an interpreter and bender of rules, and at the same time be at ease with his inner self. His conscience was too highly developed, he supposed. That was Catholicism for you. All Catholics must be guilt-ridden, latent neurotics.

MacHale recalled the first of his confessions . . . kneeling in front of a tall, wooden box, the space dark and cramped, curtained off from the remainder of the church . . . a fretwork wicket-gate sliding open above his head, revealing an amorphous, shadowy face, that wafted grown-ups'-drink-and-nicotine-tainted breath, hot and sickening, down towards his nostrils, and which he *knew* belonged to Father Mooney . . . voice trembling, heart wildly beating in his chest, so guilt-ridden he shook and quivered, as he related the mandatory preamble: *Bless me Father, for I have sinned; it is one week since my last Confession . . .*

After confession, absolution and penance, he'd skip back to class, his guilt temporarily assuaged, engulfed by a feeling of euphoria. Later that day, though, another kid would somehow bug him, and he'd maybe lash out, verbally or physically, or both, and then the guilt would be back, haunting him, until next week's confession.

But supposing he were to *die*! *Before* next week's confession. He'd sure as hell be committed there, and would roast forever in those raging fires. It was *terrifying*.

And so expert was this conditioning he'd never, to his dying day, go uninfluenced by it. Never. He'd *always* feel guilty – his mind never failed to throw up *something*, just as he was about to drop off to sleep – and he'd always be afraid of bad dreams.

Nowadays, he didn't practise Catholicism in any shape or form – much to the chagrin of his mother, whose Faith had never faltered; or *had* it? MacHale was an *only* child.

Whatever, she understood his choice. And she knew that her son would always be a *good* son, that he'd always do what was right and proper and just, that he'd always *believe* in God. His having joined the police service could be interpreted as a manifestation of this. 'God works in mysterious ways,' she'd murmured – enigmatically, MacHale had thought – as she'd admired the class photograph from training school.

She was right, too, MacHale now told himself, recalling her words, and his own experiences since joining the police. *He does* work in strange ways. But why did He *keep* giving you stick, when you *were* only doing what was right, and in good faith?

MacHale sighed and shook his head.

Then, a knock at the door brought his eyes sharply back into focus and made him jump. He glanced at his wristwatch – almost twelve-thirty A.M. 'Come in,' he called out.

The door opened and in walked Hercules, a grey sports-jacket over his half blues. 'Hello, Juan,' he smiled, and stood there, his belly arching inward, his shoulders drooping, his hands washing together. 'I wondered if you'd like a cup of coffee?'

'No, no thanks,' MacHale said. 'I'm just going to bed, and coffee keeps me awake.'

'Tea, then? I've got both, you know.'

'No. Nothing, thanks. Nothing at all.' Christ, he thought, this bloke gives me the *shits*; he doesn't look *at* you, he looks right *inside* you . . . his beady eyes roving all over. Then he noticed a love-bite on the left side of Hercules' neck, just above the collar line. That wasn't there before, earlier in the day, he told himself. Maybe Filthy Phil was right about where Hercules had got to, tonight? Of course, he *could've* been with a bird, but . . . Inwardly, MacHale shrugged. What was it to do with him, anyway, what Hercules got up to? Nothing.

'Oh, well,' Hercules said, disappointed. 'Just thought I'd ask.'

MacHale forced a smile, and watched as Hercules turned to go. But there was something he'd made up his mind to ask the older, more experienced PC. 'Herc,' he said. 'Can The Job be done properly? In *complete* accordance with the rules?'

Hercules turned and walked to the table, standing by MacHale's right side. 'What d'you mean?' He frowned. 'D'you mean – ?'

'I mean,' MacHale interposed, 'that if you *do* do The Job, properly, by the book, do you get results? Or do you *have* to bend the rules?'

Hercules thought about it for a couple of seconds. 'Well, it's a question of . . .' He paused, in difficulty, then shrugged and re-ordered his thoughts. 'Put it this way: you've got to *know* the rules, otherwise you *can't* bend them, so that – '

'But do you *have* to bend them?' MacHale persisted.

Hercules was again in some difficulty, a squirmy expression on his bony face. 'Look, Juan, you shouldn't really be asking for advice on such things. No experienced cop is gonna tell you that you've *gotta* break the law in order to enforce it . . . Let's just say that . . . well, d'you remember that song, by *Fun-Boy Three* and *Bananarama*? It was in the charts, not so long ago . . . a resurrection of an oldie?' He began humming a few bars, tapping his right hand on MacHale's left shoulder, nodding his head to the beat.

MacHale concentrated and tried to pick up on it . . . 'Got it,' he said.

'Well, there's your answer,' Hercules told him. His hand ceased its tapping on MacHale's shoulder, but briefly lingered there, its long, skinny fingers squeezing gently. Then he turned and left the room, closing the door.

MacHale shivered and instinctively rubbed away the tingling feeling that had erupted within his shoulder, as he mentally went through the song's chorus line . . . *It ain't watcha do, it's the way thatcha do it, it ain't watcha do, it's the way thatcha do it, it ain't watcha do, it's the way thatcha do it, that's what gets results . . .*

He thought about that for a fair while.

Results. They were what counted. And it didn't seem to matter too much what methods you employed, so long as they were effective. That, so it seemed, was the pro' cop's maxim. But, no, that didn't mean you had to bend rules, MacHale believed. It just meant that no one cared very much if you did. There was hope for honesty and integrity. There just *had* to be.

His eyes fell on the IB, which was lying on top of the table. He was scheduled for an attendance at CTC, in three weeks, and there was only *one* method for ensuring success, there: honest industry. He groaned, then yawned and shook his head, and didn't feel at all like studying, right here and now. He was tired, mentally and physically, and was tempted to put off until tomorrow . . . But he firmly decided, No. Make an effort; and then picked up the book and opened its pages.

Of course, the IB, a pedantic little tome, was the best known remedy for insomnia, and if you picked it up and opened it at a time when you were already half asleep, then it could be positively knock-out.

So it was, then, that MacHale came to at three A.M., his head and shoulders lying across the top of the table, saliva dribbling from the corner of his mouth. Now he felt utterly exhausted, but when he undressed and climbed into bed, switching off the light, he just couldn't sleep.

Down in the yard, below his bedroom window, a stray dog was intermittently barking and yelping . . . cars were coming and going, prisoners were shouting, banging their fists and the heels of their shoes on cell doors . . .

operational PCs were leaving and entering the nick, their PRs garbling static-ridden messages . . .

His brain became hyperactive, churning and mixing the day's events . . . ranging backwards and forwards, highlighting his fears, exploiting his doubts, slicing into his vulnerability. Time and again his body would tense to snapping point, and his eyes would burst open . . . then, his mind clear, he'd reenter the blackness, seeking restful sleep . . . But the frightening images would once again begin their mixing and churning and tossing and turning . . . until, finally, drifting . . . floating . . . into a new dimension of unconscious, mental exploitation, which he had *no* control over . . .

It *was* Schofield.

10

There was nothing to suggest it would be one of *those* days. Not at first, anyway. Outside, it was pleasant enough; the skies were clear and calm, and the sun was shining; traffic was light, and there hadn't yet been an Emercall or a shout; there wasn't even a body in the charge-room. The early-Relief Station Officer had said it was quiet for the whole of the morning, and had forecast that things would continue that way for the late Relief.

And then that woman turned up outside the nick. *That* was what started it all.

Barker rose up on his toes, and, frowning deeply, peered over the top half of the sash window in the front office. Christ, she was *still* out there, grief and pain etched all over her apprehensive, pallid face. In a moment or two, he was pessimistically certain of it, she'd have summoned up the courage to ascend the steps and walk on into the nick. And then the grief and pain would be unburdened – onto *him*.

Was she a nutter . . .? Maybe. In her mid-forties, probably, she was thin-featured, dark-haired, and wore a black, double-breasted mac and brown moccasins . . . no stockings or tights, though, and her legs, with their thick, muscular calves, were unattractively pale. That face, too: tired, strained, puzzlingly familiar, was once quite handsome, Barker felt; sort of sharp, but in a generous fashion, and probably could be very lively; big, dark eyes, as well . . .

Who *is* she? Not a tom, *surely*? Not *here*, right outside the factory. Although . . . stranger things had occurred, Barker was prompted to recall. Like that time last year, for instance, when they'd caught a breaker, screwing the CID office, upstairs; in the middle of the night. You'd have thought a nick full of coppers was the *last* place on earth that a burglar would size up for a screwing.

Barker dropped back down onto his heels, turned his head away from the window, and looked to the far end of the front office, where MacHale, seated at a desk, was entering the early Relief's stops in the Book Ninety – but one of his duties as today's ASO-cum-gaoler.

'MacHale. Come here, a minute,' Barker said.

'Sarge?' MacHale stopped what he was doing and walked to Barker's side.

'Have a look at this tart who's outside here,' Barker told him. 'See if you can sus her out.'

MacHale rose on his toes, looked out of the window, and studied the woman as she lingered by the kerb, her eyes downcast, her back facing towards him. 'Hmm,' he murmured, grimacing. 'She isn't gonna throw herself under a bus, is she, Sarge?'

'I fuckin *knew* it!' Barker snapped. 'She *is* a tom, about to make her final protest at police harassment . . . Shoot out there an give her some help . . . like, stick ya fuckin boot up her jaxy.'

MacHale didn't think Barker was serious, and he merely continued to appraise the woman. 'I don't think she is a tom, Sarge. She's not brassy enough, is she?' – MacHale hadn't yet seen any of the toms who operated in Silverleaf Park; if he had, he'd have known that looks were no indicator: some of those toms were out-and-out vagies, with stinking, unwashed bodies, lank hair, rotten teeth, and Christ knew what else; yet they *still* pulled five quid for a blow-job in the bushes, from well-to-do punters who drove up in big, flashy cars. Some *men* . . .

'Well *whatever* she is, she's givin *me* the *shits*!' Barker said. 'Hangin around out there, like that. I wish she'd either – '

'She is, Sarge. She *is* coming in.'

The woman turned to face the nick, her face now resolute, and was making for the flight of steps that led up into the foyer.

Barker moved to stand behind his desk, his face stony, his hands gripping the lapels of his tunic, mentally bracing himself, while MacHale returned to the Stop Book, his ears bristling.

She was at the public counter, now, her hands resting on top of it, her right index-finger and thumb nervously toying with, and rotating, her wedding ring – a solid band of gold. Maybe it was an unconscious manifestation of what was troubling her mind? She coughed, and sniffed, not knowing, it seemed, where or how to begin.

She'd given Barker a cue, though, toying like that with her wedding ring: it *was* a marital problem, he decided. So why the hell couldn't she write to Marj Proops? This here was a police station, not a fuckin marriage-guidance counsellor's office. Inwardly, Barker sighed, and began to feel even more irritable. He'd give her the elbow, he decided. *Schnell!* Off-load her to the social services or somewhere; *anywhere*.

The woman looked squarely at Barker, her eyes flickering. 'I'm sorry to be a nuisance, Sergeant,' she began, 'but I don't know what else to do. You see . . .' She hesitated, biting her lower lip, while her mind attempted to order itself.

'I fuckin *knew* it!' Barker almost tacitly seethed through clenched teeth. Jesus Christ, he thought, haven't I got *enough* aggravation with my *own* marital problems?

'He's gone away,' the woman continued, 'and the money's run out.' Now her lips began quivering, and her eyes filled with tears. She bowed her head and rummaged in her mac pocket, pulling out a white handkerchief, which she dabbed at her nose and eyes, sniffing back her emotion.

'Social security,' Barker flatly said, 'left out the door, down to the bottom of the High Street, turn right, third on the – '

'No, no,' the woman cut in. 'If you could just tell me when my husband will be *back* . . . I mean, if it's soon, I might just be *able* to manage.'

'What . . .?' Barker frowned and twitched his shoulders. 'D'you mean we've got your old man banged-up in the cells? Here? Is that it?'

'Not exactly,' the woman said, and she half smiled. 'I'm sorry, I've confused you. You see, I thought you knew me . . . remembered me from the Annual Dinner-and-Dance . . . The year before last. I'm sure we were introduced there.'

MacHale's ears were now popping. What had *she* been doing at a police dinner-and-dance . . . meeting Barker . . . who now couldn't remember her?

'I, er . . . I don't recall,' Barker said, a noticeable tremor in his voice. He was thinking along the same lines as MacHale.

'Let me start at the beginning, then,' the woman was now saying. 'You see, I'm Mrs Smith. *Phil* Smith's wife. And, two weeks ago, he was posted to the Falklands . . . You know, as part of the aid that was sent there, after the war . . .'

Barker, jaw hanging open, was listening with everything he'd got, while MacHale, his head having swivelled quickly in the woman's direction, was bug-eyed.

'Anyway,' the woman went on, 'he said the posting was for four weeks, and he left me *some* money, but not enough. What with the children, and the bills . . . well, I haven't been able to manage, so I wondered if I could get an advance on Phil's wages?'

Barker gulped, and almost choked on an involuntary cough; now, *his* eyes were popping, too. He could scarcely *believe* it: *Filthy Phil?* On *aid* to the *Falklands*? For the past fortnight? . . . Barker didn't think he'd ever heard such crap in all his service. What the fuck was Filthy Phil *playing* at?

MacHale had guessed. Filthy Phil was reputed to be over the side with a piece of crumpet, wasn't he? Sure, he was. So, it didn't take the brains of a lawyer to sus out that he'd moved *in* with her for a couple of weeks, having told his wife that The Job was sending him on aid to the Falklands – fairly plausible, too, because several British cops *had* been posted out there, after the war with Argentina, to assist the local constabulary.

Barker came out of the trance he'd been in. 'Look, I, er, I'm sorry, Mrs Smith, but I'll have to make some inquiries about this. Why don't you take a seat in the waiting room, for now, and I'll come back to you in a few minutes?'

'Thank you, Sergeant,' she said; and she left the counter and entered the waiting room, opposite.

'Jesus *Christ*!' Barker muttered, and he fell down in his seat, his elbows banging the desk-top. For a few seconds, he stayed there like that, his fingers writhing through his grey hair; then he stood, a philosophic look on his face, and said to MacHale, 'Go down to the Inspectors' Office, MacHale, and tell Mister Crawford that I'd like him here to deal with . . . with something *contentious*.' He smiled mischievously.

What was it that Old Crikey kept saying, when trying to justify his deriliction of duty? . . . Yes, that's it: *Delegation is the art of good management.* Well, let's just see how you manage *this* fuckin dog's dinner. *Sir!*

That afternoon, Old Crikey must've crunched, chewed and sucked his way through a couple of pounds of digestif tablets, and ground at least a centimetre off the top and bottom rows of his back teeth.

'Oh, *crikey*!' was, predictably enough, his initial reaction to Filthy Phil's adulterous chicanery, and then he ordered each operational man to drop whatever it was he was doing and go in search of Filthy Phil, who, as usual, couldn't be raised on the PR.

It was Tubby Tompkins and Snatch, in the RT-car, who first spotted him, pedalling sedately along a residential side-street, his head raised up to the left, his eyes panning the upstairs bedroom windows of the terrace houses. Silently, the Rover idled up behind him, and then Snatch flicked on the noise – *Wow! Wheeeee!* Filthy Phil's heart exploded, his helmet jumped a foot off his head, and his bike snaked, wobbling dangerously, from kerb-to-kerb, narrowly missing parked cars.

'You bastards!' he shouted, when he'd brought his bike under control and had stopped.

Tubby Tompkins wound down his window, smiling a huge smile. 'All right, Phil?' he said, very good-naturedly. 'What's the weather been like in Goose Green? . . . Any good?'

'Much crumpet out there, was there, dear boy?' asked Snatch, giggling as he leaned sideways over Tubby's gut and directed his voice out of the driver's window.

'*What?* . . . What d'you mean?' snapped Filthy Phil, his eyes narrowing suspiciously.

'Think he'd've sent us a postcard, though, wouldn't you?' Tubby said to Snatch.

'Yeah,' Snatch agreed. 'With one o' them penguins on it.'

''Course,' Tubby went on, 'he ain't due *back* for another *fortnight* . . .'

And so forth: Snatch and Tubby drawing it out, gutting Filthy Phil with their humorous taunts and jibes, until, in the end, he was panic-stricken, having been told that his missus was down at the nick, wanting to know where the housekeeping money was.

When *he* arrived back at the nick, though, his wife had gone, having been sent home by Old Crikey, who'd told her that even now a Hercules transport-plane was on its way back from the Falklands, with her husband on board; the posting was clearly having an adverse effect on the Smiths' marriage, and, from hereon in, PC Smith would resume his normal duties. *That* was a *promise*. In fact, he'd be home by eleven o'clock. *Tonight*.

Fast, these Hercules transport-planes, MacHale thought, listening to Old Crikey. But not *that* fast. A journey back from the Falklands, in one of those planes, would actually take about twenty-four hours.

Finally, Old Crikey got verbally stuck into Filthy Phil. If Smith's wife ever again – *ever* again; did he *hear* that? – appeared at that front counter, wanting to know when her husband would be back from the Falklands, or Grenada, or the Isle of Wight, or . . . or *anywhere* that wasn't within a five-mile radius of the locker room, then Old Crikey, so help him, would truss-up his body and give it over to the CIB.

Next on at the front counter was a *real* brassy-looking tom – face like a bag of spanners, shoulderlength yellow hair, heavily mascara-ed eyes, with inch-long black lashes, obscenely full, wet red lips, wearing a synthetic tiger-skin coat, open, revealing fish-net tights, gold-sequinned hot-pants, and matching boob-tube; plenty of jewellery, too . . . a gold ring on *every* onc of her red-nailed fingers, and four or five heavy-gold chains slung around her wrinkled neck – must have had a good, protective ponce, somewhere. She was probably about fifty, MacHale thought, and had undoubtedly had several face-jobs, but *still* didn't look a day older than sixty-five.

She banged her handbag down on top of the counter, and stood there, a defiant expression on her face, her breasts jutting, her gut drooping over the waistband of her pants, her left hand on her hip.

Here we fuckin go again, thought Barker, as he rose from his desk and walked to the counter. 'Yes, darlin?' he said, trying to sound interested, but sounding thoroughly pissed off.

'I've had me twat bitten by a bleedin punter,' she shrieked.

'You've had your *what* bitten?' Barker exclaimed, cocking his right eyebrow.

'Not me *what*, me *twat*,' she said. 'Look ere.' And she began raising her flabby right thigh up in the air, tugging at what little there was of the right leg of her pants, exposing a tangle of pubic hair.

'All right, all right,' Barker told her, the tip of his nose curling upward. 'I'll take your word for it. How'd it happen, then?'

She lowered her leg and leaned on the counter. 'Well, there I was, entertainin this client, back at my place, givin him the golden-fountain treatment, when all of a sudden he – '

'Just a minute,' Barker said. 'What's this golden-fountain treatment all about, then?' He was certain it wasn't in the *Kama Sutra*.

'You know,' she said. 'Where I squats over the punter, naked, and wees all over him.'

'Oh, Christ,' Barker muttered.

'Anyway,' she went on, 'he drank his fill, and then he bites me twat.' She grimaced, and rubbed a hand up and down her crotch. 'I'll be outa commission for a couplea weeks, I shouldn't wonder.'

'Take up wrist exercises,' Barker suggested.

'Now you look ere!' she protested. 'I pay my rates, too, ya know, an I'm entitled to a bitta police protection against these bleedin lunatics. I want this punter done for GBH.'

'Who is he?' Barker wanted to know.

She shrugged. 'He ain't a regular . . . But that's for *you* to find out . . . who he is, where he lives.'

'Fat chance,' Barker said.

'Well *I* ain't movin from ere till I get satisfaction!' she shouted.

Barker couldn't resist it. He turned to MacHale and said. 'You heard her, MacHale. Go an borrow a fuckin donkey from the stables. *That's* about the only thing that'll satisfy *her*.'

MacHale just looked away, unsure of how to react.

All the tom could manage was a high-pressured, 'Whooooh!' and her face glowered.

Now, Barker relented. 'Look, darlin,' he said. 'We could stand here all day, swappin verbals, and then *you'd* finish up on the sheet, for violent behaviour in a police station. So . . .' He spread his hands.

'So, *what*?' she demanded. 'What *are* ya gonna do, then? That's what I wanna know.'

'Well, for starters,' Barker firmly told her, 'we ain't gonna waste our time with a crime-book entry for assault. You know we don't stand a snowball in hell's chance of nickin the punter who bit your . . . who bit you. You just gotta accept things like that. Hazard of the job. If he comes back at any time, just give us a Bell and we'll square him up.' He looked hopefully at her.

She stared blankly at the counter top, her face sour. Then, looking at Barker, she said, 'It ain't right. This'll cost me a lotta money, ya know.'

'Simple,' Barker said. 'Go down the social security and make a claim for industrial injury benefit.'

What? MacHale thought. He's gotta be *joking*. They'll call *us* to her if she does go down there with a line like that.

Barker wasn't joking, though. He was trying to unload the tom onto someone else, that was all.

'D'you reckon it *is*?' the tom said, looking doubtful. 'An *industrial injury?*'

'Gotta be,' Barker assured her. 'You was injured doin your job.'

'Yeah,' she thoughtfully murmured. 'I s'pose I was, wasn't I?'

'There you are, then. Game, set-'n'-match. Just go down there, fill in a few forms, and you're a winner.'

Now she smiled. 'I like it. I should've thought of it meself . . . Right. I'm off, then . . . And ta. Ta very much.'

'Don't embarrass me,' Barker modestly told her, and he, too, smiled.

No sooner had Barker disposed of that problem, though, than another presented itself at the front counter.

'Yes, sir?' inquired MacHale, walking over to meet the caller, an elderly, bowler-hatted man, crimson-faced, with a waxed moustache that declared him military.

'Get me the most senior officer on duty, Constable!' ordered the man, his imperious tone and demeanour stating indisputably that he was not a person to be trifled with.

MacHale approached Barker, who was still at his desk, about to write-out a charge of drunkenness in respect of a vagie whom Pat Coles had earlier arrested. 'Sarge?' MacHale began. 'This gentleman says – '

'I heard, as well as you did, MacHale,' retorted Barker. 'He said he wants the *most* senior officer on duty. And *that* means Inspector Crawford.'

The man nodded his satisfaction, threw down his brown-leather gloves, onto the counter-top, and grunted. Something was fermenting in his mind, without a doubt, and in a minute it was going to froth over onto Old Crikey.

'Oh, *crikey*! What *now*, MacHale?' whined Old Crikey,

when MacHale arrived at his office. Then, as he reluctantly walked along the corridor to the front office, he popped another digestif into his agitated mouth.

'Ah! There you are, Inspector,' said the man at the counter, as Old Crikey cautiously entered the office. 'Colonel Reynolds, ex-Coldstreams, is the name, and I want you to step outside a moment and witness what your damn horse has done to my car.'

For a moment Old Crikey just stood his ground, staring in bewilderment at the Colonel, a little apprehensive, crunching his digestif. Then he swallowed hard and said, '*Horse? . . . My* horse? I haven't *got* a horse.'

'No, no, you fool!' thundered the Colonel. 'When I say, "your horse", I mean a *police* horse. You have stables here, don't you?'

'Well, yes, sir . . . We do.'

'Right! Get fell in behind me, then, Inspector.'

Old Crikey, looking completely inept, lifted up the flap at the end of the counter, and followed him out into the street.

Barker then jumped up from his desk, ran to the window and leaned out, looking up and down the road. MacHale joined him.

And there, a hundred yards along on the right-hand side, *was* a police horse – a bloody great chestnut thing, with huge ears – standing by a primrose-yellow Daimler Sovereign that had a crumpled-up bonnet. A Mounted Branch PC – dismounted – was in the process of examining the horse's backside, and the horse was now in the process of chewing the car's aerial.

Barker laughed until his guts ached – as did MacHale; until Old Crikey came storming back into the nick and ordered *him* to go out and report the accident.

Which is all it was – an accident. Apparently, the horse and rider had stopped at the ATS – which were showing red – and the Colonel, driving behind him in his Daimler, had pulled up about two feet back. At which point, the horse had decided to have a sit down . . . on the bonnet of the Daimler; and while the rider was examining the horse's bum, for any injury, the horse took a fancy to the car's aerial, and chewed the hell out of it. All highly embarrassing stuff for the Mounted Branch PC.

But then, that Mounted Branch PC was used to being embarrassed by his horse. Last week, old Henry – as the horse was named – crapped all over the bonnet of a hearse, at the same traffic lights, and thereby held up a funeral cortege for all of ten minutes, while Charlie Cox, the rider, galloped back to the nick to collect a dustpan and brush and a polishing cloth.

Mind you, Charlie Cox was partly to blame for that horse's unprofessional conduct while on duty, for Charlie Cox, when he came upon a wide, open space, such as Greenridge Park, began to believe he was Jim Hardy, Wells-Fargo Special Agent, and he'd lean over the horse's mane, give it a kick in the ribs, and go hell for leather to the horizon, never mind about the picnickers and the grazing deer and the courting couples . . . he'd scatter them all. Yes, that Charlie Cox fancied himself a cowboy, too.

Almost all of those police horses were deviants, in one way or another: excitable, irritable, aggressive, destructive . . . And who could blame them? How would anyone *else* feel after having been banged-up for God knew how many years, in a small stall, for the larger part of twenty-four hours of every day? It was cruel. MacHale sometimes fed them with carrots and apples surreptitiously; they knew him now, and no longer lashed out with their hooves.

Overall, then, it was a busy afternoon. Although, a good deal of what filled it was *crappy*, and *weary*, as Barker had put it. Like the seemingly endless stream of drunks.

and beggars; the two juveniles who'd been arrested by Snatch and Tubby Tompkins, for TDA of a dumper, on a building site; and the half-dozen shoplifters who'd been swagged in by the Shoplifting Squad; but the CID had brought in a pair of professional breakers, along with a van-load of stolen antiques, and the Crime Squad had fractured a five-strong team of black dippers, down the High Street. Finally, just before grub-time, the Dirty Squad came in with Roland Squires, the stooge manager of a porno shop.

People weren't often nicked for the offence of possessing obscene material, for gain; usually, their goodies were confiscated and they were merely reported, while the seizure was later forwarded to the DPP for a decision as to whether or not a prosecution was evidenced. Generally speaking, you'd get an NFA, these days, unless the confiscated materials contained shots of buggery or sodomy or kiddy stuff – for which there was a *very* hot market, indeed. However, Roland had been fractured, today, because he'd also been found in possession of some stolen kites – cheques – and credit cards.

MacHale, as ASO, got to see some of Roland's goodies, and much of the material disgusted him. Shots of straight sex, he didn't mind looking at; it only became unnatural or unhealthy if you were dependent upon porno stuff for your personal, sexual gratification. The animal stuff, he couldn't square-up to, though. How could *anyone* derive a sensuous pleasure from studying a photograph which depicted a naked woman being mounted by a dog, or a woman fellating a pig or horse? And what sort of women *were* these, anyway, who posed for such filth? All the cops – except maybe Filthy Phil – felt this way about animal porno; but they'd never admit to having been offended or disgusted by it, because that wouldn't fit the image; instead, they'd make jokes about it – like, *Christ, look at that pig's dick; it's like a fuckin corkscrew!* And so on, so that it was dealt with light-heartedly.

And then there was the juvenile stuff. Little girls, aged ten, perhaps twelve, being forced into by abnormally large men; you could tell from the poor little kids' eyes and facial expressions – despite the limitations of some of the photographic reproductions – that they'd been drugged before being subjected to this violent, sexual abuse; but that *couldn't* have made it any the less painful for them, either mentally or physically.

Finally, an article which transcended pornography: a photograph of a baby, aged ten months, maybe – certainly no older – who seemed to have a huge penis, reaching almost to its ankles. On closer inspection, though, it became clear that there must be a man, out of shot, holding the baby before himself, his erect penis placed, from the back, between the legs of the baby *girl*, to make it appear as if it were a baby boy.

So what sort of human garbage was it that did *this* to a baby? And what sort of human garbage was it that would look at this kind of pornography, get a rush from it, and buy it? MacHale couldn't even *begin* to imagine.

What he could imagine, though, vividly, was himself getting hold of these people, and kicking and punching all kinds of crap out of them . . . *killing* them. *Anything* would be justifiable . . . Then he had to stop and think less emotionally. Was *this* why the experienced cop found himself stitching-up people? An avenging angel. It must be *easy* to rationalize an unlawful act which consisted of, say, beating-up a porno merchant such as Roland Squires, because you'd be convinced that every decent, law-abiding person in the land would be with you in that act.

Where would it stop, though? In the end, you'd maybe lose your sense of direction and proportion, and your self-appointed brief might then begin to cover *anyone* who was merely *believed* to be an offender. Ultimately, you'd be going around, garotting vagies and slinging them in the Thames.

There couldn't really be *any* compromises. But MacHale was unable to stop himself adding, *unfortunately*, to that declaration.

A little later, Roland Squires found himself going on the sheet for an offence of equipped for criminal deception. Which was an unexpected bonus of an offence for the Dirty Squad. They'd sent a man along the High Street, to borrow a video recorder from Shadrack, and had then settled down for an evening's viewing in the Admin Unit; someone had broken open a bottle of Bell's, and someone else a can of peanuts, and when everyone was fully charged with eats and drinks, the first video was slotted home.

The opening scene was unusual, to say the least of it; none of the stereotyped stuff, where man meets girl in park or street, or wherever, chats her up, then takes her back to his drum and gives her one in every imaginable way – and in a few other ways, perhaps, which *aren't* so imaginable. No, here was a *desert* scene . . . late evening, with a glorious, crimson sunset over rippled dunes of flaming golden sand . . . then an Arab, leading a camel into shot . . .

'Well fan my brow,' says one member of the Squad. 'I've seen women had by donkeys, goats, pigs and dogs, and by most *other* things that've got four legs and a cock. But a *camel* . . .? He shook his head. 'Beats me.'

Actually, it didn't beat him. Because the video wasn't porno, at all. It was a travel film. Completely innocuous.

The officer stood and picked up the video's case. On its front was a colour photograph of a woman, fellating a man, so that a punter would've *believed* he'd be getting hard-core porno for his forty or fifty quid. When he got home, though, and sat there before the TV, breathless, rampant, how would he react when he realized the film was a total blow-out? Whatever he did, he certainly wouldn't complain to the law, and a complaint to Roland Squires would get him nowhere.

But if the law *should* discover that Squires was conning punters, there was revealed the offence of going equipped – to obtain property, that is, money, by deception.

Later still, then, Roland Squires found himself being banged-up for the night with one of the pro' breakers who had an aversion to kiddy porno. The officer punted Roland into the cell, saying loudly as he double-locked and bolted the door, 'Roland . . . Squires . . . Court, A.M. . . . *Kiddy* porno!'

Five minutes later, the officer would return, and he'd be disappointed as hell if Roland's nose didn't look like an over-ripe strawberry. If it were, he'd then remove and isolate Roland. But if it were not, then the officer'd probably himself do the business. Whatever, there was no way that Roland *wouldn't* have had a seeing to, by morning time. Perhaps he'd *struggled ferociously*, and had had to be *forcibly restrained*. Or maybe he'd just *fallen down the steps* while being brought in through the back entrance . . . something like that, anyway.

Pat Coles was in tears. In the canteen. She'd made an effort to eat her chicken salad – she was dieting, it seemed – but just couldn't stomach it. Not after seeing that . . . that *filth*! More specifically, not after seeing that poor baby . . . what they'd *done* to it.

Tasty Tom moved his eyes from his cards and glanced insolently across at her. 'Huh!' he spat. 'Just fuckin *look* at her. An they expect *us* to work with em. 'Magine *her* in the front bar of Mulligan's on a Friday night. While you're reachin for ya stick, *she's* reachin for a fuckin snotrag.' And he sneered, flashing his big yellow teeth.

'Yeah,' Tubby Tompkins agreed. 'They're good for two things, women . . . fuckin-'n'-cookin.'

Snatch just smiled.

'Worst thing they ever did,' Punchy Paterson said. 'Integratin WPCs . . . *Bad* mistake.'

'Oh, never mind about *her*!' Vindscreen whined. 'Let's get on with the *game*.' He was still on a winning run.

In one corner, Mathieson was sitting alone at a table, staring emptily into space, marooned on some barren island within his ice-cold head. He'd had two slices of toast for his grub; that was all. He never ate anything else *but* toast, these days, it seemed. Come six-thirty, he'd get up, pop a mint in his mouth, and make his way out, wiping the sleeve of his tunic over his watery eyes, as he headed for one of the local pubs' back room.

Over by the gas-stove was someone else whose head was all screwed-up inside – Old Crikey. He was seated at a table, hunched over today's copy of *The Observer*. By his left elbow was his wristwatch, its alarm having been set to go off in three minutes' time. He preferred his eggs to be medium hard. Now, he glanced at the stove, straightening his back and peering over the rim of the pan of gently-bubbling water, at his three eggs. Another couple of minutes and they'd be ready. He returned his eyes to the newspaper.

What Old Crikey didn't know, though – and didn't so much as suspect – was that those eggs were *stone* eggs, the kind which chicken farmers shove beneath hens, to keep them broody. Earlier on, Vindscreen had gone to the canteen fridge – where he knew that Old Crikey always placed his eggs, before taking parade – and had made the swap.

When Old Crikey's wristwatch alarm began bleeping, he pressed a button to cut the alarm, stood, removed the pan from the gas-ring, turned off the flame, and ran the eggs under the sink's cold tap. As he was doing this, he turned aside and shouted in the direction of the service counter, 'Three toast, please, Hilda . . . well done.'

Old Crikey was now back at his table, placing the eggs in little white cups that had blue circles around them – personal stock; the canteen didn't seem to *have* any egg-cups of its own.

'There we are, sir,' said Hilda, bringing over Old Crikey's plate of toast, and placing it on the table. 'Settle-up later.'

'Thanks, Hilda,' Old Crikey said, picking up a tea-spoon; then, one eye on the paper, he began tapping at the top of the first egg . . . very gently; after all, they were only *medium* hard; or so he believed. But now he was tapping furiously at the egg, frowning, grating his back teeth . . . *belting* the top of the egg, muttering, '*What the* . . . ?' . . . taking the egg out of the cup, and hitting it down onto the top of the table. 'Oh, *crikey*!' he seethed. 'What's the *matter* with it . . .?'

Meanwhile, at the other side of the room, Vindscreen and the others were having muted fits as they covertly observed Old Crikey.

Discarding the first egg, Old Crikey went through the same process with the other two, but couldn't even produce so much as a hairline *crack* in either of their shells. Finally, overcome with rage, he jumped to his feet and smashed an egg down onto the floor, chasing after it as it bounced and rolled across the room, and settled under a table.

Old Crikey, on his hands and knees, his expansive arse jutting out from beneath the table, just couldn't *understand* it: the egg *still* wasn't broken. Then, something went *click!* inside his head, and his eyes panned slowly left, upward, settling on Vindscreen, whose pursed lips and bulging cheeks were trembling with contained laughter. 'Vipas!' he shouted. 'Have you been tampering with my eggs?'

Vindscreen affected his totally-plausible look: mouth

open, eyes dilated, a trace of offence on his face. '*Me-ee*, guv? 'Course not . . . Where'd ya get em from, anyway?'

'A farm-shop, last week-end, when I was out in the country with the missus . . . Where d'you *think* I got them from?' And as he went to climb to his feet, his head clumped the edge of the table-top. A huge rush of air then funnelled in through his pouted lips, and his face screwed-up into folds and creases of loose skin, as he bent over, clamped both hands on his nut, and moaned, 'Ooh, *crikey*!'

How much *more* stick could that head of his take?

At that moment, Barker entered the canteen, carrying this evening's newspaper and holding a brown-paper bag containing sandwiches. It *was* one of *those* days. But . . . this . . . *this* took the fuckin biscuit, *this* did: here was Old Crikey, bent-over double under a table, hands on his nut, whining and muttering. The world *was* getting crazier by the hour.

'Ah, to *hell* with it!' Barker muttered, and he went back out, to eat his sandwiches in the Skippers' office, where things were marginally more normal.

Before the tour was ended, though, things would get crazier still, in Barker's crazy world.

Half an hour later, MacHale walked into the canteen, made his way down to the counter, and gave Hilda the prisoners' meal-tickets. Then he ordered a Pepsi, to drink while he waited for the meals to be prepared. Seeing Pat Coles, and the emotional state she was in, he went to her table, pulled out a chair and sat opposite her.

'What's the matter with you?' he asked, concerned. She looked as if she'd been crying.

She pushed away her untouched salad. 'Oh, I don't know. The Job's getting me down, I think.'

'Why? Why today, in particular?'

'Well, that kiddy porn, really, John. They . . .' She turned aside her head and glanced at the five PCs who were playing cards. '*They made* me look at it, in the charge-room . . . while you were putting away the charge-sheet relating to my drunk.' She made a face. 'It was absolutely awful.'

'Yeah,' MacHale agreed. 'It was.' He shrugged. 'Still . . .' And placed his right hand on her left forearm, squeezing gently . . . producing a ripple within himself, which ascended from the pit of his stomach to his throat – totally unexpected. He swallowed a mouthful of his Pepsi, and removed his hand from her arm. 'Don't feel bitter about what happened with them,' he told her. 'Just . . . just try and focus on good things . . . in yourself and in others . . .'

She smiled, patted his forearm, and said, 'You know, John, you're too nice to be a cop, really. And if you stay, it'll destroy you.' She shot a quick glance at the members of the card school, opposite, giving instance to what she'd said.

Don't *say* that, he thought. Don't *say* it. I'm gonna be a big butch macho cop, with hair on my balls . . . Like . . . Oh, Christ, like *Tasty Tom,* or . . .? No, *not* like Tasty Tom; not like *any* of the others, over there. Just a cop that doesn't get himself jived around by street-shit . . . who can hold up his own end, yet stay human, sane. 'What about *you*, though, Pat?' he asked. 'What if *you* stay?' He finished his Pepsi and put aside the glass. 'What'll it do to *you*?'

She twitched her narrow shoulders, and her breasts moved forward beneath her white shirt, pushing open her unbuttoned tunic. She *was* losing weight . . . her figure was beginning to take on a much sharper definition. 'I've never intended staying,' she said. 'I'm not a career woman.' She spread her hands, palms upward. 'Marriage? . . . Children? One day.' She lowered her eyes and looked wistfully at the top of the table . . . then aside, at the floor.

MacHale studied her profile; that smooth, pale skin; the . . . no, not retroussé, but gently-sloping nose; no make-up, either – he liked that. He didn't much care for her hairstyle, though – auburn, pulled tightly back from her forehead and formed into a bun at the nape of her neck, wisps of fine hair, astray at her temples; unattractive, but practical: no stroppy prisoner could take a handful of it and attempt to yank her head off her shoulders. Off-duty, though, she probably let it hang loose, and that, MacHale envisaged, he would like. 'Tell you what,' he said, none too confidently. 'Why don't we go for a drink, later on, after we've finished work? Not at Mulligan's, but . . . well, wherever you fancy.' He could feel his face heating up. Supposing she declined? Said she was going out with a boyfriend?

She didn't, though. She turned to face him, smiling, her eyes big and alive. 'Yes, I'd love to, John.'

A tenseness which he hadn't realized was there, oozed from his bones, and he beamed. 'Great. Ten-thirty, then.'

'Prisoners' meals!' shouted Hilda, stacking the one-trip plates, one on top of the other, on metal rims – usual stuff, for prisoners: deep orange, stewed baked-beans, mashed spuds, and lunchtime's mince, swimming in fat, together with soggy apple-pie and anaemic custard.

MacHale stood. So did Pat Coles, buttoning her tunic. 'I'll give you a hand, John,' she offered.

'Yeah, thanks, Pat.' Roll on half-past ten, he thought.

As MacHale unbolted and unlocked Roland Squires' cell door, he wondered if they'd believe him . . . the CIB, that was. They'd just have to, he decided, and accidentally-on-purpose tripped, sending the paper plates of dinner and dessert, sliding off the tray, on to the top of Squires' head, as Squires, unsuspecting, just sat there by the door, on the end of the wall-mounted bench-bed, hands outstretched to receive his grub.

Have that with me, thought MacHale . . . and with the baby girl . . . *and* with Pat. You filthy bastard! This was . . . just a *small* compromise; permissible, MacHale had impetuously decided, in a case such as this; *especially* in a case such as this.

MacHale was surprised, however, by Squires' acquiescence. The pervert merely sat where he was, impassive, flicking and clawing, from his head, shoulders and face, the messy concoction of dinner and sweet. Then, unemotionally, he said, 'I'd like a wash, please.'

'Fine,' MacHale told him, and nodded towards the far end of the small cell, to where the lavatory-pan stood in one corner. 'There's plenty of water, down there.' Then he about-turned, walked out into the cell passage, and slammed shut the door.

Now, all of his bitter feelings towards Squires had been extirpated. Well, almost all. And off he went to the next cell, humming a tune. Where did Squires get that fat lip from, though? he wondered. He twitched his mouth and eyebrows; Squires, too, must've tripped in the cell . . . or something.

At the next cell along, MacHale hesitated in opening the door; there was one *hell* of a racket going on, in there; instead, he slid open the wicket gate, and peered in . . . Two DCs were trying to stuff a prisoner's head down the lavatory-pan; the body, a skinny little, half-drowned, bald-headed man, was gasping and spluttering every time they allowed up his drenched head, and was shouting, 'No! No! . . . I'm *not* havin it! . . . I'm *not – Arrgh!*' Then, back down the bog went his head, while one of the DCs pulled the chain.

'Here,' MacHale said to the DCs. 'What about his dinner, then?'

'He ain't hungry,' MacHale was flatly told.

The last MacHale heard of it, as he moved on, was a DC, shouting, 'Either you plead, or you'll find yourself shootin head-first out a shit-'n'-slime-covered sewer pipe, on the Thames Embankment!'

And the body, spluttering, 'I can't swim . . . I can't *swim*!'

What would the guv'nor make of it? MacHale wondered – the PAS-Book and the OB, showing that the body who'd been banged-up in number-three trap, had gone on the trot – having escaped down the *toilet pan* . . .

Suddenly, there was a shrill scream, spiralling through the cell passage, from the direction of the end cell, where Pat Coles was delivering a meal to one of the drunks. MacHale nearly dropped the stack of dinners he was holding, but managed to put them safely on the floor, before running to see what had happened.

He almost collided with Pat Coles' body, as she came rushing from the end cell, her hands covering her face.

'What's up? What's happened?' he urgently said, placing his hands on her shoulders, steadying her.

Pat's hands slid away from her face. 'In there,' she whispered, shocked. 'That drunk I arrested, four or five hours ago. He's *dead*!'

He was, too.

MacHale knew it, even before he'd got to the vagrant's side and had knelt down to feel for the man's non-existent pulse. The eyes were half-closed and utterly devoid of life, while his body was cold and rigid; his mouth, gaping, was filled with vomit, so that MacHale didn't even contemplate administering the kiss of life; besides, the vagie smelled putrid, probably having excreted in his trousers as the life drained out of him. He was totally beyond recovery.

MacHale returned to Pat Coles. Her expression delegated the task of formulating their next move. MacHale glanced back over his shoulder, into the cell. The vagie was lying supine on the floor; he'd maybe had a heart attack and fallen off the bench-bed, vomiting.

'What're we going to *do*, John?' Pat wanted to know.

Her anxiety somehow endowed him with an efficient calmness. 'There's nothing to worry about, Pat,' he assured her. 'After all, no one's *murdered* him, have they? Let's face it, most of these vagies're *half* dead, anyway. It's only our nicking them, and then feeding them, that keeps them alive for so *long*. And, if they're gonna die anywhere, it's as likely to be here, in the cells, as out on the street.'

'Yes, you're right, I suppose, John,' she said. 'It's just that I got such a terrible shock. I wasn't expecting it . . . I thought he was asleep.'

'Yeah,' MacHale said. 'You weren't expecting it, and neither will Old Crikey be expecting it.'

'Sir?' MacHale cautiously ventured, having knocked at Old Crikey's office door, before entering.

'Don't *tell* me, MacHale!' Old Crikey shouted, jumping to his feet. 'Don't tell me *anything*!' And he chopped the inside edge of his right hand against his wrinkled forehead. 'I've had it up to *here*, today! Up to *here*!' And with that, he snatched up his PR, put on his cap, and stormed out, bumping aside MacHale's body as he turned left out of his office door and made for the rear exit to the yard.

We *ought* to call him *Blacksmith*, MacHale thought, not Old Crikey. Because every time something contentious happens, he makes a bolt for the bloody door . . . And howcome he's now got *two* plasters stuck on top of his head . . .?

MacHale shrugged. It was back to Barker.

'This is *your* fault, MacHale,' Barker shouted. '*You* know you're s'posed to visit prisoners in their cells, and check on them; every *half-hour*, in the case of drunks.'

'But, *Sarge*,' MacHale protested. '*I've* been – '

'Don't *argue*!' snapped Barker, and he began agitatedly pacing the front office.

What MacHale had been trying to point out was how he'd had to deal with callers at the counter, entries in official registers, CRO checks and Bailenqs on prisoners, and a score of other odd-jobs that Barker had shoved on to him. Anyway, while *all* Station Officers delegated the duty of visiting and checking prisoners in cells, the responsibility was, nevertheless, firmly *theirs*. So if anyone were going to be stuck on the dab, it would be Barker. Old Crikey, too, maybe – *if* they could *find* him, after today.

'Sarge?' Pat Coles exploratively said.

'*What?*' Barker spat. 'What *d'you* want?'

'Well, why don't we just call the District Surgeon to certify that the man's dead, then report it as per GO? The hierarchy'll understand that we were busy, and didn't, therefore, make all the visits we ought to have.' She looked hopefully at Barker, waiting for his face to be lit by her inspiration.

But it was lit by ire, if anything. 'Fuckin *brilliant*, Miss Coles,' Barker mocked, pausing before her. 'We didn't make *any* of the visits we ought to have made.' He shot MacHale a meaningful glance. 'The geezer's *stone fuckin cold!* Stiff as a *board*! . . . As dead, in fact, as *you're* fuckin *head* appears to be from the neck upwards, Miss Coles!'

Pat Coles reddened, and shuffled her feet, and stared at the floor.

'*I* know, Sarge,' offered MacHale, brightening. '*Why* don't we just drape the vagie's body over a radiator, and warm him up? Then, the doctor'll think he's only been dead for . . . What? An hour, maybe?' He found himself grinning . . . at Barker . . . at Pat Coles . . . again at Barker. This was a *world-class* idea.

'Yeah,' said Barker, nodding his head. 'Yeah . . . Oh

yeah!' But he was sardonically giggling as he paced back and forth. Then he turned on MacHale, seething. 'I can just *see* it. The doctor, havin finished his examination, pointin first to the front of the vagie's body – which is red *hot* – then to the back – which is stone fuckin *cold* – an sayin, "Well, Sergeant, this bit's been dead for five minutes, but *this* bit appears to have been dead for best part of the *day*!" You docile-lookin . . . *prick*, MacHale!'

'Well how about, then, if we – ?'

'No!' roared Barker, having divined MacHale's mind. 'It's impossible to bend *anyone* backwards over a radiator! . . . Dead *or* alive!'

'Oh,' MacHale feebly mumbled. And he, too, reddened, and shuffled his feet, and stared at the floor.

This thing was, if this *were* to be done in accordance with GO – type a lengthy and detailed report, call the doctor, attend an official inquest, conducted by the Coroner, not to mention an *unofficial* inquest, conducted by the Chief Superintendent – that would mean a hell of a lot of sweat, worry and work, all three of which Barker was averse to.

However, cops being as proficient at square-ups as they were at making cock-ups, the solution quickly came to Barker.

He stopped pacing the office, drew MacHale and Pat Coles close to him, and, in the *strictest* of confidence, related the denouement.

First of all, the vagie's property was placed back in his pockets. Then, Barker forged the vagie's signature on the receipt section of the charge-sheet, and on the section which set out details of bail, which now showed that the vagie had been released to appear at court, a week today. Finally, the van driver – Hercules was posted to this duty, today – would be ordered to load-up the vagie, drive him over to Southwell Common, on an adjoining Division's manor, and dump him on a bench.

Tomorrow, in daylight, someone would stumble across the vagie, dead, and call the police. The reporting PC would find the Form Fifty-Nine in the vagie's pocket, see that he'd been nicked for drunkenness, then bailed, and would contact the court, before the date of hearing. The post mortem would undoubtedly show that death was due to natural causes, so there'd be *no* inquests, official or otherwise. Everyone would be satisfied that the vagie, having been released from custody, had made his way over to the Common, to sleep for the night, and had popped-off on a bench.

Now *that* was what could be called a world-class idea.

No friends or relatives to allege that the police had maltreated the prisoner while he was banged-up in the cells, no Chief Superintendent to uncover lapses in procedure, and then apportion blame and consequences for those lapses, and none of those shit-stirring left-wing civil-libertarians from agitprop, alleging that the police had *murdered* the vagie.

Brilliant!

Double brilliant, in fact.

Except . . .

Hercules didn't properly engage the catch on the van's rear door, when he closed it.

While he was speeding up a gradient in a dark, deserted side-street, almost on the adjoining Division's manor, he was forced to brake hard to avoid a dog that had strayed into the road. Then, as he smacked the pedal to the metal, and accelerated away again – the violent, stop-start momentum having opened the van's rear doors – the vagie slid feet-first across the metal floor, and out into the roadway, where, a couple of minutes later, he was wiped up by a passing car.

Meanwhile, there was Hercules, in the middle of the pitch black Common, scratching his head and his arse, while staring into the back of an empty van.

On the face of it, then – a dead vagie, lying in the middle of the road, car-tyre marks all over his pulped head – there was now a FATACC to be dealt with. And GO dictated that *all* FATACCS were the responsibility of the Duty Officer.

Poor Old Crikey.

No one was about to tell him that it *wasn't* a FATACC, that the vagie was en route to Southwell Common, *already* dead, to be dumped, and had fallen out the back of the police van. Old Crikey just had to assume that the vagie, having been bailed from the nick, had got himself wiped out again on Strongbow, and had collapsed in the road, to be run over.

At first, Barker was livid, and he called Hercules every kind of skinny rat-faced poufdah that he could think of. But then, slowly, he grew to like it. It was what was known as natural justice, he believed: Old Crikey, ducking, weaving and whining his way out of having to square-up a death in the cells, only to be inescapably lumbered with it, an hour later, in an apparent FATACC. Whichever angle Barker studied it from, he saw himself still in the clear. Now, he was actually *glad* that the vagie had popped-off in the cells.

It was still one of *those* days, but maybe things weren't *quite* so crazy, after all.

By ten-fifteen, MacHale had had just about a gutful of it. There was so much *pressure*, in that front office. *Always,* there was someone, either at the counter or on the phone: reporting a suspicion, a crime, an accident . . .; something lost, missing or found.

And then there were the bodies. That charge-room was like a factory conveyor-belt; questionings for a confession; the documentation, including the written statements to be obtained; fingerprinting and photographing;

brief facts for the court; charge-sheets prepared; crime-book entries . . . and more.

At the end of a late shift, in particular, then, the Relief would sigh, thank Christ the day was over, wish good luck to the night Relief, and begin craving as much alcohol as it took to calm down.

Tonight, MacHale thought, it would take a lot to lay *him* back. As he and Pat left the rear entrance of the nick, they were each, mentally, blowing hot air and chopping the inside edges of their hands against their foreheads. *What* a day it had been.

'Well?' asked MacHale. 'Where to?'

'Anywhere,' said Pat. '*Anywhere* . . . so long as it's as far as possible away from *this* madhouse.'

11

To begin with, they went to the *Bacchs Wine-Bar*, in Virginia Street – Pat's idea; she'd been there before, after late turn.

The clientele, one or two of whom she knew in passing, were a somewhat refined crowd of business and professional people; Hooray Henries and Henriettas, were what MacHale considered them to be: fey men, and gesticulative, sonorous women, with supercilious eyes.

The candle-lit bar, with white walls, displaying very old, enamel-advertisement signs and hand-painted mirrors, was packed solid, hazy with cigar and cigarette smoke, droning with the noise of babbling voices; initially, MacHale was oppressed by these surroundings, which in turn made him feel aggressive. Eventually, though, without having pushed or shoved anyone he succeeded in making his way to the bar and ordered a bottle of the House White, having been advised by Pat that this was a safe bet for someone who was a total stranger to the delights of wine.

When they'd made their way to the quieter, back end of the bar, with their bottle and two glasses, they were fortunate enough to find a table which had just been vacated, and there they settled, facing each other, elbows on the table-top, heads close together, sipping at their wine as they chatted above the hubbub which encased them.

'You sure that's all right for you, Pat?' MacHale asked, nodding at her glass, after he'd tentatively sampled the content of his own. 'I find it rather impudent . . . with a tantalizing bouquet, and . . . yes, overall, a teasing little wine, I think.' He smiled mischievously as he affected the cultured accent and good-naturedly mocked.

She, too, smiled, but raised her eyebrows as she looked askance at him. 'Now, then, John,' she chided. 'I'm attempting to improve the quality of your social life.' She tilted her glass and peered into the top of it, sniffing the wine's aroma. 'This is nice, actually: chilled, medium dry, and with a belated warmth.'

'Hmm, yes,' MacHale agreed, thinking that he didn't actually care too much what its attributes were, so long as it was capable of putting him under the table with a gormless grin on his face. He took another sip from his own glass. 'I like it, yes. But I *don't* like the snobbery that's attached to it – wine-drinking, that is.'

'Well . . .' She grimaced. 'There is a certain amount of snobbery, I suppose. Some of these people . . .' She tilted aside her head. 'Some of them become rapt when talking of the merits or demerits of this or that wine. But me, if I find that I like a particular brand I simply enjoy it, and that means quietly *drinking* it, not looking at it and sniffing it and swilling it around the bowl of the glass, while engaging in hyperbole.'

'And what *about* these people, here?' MacHale said, turning to pan his eyes over the crowd that filled the room. 'Look at *him*, for instance.' He was nodding covertly at a George Melly clone – mid-fifties, portly, effeminate mannerisms, wearing a charcoal-grey suit with bold, orange overcheck, and a white-felt fedora – who was chatting animatedly to a svelt young thing in a mink wrap and turquoise evening-dress. 'If Tasty Tom saw *him* trolling along the street, he'd swift him in for OPD – outraging public decency.'

'Oooh, him,' Pat Coles intoned, looking at the man. 'He's the theatre critic for the *Universal Comment*. If you ever come across a copy, turn to page eleven and you'll see his photo at the head of his column. He's a very nice man, too. He's often spoken to me in here . . . fancies me, I think.' She hunched her shoulders and giggled.

MacHale almost shouted with indignation. 'You must be *joking*. By the looks of him, he doesn't know if he's Arthur or Martha.'

'Now, now. You're becoming as cynical and bitter as the others at the nick,' Pat cautioned. 'Don't categorize, or stereotype people. Give them a chance. Otherwise you'll miss out on meeting a lot of very nice, decent people.'

'Ah, maybe you're right,' he conceded, refilling their glasses; the drink was beginning to wind him down a little, blunting his sharp edges. 'But . . .' He shrugged. 'I dunno. I s'pose it's the police training – makes you wary of people. And then . . . well, you know as well as I do, if you're a cop, you can't *help* stereotyping people. How else d'you decide whether or not to stop someone in the street? Past experience tells you what characteristics the deviant groups have in common.'

'Yes,' she said. 'But don't be ignorant of the dangers. Sure, a lot of hopeless junkies have long hair, are unwashed, emaciated and ghostly pale. But not *all*. One of these, apparently wealthy, healthy characters in here, for instance, is quite likely to have a gramme of coke in his pocket. Stick to your stereotypes and you'll miss out on arresting a lot of criminals who defy classification.'

She's right, MacHale thought, surprised by her perception. He topped up their glasses, and looked at Pat's face. Her eyes were large and shimmering, and her face looked so tranquil.

MacHale, too, was now almost fully relaxed. He felt an inner warmth and security. 'You're right about it being unwise to classify people,' he told her. 'Although, having said that, if you *didn't* do it you'd find it more difficult to operate the stop-search power, wouldn't you?'

'No, not at all,' she confidently said. 'People get

stopped and searched, merely because they fit a cop's stereotype index, and about ninety per cent of them have to be allowed to go on their way, because they're found *not* to have committed any offence. Now, if the stop-search power were to be *lawfully* operated, only those people who afforded a cop *reasonable suspicion* would be stopped and searched. And that would also ensure that *all* types of people – *real* suspects – were affected by the power, not just those whom it was decided could be categorized.'

MacHale's brain was stumbling along in the slipstream of hers. Jesus, she was sharp and fast . . . had an answer for everything, but not in any way that seemed immodest. She could probably teach him more about proper, effective, professional policework, than any of the others back at the nick. Yet . . .

He put it to her: 'Pat. You seem to know The Job, inside out. You could plan strategies, *think* your way along a street. But you don't seem to get a lot of results, do you?'

She thought about it, pouting her lips and stroking the stem of her glass. 'Yes, that's probably true. But, you see, I don't believe that The Job's exclusively about enforcement. We've got *two* roles, don't forget.'

'That's right,' MacHale said. 'They told us that at TS. There's an enforcement role and a social role.'

She nodded. 'Which means that, apart from arresting and reporting offenders, we should also be assisting people who *haven't* done anything wrong.'

'Like, by dealing with civil disputes, and with lost and found property, or by seeing kids and old ladies across roads? That sort of stuff?'

'Yes. Or by socializing with people on your beat. Chatting to them, listening to them, reassuring them, showing them that we're not *aliens*, just because we wear a funny uniform and capture certain types of citizens.'

'And you'd rather do that, than nick people?'

'Frankly, yes,' she said. 'It's far more satisfying. Arresting people is destructive work . . . *depressing* work. Do too much of it, and you forget your social role, so that everyone's a suspect and you deal with them accordingly.'

'Suck back!' MacHale said. 'Can you imagine what someone like Tasty, or Punchy, would say to that? They'd say you were *anti*-police . . . a social-worker, or something.'

'I *am* a social-worker,' she returned. 'As you've mentioned Punchy Paterson and Tasty Tom, though . . . Well, they serve ideally to give life to what I've said. They're bigoted, cynical, misanthropic racists. Most experienced cops are, in my judgement.'

Strong stuff, MacHale thought. But he couldn't disagree. Although he would have if he'd believed it were necessary to keep her talking; he just loved listening to her, watching her, studying her mannerisms . . . she was captivating, the whole of her.

'You don't have to be any of those things, though,' she went on, 'in order to be a success.'

'No,' MacHalc agreed. 'But how can you thrive on your social role, when the supervisors and your colleagues scarcely acknowledge its existence, or do so grudgingly? I'm a prob', don't forget. And Old Crikey and Barker are only interested in how I perform as an enforcer. *No* one gets himself commended for promoting police-public relations.'

'Yes,' she sighed. 'That wearies me, too. *I've* been through that stage, as well, don't forget, John. And I don't see things changing, unfortunately. The poor quality of the guv'nors has a lot to do with it.'

'How d'you mean, Pat?'

'Well, at the top, they're only really interested in figures. You know: how many arrests are made, how many stops are done, how many traffic offenders are reported. So, if the top men are chasing the middle-ranking men for results, this ensures that the PCs are chased for results.'

'Yes. And while the top and middle men are always calling for results, they *never* take you out and show you either what *they* want or how *you* should obtain it.'

'That's always been the case,' she assured him. 'The supervisors and the lack of supervision are appalling. That's why there's so much bad practice. Look at today's events at the nick, for example.'

MacHale reflected, and winced, as he shook his head slowly from side-to-side; and hadn't he himself succumbed to bad practice, by unloading a tray of dinner onto the head of Roland Squires? He took a big swallow of his wine, and wondered if he should ask *her* the question which had nagged at him since the Schofield job.

She was taking a delicate mouthful of her own wine, savouring its taste, while her eyes roved over his dark features. She put down her glass, frowned, and said, 'What's the matter?'

Yes, ask her, he decided. And he shifted his weight on his seat, turning sideways-on to her – an unconscious manifestation of his unease. 'You agree you've been through the stage I'm now going through,' he said. 'So tell me all about verballing, about fit-ups. How you encountered and dealt with them.' There, it was out.

Her eyes grew larger, and her head and torso rose slightly. 'My God, *that* was abrupt,' she said. 'What made you ask?'

'Schofield,' he told her. 'You remember that villain I was involved with, on nights? The one with the Jag which turned out to be a ringer.'

'Yes.' She was frowning more deeply.

'Well, when I got to the nick, with Schofield, I was left in no doubt, by Tubby Tompkins and Snatch, that I'd be expected to verbal him. Say I was positive he'd been driving the Jag, when, in reality, I just didn't *know* who'd been driving it. When I refused to do it, they got annoyed and left me to it. And, at the end of the day, Schofield was kicked out.'

For a moment, she was silent, and looked aside and down as she soaked up what he'd said and formulated her response. 'Well,' she began, looking up. 'The truth of it is that verballing is probably the most prevalent form of corruption within the police. It's institutionalized, in fact. I discovered that, very early on in my service.'

'*Institutionalized*?' he said, incredulous, and turned fully to face her once more. 'You mean, *everywhere*? . . . As bad as *that*?'

She nodded. 'I'm afraid so, John.'

'But *why*? . . . *How*? Doesn't anyone want to put a stop to it? Deter it?'

She emitted a hollow laugh. 'You're kidding. Officially, it does *not* exist. And no one in authority is going to attempt to rectify or eradicate a problem which isn't, in his eyes, *there*, is he?'

'But . . . Is *everyone* at it, then?'

'*We're* not,' she said. 'Although, I must admit, we're rare birds, indeed. Let's just say that nearly all of the practical street-cops have got verballing down to a very fine art. After a while, they do it naturally, instinctively, and none sees it as criminal.'

'But *why*?' he reiterated. '*Why* do they do it?'

She shrugged. 'It's not difficult to see why, really. No one, a cop or anyone else, likes to stand idly by while another, an adversary, scores points off him. So, if a cop catches someone *almost* bang to rights, he'll – what shall we say? He'll fortify the available evidence, so as to try and create an unassailable case. No experienced cop would've let Schofield off the hook, as you did.'

'You're not suggesting I *should've* verballed Schofield, are you?'

'Oh, no,' she said, reaching across the table to pat his forearm. 'My God, no. I would've done exactly as you did.'

'How about fit-ups, though? How prevalent are they? As opposed to *part* fit-ups, which is what verballing amounts to.'

'I don't really know. I don't suppose anybody does. But *pure* fit-ups are more the CID's style. The crime-squads, you see, where every detective gets his grounding as a plainclothes PC, demand results of their members, too. A PC who wants to be a *D*C must, therefore, show that he's capable of nicking villains, for crime.'

'And?'

'Well, they work in pairs, generally, and they'll go out on the streets, find themselves a likely-looking body, say a near-vagrant type, and give him three car-door handles. Say they saw him pulling at car doors, which infers he was going to steal from inside the car, or cars.'

'You mean they just – ?'

'Yes,' she said. 'And, most times, their victims are men of bad character, anyway; people with long criminal-records. When they get to court, they stand no chance. It's their words against the words of police-officers who have, on paper, *impeccable* records.'

MacHale was astounded.

'Let me tell you, John,' she earnestly said. 'When you've been in The Job as long as I have, you'll look at a CID officer, and ask yourself if he's *straight,* not if he might be bent.'

'That bad, eh?'

'That bad.'

'But why should *we* have to put up with it?' MacHale said. 'Couldn't we do something about it?'

Pat shook her head. 'No way. We totally honest cops, are in a tiny minority. And, as I've told you, these sorts of thing – verballing, fit-ups – just *don't* occur, officially.

You might be able to act, in an individual case, where you had incontrovertible evidence, but you'd *never* change the *system*. You'd only succeed in making your own life unbearable, thereafter. The others, in one way or another, would crucify you.'

'You believe that?'

'I *know* it.'

'Why? . . . What would they do?'

She twitched her shoulders. 'One day, maybe you'd arrive back at the section-house, and find the CID waiting to turn-over your room. They'd maybe come up with a bit of cannabis you'd never seen before. And how would you wriggle out of that?'

'I don't s'pose I would, would I?'

'No, you wouldn't.'

For a while, MacHale was silent, digesting what she'd said. Then he sighed, and gazed into her eyes. 'I feel like getting drunk. I mean, legless, roaring, shouting, *violently* drunk.'

'I've got a better idea,' she said, smiling. 'Something which won't give you a world-class hangover, and which'll be far more therapeutic.'

'*Oh?*' he said, smiling and fluttering his eyebrows. 'What?'

'A walk . . . down by the river.'

'Oh,' he repeated, but flatly, this time. Then he smiled again. She'd blushed. 'Why not?' he said. There was no more drink to be had, here, anyway: the bell for last orders had just sounded, and the bar staff were beginning to clean the tables.

They drained their glasses and left the bar, cutting through a series of quiet, residential side-streets to reach the embankment, half a mile away. The night was still, with a refreshing bite to the air, and a full moon shining from the clear skies; anything seemed possible.

'D'you think it really does bring them out of the woodwork?' MacHale said, looking upward.

'Who? What?' she asked, following his gaze.

'The full moon. They say it draws out all those who're mentally unhinged, don't they?' He came to a halt, still looking up at the sky, and she paused at his side, hooking her left arm through his right arm. Their upturned faces were awash with a translucent silver glow.

'Well,' she said. 'They are called *luna*-tics, aren't they?'

'Hmm,' he murmured, and they strolled on, now approaching the brightly-lit bridge, at the end of the road, which gently arced over the Thames, to the south bank. 'They *are* out tonight.' He turned his head and cocked an ear to the night. 'Listen . . .' In the distance behind them were the howls of emergency services' sirens and whip-tones . . . police, fire, ambulance, each of the three services' vehicles emitting a slightly different noise – only an experienced ear could immediately tell which was which. He felt glad that, for this night, at least, he wasn't a part of it.

They walked away from the madness that was behind them, and crossed the road in front of the bridge; then they carried on, turning right, and strolled slowly, silently along the embankment, their arms linked, their thoughts savouring each other's company.

'Beautiful, isn't it?' he softly said, looking to the river. Gently-undulating sheets of moonlight were glancing off peaks, falling into troughs, all over the broad expanse of jet-black waters, from bank-to-bank.

'It's got a magnetic quality,' MacHale continued, looking down over the top of the embankment wall. 'You look at the black, twinkling water, and it sort of pulls you inexorably towards itself.'

'It does seem to, I must agree,' Pat said. 'You can imagine yourself jumping . . . falling through it, and entering another world.'

'As so many do, every year.'

'Mind you,' Pat went on, shivering. 'If you see one come out, after its been down there for a week, your imagination takes an entirely different turn . . . along with your stomach.'

'Yeah,' MacHale said. 'I've *had* one: it was an old boy, and he just popped up to the surface, one Sunday afternoon, all black and bloated and – '

'Ugh! Stoppit!' she said, pulling a face.

But MacHale was wallowing in it. '. . . and his fingers were hanging off his hands, all yellow, and that, joined only by little strips of flesh to his knuckles . . . those the fish hadn't gobbled up, that is.'

Now, she had her hands clamped over her ears, and was walking away.

He went after her, laughing, pulling her to him as he placed his right hand around her waist and apologetically squeezed her. 'Sorry,' he said.

'Why is it, when cops get together, off-duty, they always end up talking shop?' she wanted to know.

MacHale shrugged. 'Dunno. The Job's such a big part of our lives, I s'pose.'

'It's too much, you know,' Pat told him. 'I don't think *I'll* be able to take a lot more of it.'

'Why did you join, then?'

She arched her eyebrows and mouth, and tapped her head, sideways, down onto his shoulder. 'Well, excitement was a factor, I think. And variation, too . . . never knowing what you'd be called upon to do, from one day to the next. Much better than a nine-to-five routine. Money, as well. The money *is* good, for a woman.'

'And these factors are now outweighed by the disadvantages?'

'I think so, yes. Shiftwork, for instance. It's debilitating. And the relentless pressure. It's a *young* person's job, John; and the older you get, the more afraid of it you

become, not knowing what's around the corner – but always apprehending the *worst* – and acutely aware that there're people out here who'd be quite prepared to kill you if you threatened their liberty.'

'One man's excitement is another man's fear,' MacHale said, rehashing an aphorism and creating a new one. 'That's it, isn't it? Take Mathieson. *He's* afraid of police-work, now. *All* of it.'

'That's my point,' she said. 'Mathieson's *only* twenty-*eight*. Each one of us is in real danger of becoming just *like* him, too.'

MacHale wasn't sure. In Mathieson's case, there was a little something more. There had to be. His private life, maybe, which, by all accounts, was a total write-off. It was true, though, that nearly all of the older cops had prematurely retired – Snatch *was* an exceptional man, because most of the PCs he'd joined with, at TS, were now in non-operational, nine-to-five sinecures, which demanded not a shred of police training or expertise for their accomplishment; they were paper-sifters and distributors, with no pride in themselves as cops.

'You're probably right, Pat,' he said. 'Streetwork certainly *appears* to be a young person's job. But there's promotion for older officers who're industrious, and that legitimately affords less involvement in practical duty, where the stress is. Make Inspector, and you can relax . . . well, a bit.'

'You can't be serious,' she laughed. 'Look at Old Crikey. If *that's* what promotion does to you, *no* thanks. Anyway, it's a *man's* job. Women just aren't accepted. None of the other PCs want to work with me, because they think my physical limitations are an impediment to me and to them.'

'I don't agree,' MacHale said. 'What a man can achieve with brute force, a woman can achieve with tact and diplomacy.'

'Not often,' she said. 'No, they're right, really. I *am* useless in a no-holds-barred punch-up. Gone are the days when men respected women officers. I'm just as likely to be assaulted by a villain as you are. What I object to, though, is not being given the opportunity to prove myself. The Commander, for instance, had a directive put out, which established that no WPCs will be employed at football matches or on demos which are likely to become violent. That's cosseting. And no woman wants that.'

'But what if you go? I mean, leave. What'll you do, then?'

'I'm not sure,' she said. 'You see, I'm a country girl, from a tiny village near Henley-on-Thames, in south-east Oxfordshire. A lot of well-off people have big, riverside houses down there, too . . . pop and show-business personalities.'

'Yes, I know the place,' he told her. 'I've never been there, but I've heard of it. They have that yearly regatta on the Thames at Henley, don't they?'

'Yes, that's it. But the village where I'm from is about five miles north of there. Broad Cross, it's called. A very small place, with a lovely, olde worlde, main street, which has a pub – naturally – antique shops, and other little businesses. There's a church, too, of course.'

'Sounds okay,' he said, imagining what the village must be like.

'That's what my father thinks,' she told him. 'He adores the place. They – he and my mother – own a restaurant-cum-teashop, in the main street. A marvellous, red-brick old building, with bay windows that have those opaque bulls'-eyes in some of their squares of glass; and, inside, oak-beamed ceilings, with a tall, wide, brick fireplace in the restaurant room.'

'So why didn't you work *there*?'

'Oh, I did,' she said. 'Until I joined the police. It was

the lure of the city, I suppose. Every youngster, in every country in the world, experiences it.'

'So why not return, if you're fed-up here?'

She was silent for a while, her eyes downcast as they strolled leisurely on by the river. 'Return to what?' she said, at length. 'I may *have* to return, but . . . You see, my parents are retiring, soon, and the business is mine, if I want it. It's a good business, too, with particularly busy summers and weekends, and a company of long-time, trustworthy staff, so that the proprietor's job is only supervisory, really . . .'

'So what *is* the problem?' – he'd sensed there was one.

'It's a closed community, John. What would my prospects be for . . . well, you know, marriage and things, if I were to go back? There was no one for me, before I left, and that position won't have altered.'

'Well . . .' He broke off, hunching his shoulders, not knowing what to suggest because his feelings about what she'd said, and about what she *hadn't* said, were so difficult to convert to words; come to that, he wouldn't actually *want* to say much of what he was thinking and feeling; not yet; maybe never. Maybe he wasn't *entitled* to think that it would be so awful not to see her again, if she did go away?

'You must come down there with me, some time, John,' she said, breaking the silence. 'In the spring, perhaps, during a week-end leave. You'd like it.'

'Yes,' he enthusiastically said. 'I think I would.'

By now, they'd walked almost a mile, and were approaching an all-night coffee-stall which had a permanent place in a lay-by on the opposite side of the road. Here, the kerbs were lined with gleaming, powerful motor-cycles, and the stall, a white-painted box on wheels, with a brightly-lit serving hatch, was surrounded by groups of young, denim-and-leather-clad bikers, who were chatting and admiring one another's machines; one or two vagies were there, as well, shuffling up and down the pavement – on patrol, as it were – waiting their chances to pounce upon and squabble over a discarded, part cup of coffee or hamburger or hot-dog.

'Fancy a coffee, Pat?' MacHale asked.

'Please,' she said.

He left her standing by the embankment wall, while he crossed the road and bought two coffees and two hamburgers.

'Hey,' she said, on his return. 'What're you trying to do to my diet?' She was looking at the burger which he'd put on offer to her.

''S'okay,' he assured her. 'It's got salad in it.'

'Hmm . . .' She was dubious. But once her nostrils had caught the mouth-watering aroma of the meat and onions, her stomach was hooked, and she accepted the burger and ate heartily, resting her polystyrene cup of coffee atop the embankment wall.

'Lovely,' she said, in-between a couple of sips of coffee. When she'd finished, she accepted the offer of his handkerchief to wipe her lips and fingertips. 'Really nice.'

She checked her wristwatch. 'It's getting on for one o'clock. We'd better make our way back.'

They returned the way they'd come, now walking a little more quickly, their arms having found each other's waist; it was a peaceful, satisfying intimacy, with a great potential, so long overdue it seemed unnaturally natural on their first night out together.

At the bridge, MacHale stopped a black cab, and put Pat in the back seat, thanking her for her company, and then wondering if she'd think him old-fashioned for having done so. As the taxi drew away from the kerb, he stood there, waving, smiling as he saw her turn aside in the back seat and blow him a kiss from the window.

And when the cab was out of sight, he was still there,

motionless, his eyes staring, his head moving gently, almost imperceptibly, from side-to-side.

It had been a terrific evening. Nothing special, but *still* terrific – which seemed absurd, paradoxical; but that was just how he felt about it, because he'd been close to someone whom he'd discovered he liked very much.

Funny, though, he thought. Until now, he'd never really so much as suspected that he might be attracted to Pat Coles, not in this way, the way he was now experiencing it; he supposed he'd considered women as . . . well, sex objects; but while Pat Coles, physically, wasn't page three of *The Sun*, she had other qualities which, in MacHale's eyes, made her the centrefold of *Penthouse*. And with a woman like that, there could be *real* intimacy; in so many ways.

Yes, there could be. His eyes pulsated and came back into focus, as he stirred himself, crossing the road to make his way back to the section-house.

When he climbed into bed, just before one forty-five A.M., he was half smiling, and was fast asleep within ten minutes.

And for the first time in a long time, he didn't come crashing awake before dawn, his eyes rolling around in their sockets, his body dripping sweat.

12

He was still thinking about her at three o'clock the following day, as he left the nick and walked south along the High Street, making for Two Beat, accompanied by Vindscreen, who was posted to an adjoining beat.

She hadn't been on parade, though, this afternoon, because Barker had posted her to comms, as stand-in for Blinky, who'd reported himself UC-sick with a cold. MacHale had intended finding an excuse to go along to the comms room to see her, maybe again ask her out for a drink, tonight, but Old Crikey came charging into the canteen, ten minutes after parade, and ordered everyone out, on the double. So, he'd have to try and see her, later on . . . perhaps at grub-time.

'What d'you s'pose it is that brings a couple together?' he asked, as he and Vindscreen strolled slowly along, their hands clasped behind their backs, the sunlight glinting on the silver-coloured badges of their helmets.

Vindscreen glanced at him, and shrugged. 'Depends what their predominant needs are at the time *it* clicks with them, I'd say. So, *it* might be a sexual attraction, initially.'

'But what's left when that's been explored and exhausted, because no relationship can endure on sex alone?'

'Yeah, don't I know it, too,' Vindscreen ruefully said. 'My bird's terrific in bed, but that's as far as it goes. She can't cook and I can't have an intelligent conversation with her. At first, it never mattered, 'cause the attraction was purely physical, but now . . .' He affected a sour expression and slowly shook his head.

'But what if a couple *were* welded together by a mutual

admiration for each other's intellect or personality?' MacHale went on. 'They could later discover that they were far from compatible, sexually . . . Not that every relationship between two people, *demands* sex for its consummation, but if two people are really close, and very fond of each other, then the relationship might be . . . I dunno . . . *refined* by a mutual, sexual fulfilment.'

'Mmm', Vindscreen thoughtfully murmured, turning sideways-on and falling slightly behind MacHale, to allow passage in the crowded street, for a short, fat woman who was weighed down with an armful of shopping. 'Maybe a relationship shouldn't become sexual till there's a mutual love? Then, sex *would* refine it.'

'What *is* love, though?' MacHale wanted to know. 'I mean, how d'you define it? How d'you *know* if you're in love with someone?'

Now, Vindscreen looked suspiciously at MacHale . . . and smiled knowingly. 'Okay, who's the bird, then? Anyone *I* know? This *is* what it's all about, innit? You've pulled one, and she's mesmerized you.' He chuckled and jabbed his elbow at MacHale's ribs.

'No, no,' MacHale earnestly protested, and felt his face growing hot. 'It's just that . . . well, I was just wondering . . .'bout things.' He felt embarrassed, too, of course, and fearful of exposure; primarily because if the supervisors should discover that he and Pat were at the beginning of a personal relationship, they'd split them up and have one or the other transferred to a different Division, on the grounds that their commitment to each other would be likely to vitiate their commitment to The Job. So it could, too, if he and Pat were irresponsible, and neglectful of their duties. Only last week, the Duty Officer at an adjoining nick had caught a PC and WPC making love in the back seat of the RT-car, at three in the morning, in a dark and deserted side-street.

But in this case, the PC was a married man, as, indeed,

were so many PCs who fooled around with female officers while they were on duty. If MacHale and Pat started going steady, though, they could fool around all they wanted, while *off*-duty. Although, it'd be no use telling that to Old Crikey, if he should find out that they were emotionally involved with each other; he'd more than likely keep Pat – everyone knew the old fool himself fancied her – and get shot of MacHale.

So, no one must get to know of their burgeoning relationship; they'd have to be very discreet.

'Anyway,' Vindscreen said. 'If I was you, I wouldn't try to define your relationship with a bird you fancy and make some headway with. Just let it happen naturally. And if, after a few months, you're still thinkin fondly of her throughout the day, and just longin to get home to see her, to be with her – and not just so's you can climb all over her – then you'll *know* it's okay, that it's happened, that she's the one. After that, you can start analysin the relationship, workin at it to make sure it lives on . . .' He twitched his shoulders, and sniffed, adding, 'I s'pose.'

There'd been a hint of yearning, of regret, in his voice, MacHale thought. Vindscreen was right, though, he decided, about it not being a good idea to attempt to define a relationship, at its onset. There wasn't much point, and it would probably lead to unfulfilled expectations. So, he'd just allow himself and Pat to develop naturally. Besides, the feeling he'd generated within himself, yesterday, in the canteen, when he'd touched her arm, just couldn't be properly analysed and interpreted and put into words. It simply demanded that he should spend more time with her, in the privacy of the world outside The Job. For now, then, he'd simply settle for the conviction that they were quite fond of each other, and *were* going somewhere together – after all, he reassured himself, she had blown him a farewell kiss from the rear seat of the taxi last night.

That settled, his head cleared, but was immediately refilled by the rumbling thunder of traffic as it passed slowly, inexorably by, crowding all four lanes of the wide, one-way street.

He experienced an irritant buzzing in his inner ear, and could feel the flagstones vibrating beneath his feet as he and Vindscreen slowly moved, sidestepping, faltering, pausing and walking on, through the bobbing, weaving tangle of faces. One of these days, he was sure, the combined shockwaves of noise, emitted by these huge juggernauts, tall buses, squat coaches, small cars, and vans of every size and description, would succeed in shattering one of the massive plate-glass windows of the shops which lined either side of the Street.

That was why MacHale and Vindscreen were walking along by the kerb's edge: neither wanted to be vulnerably close to one of those enormous panes. Mind you, walk by the kerb, and you were then in real danger of either tripping or being jostled off it, to fall beneath the tall, fat wheels of one of those giant container-lorries.

Which reminded MacHale. 'D'you remember that woman, a couple of months ago?' he asked Vindscreen. 'The one who came running out of the greengrocer's shop, just up by the nick, at eight-thirty in the morning, clutching a pound of golden-delicious apples.'

'Do *I*?' Vindscreen said. 'How could I *forget* it?'

The woman's right, stiletto-heeled shoe had become lodged in a gap between the kerbstones as she'd run for the bus, and she'd gone sprawling sideways into the road . . . just as a French juggernaut, on its way to New Covent-Garden Market, was thundering by.

The rear, triple wheels of the juggernaut's nearside had passed over the thighs of her legs, the wheels acting as a guillotine against the edge of the granite kerb, ripping the flesh and crushing the femoral bones. The driver didn't even feel so much as a bump, though, and carried on along the road, with the woman's right, lower leg being flailed and ground between the tops of the second and third wheels and the upper ridge of the metal mud-guard; the left leg was lying by the woman's side, in the gutter.

Her screams were terrible, too, rising above even the harsh din of traffic, and when MacHale and Vindscreen arrived at the scene, having been summoned by a cata-tonic bus-driver who'd seen what happened, they found her, just sitting there, amid a scattering of pulped apples, clutching the ragged ends of her thighs, screaming, '*Where're my legs? . . . Where're my legs? . . .*' The arteries were severed, of course, and there was blood, *everywhere . . .*

The spectacle was one which drew and held a large crowd of onlookers. Fortunately for MacHale, too; because while he was diverting traffic and dispersing the ghouls, it was left to Vindscreen – ably assisted by the greengrocer, who had a first-aid kit in his shop – to administer first-aid, a task which MacHale, when it was all over, had told himself *he* just couldn't have accomplished; he'd felt so sick, so deeply shocked.

Vindscreen, then – and the greengrocer – had done a magnificent job, that day. But for a couple of days thereafter, Vindscreen was uncharacteristically reticent, and he'd sat for long periods in the canteen, just staring emptily into a full cup of tea, watching it grow stone cold; after an hour or so of this, he'd risen, sighed heavily, and walked on out to the streets.

MacHale wondered how he'd react now, if he were alone in the High Street, and a similar incident occurred. He'd just *have* to take charge and get on and deal with it, he supposed.

Maybe his worst fear, though, was that, someday within

the next twenty-nine years, he'd be walking peacefully by a house, and he'd be dragged on in to assist a woman who was in the final throes of labour. What the hell would he do about *that*? Now that really *would* be a world-class crisis, if ever there was one. He supposed, for starters, he'd order-up some hot towels and boiling water . . . oh, and a bucket, for all the blood – well, that's what they always did in the movies, wasn't it? So it must be right. Trouble was, they never actually showed you what happened *next*, did they? What were you s'posed to *do* with all those hot towels, buckets, and gallons of boiling water? That was a *complete* mystery – to MacHale, anyway.

Reaching the end of the High Street, MacHale and Vindscreen turned right and began making their way west along Martin Lane, a much narrower road, with only two lanes of traffic – one in each direction – which, in the eastbound lane, was stationary and tailed back for at least a quarter-mile.

'Hang on a minute,' MacHale said, as they turned the corner, and he walked over to the traffic-light-controlled junction, where he'd spotted an old lady, hovering at the kerb, bewildered and overwhelmed by the crush of people and the noise of traffic. She was actually trembling, clutching her handbag before herself, and no sooner had she made up her mind to cross, than she wavered and took a few faltering steps backward, biting her lower lip and looking scared half to death.

'Wanna go over, luv?' MacHale asked her, appearing at her right side, smiling winsomely and gently gripping her elbow.

'Oh, ta, dear,' she said, looking up at him, and as he led her at a snail's pace – a snail with ingrown toenails and deformed feet, that was – across the road, she began relating the story of her life . . . how she'd *lived* round here all her life, and how it never used to be like this, and how much traffic there now was – *makes yer winders rattle, dear, and makes the ornaments jump all along yer mantlepiece, as well as givin the cat diarrhoea and the budgie hypertension* – and how you don't know nobody any more, and how the Asians have taken over all the little shops, and how the blacks have multiplied and how bad the crime-rate is, and . . .

'Okay, love?' MacHale said, cutting through her monologue as he set her down on the pavement. 'I'd like to stay and talk, but I've got to get back along the road to join my colleague. Mind how you go . . . Cheerio.' And he was away, anxious to recross the junction while he'd got green in his favour.

Maybe he ought to have stayed and talked, though? Hadn't Pat told him, only last night, that they mustn't neglect their social role, that they should socialize with people on their beats . . . chat to them, listen to them, reassure them? True enough, he conceded, and felt a twinge of remorse for having . . . yes, that was what he'd done, really; he'd *dumped* the old dear. But supposing, while you were socializing, you missed a red-hot knock-off, just around the corner? Figures were what counted for most, so far as a prob' was concerned.

'You wanna be careful, y'know,' Vindscreen told him, when they were again together, continuing their way along the Lane. 'Seein old dears across roads can be highly dangerous.'

'Oh?' MacHale said.

'Yeah. The last time *I* saw an old dear over the road, she whacked me over the nut with a stick of French bread.'

MacHale tossed back his head, and laughed at the thought of it. 'Why'd she do that, then?'

'Because she never wanted to *go* over the road, did she?'

'Well . . .' MacHale paused, bemused, and shrugged.

'When I saw her,' Vindscreen explained, 'she was standin at the kerb, all hunched over and squintin her eyes, as if she couldn't even *see* across the road, never mind walk there. So, up I goes, grabs her arm, and breezes her across, quick as you like, assurin her it was all part of the service . . . my *pleasure*, in fact. Then, she bops me one with the loaf, breakin it, and knockin my helmet off.'

'But if she didn't want to cross, what *was* she doing, standing at the kerb, like that?'

'Turned out she was peerin over at the greengrocer's shop, wantin to see how much his spuds was for a pound, comparin his prices with what she'd paid for the spuds she'd already bought, up the High Street. Which reminds me, talkin about spuds: d'you hear that one about the potato that got run over by a bus?'

Here we go, MacHale thought, smiling in anticipation. 'No, go on.'

'Well, when the potato wakes up in hospital, the doctor goes, "There's some good news, and there's some bad news, I'm afraid. Which d'you want first?" And the potato goes, "Gimme the good news first." And the doctor goes, "Right. You're gonna live." The potato looks at him, all funny, like, then goes, "So what's the *bad* news, then? I'm gonna *live*." And the doctor goes, "Well, you're gonna be a cabbage for the resta your life."'

For a while, they walked on in silence, taking in their surroundings. There were fewer shops, now, along here, and, as a consequence, fewer people; although, early in the mornings, a good many housewives made their way along the Lane, to buy their fruit-and-veg from the barrow-boys who traded from kerbside stalls at the edge of the north pavement, about half a mile west of the High Street.

'You know,' Vindscreen said. 'A few years ago, this Lane was lined on both sides with terraces of small shops, each with a flat above it. But look at it now.'

MacHale looked about himself. 'Yes. It won't be too long before the whole lot are gone.'

There were wide, jagged gaps in the terraces, half filled with piles of brick and rubble, and beyond, to the left and right, where similar streets had once stood, there were broad expanses of churned-up clods of earth, enclosed by low, corrugated-tin fences; between the gaps in the terraces there were small, rundown businesses, anticipating their own, inevitable fate: cafes, second-hand-furniture shops, old-clothing shops, one or two fruit-and-veg shops . . . a used-book shop, all with grimy windows – some cracked – blistered paintwork, lopsided doors and black, crumbling brickwork.

Now, to their right, where there was a huge gap in the old terrace, MacHale saw the beginnings of the result of this progress into the Twenty-First Century: set far back from the road, and presided over by three, towering cranes, four skyscrapers were rising from the rubble, surreptitiously vibrating upward, it seemed, from a cacophany of noise produced by pneumatic drills, dumper trucks, concrete mixers, and earth movers.

'Another Rat-Farm in the making,' observed Vindscreen.

MacHale nodded his agreement, and they continued on their way.

As they approached the line of traders' stalls, they took in the smell: exhaust fumes, naturally, and the blunt, *furry*, faintly musty odour of dirt and grime which clung to the decaying brickwork of the old buildings, but tinged, now, with the sweet aroma of apples and onions and fresh-cut flowers, and wet fish.

MacHale braced himself, mentally and physically. These barrow-boys were a scabrous lot of bastards; one or two of them were ex-boxers, but all were graduates of the gutter and the street, each with a first-class-honours degree for drunkenness, public brawling and petty thieving.

If they sensed that you were of a timorous disposition, they'd piss all over you, cop or not.

This afternoon, though, they all seemed fairly torpid, as they chatted in ones and twos, or leaned or sat by their stalls, their leathery complexions inflamed by years of exposure to the elements, not to mention their daily sessions, at lunchtimes and during evenings, at the *Flag and Lamb*, across the road from where they traded; they all seemed to have claw-lie fingers, too, thick and hooked, and calloused hands that were permanently dirt-ingrained, and each wore a cheesecutter cap, denims or cords, and navy-blue donkey-jackets, with mufflers or cravats.

Very basic men they were, MacHale thought . . . animalistic, really; they appeared to live only for money, drink and sex – in that order, too, probably – and the easier these were obtained, the better they liked them. They all talked backchat, or arsey-versey, as well, which was a London traders' sub-language whose vocabulary consisted of normal English, but spelt and pronounced backwards. Hence, if one of the traders had a difficult customer, or one he didn't much like, and whom he considered a prat, he wouldn't actually *call* him a prat, because he wanted the man's money; no, he'd just turn to the trader next-door, force a smile, and say, 'Got a tarp, here, mate; giving me orgga.' – *orgga*, being aggro, of course.

In contrast to their keepers, the stalls themselves were always very well maintained – high, triangular mounds of clean, shiny fruit, with troughs of washed vegetables, all bedded on a thick lawn of bright green, artificial grass – but it was the wet-fish stall, in particular, which always caught MacHale's eye, especially first thing in the morning: a large centrepiece of gaping dogfish, curled prawns and lobsters, mackerel and whitebait, and red-and-yellow starfish, all arranged in an intricate, circular pattern, with the remaining offers set out in neat rows on white-plastic trays amid chunks of glistening ice.

As MacHale and Vindscreen passed-by the stalls, they received respectful nods of the traders' heads, which they returned; but the relationships were uneasy, MacHale found; the cops knew that the traders were all petty villains, who short-changed customers and palmed them off with bad produce if they weren't regulars, and there were often problems with rubbish blocking the footway; for their part, the traders felt that it was accordingly wise to acknowledge, with a modicum of respect, a cop's authority and presence on the street; but never would they trust or like him.

'A lot of those traders used to be GTP,' Vindscreen commented, looking back over his shoulder after he and MacHale had cleared the line of stalls.

'GTP? What's that?' MacHale queried.

'Good To Police,' Vindscreen explained. 'They've always hated us, but one or two of them used to throw you an apple as you walked by, or maybe the fish man'd give you a bag of prawns . . . or Charlie Lightfoot, on the flower stall, would go into you with a buncha carnations for the wife.' He shook his head. 'Not these days, though.'

'Howcome, then?'

'Oh, it was down to Tasty Tom, I think. He killed the goose. Used to come down here every day, regular as prunes, an go along the row of stalls, loadin himself up with fruit-'n'-veg. They just got naused off with him takin the piss, I s'pose.'

'Is it right, anyway, though?' MacHale said. 'I mean, even taking an apple . . . one apple?' He now glanced back over his shoulder at Charlie Lightfoot, the middle-aged man who ran the flower stall; Charlie was an ex-trackside bookie who'd become a *kerbside* bookie.

'Take Charlie Lightfoot,' MacHale went on. 'We all *know* he's running a book at that stall of his, and *he* knows we know. So if he does stuff a bunch of daffs up your kilt, he's gonna expect something in return, isn't he?'

'Like what?'

'Like we don't nick him . . . or his runners.'

'*We* wouldn't be nickin him or his runners, anyway,' Vindscreen pointed out. 'That's plainclothes stuff, nickin bookies.'

'Yeah, but Charlie Lightfoot doesn't know that,' MacHale said. 'He thinks he's vulnerable to all cops. And no one'd stop me nicking him, if I had the evidence.'

'Na, you're bein too . . .' Vindscreen contorted his face and gesticulated with his hands. '. . . too *straight*. It don't do any harm to be friendly with people, or to allow them to be friendly with you. An what if you *do* turn a blind eye to a small breach of law, like a couplea boxes on the footway, or a fifty-P bet here-'n'-there? There's more important stuff to worry about, I reckon.'

MacHale couldn't agree, although he thought it unwise to fully submerge himself in his protests; after all, he didn't want to make a name for himself as a . . . a caped crusader, or something. But he was in no doubt that they were talking, here, about a division of loyalties, a debasing of professional integrity, and, what's more, a breach of the Discipline Code.

Vindscreen, however, interpreted MacHale's silence as uncertainty, and he went on: 'Every Division's got people who're GTP. We've got loads, here. The take-aways, the clothing shops . . . *most* shop-owners like to favour the law, 'cause we're lookin after their properties. We've even got the MPCS *arrangin* for us to obtain discounts on bought goods. That's The *Job*, John, for Christ's sake, *tellin* us it's okay.'

'But how d'you nick a bloke who's done you a favour?'

'You don't,' Vindscreen retorted. 'If you've taken a small bung from a bloke, you've got a relationship with him, and that enables you to *advise* him if he steps outa line. There's no *need* to hit him with the law.'

'I can't agree,' MacHale said, and to hell, now, with what *anyone* might think; he felt too strongly about this to keep quiet. 'Look at Shadrack, down the High Street, for instance. He actually *believes*, just because he gives discounts to police, that he's *immune* from the parking laws. He's a piss-taker, just like most of them are that offer you this, that and the other. No, the only way is to be straight; treat everybody as equal; don't compromise yourself.'

Vindscreen sighed, then smiled sardonically. 'We could argue all day, over this, John. But there's no point, is there? Your mind's made up, innit?'

'Yes it is,' MacHale told him. 'And *you* can't tell me I'm *wrong*, either, because – '

'No, no, you're right,' Vindscreen interjected. 'You *are* right. *Officially*. All I'm sayin is there's no harm in bein flexible. But, okay, you're still a prob', and you're head's still burstin with law and procedure and instruction; for the first couplea years, you've gotta play it by the book, I s'pose. But after that, you begin to realize it's futile, that you *can't* do The Job by the book, that you're outnumbered and you're losin.

'Then, you change; you go one of two ways: you either bend or break. But just remember this: if you're too rigid, you *can't* bend; you'll just snap . . . you'll crack up.'

That's crap! MacHale thought. He wasn't obsessed with being a *goody-goody*, or with winning the war against crime. It was just that . . . well, at the end of the day, he knew that he couldn't experience any sort of job-satisfaction, without a tenacious professionalism. And then, suddenly, another of those wingeing pangs of guilt . . . Yesterday. In the cells. Roland Squires . . . If Vindscreen had known about that incident, he'd've said that MacHale was a hypocrite.

Which only served to reinforce MacHale's belief that there were no shades of honesty and integrity and professionalism. A cop had to be either bent or straight; there was no in-between.

The two of them walked on in silence, now, each with his own, not too disparate, thoughts. MacHale wasn't ashamed of his stance, and neither did he doubt its validity, but he was concerned lest it should pick him up and set him down at too great a distance from his colleagues.

Maybe, then – at least for a while – he should try and acquiesce in the belief of his older colleagues and the supervisors, which had it that probs, like little boys and girls, should keep their fuckin traps *shut*, till they're old enough to know what they're *talkin* about, by which time the ink on their warrant cards might've dried out, as well.

At length, Vindscreen broke the uneasy – for MacHale, anyway – silence. He nudged MacHale in the ribs, nodded in the direction of the pavement across the road, and said, 'Have a look. Here comes Dog-End Dan . . . dirty old sod.'

MacHale glanced across the road, pausing by the kerb's edge.

He was a hunchbacked old boy of about seventy-five, with a cadaverous complexion and several days' growth of silver stubble around his chin and sunken cheeks; as usual, he wore a shabby brown-tweed sports jacket, blue trousers whose bottoms flapped about three inches above the tops of his scuffed brown-leather boots, and a battered grey trilby that was now almost black with a shiny crust of dirt and grease; his eyes, permanently downcast, were trained on the flagstones and in the gutter, while his hands were mostly buried deep in the bulging, sagging pockets of his jacket.

No one at the nick seemed to know what his true name was, but the local cops, oblivious of the pun, had *nick-named* him Dog-End Dan, because he'd never pass-by a discarded cigarette butt, without stopping to pick it up. He was at it, even now, MacHale saw: he'd halted, taken his hands from his pockets, and was reaching down into the gutter to claim a couple of filter-tips that each had a quarter inch of unburned tobacco . . . upright again, he was now picking at the dog-ends, removing the paper and tips before dropping the loose tobacco into his right-hand jacket pocket. Then he was off, his eyes scanning the pavement as he shuffled slowly along. Later, when he neared the High Street, he'd probably sit at the public bench outside the County Court, and there, with his rolling machine and a packet of green Rizlas, begin recycling the roadside Virginia.

Pedestrians were often to be seen frowning at Dan's insanitary habit, and giving him a wide berth as they passed him; a few, though, would stop and press money on him, assuming that he'd been forced by hard times to scavenge for his smokes.

But Dan *wasn't* a smoker, at all. He was an inmate of the old folks' home, over in Carter Street, and the tobacco he'd collected from the gutter, to make into rolled cigarettes, was later sold by him to those of his fellow inmates who were smokers.

So, Dan wasn't the poor old impecunious pensioner that most people took him to be; he was a snout baron at the old folks' home, and probably had about three-hundred grand, tucked away in a Swiss bank-account – or so the cops reckoned.

MacHale and Vindscreen turned away and moved on.

''Ere, that reminds me,' said Vindscreen. 'D'you hear that one about the penniless hunchback who went to the money lender and said, "Can I borrow a couplea quid till I get m'self straight?"' He looked at MacHale, and fluttered his eyebrows, Groucho-Marx-style. 'Like it?'

'Not a lot,' MacHale told him, smiling. Vindscreen was back on form, again.

'Ya know, the streets're chocker with wierdos and nutters and eccentrics,' Vindscreen observed. '. . . And not *all* of em are from the nick, either.'

'Oh, I dunno,' MacHale lightly said. 'There's Old Crikey, and Tasty Tom, and poor old Mathieson, and . . .'

'What about John Purvis, though?' Vindscreen asked. 'No one at the nick can touch him for nuttiness.'

MacHale felt nauseous at mention of the name. Purvis was a filthy old vagie whose grimy, weatherbeaten face was practically lost beneath a huge, greasy and matted white beard that almost reached down to his waist, and who, whatever the weather, wore at least *four* ragged overcoats that were wired and strung to his dirty, skinny body; whenever he spotted a cop, he'd fish into one of the pockets of his coats, bring out a battered old Bible, hold it on high, and bellow, 'Ya *dead*! Ya gonna get ya *soul* kicked in! . . . Ya *dead*!'

Then there was Eli Jones, another old vagie who smelled like a compost heap and looked like a down-at-heel scarecrow; he'd always approach a uniformed cop, too, and, after glancing furtively about himself, urgently whisper, '*Special Branch! Anything to pass on?*' Then he'd scurry away, giggling dementedly, his hands clamped over his ears.

These were but two of the scores of regulars who'd been around the ground for many years, and, in addition, there were always those who were passing through, en route to . . . nobody knew where. Go down to the railway or coach stations, and you'd see them at all hours of the day and night, lying around drunk, depressed, creating disturbances, accosting passers-by for money, or even attempting to hire out, for sex, their filthy, malodorous bodies, so's they could earn the price of a drink or a packet of cigarettes; and, as was the case with the down-and-out toms, they had their takers, too.

'Talkin of nutters,' Vindscreen said. 'What happened to George Scott, that ever-ravenous half-wit who lobbed a brick through Old Crikey's window?'

'Oh, he was RIC for a nut-'n'-gut report,' MacHale said. 'He'll probably be committed for compulsory treatment. All a waste of time, really; he won't be cured, or deterred.' He paused, then added. 'It was you who put him up to smashing that window, wasn't it?'

'*Me-ee?*' Vindscreen intoned, affecting indignance. ''Course I never.' But an unstoppable grin was widening his mouth and cracking his cheeks and narrowing his eyes, as he added, 'No, *I* told him to lob a *milk-bottle* through the window.' Now he was laughing quite openly, having assumed it was safe to admit his guilt, because old George had ducked his nut at court, and there couldn't be any comebacks.

'I knew it was you,' MacHale said. 'You could've dropped me right in it, there, doing that. S'posing he'd gone bent on me, at court?'

Vindscreen shrugged. 'He didn't, though, did he? Although, I will concede he *could* have. In fact, those sorta bodies are more'n likely to. That's why it ain't *worth* nickin em. Any of em could be nicked, at any time, but why bother? It's just pointless.'

There was a lot of truth in that, MacHale thought.

Any of them *could* be arrested at any time: for drunkenness, for vagrancy offences, for importuning or soliciting, for breaching the Peace, or as a means of having them compulsorily committed and detained for treatment under the provisions of the Mental Health Act. But it was futile, really, to arrest them, because they just couldn't be deterred; they had nothing; they had no pride or self-respect; therefore, no guilt or shame, either. The courts, most often, would merely fine them, but as few if any of them had money, they'd merely serve a day's detention as an alternative, and, come tomorrow, they'd be back. There was always the danger, too, that they'd die or commit suicide while in police custody, or attempt to dismantle or set fire to their cells, with implements – such as bottle openers – or matches, which they'd concealed in the crevices and orifices of their decomposing bodies . . . bodies which arresting officers tended, for obvious reasons, to search as perfunctorily as possible.

Of course, probs, like MacHale, were expected to nick such people, from time-to-time, just to keep their figures up to strength. But no prob' actually relished the duty.

'It's pointless nickin any of *this* lot, an all,' Vindscreen was now saying, nodding his head at the mini-procession that was slowly progressing along the pavement, towards himself and MacHale.

'Ah, Harry Krishna's firm,' said MacHale, and he and Vindscreen moved to the back of the pavement, standing with their shoulders against the brick wall, their heads turned to their right.

Slowly, methodically more than rhythmically, the eight-strong procession jigged along. Each of the young men had a shaven head – just a little pigtail, sprouting incongruously from his crown – and each wore a flimsy, orange-cotton sari, with rubber flip-flops on his otherwise-bare feet. On they came, banging and flourishing their tambourines, their leader waving a smouldering joss-stick, in unison, chanting, '*Hare Krishna, Hare Krishna, Hare Krishna, Hare Krishna, Krishna Krishna, Krishna Krishna . . .*'

And then they were past MacHale and Vindscreen, completely unaware of the law's presence on the street.

They looked so tranquil-eyed, MacHale thought, so at peace with themselves and the world. MacHale was reminded of what Bernard Levin had said of Jehovah's Witnesses: they were waiting around for Judgement Day, with the smugness of a man in the dry season who knows that his neighbour's house is not insured for fire.

'When they get to the High Street,' Vindsdreen said, watching after the procession, 'they'll probably stop and gather in a circle, and one or two of em'll start frontin passers-by, attemptin to . . . *What* is it they're doin?'

MacHale thought about it, then offered: 'Attempting to convert people to the most celebrated of the Hindu deities.' He was only half sure he was right, but sounded completely authoritative.

'Yeah, tha's it,' Vindscreen gratefully said. 'Trouble is, if you do em for footway, they never plead. The buggers're renowned for it.'

'Don't I know it,' MacHale responded. 'The last time I claimed one, he just stood in the box, chanting *Harry Krishna*, and refused to plead, either way.'

Now they were passing the green-painted iron-spear railings of Martin Park, an undulating spread of grass, broken up by circular beds of shrubs, and clumps of tall silver birches and firs. It was rectangular in shape and encompassed an area of about a quarter square-mile. In the centre of the Park there was a kidney-shaped boating lake, and a cafe, and if you hired yourself a deckchair and sat down there on a hot, summer's afternoon, closing your eyes and listening to the sounds of splashing water, singing birds and playing toddlers, you could imagine you were miles away from the city and its oppression.

If you could *bring* yourself to close your eyes, that was. MacHale didn't think he'd be able to, not even if he were in full uniform. *He* knew just how many crimes were committed in the Park: muggings, indecent exposures, indecent assaults, thefts . . . Christ, a man couldn't even go for a slash in the public toilets without fear of having his joint grabbed at by some raving fruit. And last week . . . that was a bad thing: a young girl of seventeen was surrounded by a gang of five black kids, just before dusk, as the Park was closing; one held her down, one raped her three times, and the remaining three just looked impassively on; as they were finishing, another, older, black man came on the scene, and they ran away; now, he knelt by the girl's side and asked what had happened – although it must have been all too obvious what had happened – and then he, too, raped her. You weren't supposed to *say* things like this, but every cop *knew* that blacks – young blacks – had, for a very long time, been disproportionately – in relation to their numerical ratio, black kid to white kid – involved in street crimes, particularly robbery from the person. So while the lefties and the do-gooders threw up mitigating factors – such as unemployment and disadvantage and discrimination – no person had better suggest to the *cops* that, from next Monday, it was Be-Nice-To-Niggers Week.

'D'you think the CID'll ever catch them,' MacHale asked. 'Those slags who raped that girl, I mean?'

'Na, there's not a lotta chance, really,' Vindscreen said. 'She can't ID em. All spades look the same, to her, so she reckoned, and the older one was wearin a woolly hat, anyway – pulled right down over his boat. It's a pound to a pincha shit, though, that they all live down there, on the John-Selwyn Estate.' And he pointed ahead, to the near distance, to the western side of the Park, where four twenty-storey high, glass-and-concrete tower-blocks rose up to deface the pale, grey-blue sky.

'You mean the Rat Farm,' said MacHale.

'Yeah, the Rat Farm.'

They're hideous monsters, too, MacHale thought, as

he looked across and upwards at the four tower-blocks, and so are *most* of the people who *occupy* them.

A majority of the block's residents were black, and a majority were unemployed, too, owing thousands of pounds in unpaid rent and rates, little or none of which the local Council could ever hope to recover; of course, the Housing Department could've commenced proceedings to evict the indebted families, but had they done so, they would immediately have assumed responsibility for them as homeless persons in their Borough, and, accordingly, the obligation to *re*house them. They could, too, have commenced proceedings to levy distress on the debtors' possessions; but such deprived families had little or nothing that was of any value. An impossible situation, then, so that all the Council could hope to do was cajole the debtors into making small weekly or monthly repayments, and just live with the knowledge that most of the arrears would take *two* lifetimes to clear.

By the end of the decade, though, the Estate would either have been demolished – by the Council, if the resident vandals hadn't beaten them to it – or would have fallen down of its own accord; bits and pieces, like concrete wall-panels, were forever breaking loose and crashing down onto walkways. Just like so many other inner-city estates, the Rat Farm was a crumbling monument to the total lack of ingenuity and foresight of the 'Sixties' planners and architects. The consequences of this so-called answer to the housing-shortage problem were devastating.

Mothers didn't dare let loose their kids to play on the communal green, far below, because how could a mother supervise and protect her child, from a hundred feet up in the air? No one knew his neighbour, either, because people only ever encountered one another in the lifts which stank of urine, were covered in obscene graffiti, and littered with rubbish; or, more usually, because the lifts were almost permanently vandalized and out of order, when passing, breathless and agitated, on the stairways, which were in no better state than the lifts. The walkways, badly lit and foreboding, were a mugger's paradise, and the underground car-parks were used only by car thieves – for stripping lost-or-stolens, or for ringing them – vagrants, prostitutes, glue sniffers and junkies.

Here, then, there could be no community spirit, because the people were depressed and *dis*pirited, and resigned.

Always there was noise, too, which intensified at night and during the early hours of the morning: of hooligans and vandals; of drunks, and of throbbing music, punched out by huge ghetto-blasters; of domestic disputes and assaults; of wild parties, which often lasted for as long as three days and nights during summer months; and of barking dogs, frustrated by their incarceration, kept not as pets but as deterrents against muggers and burglars – there were probably more Alsatians and Dobermans to the square mile, here, than anywhere else in the world, MacHale believed; and this despite a Council Regulation which forbade any tenant to keep a dog or cat inside his flat. But a man had to take some measures to protect his property and his family. Christ, things were so bad around here, they even had to padlock the refuse bins to the pavement, down below.

Until recently, a favourite pastime of the kids was to make bogus Emercalls which'd take the cops to the top floors of the blocks; and while the cops were there, the kids were setting fire to their RT-cars, on the Estate roads. Nowadays, however, the cops always left two of their number on the forecourt of the blocks, to guard the vehicles, whenever they responded to a shout.

'D'you think the people in there would be able to alter with their surroundings?' MacHale asked, as they approached the Estate. 'I was just wondering, is it living in there that's made them what they are, or are they naturally anti-social and criminally-minded?'

'Na,' Vindscreen firmly said. 'People're cast in moulds. They *can't* radically alter themselves. And if you don't believe that, then you oughta go and take a look at one of them new developments on the east side of the ground, where the old, terraced houses've been gutted and refurbished.'

'Over in Longhill Street . . . and Churchill Street?'

'Yeah, those places, where people's livin conditions've been reverted to the style of the 'Fifties, in as much as they've all got gardens and plenty of space, and a chance to mix and get to know one another and take a pride in themselves and their properties.'

'And? What's the result?' MacHale asked. 'Those places seem pretty respectable to me.'

'Na,' said Vindscreen. 'Take a look at the crime-books. Vandalism's not as bad, but everythin else – robberies, thefts and screwins – is no different. The only statistic which's been really drastically reduced is the one which relates to death by suicide.' He shook his head. 'Na. Slags are slags. If ya put em in a *palace* they'd turn it into a slum.'

'I'm not so sure,' MacHale said. 'It's a social problem. The people have got to be educated. It should be a multi-agency approach, like the Commissioner said, with the police, the social services, architects and planners, the communities and local authorities, all working together to – '

'Look! Over there!' Vindscreen suddenly cut in, coming to a halt and pointing to his right, in the direction of the communal green that was spread before the entrances to the Estate's four tower-blocks. 'The little bastards!'

MacHale halted beside Vindscreen, following the direction of his pointing arm, to where a group of four black kids were taking it in turns to hurl a thick-bladed throwing knife at the trunk of a newly-planted silver birch which had already been stripped of most of its branches.

The kids spotted MacHale and Vindscreen, and fled, making for the concrete ramp that led down into the subterranean car-parking area.

'Shall we go after them?' asked MacHale. 'We might be able to nick em, for criminal damage or something.'

'Na,' said Vindscreen, watching as the kids disappeared. 'Wastea time, innit? The Juvenile Bureau'd only caution em. Besides, we'd never catch em, now, not down there in that pitch-black, concrete rabbit-warren.'

Yeah, thought MacHale. They'vc got a knife, too. Maybe *they'd* catch *us* if we ventured down there?

They shrugged away the problem and crossed over the road, turning left and walking south along Denmark Street, down towards the red-light area of the ground, which was a mixture of small businesses – mostly cafes, restaurants and sandwich bars, run by Italians, Spaniards and Greeks – sex-book shops – most run by Maltese – and private flats – most occupied by call-girls. Maybe they'd get to caution a tom; although most of the girls, on spotting the law, would scuttle away into a cafe or sandwich bar, until it became safe to reemerge; the same went for the rent boys, who mostly congregated outside the foyer of the run-down Regent Hotel, waiting for their pick-ups.

'He's GTP,' said Vindscreen, looking at the window of an Italian patisserie, across the street. 'Just go up the alley at the side of the shop, knock at the door, and you'll get all the hot, strong coffee you can drink, all the sweet pastries you can eat, and a loaf or two, as well, to take away. Only on nights, though, when the guv'nor, Rossi, is there, supervisin the bakin of the bread and cakes.'

'Oh, I'll remember it,' said MacHale, determining that he'd never, in fact, bother to use the place.

'But don't have any pie,' warned Vindscreen.

'Oh? Howcome?'

Vindscreen smiled. 'I remember the first time I met Rossi. Tasty took me in there at two o'clock, one mornin. There they were, him and Tasty, chattin away – Tasty sippin coffee, Rossi makin a cherry pie – when Rossi suddenly takes out his top set and decorates the pie-crust; then he pops em back in and carries on chattin as if nothin untoward had happened.'

'Did he *really*?' MacHale said, amused but only half convinced that this wasn't just another of Vindscreen's jokes.

'Yeah, straight up,' Vindscreen assured him. 'But if ya think that's anythin, ya shoulda seen what he *rolled* the pastry with.'

I'm *definitely* not going in there, MacHale affirmed.

'Here, what about that, then,' Vindscreen said, pausing by the window of a sex-aids' shop, and nodding at a life-size, red-bikini-clad rubber doll that was lying, face up, amid a display of vibrators, creams, oils, magazines, and various other weirdly-shaped and brightly-coloured gadgets that were *guaranteed* to improve your amatory exploits. 'D'you fancy it?'

MacHale arched his mouth and tilted his head, sniffing. 'Can you actually . . . well, you know, *give* it one?'

''Course ya can,' Vindscreen said. 'It's got a latex one, under those red-silk drawers, with real pubes. And look at how the lips and mouth are shaped . . . all poutin and gapin.'

'But it's *dead*,' MacHale said. 'You might just as well stick your joint in a wet loaf of bread.'

'Yeah, you're right, really,' Vindscreen conceded. 'Mind you, one of those red-rubber alarm-clock-dolls that I've seen elsewhere'd be okay.'

'And *what* d'you do with *that*, then?' MacHale asked, falling in head-first.

'Well, you take it to bed, wind it up and set it, and it's guaranteed to give you a rude awakenin, in the mornin.'

MacHale grinned.

'Come on,' Vindscreen said, turning away from the window. 'Let's go and stand in Rossi's alley, see if we can't spot ourselves a tom.'

They got a break in the traffic and crossed the road, taking up an outward-facing position in the entrance to the arched alleyway.

'They'll've spotted us, coming in here, won't they?' MacHale said.

'I'd be surprised if they *haven't*,' Vindscreen told him. 'By now, they're all performin on the other side of the block, where we can't see em.'

'So why're we here, then?'

'Well, there'll be a couple who're away on the job . . . down the underground car-park at the Rat Farm, or along one of the quiet mews, or at one of the bed-'n'-breakfast places down the road. *They* don't know we're here, so they'll come right back and start performin again.'

'We hope.'

'They will.'

Vindscreen was right, too.

To their left, about twenty yards away on the opposite side of the road, a gold-coloured Cortina had drawn-in to the kerb, and a curly-haired brunette was now alighting from the passenger's side at the front. She wiggled her backside, tugged down at the hem of her green-satin micro-skirt, then turned, bent forward, smiling, and spoke to the car's Negro driver, sticking her head through the open window of the passenger's door. A moment later she straightened up, and watched as the Cortina accelerated away.

'Her ponce, d'you reckon?' MacHale said.

'Na,' replied Vindscreen, without forethought. 'No

ponce I've ever seen or heard of would drop his tom right on her manor. Ponces are furtive, background people . . . very wary of bein spotted or tailed.'

'Must've been a punter, then.'

Vindscreen nodded his agreement, and kept his eyes on the tom.

She was attractive enough, MacHale considered – from twenty yards away, that was; but he suspected that if he were face-to-face with her, he'd see the deep folds of flesh that ran from her nostrils to the corners of her mouth, the heavy, dark pouches that sagged beneath her glassy blue eyes, or the jowly aspect of her throat and upper neck. She looked a good fifty; but she was probably no more than about thirty-eight.

As he observed her, Vindscreen affected a sour expression. 'You could go potholin in that face,' he remarked.

'Or mountain climbing,' added MacHale, looking not at her face but at a lower part of her body.

Apart from the green-satin micro skirt, which was corrugated with horizontal creases, she wore a pair of glossy-red stilettoes which made her plump white legs sag at the knees, and a crimson-satin T-shirt that could hardly contain her huge breasts. As she wiggled slowly along the road, her buttocks sliding up and down beneath the tight skirt, her shoulder-bag swinging at her right side, her arms were folded across her chest and her hands were massaging the pale, goose-pimpled flesh at her elbows . . . which drew the eye to a red butterfly tattooed on her left bicep, beneath a round, pock-marked innoculation scar.

'D'you know her?' asked MacHale.

Vindscreen shook his head. 'Na. Never seen her before. Must be a transfer from a hotter climate . . . Kings Cross, maybe, or Bedford Hill.'

She'd stopped, now, and was leaning nonchalantly back

against the wall adjacent to a closed door that entranced a bookie's shop, her arms still folded, her right leg raised up high behind her, bent at the knee, with her stiletto pressed flat against the brick wall. Now she was fumbling in her shoulder-bag . . . taking out a packet of cigarettes . . . popping a long filter-tip into her mouth, placing the packet back inside the bag . . . leaning forward to ask a male pedestrian for a light; the man halted, took a lighter from his trousers pocket, and ignited her filter-tip . . . then turned aside his head to listen to something she was saying . . . shook his head, negatively, and walked on, taking a glance back over his shoulder before he'd gone twenty paces, shaking his head once again.

'We can't nick her if we don't know her, can we?' MacHale said.

Vindscreen looked squarely at him. 'Haven't you dealt with a tom, then, before now?'

'No, I haven't. As you know, we can't approach them by ourselves, unless we get a complaint from a solicited man, and whenever I've seen one, working, I've always been alone.'

'Yeah, well . . .' Vindscreen's shoulders rose and fell, and his expression was one of unease. 'You don't *have* to do it by the book, y'know. I mean, there are ways round it.'

'What're you trying to say?'

'Okay, so we're *s'posed* to be in pairs, and in uniform, when we do toms . . . when we nick or caution em. But . . .' He paused, reordering his thoughts. 'Let's start at the beginnin. We can only nick a tom who's got recent convictions for tommin, right?'

'Right.'

'Or one who's been cautioned on at least two occasions, right?'

'Yeah.'

'The idea bein, I s'pose, to try and preclude, as far as

possible, our goin up and nickin or cautionin a tart who's respectable; say, an ordinary woman who's just hangin around, waiting for her ol man or her boyfriend.'

'That's probably it, yes,' MacHale agreed.

'But those regulations, or instructions – because they ain't *law* – are a damn nuisance, and unnecessary, too.'

'How so?'

Vindscreen nodded in the direction of the tom who was along the road. 'Take her. We don't *know* her, but there's no doubt at all that she *is* a tom and that she's got plentya form for it. Yet if we do it by the book we've gotta go up to her, tell her what we've seen her doin, caution her, and – and this is a gutbuster – ask her if she'd like an appointment with a social worker or the Sally Army, or some other buncha do-gooders who'll attempt the fuckin *impossible* and try and convert her; then, *we've* gotta let her *go*.'

'Well?' MacHale said. 'I know that no tom actually would agree to be referred to a women's organization, for help and advice, but after she's been cautioned, the official form, when it's returned from the central index, might show she's either got form or been cautioned elsewhere; *then*, we *can* nick her, next time we see her, *without* ourselves giving her another caution. That's right, innit?'

'Well . . . yeah. But it's a wastea *time*; if you go up and caution a tom, what's she gonna do?'

MacHale began thinking hard, but couldn't find the answer.

'I'll tell ya, then,' Vindscreen said. 'She's gonna go on the trot, and start workin somewhere else, so that if you *do* do it properly, you'll *never* nick a tom. She'll bugger off, then go all round the MPD, collectin her one or two cautions in each Division.'

'So what're you advocating?'

'Well, there're two unofficial methods of dealin with

em. One, we go up, tell her we know she's tommin, then do a name-check on her. If she comes back, Known, with a club number, we get the nick to do a Collator's check on her address. Then, when we're told she's got recent previous for tommin, we claim her.'

'But what if she hasn't got recent previous for tomming?'

'We let her go. Then, when we get back to the nick, we put her in for a caution. But we don't actually *tell* her she's been cautioned, so's not to frighten her off. Tomorrow, when we find she's back again, we put her in for a second caution – as before, without tellin her; in fact, we don't even go *near* her, this time. Then, on the third day, when we again see her loiterin or solicitin, *bang*, we tell her she's ours, and put her on the sheet.'

'That's illegal, innit?' MacHale said.

'No, not at all,' Vindscreen confidently said. 'It's against instructions and procedure, but that's definitely not unlawful. Ya see, the cautionin and arrestin procedures arose from a Commissioner's instruction, on advice from the Home Office. It dates to the time when, in the 'Twenties, some Hooray Henry, name of Money, was caught in Hyde Park, havin it off with a tom. He had so much poke, though – financially and socially – the court slung the charge, and there was a public outcry about police malpractice – usual, typical sorta crap, when a well-known person, who's caught bang to rights, starts lookin for an outer. Well, this Money geezer got his outer, only to be nicked, some time later, for doin the *same* sorta *thing*, on a train.'

'Hmm,' MacHale said. 'Interesting.' He thought about it for a while, then said. 'And what're we gonna do with *this* tom?'

'We either go up and do a name-check on her, and nick her if we find she's got form, or we leave her alone, go away, and enter her up – on description, pars refused

– in the caution book. Then, tomorrow, I'll see if she's back. If she is, I'll put her in for another caution. Then, the day after tomorrow, if she's still around, I'll claim her.'

'You reckon it's better to put her in for a couple of bogus cautions, do you? Rather than do a name-check on her?'

'Yeah, it is, really,' Vindscreen said. 'If we stop her for a name-check, we might just find she's clean, and be unable to nick her. Then she could get scary and move away to another Division. If we just award her a couplea cautions, though, we're certain to be able to nick her, day after tomorrow.'

'And you want me as a witness?'

''Course. There's gotta be two of us for a caution. You know that . . . Not bottlin out, are ya?'

'No, no,' MacHale quickly responded. 'It's just that . . . well, I'm a prob'. S'posing we got found out? I'd maybe get the sack.'

'Don't be silly,' laughed Vindscreen. 'It'd be her word against ours. And who's gonna believe a slag like that? She is a *tom*, y'know. Anyway, I'd take the can back for you, you know that. It's a blow-out, now, anyway,' Vindscreen continued, looking along the road. 'She's pulled one. It'll have to be a caution, on description.'

MacHale glanced around the wall of the alley, and saw that the tom was just climbing inside a primrose-yellow Rover . . . And now the Rover was driving away.

'Well?' Vindscreen asked. 'D'you wanna go witness?'

MacHale considered the proposition. It *wouldn't* be unlawful, so they couldn't bang him up over the wall, if he and Vindscreen were to come unstuck. But then again . . . 'No, I can't,' he said, his mind made up. 'It's not that I'm frightened, or – '

'Well *what*, then?' demanded Vindscreen, staring intently at MacHale.

'I just wouldn't be able to carry it off,' he told him, a note of pleading in his voice. 'If it came to an up-'n'-downer in court, I'd let you in for it. I just wouldn't be able to tell lies, say that we went *up* to her and actually *told* her she was being cautioned, when we *didn't*. I'd drop you in it, because anyone looking at me would straightaway know I was lying.'

That wasn't the whole of it, though. At the heart of it was the deep-rooted truth that he found inherently repellent the idea of breaking one set of rules in order to enforce another set. And how could he add to the guilt he already felt about Roland Squires?

Vindscreen had been studying MacHale's face, soaking up what he'd heard. Then his shoulders rose and fell. 'Okay. Whatever you say.' He glanced at his wristwatch. 'I've gotta be away, now, as it happens. Got a traffic-point. See ya later.' And he turned away and walked out of the alley.

For a while, MacHale remained there, dissecting what had occurred . . . his stance, Vindscreen's reaction to it . . .

Dejected, he at last felt forced to leave the alley, because movement dissipated depression, to a degree; he really wanted to run, to feel the air, fresh and chilly on his face, but then he thought again of Pat, and knew that here, at least, was an ally, and this sustained him, made him determine not to give in. You *didn't* have to be a cowboy to do The Job.

He crossed the road and began aimlessly walking back the way he and Vindscreen had earlier come. But it was too busy, here: too many people and cars and taxis and buses, emitting a concomitant drone of noise that precluded clear, undisturbed thought. So he turned left, past the sex-aids' shop, and began strolling down Harper's street, a narrow, quiet road, the tall, windowless wall of the Astoria Cinema running along the entire length of its right side, and, on the opposite side, several small-business premises and a large square of wasteland that had recently been covered with tarmac and converted to use as a public car-park for shoppers and office workers.

Set in the Astoria's wall were several recessed doorways, exits from the cinema, which were bar-bolted on the inside; often, a cop would find groups of kids in these doorways, waiting to be let in, free of charge, by a friend who *had* paid, around the front, or by an exiting film-goer. No kids here today, though . . . only a snoring drunk, in the first doorway, lying sideways, in the foetal position, on the urine-stained concrete.

MacHale paused at the drunk's feet, wondering if he should claim him and call up the van; he could always do with a body, even if only for simple drunkenness. But no, he decided; today, now, he just couldn't be bothered.

Instead, he kicked gently at the vagie's holed and battered shoes, trying to rouse him. At length, the snoring spluttered, then ceased, and the vagie's bleary-eyed head moved sideways and up; then he rolled onto his stomach and climbed up the wall, until he stood, hunched over, shivering and pulling his greasy brown mac about his skinny body. After bending unsteadily to check the row of empty cider-bottles that lined the side of the entrance, he reeled past MacHale, trailing a thick smell of stale sweat, vomit and drink, and meandered up the road, head down, coughing, spitting and cursing.

MacHale called him back. The vagie hesitated, turned, and looked apprehensively at MacHale. MacHale walked towards him, his right hand dipping into his trousers pocket, to pull out some loose coins. But the vagie apparently thought he was about to get some stick, and turned and began trying to run for it. MacHale walked more quickly, caught the vagie, and turned him round by the shoulder. 'Here, pop,' he said. 'Have this with me,' and he pressed a fifty-P piece into the vagie's hand. 'Get yourself a sandwich or something.'

For a second, the vagie looked disbelievingly at MacHale; it definitely *wasn't* Christmas, and cops just *didn't* ever do what this cop *seemed* to be doing. But it was real enough, all the same, never mind the Why? of it, and now the vagie smiled a toothless smile, snatched at the fifty-P, kissed it, said 'God *bless* ya, son!' and was doing a runner, up the road, weaving from side-to-side, and bouncing off the cinema wall.

'Don't waste it on drink, either,' MacHale called after him, at the same time, knowing full-well that this was exactly what the vagie *would* do. What the hell, though? The poor ol' bag o' bones needed drink to stay alive, never mind in one piece.

Now, MacHale felt a whole lot better. Virtuous? Yeah, he decided. And why not? It was a *good* feeling, knowing that you'd helped out someone in need; so much better than feeling a sense of perverse satisfaction at having pulled a few strokes in order to get a body lodged in the cells.

On he moved, halting by the second of the recessed doorways, to glance in . . . and be disgusted by the half-dozen used condoms that had been deposited there – obviously, some of the toms, or maybe it was only one, were entertaining clients, here, probably during the hours of darkness. Later on, perhaps, he'd come back and find a couple, on the job: that'd be a pair for OPD, or insulting behaviour. Which reminded him of the time when old Snatch had lifted a pair for OPD, having caught them at it in Silverleaf Park. The evidence was that the tom, while sitting on a bench, in the darkness, had masturbated a punter who'd sat next to her. The tom protested her innocence, though, as did the punter, and Snatch's notes of evidence went into some detail: how he'd been hiding in a bush, next to the bench, and how he'd overheard the business conversation between tom and punter, and how she'd then manually manipulated his penis, using the right thumb and index-finger of her hand.

Next morning, at court, the two defendants sat impassively listening to the evidence, and Snatch must've thought he'd got a stone bonker. But when the tom was asked if she wanted to question Snatch's evidence, the roof fell in; triumphantly, she held aloft her right arm, and shrieked, '*Aha!* Got yer there, ain't I? It's *lies*, it's *lies!* I ain't *got* no bleedin thumb on me right 'and, 'ave I?'

And neither had she – it had been amputated, apparently, as a result of a factory accident, some years previously, and Snatch hadn't noticed, after he'd nicked her, because he hadn't taken her dabs or paid any attention to her hand.

However old Snatch had a good reply: 'Well, it was *dark*, Your Worship, and I was some feet *away* from the defendants, therefore I must have mistaken two fingers for a *thumb* and finger.'

The court liked that explanation, and the two defendants went down. Clearly, though – so far as Snatch's colleagues were concerned – Snatch had fantasized most of the 'evidence'.

So, there was a lesson to be learned there, MacHale believed. Not, as the others would have it, to be more careful in such situations, but to refrain from practising such conduct.

As he neared the end of the road, MacHale looked across to the car-park, wondering if he should walk across and check some excise licences . . . maybe turn up a theft and fraudulent use; a ringer, as well, if he was lucky. And then he saw a swift movement at the front of a huge, green lorry . . . a pantechnicon, which was parked at the front of the tarmac area, parallel to the roadway.

He stopped, and intensified his gaze, thinking he might just have been mistaken . . . But, no, he hadn't been. The dark figure again moved around the front of the lorry, looked at MacHale, motioned agitatedly with right arm, and once more moved out of sight.

It was Punchy Paterson, bare-headed, and red in the face.

What the hell's *he* up to? wondered MacHale . . . And what does he want me for?

There was but one way to find out, so MacHale moved quickly across the road, into the car-park.

13

'C'mere!' Punchy urgently whispered. 'And take your helmet off.'

MacHale took off his helmet and, hunched over, followed Punchy around the front of the green pantechnicon, then along its far side, until they were standing near its rear end, opposite a grey Leyland Sherpa van that was parked close alongside.

'Look,' Punchy said, crouching forward and peeping tentatively around the rear of the Sherpa, across the wide expanse of car-park. 'See him?'

MacHale leaned forward and peered over Punchy's left shoulder. There were row upon row of parked vehicles, abreast of one another in close order, the sunlight bouncing across their shiny-metal rooftops. But there was no one in sight. 'Where?' he asked, squinting his eyes against the glare.

'Over *there*!' Punchy irritably snapped, pointing to the middle distance. 'Behind that BMW.'

MacHale's gaze followed the line of Punchy's left arm, to a dark blue BMW that stood in a long line of vehicles, about fifteen yards away; his brow was creased, and his eyes began to smart, he was staring so hard, so intently . . . Then he spotted him: a young white kid, about twenty, who had long, curly dark hair, and who wore a red tracksuit top . . . MacHale was unable to see below the bottom half of the kid's chest, because that portion of him was obscured by the BMW . . . But now he'd altogether disappeared, again . . . He must've ducked down, MacHale thought.

'See it, see it?' Punchy said, excited.

'What?' asked MacHale, not taking his eyes off where he'd last seen the kid.

'The *BMW*,' whined Punchy. 'Whaddaya think? It rocked from side-to-side. Just then, as he bent forward. The thievin little git's tryin the door-handle.'

MacHale stared even more intently, but the sunlight, glinting up as a blinding white-gold Aurora where it struck the BMW's dark-blue roof, made him look briefly aside and blink his eyes. 'I can't see *anything*, now,' he told Punchy. 'What was he doing before I got here?'

'Tryin fuckin car-handles, that's what,' Punchy wheezed, moving even lower down and resting his palms on his knees. 'He's a TDA-merchant.'

'Why didn't you give me a shout, on the PR, then?' MacHale asked, lowering himself to Punchy's position. 'I've been in the area for a while, now.'

'Fuckin PR's up the spout,' Punchy hissed. 'Flat battery, I s'pose.'

'Oh.'

'Look, look! There he goes!' Punchy said. 'Along the side of the BMW . . . Now he's at that Vauxhall . . . the red one.'

'Got him!' MacHale said. The kid was now standing by the driver's door of a red Vauxhall Cavalier . . . his head, slowly moving in an arc, his eyes panning the area, apparently looking out for anyone who might be observing him . . . Now he was bending forward, peering, it seemed, into the interior of the Vauxhall.

'It *moved*, it *moved*!' wheezed Punchy. 'He's had a tug at *that* door-handle, too!'

He's imagining things, thought MacHale. The Vauxhall definitely *hadn't* moved, so far as he himself was concerned. 'You sure?' he said.

''Course I'm sure,' Punchy indignantly retorted. 'Whaddaya think, I'm *blind* or somethin?'

MacHale shrugged in silence.

Now the kid had moved around to the Vauxhall's passenger door . . . He was wearing bleached denims, and white trainers, and his hands were thrust deep in the pockets of his tracksuit top. Again, his eyes panned the area before peering in through the closed windows of the car.

'We gonna give him a pull?' MacHale wanted to know. 'He's definitely up to something.'

Punchy tut-tutted exasperatedly. 'The original fuckin brain-transplant donor, ain'tcha? '*Course* we ain't gonna pull him. Patience is what's wanted, here. Give him enough rope and he'll hang himself. Let him try *fifty* door-handles if he wants to.'

'Oh, yeah . . . I s'pose you're right,' MacHale weakly said, feeling incompetent. One of his instructors at TS had said that too many officers jumped in too quickly when observing suspects, and thereby deprived themselves of evidence which would probably have been gained had they continued to wait and watch. *Now* he remembered that advice.

'Come on, come on,' Punchy impatiently whispered, his fists clenched and making short jabs at the air; his shoulders were twitching from side-to-side, as well . . . and his head was weaving and bobbing; it was as if he were back in the ring, shadow boxing.

The kid was now walking slowly, casually, along a line of cars, his hands still in the pockets of his tracksuit top, his eyes to his front.

'Shee-it!' seethed Punchy. 'He's been disturbed.'

A middle-aged, bald-headed man, wearing a dark suit and carrying a black briefcase, was walking along towards the kid; an office worker, MacHale thought, leaving for his home. And now there were voices to be heard from the direction of the road, on the far side of the green pantechnicon . . . growing louder, nearer . . .

Punchy stood, and put on his helmet, MacHale following suit . . . and then a group of men walked by, making for the middle area of the car-park, each of them holding a bunch of keys, one man twirling his bunch at his side as he chatted to his colleagues.

'That's *that*, then,' Punchy said, his voice bitter. 'It's a fuckin blow-out, *now*, innit? All the office workers are startin to leave for home.'

Covertly, they peeped around the rear of the Sherpa, following the progress of the group of men who'd just passed by them, saw that the kid was walking *towards* the Sherpa, and pulled back, out of sight.

'Wait till he's on us,' whispered Punchy. '*Then* we'll give him a pull . . . And it's down to you, too, if he does a runner. Okay?'

'Okay,' MacHale confirmed.

And now the kid was walking by the rear of the Sherpa. He glanced right, as he passed, somehow sensing that he was about to be pounced upon, and momentarily broke his step, his jaw falling markedly lower, his hands leaving his pockets. Then, as he was about to go on the trot, Punchy sprang at him, lifting him right off the ground, swung him around and sent him crashing against the side of the Sherpa, which rocked violently under the force of the kid's impacted body.

'*Gotcha*, ya greasy little shit!' shouted Punchy.

For Christ's sake! MacHale frantically thought. He's only *dented* the side of the bloody van . . . S'posing its *owner* returns?

The kid, having slid down the side of the van, was sitting on his backside, his mouth gaping, staring up in bewilderment at the huge wedge of cop who towered above him, arms akimbo, a wicked snarl twisting the mouth of his battered face.

'*Name?*' Punchy menacingly said.

The kid swallowed hard and drew the back of his right

hand across his lips. 'What *for*? *Why*? *I* ain't done nothin, man.' Then he took note of Punchy's altered features: the lips, compressed tightly; the eyes, narrowing, reflecting violence; the left brow, arching upward. 'Lee . . . Lee Cooper,' he quickly said, his eyes flitting to MacHale . . . back to Punchy, settling on Punchy.

'Okay, Lee Cooper,' growled Punchy. 'Get off your arse, and roll over on your stomach.'

The kid did as he'd been ordered, turning over and lying prone, his head to one side, his eyes, showing white and dilated and bloodshot, trying to see behind and upward, to where Punchy was standing.

'Yeah, I thought as much,' Punchy said, and he leaned back and kicked the kid, hard in the buttocks. 'Lee Cooper, my *arse*! . . . Named ya jeans after ya, did they? . . . Naw; try ya *right* name!'

'Okay, okay,' winced the kid. 'Harvey . . . Frank Harvey.'

'Address?'

'Twenny-Eight, Wendover Road.'

Punchy glanced at MacHale. 'That there's the homeless-youth project, ain't it?'

MacHale nodded affirmitively. 'Yeah, it is.'

'That scores as NFA, then,' Punchy told the kid. 'Now, what's your age?'

'Nineteen. Twenny, almost.'

'So you ain't a juvenile. That's terrific. What sorta car you got?'

'*Car*? *I* ain't got no car.'

'Howcome you're in here, then, if you ain't got no car. *This* is a *car-park*.'

The kid shrugged. 'Just lookin around. I like cars. I'm interested in cars. Can I get up, now . . . please?'

'Kick ya shoes off, first.'

The kid kicked off his trainers and Punchy swept them aside with the toe of his right foot. 'Okay, get up.'

Good idea, that, thought MacHale, making him take off his shoes; now he *can't* do a runner.

The kid was now standing against the side of the Sherpa, his back masking the dent in its body panel, his hands clasped before him. 'Can I go, now?'

'Can you *hell*!' Punchy told him. 'You're nicked, my son. Only place you're goin is to the factory.'

'*Nicked?*' intoned the kid, his face going into shock. '*Whafor? I* ain't done no crime. I was just *lookin* at cars, is all. I told ya.'

'Don't gimme that crap, ya little scrote,' growled Punchy, leaning forward to eyeball the kid. '*I saw* ya. Ya tried the door-handles of four different cars, out there . . . A Merc', a Datsun, a BMW and a Vauxhall.'

'*Me-ee?*' protested the kid, looking alternately at Punchy and MacHale. 'I never *touched* no cars.'

'Turn ya pockets out, then,' ordered Punchy.

The kid hesitated.

'*Now! Right* now!' Punchy bellowed, showering spittle in the kid's face, making him blink and turn away his head.

Hurriedly, the kid complied, and out of the pockets of his denims there came a packet of blue cigarette-papers, a packet of gum, a front-door key, an unemployment-benefit card, bearing the name, Francis Harvey, and some loose change amounting to no more than a pound. The pockets of his tracksuit top were empty, though, save for a fluff-clogged black comb, which he produced from the one on his right. 'That's the lot,' he told Punchy, holding forth, for inspection, his possessions.

'Check,' Punchy now told MacHale.

MacHale began dipping into the kid's pockets. The tracksuit top was clean, so were the front pockets of his denims; but in the rear, left pocket, he found a worn old ignition-key for a Ford car – a key which could have gained the kid entry to *any* car that was, say, over eight years old, with worn locks on its doors. MacHale handed the key to Punchy.

'Well, well, well,' Punchy said, examining the key. 'Now what might this be for?' He glared at the kid.

The kid lowered his head, and stared at his white-socked feet, a black-nailed big toe, protruding from a hole in the wool of the right sock. 'Nothin,' he said, looking up again. 'Just an old key I found, is all . . . Ain't no use to no one.'

'So whaddaya keep it for?' Punchy wanted to know.

The kid shrugged. 'Dunno,' he quietly said.

'For screwin *cars*, is what *for*,' Punchy told him. He looked at MacHale. 'Get on to the nick and order up the van.'

MacHale moved away to dispatch his message on the PR, leaving Punchy to guard the kid.

'Five minutes,' MacHale called to him.

Punchy nodded his satisfaction. 'Lovely . . . And just leave the evidence to me, when we get him in. Okay?'

'Okay,' agreed MacHale, thinking that Punchy had better *have* some evidence to present to the SO, because he himself had none.

'What the fuck's goin *on* here?' pleaded the bewildered skinhead. 'You just *can't* be serious . . . I mean, this *is England* . . .' His hands were 'cuffed behind his back, and Tasty Tom was shouldering and shoving him across the yard, in the direction of the stables, where, so Tasty had *said*, he was going to be executed . . . . fuckin *executed*! Tasty *must've* been joking, though . . . *Surely?*

But he wasn't. He pushed the kid on before himself, saying, 'It's a new law, passed this mornin. Anyone who don't admit his guilt, we execute. Saves the courts wastin all that time, *findin* em guilty.'

'That's right, dear boy,' confirmed Snatch. He was walking behind Tasty and the prisoner, carrying a .38

Smith & Wesson revolver, which Tasty had borrowed from the front office, while Barker was otherwise engaged – he'd told Barker, when asking for the SO's bunch of keys, that he wanted some fresh IRBs from the safe, but had instead burgled the firearms' cabinet.

'New *law*?' said the skinhead, not believing it, unsure of whether he should laugh, cry, or just *faint*. 'You're *crazy*. Ya *can't* . . . well, *execute* people no more.'

'You're right,' agreed Tasty, leering sardonically. 'But stringin-up shit like you's called *justifiable* homicide.'

'Na, na, I *don't* believe this,' mumbled the skinhead. 'It's a . . . it's a game, it's *gotta* be.'

'You'll see,' Tasty told him. 'You'll see.' And he halted the skinhead outside the stable doors, unlocked the 'cuff that was fixed to the skinhead's right wrist, passed it behind a drainpipe, and refixed and locked it. Now, Snatch handed him the revolver, and both cops took several paces backwards.

'Right,' said Tasty. 'It's make-your-mind-up time. Either ya plead to possessin that offensive weapon, or ya gonna get ya brains blowed to the dark sidea the fuckin moon.' He levelled the shooter at the skinhead, both hands gripping its butt, and added, 'Which'll it be?' – the shooter hadn't actually been loaded by Tasty, but the *skinhead* didn't know that.

The skinhead's face was now ashen, but he still said, '*No!*' – he *still* couldn't believe they were going to shoot him.

'Either ya plead or ya'll go to a higher court for sentence,' Tasty warned. His right index-finger was pressuring the trigger, and his left eye was shut tight as he sighted the shooter on the skinhead's nose.

'Come on, dear boy,' shouted Snatch. 'This is ya last chance.'

'No, no, *no*!' yelled the skinhead.

'Right, ya gonna fuckin *get* it, then,' Tasty said, and he

began squeezing even harder at the trigger . . . slowly, determinedly, his legs spread, his body in a half squat.

The skinhead stopped struggling, turned sideways and blinked furiously, trying to shy away . . . and then screamed one *hell* of a scream, as he heard a loud report, and *saw* flame and smoke, boring from the shooter's barrel; then he fainted, and his knees hit the concrete yard, as the 'cuffs slid with the weight of his body, down to the bottom of the drainpipe, while the discharged bullet, whooshing through the air towards where his head had been, ricocheted off the brickwork of the wall, tearing out a chunk, and went Christ knew where . . .

Snatch just stood there, his mouth hanging open, not believing it, as he looked at the unconscious skinhead . . . the hole in the brickwork . . . the bewildered Tasty Tom.

'Well fuck a duck an bugger a bat,' mumbled Tasty, peering down the barrel of the smoking shooter. 'It wasn't *s'posed* to be loaded . . . *Someone* must've left one in line with the *barrel* . . .'

And then the Transit swept into the yard, its driver, Hercules, blasting the horn, lest another vehicle should be about to leave.

'What the fuck's goin *on* here?' said Punchy Paterson, echoing the very words the skinhead had uttered when first led out into the yard.

'Dunno,' said Hercules, bringing the Transit to a halt.

'They've *shot* a *prisoner*!' exclaimed MacHale. '. . . *Murdered* him!'

'Oh, Christ,' wailed Francis Harvey, sitting in the back of the Transit. 'Are they *allowed* to do that?'

Punchy Paterson looked over his shoulder, from the front passenger seat. 'New law, passed this mornin,' he told Harvey. 'Anyone who don't admit his guilt, we execute. Saves the courts wastin all that time, *findin* em guilty.'

'Oh, Christ,' repeated Harvey, and he began shaking from head to toes.

'Watchya got, then?' Barker wanted to know as he walked from the front office, eating an apple. He looked first at Punchy Paterson, then at the kid, Harvey, ignoring MacHale's presence.

'Sus and goin equipped, Sarge,' Punchy replied, removing his helmet and placing it on a nearby desk. 'Four handles on car-doors in Harper's Street . . . the car-park opposite the Astoria.'

Barker bit into his apple, speaking as he ate: 'You mean . . . interferin with motor vehicles,' he corrected, between chews and swallows. 'Sus went out the window . . . a couplea years ago . . . Remember?'

Punchy shrugged. 'Same thing.'

'Yeah, I s'pose. What's the goin equipped?'

Punchy held up for Barker's inspection, the Ford key. 'In the back pocket of his jeans. But he don't *own* a car, and he don't *drive* a car . . . unless it's one he's nicked, that is.'

Barker turned aside and lobbed the apple core into the corner of the charge-room, spitting out a pip before turning back to face Punchy Paterson. 'Any property in the motors, was there?'

Punchy nodded. 'Radios, cassettes . . . stuff in the boots, too, I s'pose. I've got all the index numbers, so's we can check, if need be.' He had, in fact, checked the interiors of the vehicles in question – from their outsides – while awaiting the arrival of the van.

'Okay,' Barker said, satisfied. 'I've just gotta bail out that Clone Queen, over there, and then I'm yours.' He nodded towards the wall bench, where Hercules, seated, was in conversation with a homosexual he'd earlier arrested for importuning in a public toilet.

Barker, hands stuck in pockets, sauntered back to the front office.

As they waited, the charge-room door swung inward, and Tasty Tom, assisted by old Snatch, struggled in, carrying a half-comatose skinhead who was groaning and muttering that he'd be prepared to plead to *anything*, just so long as they promised not to take him out again into the yard, and make a *proper* job of getting him his brains blowed to the dark side of the moon.

Now, Punchy led the kid, Harvey, into the detention room, where he sat him down on a rickety wooden chair, and stood before him, sizing him up. 'Okay, Frank,' he began, his tone unusually docile. 'Ya know what you're in the frame for, so let's not waste time. If ya duck ya nut and make a statement, things'll be sweet. There *might* even be a bitta bail, later on. Whaddaya say?'

The kid spread his hands and affected a wide-open expression: dilated eyes, creased brow, half-open mouth. Tacitly, it said, What can I *do*?

'You are bang to rights,' Punchy assured, mimicking Harvey's expression.

'So what's the hassle?' Harvey came back, looking alternately at MacHale and Punchy. 'It's two to one, which means I'm a million to go down, I s'pose. But I ain't pleadin to nothin I ain't done, am I?' His expression and tone of voice reflected sincerity and a reluctance to displease, but somewhere there, there was a trace of restrained resentment and defiance.

For his part, Punchy affected nonchalance, and twitched his shoulders and stuck his hands in his pockets. 'Makes no difference to us. Might just be easier for *you*, if it's gonna be a plea.' Now he addressed MacHale: 'Get his full pars and do a name-check on him. I'll bag-up his property and put him in the bin, till he's ready to be stuck on the sheet. He'll come round sweet. Eventually.'

'Will do,' MacHale eagerly said – the VDU – on which

the name-check had to processed – was in the comms room; and so was Pat. At the same time, though, as feeling a lift in his spirits, he felt a little uneasy about this job. Certainly he was a witness to the kid's presence in the car-park, and to his possession of the Ford key; also, he could corroborate Punchy's questioning of the kid, when they'd pulled him as he was about to leave the car-park.

But was the kid really *guilty* of what he was about to go on the sheet for? Had Punchy *really* seen him trying several of the cars' door-handles? And what was more, would Punchy expect him, MacHale, to corroborate *that*, as well?

He couldn't. All he could tell was what he'd seen and heard . . . Which fed him straight into another dilemma: what if they were cross-examined on an allegation that the kid had been assaulted? Punchy *had* tried to lob him through the side of that Sherpa van . . . and he *had* kicked him in the buttocks. Cops were expected to protect one another, but MacHale was convinced he just wouldn't be able to look the Magistrate in the eye and *deny* the kid was hit by Punchy. And the only person who would understand why would be Pat.

After questioning Harvey, and eliciting the information he required for a name-check, MacHale left the charge-room and made his way along to the comms room, holding a message-pad form with details of the kid's pars on it.

She was seated at a desk, when he entered the room, sifting through the AS-messages, a ball-point pen jutting from the corner of her mouth.

She glanced up, looked back down at the message-pad, then did a double take, smiling broadly and removing the pen from her mouth. '*Hello*, John,' she enthused, leaning back in her chair. 'Where've *you* been, all day?' Her tunic was slung around the chair's back, so she was in shirt-sleeve order, the shirt, crisp and white and shiny, smelling of a fabric softener.

'Oh, out-'n'-about,' he told her, returning the smile as he moved to stand by her side. 'I've just come in with a body. Well, it's Punchy's body, actually . . . I'm just a witness.'

'Of course,' she said. 'You asked for the van.'

'Are you busy in here?' He looked at the messages, stacked neatly in their binders, on the desk; the SMs had several slips of paper protruding from their binder, denoting places where there were outstanding entries that would either have to be marked with results or handed over to the next Relief at the end of this tour. 'You seem to be in control of everything.'

'Naturally,' she said. 'I shall want a charge-number in respect of your message for the van, too.' And she smiled a modest smile.

'Big head,' he joked.

She laughed and then glanced at the message-pad form in his right hand. 'So what can we do for you?'

'A name-check is what I'd like, actually, Pat. On Punchy's body.' He gave her the form.

She looked at the details of the prisoner's full name, age, date of birth, place of birth, and height . . . a note of a distinguishing mark, too, which was the small scar Harvey had on the bridge of his nose; not that there were likely to be too many *Possibles* on someone with the name Francis *Elvis* Harvey.

She took the form across to Dave Hall and asked him to do the check. Hall got to his feet, winced, rubbed his gut, where he'd been scarred by his operation for the removal of a growth, and walked on over to the set, pulling up a swivel chair and putting on his glasses.

God, how I'd love to make love to her, thought MacHale, as she returned to stand before him; it was those eyes, those mischievously jovial, hazel eyes.

He coughed embarrassedly, and pulled his right index-finger around the inside of the collar of his shirt, as if it were too tight – and maybe it was, temporarily, because his throat had swelled up in response to what he'd felt for her. 'I was just wondering, Pat,' he began, hoping that his face didn't look as flushed as it felt hot, 'if maybe we . . .' He broke off, gulping words and saliva. She'd turned away and was looking in the direction of the teleprinter room, which was located at the far side of the comms room; the machinery in there had just been activated, and was clattering noisily, like a whole pool of touch typists who were on piecework.

'Just a minute, John, please,' she told him, walking towards the teleprinter room. 'It might be an Emercall.'

Oh, *hell*! he inwardly cursed. *Now* I'll have to start all over again. He followed her. The teleprinter room, despite its noisy atmosphere, was, anyway, a far better place to proposition her, he'd decided; in there, there were no witnesses or eavesdroppers.

She leaned over the top of the long machine and reached out to pick up the loose end of the type-roll, examining its face. 'Early-warning list for the Bailey and Crown Courts,' she commented.

She dropped the teleprinter paper and turned aside, looking at him, studying his flushed face and his apprehensive expression. 'What's the matter with you?' she asked.

'What? Oh, nothing,' he quickly said, his left hand now moving involuntarily to finger the knot of his clip-on tie.

'You'll be all right, tonight, then?' she said.

'*Tonight?*'

'Yes, tonight,' she repeated. 'I thought we'd arranged to meet, after work . . . Last night, during our walk.'

'*Did* we?' he said, amazed. '*I* don't . . .' And then he fell in: she'd intuitively identified his predicament and had come, as diplomatically as she'd known how, to his aid. 'Yes, yes, of course,' he apologetically gushed.

She was smiling. 'Good. I'll see you later, then.' Now the teleprinter reclaimed her attention, and she turned away and sat before it, studying its output.

'Great,' he said. 'Ten-thirty, at the yard gates. See ya.' And he bounced out of the teleprinter room, reexperiencing the intumescent expectation of a kid on Christmas Eve.

He was halfway out the door of the comms room when he heard Dave Hall, calling him back. He stopped, and popped his head around the door. 'Yes, Dave?'

Hall held up a message-pad form, fluttering its paper. 'Your name-check: Known but Not Wanted.'

'Oh, cheers, I'd forgotten it,' MacHale said, and collected the piece of paper.

He then went back to the door of the teleprinter room. 'By the way,' he said to Pat. 'Where was it that we'd decided to go, tonight, when we made the arrangement, *last* night?' His tongue wasn't in his cheek, but maybe he looked conspiratorially smug.

'My place,' she smiled. 'For a TV supper.'

'I like it,' he said.

TV supper, he thought, as he returned, spring-heeled, to the charge-room . . . At *her* place. A shiver of excitement then ran through him.

When he reached the charge-room, he found himself in the middle of a well-stoked argument that was taking place between two DCs, with Barker acting as referee; while, below the wall bench, Old Crikey, Punchy Paterson and Hercules were huddled together, kneeling over the body of a young black kid – a robbery suspect – who was lying three-quarters prone in a thick red pool of blood, his right arm held high in the air, by Hercules, his ebony complexion turning a ghastly shade of caramel.

'It's *down* to *you*!' one DC shouted at the other DC.

'Down to *me*! Don't talk crap! *You* were s'posed to be searchin him!'

'And *you* were s'posed to be holdin his arms!'

'Well how the fuck did *I* know he'd pull out a blade and stripe his wrist?'

'All right, all right!' snapped Barker, moving to separate the two protagonists. 'Never mind *whose* fault it was. It's done. And now *we've* gotta square it up.'

Old Crikey looked back across the room, at the two DCs and Barker, his face screwed-up with anguish, as he began raising himself to his feet. 'Where's that amb – ?' But that was as far as he got, before gouging a chunk out of his nut, as it struck the ridge of the wall bench; he fell back down onto his knees, sucking in a huge gasp of air, which rushed back out as, '*Kerrrr-ikey!*'

With one hand clamped over his nut, he started shouting at Punchy Paterson and Hercules, 'Keep his arm up high! . . .' – another gasp of air as he felt a rush of pain to his head – '. . . and keep your finger on that pressure point! . . .' Then, after a further gasp of air, he jabbed the finger of his free hand at the two DCs, and yelled, 'As for *you* two: get out of my *sight*! *Now!*' Finally, he stalked off out to his office, wincing and muttering, looking for a first-aid box – for *himself*. After allowing Old Crikey sufficient time to get well clear, the DCs followed on, resuming their argument over whose fault it was that the black kid had striped his wrist.

By Christ, thought MacHale. Poor Old Crikey's nut hasn't half taken some stick, lately. Maybe he ought to get it comprehensively insured? Or start wearing a riot helmet, while he's inside the nick?

'MacHale!' shouted Barker, startling MacHale. 'Don't just *stand* there, dreamin like a schoolgirl on heat. Get y'self prepared to accompany that ambulance, when it arrives.'

'But . . . I've got a body in the detention room,

Sarge,' MacHale protested. 'I've got notes of evidence to compile.'

'Never mind about *that,*' Barker irritably snapped. 'That can wait. You can refer to Punchy's IRB, when you get back.'

Inwardly, MacHale tut-tutted and cursed, and then the ambulance crew walked in, carrying a stretcher, and red blankets, and the black kid was quickly wrapped and strapped and carted away, MacHale walking by his side, wondering why the two DCs couldn't have been deputed to accompany the prisoner . . . *their* prisoner.

MacHale climbed into the ambulance and sat opposite the black kid, whose torso was soaked in thick, arterial blood. MacHale could scarcely bear to look at it . . . and didn't have to, so averted his eyes. He'd been turned over, for as long as he could remember, by the sight of a lot of blood, although he'd never confess that to another, and was loath to confess it to himself.

The ambulance accelerated smoothly and quietly across the yard . . . down the ramp, its two-tones and blue light cutting through the dark evening as it entered the main street. MacHale's eyes blanked off, and he remembered how Sister Mary had told them that when they received Holy Communion they must never dare bite the Host; it was the *body* of *Christ*, to be consumed by osmosis on the still tongue of the mouth. And just to be *sure* they'd never, ever forget the lesson, she'd mesmerized them with the cautionary tale of a small lad who *had* dared chew the Host, and whose mouth had immediately become a gusher of the red-hot thick blood of Christ; the little lad had *drowned* in Christ's blood . . . and, for his sin, was committed to the raging fires of *hell*!

But how *could* this God, who was credited with supernatural qualities of pity, understanding and forgiveness, at the same time be so wickedly cruel as to cast an errant child eternally to hell? MacHale had rejected this God in favour of his *own* God, who was all which He ought to be; He smiled fondly upon you if you tried your utmost to do what was right and proper and just, and He understood if you should err, and seek forgiveness.

But always the spectre was there, haunting MacHale. And even now, as the ambulance careened and shrieked its way through the rush-hour traffic, he felt sick and guilty and ashamed.

14

The black kid had lost a considerable quantity of blood, but was in no real danger of dying. On admission, he'd undergone emergency surgery, and was now confined to a private room on the third floor of the hospital, where he was bedridden, surrounded by anxious relatives – obese Negro women with gaily-coloured bowler-hats, and skinny little Negro men with baggy suits – who were invoking the name of *their* God, and making promises as to future conduct, which they'd be either unable or unwilling to fulfil, should the kid be spared.

Outside the room was an equally anxious MacHale, whose restless pacing of the wide, brightly lit, deathly silent and deserted corridor, with its high ceiling and white-gloss walls, was intermittently broken by pauses at the room's closed door, when he'd peer in through the small square of wired glass, at the kid's bed. Supposing the kid were now to try and finish off the job, by jumping out of the window? He wasn't chained to that bed in there, and the room's window wasn't barred or locked.

It'd be down to MacHale, too, if he did finish up as a shovel-and-binsack job, down below, on the concrete surface of the hospital's car-park.

MacHale left the door and continued his slow, aimless pacing. It wasn't *only* the possibility that the kid might top himself, which had made MacHale eager to get away from here. It was already half an hour past his scheduled booking-off time, and he still hadn't been relieved by a night-duty PC. When he'd phoned the nick, at half-past ten – thirty minutes ago, now – he'd been told by the night-duty Reserve that the late Relief was being held back until one of its members, who'd failed to report for booking-off, was accounted for; the Reserve hadn't known who it was that had gone missing, only that every available officer was standing by to undertake a sweep of the streets, in an effort to locate him.

Wonder if it's Old Crikey? MacHale had afterwards thought. All those cracks on the nut, lately, might've sent him *right* over the top; he might've gone and chucked himself in the Thames; and nobody'd know for sure, till some ol' vagie, who regularly scavenged on the embankment, first thing in the morning, was nicked for impersonating a Police Inspector.

'Found you at *last*,' said a voice, cutting through MacHale's thoughts. 'It's just like Hampton Court maze, in here, innit?'

MacHale stopped pacing, and about turned. It was his relief, Steve King, a night-duty officer, who was carrying a white-plastic lunch-box, a couple of paperbacks, and a PR. 'Yeah,' agreed MacHale. 'You could easily get lost in this building. Glad you found me, anyway.'

King walked over to the door that entranced the black kid's room, then leaned forward and peered in through the square of glass. 'Who's that firm of hot-gospellers in there?' he wanted to know. 'The spook's family?'

'Yeah, family,' MacHale confirmed.

'Hmm. He gonna kick it, is he?'

'Na. Shouldn't think so.'

'Pity,' said King, disappointed. 'He's got fifteen handbag-snatches down to him, y'know. Last month, I was up here with one of his victims, an old dear, about seventy, with defence wounds all over her hands, and a broken nose, where he'd put the boot in on her. One of her fingers was just hangin off on a stripa skin . . . Black enamelled cunt, *deserves* to die.'

Although MacHale didn't disagree, he did warn King

that the kid might die, anyway, if he took it into his head to take a dive out of the window.

King smiled. 'If he gives *me* a Bell, first, *I'll* shoot in there and give him a fuckin *hand*, no problem . . . By the way, where's Hitler in drag?'

'*Who?*'

'You know: the Sister-in-charge. They're all a bit that way, these Sisters-'n'-Matrons. Think they're runnin fuckin Guards' Depots, not hospitals.'

MacHale laughed; then pointed along the corridor and said, 'Way down there's where the Sister is. First on the right, in the ward.'

King took a manila envelope from the breast pocket of his tunic. 'Better give her this, I s'pose.'

'What is it?'

'Oh, just a notice, informin her that chummy in there is a prisoner who'll be taken charge of by us when he's fit to leave. We have to serve it on the hospital, so's they know what's what. 'Kay, then. You'd better shoot off,' King told him. 'There's a GP, waiting in the car-park.'

'By the way, Steve,' MacHale said as he started to go. 'I forgot to ask. Who was it that failed to book-off at ten-thirty?'

'Oh, that,' said King. 'That was nothin. It was just that piss-artist, Mathieson. Quite amusin, really. Apparently, he got his head down in a lost-or-stolen van, during the evening and while he was bombed-out in the back of the van, the owner of it came along to pick it *up*. He signed for it at the front office, then drove it *away*.

'And fuckin Mathieson, a couple of hours later, wakes up, locked in a garage in the middlea fuckin Wimbledon, about ten miles off his beat.'

MacHale folded up with laughter, imagining it. 'And what happened then?'

'Apparently, it was a greengrocer's van, and the garage is tacked-on to the shop. So, Mathieson, *eventually*, finds a side door, *into* the shop, where he Bells the nick, who have to turn out the keyholder to set him free.'

MacHale was still chuckling when he reached the car-park.

On his arrival back at the nick, he discovered that Pat had left for home.

She's blown me out, he thought, feeling miserable. But his spirits lifted when he went to his corres' tray in the Collator's office and found that she'd left a message for him: he was to call at her place when he'd finished duty at the hospital, no matter how late the hour.

He left the Collator's office and made his way downstairs to the charge-room, where the night-duty Station Officer, together with two of the four Section Sergeants, was knee-deep in bodies, arresting officers and paperwork. MacHale walked across the room, sidestepping a tangle of raucous drunks who were enmeshed with their arresting officers, and was halfway through the door to the front office when he was called back by the Station Officer, who was seated at a desk, doing some one-fingered typing.

'Sarge?' MacHale stood at the SO's side.

The SO paused in his work and glanced up. 'Punchy Paterson asked me to deliver some corres' to you. You'll find it on my desk in the front office. You've gotta do an IRB or somethin. For a body you nicked, earlier on.'

'Oh! . . . Yes, Sarge,' MacHale said, touching his left temple and rolling his eyes, ceilingward. 'I'd forgotten about that. Shall I give it to you, for checking, when it's done?'

The SO shook his head. 'I don't wanna see it.' He'd resumed his typing. 'I'm up to my eyes, here. Anyway, if I was you I'd leave it till tomorrow. Shoot off home, now, and sleep on it. There's no panic.'

MacHale briefly hesitated. 'Well . . . if you say so,

Sarge.' Notes of evidence were supposed to be completed at the *time* of an incident, or as soon afterwards as possible; in fact, MacHale should at least have begun to compile them while he was kicking his heels at the hospital.

'I just *did* say so,' remarked the SO, not looking up, and having indicated, with his tone of voice, that the matter was ended; he was under considerable pressure, here.

MacHale walked into the front office and collected the corres' from the Sergeant's desk – case-history folder, copy of charge-sheet, and Punchy's IRB; no statement under caution, though, which meant that Harvey hadn't been induced to make a plea, in writing; which, in turn, undoubtedly meant that he'd decided he *wasn't* pleading.

Then MacHale took the Book One from the long shelf of official registers, and looked up Pat's name, making a written note of her address and telephone number, which she had forgotten to give him. Then he dared to use the SO's telephone to call her up and tell her he'd be over in about three-quarters of an hour, after he'd completed his IRB – *no* Sergeant could legitimately tell him to breach the Discipline Code, he'd decided.

When he'd made the call, he returned to the now-deserted Collator's office, and sat at a table, taking off his tunic and slinging it around the back of the chair; then he snapped-off his tie and rolled-up the cuffs of his shirt. She was pleased he'd still be coming, and had said she'd start preparing some food; there'd been music playing in the background, too . . . it had sounded like Cliff Richard . . . Had she let down her hair? he wondered . . . And what was she wearing . . .?

Reluctantly, he forced himself back to the paperwork before him on the desk; then he took an unused IRB from the fold-over wallet which he kept in the back pocket of his trousers, and got down to work.

First, he examined the copy charge-sheet, and saw that Harvey was on for two offences: Unlawfully Interfering with Motor Vehicles, contrary to Section 9(1), Criminal Attempts Act, 1980; and Going Equipped for Theft, contrary to Section 25, Theft Act, 1968. Then he began reading Punchy's IRB, wondering how much of the evidence he would be able to corroborate.

The notes began, 'On DDTP, saw acc. in centre of car-park, standing next to a white Merc' sal. After looking about himself, for sev. secs., acc. moved his L. hand to driver's door of veh. I saw veh. rock from side-to-side. Acc. then moved around veh. to passenger door. Again, his L. hand touched veh's handle, and, as bef., veh. rocked. Acc. then moved along line of vehs. to a red Datsun sal., pausing at its driver's door. He looked about himself, backed up to door, placed R. hand beh. his back, and jerked forward with his upper body. The Datsun rocked. Now acc. walked along to a blue BMW sal. and stood at passenger's side. He glanced up and down, then bent forward and looked into veh. At this stage, I was joined by PC MacH. and together we kept acc. under obs.

"Acc. stood up by side of BMW, then ducked down, and I saw the veh. rock back and forth. Next, acc. moved along side of BMW, to a red Vaux. Cav. sal., his head moving around in a circle as he looked up, down, and around park. Then he bent forward and looked inside the veh. His body was obscured by veh., but as he bent I noticed veh. rock to and fro. Acc. then stood and walked to passenger side of veh., his eyes roving the park. Once again, he bent forward and looked in thro. closed windows of veh. before standing and moving away.

"Then, a man, wearing a dk. suit, ent. car-park and walked towards acc. Acc. began walking away. A group of five men then ent. car-park, and acc., on seeing them, began to leave. Myself and PC MacH. stopped acc. . . .'

MacHale looked up to the ceiling, his eyes vacuous. *He* didn't know if Harvey had tried the door-handles of a Merc' and a Datsun; when these incidents were alleged to have taken place, MacHale wasn't even present. Neither could he say that Harvey had tried the door-handles of the BMW and the Vauxhall; he hadn't seen those vehicles rock from side-to-side. In fact, at the time, he was certain that Punchy had imagined having seen them move. What he could say, though, was that he'd seen Harvey at the side of the BMW, bending down; he'd also seen him move on to the Vauxhall and look inside it.

He lowered his eyes and continued reading Punchy's notes of evidence, which now proceeded to recount the Q-'n'-A session which had taken place after Harvey was stopped. And the more MacHale read, the more disturbed he became. The account was almost wholly fictitious. Harvey had been verballed, to a degree almost beyond belief:

Q: I've been watching you for the last twenty minutes. First, I saw you try the driver's door-handle of a white Mercedes. Then you tried the passenger's door-handle. Moving on, you went to a red Datsun and tried the handle of that vehicle, as well. Next, you walked to a blue BMW, looked inside it, and the vehicle rocked. Finally, I saw you go to a red Vauxhall and look inside that vehicle, which also rocked to-and-fro. I think you were trying to steal a car, or steal from a car. What have you got to say to that?
A: No. No. I'm sorry, officer, you're wrong.
Q: Do you own any of the vehicles in this park?
A: Acc. hesitated, then said, Well, no, I don't.
Q: Then why are you here, in the park?
A: Waiting for a mate. He said he'd meet me here, after I'd been to the pictures.
Q: What's his name, then?
A: (After a long silence) Dunno, do I? I just met him in a snooker hall, a couple of days ago, and arranged to meet him here tonight. We was going clubbing, up West . . . Wait a minute . . .. Craig's the name of the bloke. That's right, Craig.

Q: And where does he live?
A: Dunno. Never asked. Bermondsey, I think.
Q: Has he got a car?
A: Yeah, 'course he has.
Q: What make and colour?
A: Dunno. Haven't seen it, have I? He just said to wait here and he'd pick me up.
Q: At what time?
A: Four o'clock.
Q: It's now a quarter to five. Where is he?
A: Let me down, I s'pose.
Q: Why didn't he arrange to pick you up at the snooker hall, where you'd first met him? Why here?
A: 'Cause I'd arranged to go to the pictures, hadn't I? Like I said. Over there, the Astoria.
Q: And did you go?
A: Yeah. Earlier on.
Q: What film is showing?
A: N/R.
Q: Well? You said you saw the film.
A: Acc. shrugged. I must've fell asleep, mustn't I? Missed it.
Q: (After C) As I said before, I believe you were here to steal.
A: Acc. stared at his feet and made N/R.
Q: What have you got in your pockets?

Acc. emptied his pockets, which contained no property of relevance to the charges.

Q: (To PC MacH.) Check his pockets.

PC MacH. then checked accused's pockets, and, in the rear pocket of accused's denims, found a key. (Exhibit JM/1.)

Q: (By PC MacH. in P-and-H of acc.) Look, there's this.
Q: (By me, to acc.) This is a Ford car key. Do you own a Ford car?
A: No.
Q: Have you ever owned a Ford car?
A: No.
Q: Do you know anyone who owns a Ford car?
A: No . . . Wait a minute, yeah. 'Course, that's right, innit? Craig's got a Ford, hasn't he? He must have given me the key when he paid me for losing at snooker. That's it. It must've been in with his loose change. And that's why he ain't turned up: he can't start the car, can he?
Q: And how, then, would he have driven it away from the snooker hall, after he'd paid you, if he didn't have the key?

A: Oh . . . I dunno, do I? Maybe he had a spare or something.
Q: A moment ago, when I asked you what type of car Craig's got, you said you didn't know. You said you'd never seen his car.
A: (After a lengthy pause) Oh shit! Okay, all right. What's the fucking point?
Q: Now do you want to tell me why you are in the car-park? Why you're really here, I mean?
A: It's obvious, innit?
Q: Well, I want you to tell me.
A: I dunno . . . I was hard-up, wasn't I? Borasic lint – skint. I was just looking for a radio, I s'pose. Something I could nick, and then knock out for a few quid.

Arr. acc. To stn. CCC. No reply.

Jesus Christ, MacHale thought. You could put this lot up for the Pulitzer Prize.

Then he was struck by an attack of panic. What the hell was he now going to *do*? All he knew for certain was what he *wasn't* going to do. He stood, clipped on his tie and rolled down the cuffs of his shirt. Then he went down into the basement of the building, to the locker room, hung up his tunic, put away his helmet, and shrugged into his anorak.

Pat would know what to do, he was sure. She *had* to know what to do.

MacHale paid off the taxi and stood on the pavement, glancing at his wristwatch – twelve-twenty A.M. The street, dark and empty of people, was lined either side with semi-detached houses, wide, four-storey-high blocks of flats, chestnut trees, and vehicles, parked bumper-to-bumper.

A light, chilling breeze rustled the heavy silence, swishing through leaf-buds and twigs in the tall trees. He shivered, and stuck his hands in his trousers pockets as he moved across the pavement and passed in through the swing doors of the block's foyer, halting in front of the lift, and jabbing a forefinger at its illuminated *Call*-button.

When the lift reached the third floor, he stepped out and turned left along the brightly-lit corridor, his rubber-soled boots squeaking on the highly-polished, grey-vinyl tiles; but he'd gone the wrong way: Pat's number was twenty-seven, and while the door of the first flat he came to was number twenty-five, the next door along was twenty-four. He retraced his steps, and arrived at Pat's door – painted glossy red, with brass furniture, and a coconut-fibre mat beneath it, imprinted with the word, *Welcome*. He stabbed at the bell-push, and waited, his hands moving over his hair, smoothing it, a finger now wiping the inner corner of each of his eyes . . . his left hand adjusting the knot of his tie.

The door opened halfway, and she peered out, opening fully the door when she saw him. 'You've arrived, at last, then,' she smiled, and stepped aside as she waved him in.

'And to prove it, I'm here,' he replied, forcing a return of smile as he wiped his boots on the doormat and moved in past her to stand in the warm, narrow hallway. He immediately noticed that she'd let down her hair; it looked great, too, he thought, falling in shiny, undulating tresses around her shoulders; so much better than that regulation bun she wore for duty. She was dressed in a wine-coloured sweater – no bra, either, he believed – and tight-fitting blue denims; her feet were bare.

'This way,' she said, walking past him and making for the first door on the right.

He followed, his eyes falling to her buttocks and legs; the denims really looked good on her; maybe she was still a little too wide at the hips, but there was terrific definition there, all the same.

'Sit down, John,' she told him, pointing to a brown-cord three-seater settee against the right wall of the softly-lit living room. 'I'll get you a drink from the fridge.'

'Thanks. Just what I need,' he said, watching her movements as she left the room. Then he took off his anorak and draped it over an arm of the settee, before sitting and unclipping his tie, then loosening his shirt collar.

Very nice, he thought, as his eyes roved the room. To his right, the wide, picture window was covered by dark-red velvet curtains, while before him, against the far wall, was a large, dark-wood unit, with leaded door-glasses, which contained an array of leather-bound books, a brass carriage-clock, china, copper and brass ornaments, a TV-set and a stereo music-centre; there were two armchairs, as well, flanking the settee, one a recliner, and both in a matching brown-cord, and at his left side was a glass-top coffee table which bore a tray, covered with a square of white, starched linen; resisting an urge to pick up a corner of the square of linen, he merely supposed that beneath it was a plate or two of sandwiches. The surrounding walls were decorated with a white, embossed paper, hung with framed, landscape prints and bird portraits, and the floor was wall-to-wall with a deep-pile carpet which matched the curtains.

'Do you want ice, John?' she shouted from . . . the kitchen, he supposed.

'What's the drink?'

'Lager.'

'No, thanks.' – ice in *beer*? What was she *thinking* of? Most of today's beer was watery enough as it was.

She returned to the room, carrying two empty plates, a pint mug of frothy lager and a small glass of white wine. 'There we are,' she smiled, bending and holding forth the mug.

'Oh, thanks,' he said. He took the beer, raised it carefully to his lips, and downed about a third of it, straight off. 'Terrific,' he sighed, licking froth from his upper lip, then set down the mug on the coffee table.

She put the plates next to his mug, then sat beside him, pulling the coffee table up to their knees. 'Sandwich?' She removed the square of linen from the tray, folded it, and placed it aside. 'There're all sorts, here: cheese-'n'-tomato, ham-'n'-pickle, prawn-'n'-lettuce – my favourite, they are – and . . . let's see.' She lifted up the corner of a sandwich, and inspected its content. 'Yes. Dressed crab . . . Wholemeal bread, too, and a low-cholesterol spread.'

'Not at the moment, thanks, Pat,' he said, sounding tired, and leaning forward to take another swallow of lager. 'I'm not all that hungry, really.'

'Oh.' She looked quizzically at him, very briefly, then let it go. 'Later, perhaps, then.' She picked up last evening's paper, and began opening it at the TV-page, then stopped and said, 'Ooh, that reminds me: did you hear about Mathieson, tonight? What happened to him?'

'Yes,' he said, making himself smile at the recollection of it. 'Steve King told me, at the hospital.'

She shook her head, smiling, and resumed her inspection of the paper's TV-page. 'Shall I put the telly on?'

'What's showing?' he asked, not sounding bothered, one way or the other.

Her eyes roved up and down the page . . . then she tilted her left wrist and glanced at her watch . . . looked back at the paper. *'Night Thoughts,'* she dismally said. 'Something to do with religion, I suppose.'

'Oh Christ,' he wearily muttered.

'Yes, that's it,' she laughed.

For a while, there was an uneasy silence. Then she stood, walked across to the unit, and began taking LPs from the stack that was adjacent to the music centre, holding them up for his inspection. 'Shall I put one on, John? There's a varied selection, here: Cliff Richard, The Beatles, Elton John, Bob Marley . . . UB-Forty . . .'

He shrugged non-committally. 'If you like.'

She replaced the LPs and returned to sit at his side,

turning inward to face him and heaving out a sigh. 'Okay. What's the matter? Something's wrong, I can tell . . . Isn't there?'

'Yeah,' he admitted, staring at the carpet, relieved that she'd at least asked.

'Well what, for heaven's sake?' she said. 'Maybe I can help . . . *if* you'll tell me. Is it something *I've* done . . . or *said*?'

'Hell no,' he earnestly responded. 'It's nothing that's down to you, Pat.'

'Well *what*?' she repeated.

He had difficulty understanding why he was reluctant to unload the problem. An hour ago, at the nick, when he'd been confronted by it, he hadn't even considered *not* telling her; in fact, she was the only person who *could* be told. He supposed that it was the nature of their relationship which was holding him back. The *man* was expected to be the torch-bearer of a heterosexual relationship, wasn't he? *He* was supposed to be the one who shouldered the difficulties and hefted the responsibilities and resolved the problems; reverse that role and maybe the man would be emasculated – or would feel as if he were.

But that was ridiculous, he decided: Pat was the one, so far as their profession was concerned, who had most of the experience.

He took a swallow of his lager, followed by a deep breath. 'It's that job I had with Punchy Paterson,' he began. 'As you know, I had to escort that black kid to hospital, so I wasn't present when Punchy made his notes. He didn't even *discuss* the evidence with me, beforehand. Come to that, he didn't even discuss the evidence with *Barker*, when we brought the body to the nick. He just said the offences were sus and going equipped, and Barker accepted it.'

'Typical,' she sagely nodded. 'Arresting PCs are *supposed* to make their notes of evidence as soon as they get to the nick, and then read them out in the presence of the body and the SO, so as the SO knows what facts'll be presented at court, and whether the alleged offences can be charged and substantiated. But *do* they? *Never* . . . Of course, you already know *that*, though.'

'Don't I just,' he agreed. 'Anyway, Harvey – that's the body's name – was charged and binned-up, and Punchy left the case-papers on the SO's desk, so's I could refer to his IRB when I got back from the hospital. But he's verballed him, Pat. It's a pack of lies, from start to finish, and he obviously expects me to back him up.'

'Oh *does* he, now?' she defiantly said.

'Well, yeah. Of course he does. But . . . I mean, how's it gonna look, tomorrow morning, at court, if Punchy gets up in the box and gives his spiel, and then I follow on and say something entirely different? No doubt the kid *is* guilty, but – '

'That's how these problems arise,' she cut in. 'Officers themselves deciding guilt, when the defendant ought to be given a straight run on the legitimately-available evidence.'

'I can see that,' agreed MacHale. 'And, here, the ridiculous part of it is that the legitimately-available evidence might just have been sufficient to get a conviction. Harvey was *in* the car-park, he *was* looking inside cars that didn't belong to him, and he did *have* an old car-key in his possession, too – a jiggler.'

'Tell me the story, from start to end,' she said. 'Then we can try and work out what to do.'

He took the case-papers from his anorak and went through everything, carefully pointing out where Punchy Paterson's evidence was at variance with what had, to MacHale's certain knowledge, actually taken place.

When he'd finished, she leaned back and clasped her

hands behind her head, thinking . . . At length, she said, 'You know, John, the irony of it is that if Punchy had *really* asked all of those questions which he later invented, he'd probably have *got* those answers from Harvey, in response . . . Or very similar ones, anyway.'

'Why didn't he, then, Pat? That's what I don't understand. Soon as he found out that Harvey didn't own a car, and that he had that key, he nicked him. Christ, we thought old Snatch was a bit on the swift side, but *this* . . .'

'Most cops're that way,' she said. 'Too eager, too impatient. Just can't wait to get their prize back to the nick, and show it off. A bad lack of skills in questioning is a problem, too. They often run out of questions, and resort to threats and violence.'

'That's Punchy, all right, anyway,' MacHale said. 'And a few of the others, too. What am I gonna do, though, Pat?'

'Well, for a start, you're not going to tell lies for Punchy Paterson.'

'Right.'

'So that leaves two choices, really.'

'Which are?'

'First,' she said, 'you go, immediately, right here and now, to CO, and ask to see the night-duty Reserve at CIB-Two, telling him everything you've told me. Punchy'll be seen, suspended from duty, and the matter'll be investigated.'

'Jesus Christ!' exclaimed MacHale, horrified by the idea of such consequences. 'I can't do *that*! What'll the others say? . . . What'll they *do*? They'd crucify me. *You* said, last night, they'd crucify anyone who made allegations like that. You said the CID'd maybe find a piece of dope in your house, or something. You *said* that, Pat.'

'And I believe it, too,' she returned. 'But that course of action is *open* to you.'

'Tell me about the second one,' he quickly said.

'Okay. You write-up your IRB, including only those facts which you know for *sure* go with Harvey's case . . . how you saw him, in the car-park, and how you found the key. Then you put down the Q-'n'-A session as *you* heard it, leaving out all the verbals.'

'And after that?'

'Tomorrow, if Harvey admits his guilt, that'll be the end of it. No one'll check the IRBs and see that yours differs from Paterson's. But, most important, you get hold of that Paterson, afterwards, and leave him in no doubt as to what you think of him. If you don't, he'll pull a stroke like this again, some time.'

'What if Harvey *doesn't* plead, though? What then?'

'Well, okay then. As soon as you get to court, see Paterson and tell him it's not on. Tell him he's verballed Harvey, and that you're having nothing to do with it, that your evidence'll be reflecting what really happened.'

'But, as I said before, Pat, how can I follow him into the box, and tell the Magistrate a different story? It's crazy.'

'You won't have to,' she assured him. 'When Paterson hears what you've got to say, *he'll* change *his* story, so that *his* evidence corroborates *yours*. He wouldn't dare chance your not backing him up, in the box.'

'Either way, though, Punchy gets away with it. He won't alter his ways, will he? He'll maybe just be more careful, that's all.'

'That's something *else* I told you, last night,' said Pat. 'How the system'll never be changed. Don't forget, this has all been going on since Eighteen Twenty-Nine; it's as old as The Job itself.'

'And *what* a job,' he said. 'What an *eye*-opener it's been for me, I can tell you.'

'Same for everyone,' she pointed out. 'When you're dealing, day in, day out, with dirt and scum, some of it's bound to rub-off. It's just a pity that those of us who strive to keep ourselves clean are in a minority.'

'You must've had these difficulties, then, Pat,' he said. 'When you were a prob'. I mean, older PCs expecting you to pull a few strokes.'

For a moment, she was reflective. 'No. Not *really*. You see, a WPC is automatically rated as useless and untrustworthy, right from the beginning. They – the men – don't believe she's *capable* of The Job, therefore they don't *expect* her to do it. They're often tolerant, in a patronizing way, and maybe over-protective. During my probationary period I was just expected to take all of the shoplifters, search all of the female prisoners, and do all of the MISPER inquiries.'

'So you never found yourself with a problem like I've got?'

'No, never,' she said. 'But it's not a problem, anyway, John. You're still establishing yourself, you see. Once they realize you won't bend, that you've got integrity, they'll accept you for what you are and let you get on with things in your own way.'

'Hmm,' he thoughtfully murmured, his eyes blanking off. She should have added a rider, he believed: *but they'll also despise and distrust you, because you represent a threat to their security*. And then what might they do . . .? He hoped he'd never find out.

'You'll see,' she brightly went on. 'Everything'll work out okay. Now, finish that IRB, and then we can enjoy what's left of the evening.'

'Night, you mean,' he corrected, glancing at his wrist-watch; it was three minutes after one A.M.

She glanced over at the carriage clock on the unit. 'Morning, actually, if you *want* to be pedantic about it.' She smiled, and stood, picking up their glasses. 'While you're making a start, I'll get us some more drinks. Have a sandwich, too, John.'

'Yeah, thanks,' he said, and reached for a crab-filled one. Now he felt easier, more loose inside. Perhaps everything would work out okay.

She returned with the drinks and sat beside him, watching, nestling against his side as he leaned back and began completing the IRB, resting it on his fold-over wallet, as he wrote. Her presence was warm and perfumed, reassuring, and pleasantly distracting.

'Here,' she said. She'd picked up a sandwich and was holding it to his lips. 'Have a bite.'

He bit into it. 'Mmm. Nice . . . Prawns?'

'Mm-hm.' She was eating the remaining half.

'Why don't you take off your boots, John? Rest your feet on the coffee table . . . make yourself comfortable.' Her feet were already on the table, the left crossed over the right, but now she uncrossed them and stuck out her left foot, carefully repositioning his glass of lager so as to make room for his feet.

He bent forward, undoing the laces and kicking off the boots. 'That's better,' he sighed, wiggling his toes as he leaned back on the settee and crossed his feet on top of the table. 'Now where was I?'

Ten minutes later, the IRB was completed, their drinks were finished and the tray of sandwiches had been reduced to a scattering of crumbs on their two plates. She cleared the coffee table and went to the kitchen, while he walked over to the wall unit and placed an LP on the music centre's turntable – The Shadows, *String of Hits*. When she returned, she stood in the centre of the room, her head cocked aside, listening, nodding her approval of his choice.

'Lovely music,' she sighed, and lowered the dimmer switch that controlled the room's lighting, so that soft gold light contrasted with deep black shadow, all around.

Then she sat close to him, placing her left arm around his shoulders, her left leg over his right leg, the toes of her foot caressing his toes, her face pressed gently against the side of his. Her eyes were closed and she softly murmured her deep satisfaction.

He wrapped his arm around her waist, and she settled back against it; then he turned into her, and eased a sonorous groan from deep within his chest; it took with it the whole of the day's tension, and he began floating with the music . . . penetrating, highly emotional.

Their breathing had quickened . . . their bodies were pressed desperately close together, their comforting, reassuring holds on each other had become tighter, progressing to caresses . . . exploratory excursions, back and forth . . . more urgent by the second; they were fast approaching the point of no return . . .

They made love with the music . . . sweet, sensual . . . rhythmic, with peaks and troughs . . . climaxing with a vibrant flourish which continued its reverberation before fading gently away . . .

When the music had ended, they lay back naked on the settee, in near darkness, their glistening bodies intertwined, his dusky flesh contrasting starkly with the smooth, creamy whiteness of hers. There was total silence, now; an intense peace; a mutual plateau of well-being. A diamond teardrop glistened in the corner of her right eye. She brushed it away, and smiled an ethereal smile, then held him closer to her.

'Oh, *John*,' she whispered.

'Don't speak, Pat,' he softly said. 'You'll break the spell.'

15

He arrived at ten A.M. at the court-house, and made his way to the door of the gaoler's office. The foyer of the building was already filling up with officers, and non-custody prisoners who'd surrendered to their bail, as well as timorous civilian witnesses whose apprehensive eyes said, What the hell've I let myself in for, here? By noon, those same eyes would be reflecting impatience and anger, and the resolve, *Never* again.

'Whaddaya got, son?' asked the Sergeant gaoler, studying a long, five-page list of typed names and cases, which was on a clipboard in his left hand.

'Harvey,' MacHale said, taking off his anorak and hanging it on a bentwood stand in the gaoler's office. 'Interfering with Motor Vehicles, and Going Equipped. PC Paterson's the officer in the case, though; I'm just his witness.' He began putting on his tunic – which he'd carried with him to court, slung over his right arm.

'Harvey . . . Harvey . . .' mumbled the Sergeant. 'Got it.' And he pencilled a tick by Harvey's name. 'Paterson here yet, is he?'

'Haven't seen him, Sarge.'

'Okay. A bit previous, yet, maybe. Tell him to report to me when he arrives, so's I know he's here.'

'Will do, Sarge.'

'By the way,' said the Sergeant. 'Is Harvey pleading? Helps if I know . . . So's I can juggle the list.'

'Dunno, Sarge.'

'Better go and put it to him, then.' The Sergeant nodded in the direction of the cells; the cell-passage door was unlocked and wide open.

MacHale walked along to the passageway and strolled slowly down it, looking at the names which were scrawled in chalk on wall-slates adjacent to each of the twenty-odd cells that lined the white ceramic-brick-tiled wall to his right; at his left side there was a bank of tall, barred windows, their lower halves having been slid up to admit fresh air.

Harvey was banged-up in the sixth cell along, and MacHale slid open its wicket gate and peered in to the gloomy interior, pulling quickly back, and gasping as his nostrils were blasted by a rush of hot, fetid air. In all, there were four bodies inside the cell: three, dirty and dishevelled vagrant drunks – one lying along the wall-bench, two stretched out beneath it, on the floor – and Harvey, who was leaning forlornly against the far wall, his eyes downcast.

'C'mere, Frank,' MacHale called out.

'Uh?' Harvey's head shot up, and he shouldered himself off the wall, before walking quickly, the few paces to the open wicket gate.

'All right?' said MacHale. 'How're you doing?'

'How am I *doin*?' retorted Harvey, incredulous, casting a backward glance over his shoulder. 'Are you kiddin? It fuckin *stinks* in here. Lemme out, will ya?' There was stubble around his chin, his eyes were sore and heavy-lidded, and his face was shiny with grease-laden sweat.

'Sorry, Frank,' MacHale told him. 'I don't have the keys.'

'Well gimme a smoke, then.'

'Can't. I don't smoke . . . Sorry again.'

'Jesus Christ!' snapped Harvey, scratching his tousled head. 'How long's it gonna be before I do get outa here?'

'Not too long,' MacHale assured him. 'Soon as the court gets under way, you'll be taken along the corridor to wait your turn.'

'*How* long?'

MacHale glanced at his wristwatch – ten-fifteen. 'Another fifteen minutes, maybe. They generally start at about ten-thirty.'

'An what's gonna happen when I get in there?'

'That's up to you, Frank. If you plead, it'll all be over this morning.'

'Fuck that!' spat Harvey. 'I ain't pleadin to somethin I never *did. I'm* askin for trial by judge-'n'-jury.'

'You can't,' MacHale told him. 'Tampering with Vehicles isn't an indictable offence; it can only be dealt with here at the lower court. And if you elect trial on the Going Equipped, which *is* indictable, we'll drop it out, using your possession of the key as evidence of intent to tamper with cars.' He supposed that's what they'd do, in such circumstances, but wasn't entirely sure; as Going Equipped was the more serious of the two offences charged, maybe Harvey *could* elect trial on that one, thereby obliging the prosecution to drop out the *Interfering with Vehicles*? Still, what MacHale had said *sounded* plausible enough.

'You dirty bastards!' growled Harvey. 'I'm gonna *complain* about *you*. You ain't getting away with pullin a stroke like this.' He turned away from the door, and began agitatedly pacing the cell.

MacHale's gut fluttered. If Harvey did complain, the truth would have to come out, because there was no way that MacHale was going to cover up for Punchy Paterson; he turned to see Paterson striding along the cell passageway. He looked hung-over and irritable, too; he'd probably spent half the night in Mulligan's back bar, MacHale thought.

'*Well?*' Punchy snapped at MacHale. 'What's the SP? Is he duckin his nut, or what?'

MacHale turned aside his head to avoid breathing Punchy's sour breath. 'No, he's not. Matter of fact, he's gonna *complain* about us, so he says.'

Punchy stooped and looked in through the wicket gate. 'Harvey!' he shouted. 'Get your arse over here! *Schnell!*'

'Yeah? Whaddaya you want?' sneered Harvey, pressing his face against the open, wicket gate.

'I hear ya not pleadin. That right?'

Harvey nodded resolutely. '*Right* it's right. I'm *fightin* you bastards. *All* the way.'

'That a fact?' said Punchy, feigning surprise. 'So we can't do ya no favours, then, can we? Makes no difference to me, though.' He shrugged, turned on his heel, and began walking away.

'Hey! Waita minute!' shouted Harvey. 'Come back!'

Punchy returned to stand before the cell door. 'Yeah, Frank? What is it? Somethin botherin you?' It had taken a real effort, but he'd affected a gentle, avuncular expression and tone of voice.

'Well . . .' Harvey began, looking unsure of himself, concerned. 'I mean . . . What's gonna happen? What'll I get?'

'Lemme tell ya, Frank,' said Punchy, oozing sincerity that was wholly counterfeit. 'Ya can have it on ya head or ya toes. If ya deny the charges, ya'll go down, anyway. All the evidence is there, my son. Only thing is, it won't be dealt with *today*, if ya deny em.'

'Whaddaya mean?'

'I mean, ya'll be remanded in custody. No bail. A couplea weeks in Brixton, to think things over. An when ya get outa *there*, ya arse'll be big enough to drive a fuckin *tube* train through, nice young boy like you . . .' He paused, watching Harvey gulp air and saliva. 'If ya plead today, though, it'll all be over this mornin. Probably give ya Probation, or a Con-Dis or somethin.'

'Ya *mean* that?'

'Sure I do. Okay, so you've got form, but its petty an unrelated.' He took a piece of paper – a Six-O-Nine – from his trousers pocket, unfolded it, and read its detail:

'"Shopliftin, five previous; Threatenin Behaviour, three previous; an one Criminal Damage." Right?'

'Yeah, right,' agreed Harvey. 'All pretty unrelated stuff, like ya said.'

'So what's the problem, then?' Punchy said, spreading his hands, palms upward. 'I told ya: it'll be a Con-Dis or somethin. An there's still a place for ya at the project. I checked up, this mornin, and they're willin to take ya back. Whaddaya say, then?'

'How bouta brief, though?' Harvey cautiously responded. 'Maybe I oughta have a mouthpiece when I stand up in there.'

'Yeah, sure,' Punchy told him. 'Ya can see the duty solicitor. Mattera fact, *he'll* be lookin for *you*, toutin for business. But he'll see to it for certain that you're RIC for a week.'

'Howcome. Whaddaya mean?'

'He's a bent bastard. Only interested in as many appearance fees as he can screw outa your case. So, he'll tell ya to deny everythin and apply for legal aid. That way, ya'll get a laydown for a week at least . . . an finish up with an arse so *big* they'll be able to drive an *artic* up it. Na, row him out, Frank, an throw ya hands in the air. Everythin'll be sweet, that way.'

'You ain't bullshittin me, are ya?' Harvey asked, narrowing his eyes.

Again, Punchy spread his hands. '*Frank*,' he earnestly said, with just a shade of indignance. 'Whaddaya *sayin*, my son? I'm kosher. Straight up. Stand on me.' And he winked at Harvey.

'Okay,' Harvey sighed; his arse was *already* feeling sore as hell, just *thinking* about a week's laydown in Brixton. 'I'll take a chance. Duck my nut . . . You gotta smoke on ya?'

'Terrific,' Punchy smiled. 'Yeah, sure I gotta smoke on me.' He took out his tobacco tin, rolled Harvey a thin cigarette, handed it in to him, and lit it. 'See ya later.' He slid shut the wicket gate and turned to MacHale. Now his expression was its usual self – long, dark; minatory eyes – and his voice took on a conspiratorial note as he spoke: 'D'ya do that IRB last night?'

'Yes,' MacHale told him, and his heart began beating faster as he reached into the back pocket of his trousers and took out the case-papers. He handed them over to Punchy. 'But I'm not happy about it.'

'Whaddaya mean, y'ain't happy?'

MacHale swallowed hard and felt his face reddening. 'I mean that as far as I'm concerned, your notes of evidence don't reflect what actually took place. The Q-'n'-As are a load of verbals, and I'm not going to corroborate any of it.' – he'd blurted it out.

'What the fuckin hell're you *talkin* about?' Punchy seethed, and he pushed MacHale further along the cell passageway, out of the hearing of Harvey.

'What I'm saying,' MacHale told him, 'is that you're not making *me* part of a conspiracy to pervert the course of justice. *You* can do what you want, but *I'm* not getting involved in it any more than I have already.'

For a couple of seconds, Punchy just stood there, staring in complete bewilderment at MacHale. Then he said, 'I don't *believe* this . . . Where's ya *loyalty*? Harvey's as guilty as *hell*, an you *know* it. Whaddaya want, him to get a result or somethin? D'ya want him to walk outa here, and go an mug an old lady . . . maybe *kill* her?'

'That's ridiculous!' MacHale said, raising his voice. 'You're not making *me* feel guilty for being straight . . . honest.'

'Okay, okay,' Punchy said, patting, with both hands at the air, and backing off a little. 'After today, ya can do whatever ya want. Go y'own way. But you'll learn. You'll soon find out that ya *can't* be straight in The Job – leastways not if ya gonna get things done. It's a *fight* out there. Us against them. There *ain't* no rules in war. Slags like *Harvey* don't play to no rules, do they? Go soft on em, an they'll piss all over ya.'

'I'm sorry, Punchy,' MacHale insisted. 'It's not on. What you've said is very appealing, but it doesn't constitute a defence to a charge of Perjury. You're on your own, here.'

'That's it, then, is it?' Punchy said, clenching his fists and speaking through taut lips. 'Jesus *Christ*, what a spineless, gutless little fucker you *are*, MacHale! Ya make me *sick*!'

'Here,' MacHale said, outwardly unmoved by the outburst, and handed Punchy his own IRB. 'This'll show you what evidence I'll be giving if it's not a plea. Maybe *you* should corroborate *me*.'

Punchy snatched MacHale's IRB, tore it in half, and threw the pieces at his feet. 'Stick it up your *arse*!' he shouted, and then stormed off along the passageway.

MacHale closed his eyes, tilted back his head, and took a deep intake of breath, easing it out as a long sigh of relief. It hadn't been half as difficult as he'd imagined, and he felt stronger for having accomplished it; he *knew* he was right in what he'd done. He wiped the back of his hand across his hot forehead, glanced at it and saw that it was glistening with sweat. Then he picked up the pieces of his torn IRB, walked down to the far end of the passageway, and drank several mouthfuls of cold water from the tap above the wall-sink; after that, he rinsed his face, dried it on the grubby, twisted roller-towel, and made his way back along the passage. He'd decided he'd sit in the court and just wait for Harvey's case to be called.

The usher, a white-haired elderly civilian who wore a black-cotton cloak over a dark suit, rose from his tiny enclosure by the right side of the witness box, turned to the members of the public who were packed into the rows of benches at the back of the court, and called out, 'All rise!'

The court rose, and there was a hushed, respectful silence as the Magistrate and his clerk walked from a side door at the front of the court, and took-up their places.

First, the drunks and the footways and the gamers, then the remands, then the charges. MacHale was sitting on the police benches, in front of the public enclosure, and before him, slightly to his left, stood the dock, which was positioned immediately in front of the clerk and the Magistrate. The large, square room, with its windowless, oak-panelled walls and high ceiling, was lit by a chandelier, and it smelled pleasantly of furniture polish.

'Charge number one, Your Worship: Daniel Rafferty,' announced the gaoler, consulting his clipboard; then, turning towards the door, he pulled it open, shouting, 'Rafferty!' and stood aside to admit the day's first case, pointing Rafferty in the direction of the dock.

The clerk then read out the charge – found drunk in a public place, yesterday afternoon – Rafferty said, 'Guilty, sir, oh yes, sir, guilty,' in an obsequious, Irish brogue; the court Inspector rose from his enclosure at the left side of the witness box, said, 'No trouble, Your Worship,' and the Magistrate, Claud Harris, followed on with, 'A pound or a day.'

It had taken no more than two minutes for Rafferty to be weighed off and disposed of. But tomorrow he'd be back, and the whole process – or ritual, really – would be repeated. Maybe next week, when the Magistrate got fed-up of seeing Rafferty in the dock, he'd award him a fourteen-day laydown; then, Rafferty's face wouldn't be seen for a couple of weeks, although on the fifteenth day he'd be back once more charged with drunkenness, looking a lot fitter and healthier, after a fortnight's free bed-'n'-breakfast, with no alcohol. All pretty senseless, really.

And so it went on for the next half an hour, as a stream of pitiful, rag-shrouded, terminally-ill-looking, dehydrated vagies, their fleshless limbs afflicted with uncontrollable shakes, were fed in and out of the system.

And now, standing in the dock, charged with D-'n'-D, was a haggard-looking, unshaven and dirty face which MacHale found familiar. 'Shouting, swearing and waving his arms,' said the court Inspector. And then it came to MacHale: the face belonged to that poor old vagie whom he'd taken pity on, yesterday afternoon, and had given fifty-P to buy a sandwich. He might just as well've been nicked by me, MacHale told himself. At least, that way, I could've ensured he actually *got* a sandwich; and the charge would've been only *simple* drunkenness, costing him a pound or a day.

As it was, the vagie drew fourteen days at the 'Ville, and MacHale drew a small piece of regret. Another stream of disintegrating vagies: begging, petty theft, drunkenness; and two cases of criminal damage. MacHale folded his arms across his chest, and stretched out his legs. His interest in the proceedings was running short, and it would be some time yet before Harvey was put up. He began to wonder if Pat would be thinking of him, now . . . about how he'd made out with Punchy. His mind wandered back to last night. It'd been great, and it could only get better, he believed. It was curiously fortifying, knowing that someone else was a large part of you; you could draw on their reserves as well as your own. He pulled down the cuff of his white shirt, examining it: dazzlingly clean. She'd actually washed it for him, first thing this morning, while he was in the shower; now it smelled of perfume . . . something she'd added to the wash, so she'd said. He could get used to that, too: perfumed shirts, and close companionship, and cooked breakfasts, and . . . well, everything that went with cohabitation. Strange how it had worked out, he mused, and so quickly, so spontaneously. He'd never dared hope it'd turn out that way. He'd considered it, of course but thought it might be better if they were to hold off until they were both absolutely certain of their commitment. Now, though, he couldn't wait to do it again, and was sure that she must feel the same way. This morning, she'd said it was wonderful; embarrassedly, he'd agreed . . .

His eyes came alive, and he looked towards the witness box, where a very plain-looking, dark-haired girl of about thirty-five was giving evidence in a case of indecent exposure; she wore a faded, navy-blue mac, belted at the waist, its right lapel displaying a tin badge which depicted a hand, closed save for the index finger, which pointed skyward – *One Way*, a Christian symbol, denoting the path to God and Heaven. She's an ex-convent girl, MacHale decided. She was very pale-complexioned – without make-up – and clearly unnerved, pausing between sentences, to bite her lower lip and look to her feet. Her evidence was being led by the officer in the case, a crime-squad PC, who was having some difficulty, it seemed, in eliciting from her exactly what she meant by '. . . his . . . his *thingy*,' when she said, '. . . he ran into the shop, opened his mac, and waved his . . . his *thingy* at me.'

The defendant, a Greek, named Kris, was smiling, enjoying her difficulty and embarrassment, it appeared, as much as he'd enjoyed waving his joint at her, when he'd run into the shop where she worked.

'Look, Miss Ryan,' the prosecuting PC said, sighing impatiently. 'You must *tell* the court, *exactly* what you mean by "thingy".'

'His, his . . .' Again, she paused, her face reddening, her hands clasped tight together before herself, her fingers white-knuckled and wriggling. 'It was . . . it was his *willy*!' – there, she'd at last brought herself to say it;

she'd blurted it out – what was probably the most disgusting word she knew or had heard of – and was now staring at the floor of the witness box, her body quivering.

'Miss Ryan,' the PC said. 'I'm afraid that *this* description advances us not a jot further. *What* do you *mean* by, "*willy*"?'

She looked up, her face devastated by embarrassment . . . at the PC . . . at the Magistrate . . . at the row of solicitors who were seated on tiered benches, across from her . . . at the public gallery . . . back at the PC. Everyone's eyes were adhering to hers. What the hell *did* she mean? No one believed the prosecution's PC was being pedantic in attempting to elicit her *exact* meaning. Before the court knocked down a man for indecent exposure, there had to be no doubt that he had, in fact, committed the offence. Her idea of a "thingy" or a "willy" might be at total variance with everyone else's idea.

'Well, Miss Ryan?' put in the Magistrate, cocking an ear and a glass eye in her direction. 'Do you mean, *penis*? Is that what you mean? The defendant waved his penis at you?'

'Yes, yes, sir,' she gushed, greatly relieved. 'That's what I meant. He waved his . . . *that* at me.' She still was unable to bring herself to say *penis*.

'Thank you very much, Miss Ryan,' the PC indulgently said, and he sat down with a thank-Christ-for-*that* expression on his face.

Now it was the turn of the defendant's brief, who sprang to his feet, pomp and circumstance all over his thin-featured, shiny young face, and began to cross-examine in a high-pitched, crystal-clear voice that was full of arrogance. 'Miss Ryan . . .' A fawning smile parted his lips, and she was momentarily disarmed. 'Have you ever before *seen* a man's penis? That is, prior to the day on which you allege my client flaunted his, on the floor of the fish-and-chip shop where you are employed as a counter-hand.' His head swivelled slowly, to the left . . . to the right, his supercilious eyes ensuring that all present were closely attending to him.

Snotty-nosed git, thought MacHale. She's gonna say, 'No,' and he's gonna come back with, '*Well*! How on earth can you say that you saw my *client's* penis, then? You don't know what a penis *looks* like, Miss Ryan.'

But Miss Ryan floored him, saying, 'As a matter of fact I have, sir. Yes. Your client came in the shop, two days earlier, and did the very same *thing* at me!' She was pointing a shaking, accusing finger at the defendant, whose expression said, *Who? Me-ee? Never!*

Good for you, Miss Ryan, thought MacHale.

Claud Harris, the hoary old Magistrate, turned aside his head and cocked a predatory eye – his good one – at the brief: Follow *that*, it challenged.

The brief tried his best, too, but was unable to shake her, and she went on, albeit hesitantly, to describe how the defendant had thrown open his mac to reveal that his fly was undone, and how he'd then leaned back, shouted, '*Yoo-hoo!*' and waved his – now she brought herself to say the word – penis at her. She was gaining strength, it seemed.

After that, the brief tried a different tack. Perhaps she'd been utterly mistaken? Perhaps it was the defendant's *finger* she'd seen? Why of course. That was it, wasn't it? He'd had a loose zip on his fly, and, as he'd opened his mac to pull up the zip, his index finger outstretched, she'd – naturally enough – mistaken it for his penis. 'Are you *certain* it couldn't have been his finger, Miss Ryan? Think carefully, now. My client's liberty is at stake, here, don't forget.'

Miss Ryan thought most carefully before giving her considered response: 'Have *you* ever seen an index finger that's covered in pubic hair, standing up, and about *this* long?' – she bunched her hands, stuck out her own index fingers, and held them before herself, about fifteen inches apart.

Surely it couldn't've been *that* long? thought MacHale. The PC sitting next to him, nudged him in the ribs, leaned over, and whispered, 'Surely it couldn't've been *that* long?' And the question was repeated many more times among the onlookers in the public enclosure, too, before the air again settled inside the court.

Claud Harris, though, congratulated Miss Ryan: 'Very well put, m'girl.' Then, to the brief: 'Anything *further*? Or may the witness be released?' his tone indicating that there'd better *not* be anything further, and that the witness better had be released.

'No, no, Your Worship,' mumbled the brief, now totally deflated. And he sat down heavily on the bench and began sorting papers.

Next on was the arresting PC, who gave evidence of his interviews with the defendant, and the brief didn't even rise to make an effort at cross-examination. The defendant, who declined to give evidence on his own behalf, was duly convicted, then remanded for reports.

Then MacHale's heart attempted to break loose from its mountings as the gaoler returned to the court, saying, 'Charges thirty and thirty-one, Your Worship: Francis Harvey.'

Harvey entered, made his way to the dock, and stood there, motionless, his hands clasped behind his back, his head held high, while Punchy Paterson walked around to the witness box and respectfully asked for a summary trial.

God, let him plead guilty, thought MacHale. The clerk was now telling Harvey that he could have the cases dealt with here and now, but that he also had the right to elect trial at a Crown Court on the charge of Going Equipped, if he so chose; however, if he should choose summary trial, the Magistrate, after hearing of Harvey's past character and record, could then commit him for sentence to the higher court, if it were apparent that this lower court's power of punishment would be inadequate.

'I'll have em dealt with here, sir,' Harvey told the clerk, and the clerk then proceeded to read out each charge, asking Harvey how he pleaded. 'Guilty . . . Guilty,' answered Harvey, in answer to each one.

MacHale momentarily closed his eyes and sighed relievedly.

Now, Punchy was relating the brief facts: Harvey had entered the car-park opposite the Astoria Cinema, intending to steal valuable and removable property from unattended vehicles; and to facilitate this intent, he'd had possession of a worn old key for a Ford motor-car; however, after having tried the door-handles of four vehicles, which were securely locked, he was disturbed by a group of office workers, returning to collect their vehicles after a day's work, nearby; on leaving the car-park, Harvey was stopped by police, and readily admitted his unlawful intent; he'd been most cooperative, on arrest, and subsequently, and had seemed extremely repentant; when he was charged and cautioned, he made no reply.

Readily *confessed*? thought MacHale . . . *Cooperative*? Repentant? What a load of crap! Punchy Paterson had obviously promised Harvey that he'd put in a good word for him, in exchange for a plea; he'd probably have said almost anything, in exchange for that plea.

Punchy had now disclosed Harvey's previous convictions, and had related his antecedent history, and Claud Harris was about to deliver the sentence.

'Harvey,' he began, an ominous ring to his voice. 'These are most serious offences, and I am going, therefore, to remand you in order that you may seek legal representation. Which is an indication to you that I am seriously considering the imposition of a custodial sentence.' He looked to the gaoler.

'Twenty-fourth of next month, sir,' the gaoler responded, having consulted his diary. Then, bail was fixed, with a requirement for a surety – to be later nominated by Harvey, and either approved or disapproved of by police and the court – and that was that.

Harvey was led out, his face black with rage, to the gaoler's office, with Punchy falling in behind him; he'd be banged-up in the cells until his surety had been produced and accepted. Come next month, he'd probably be sent over the wall for sixty days.

MacHale left the court and went along to the gaoler's office to collect his anorak.

'Thanks, MacHale,' Punchy sarcastically told him. 'Thanks for everythin. Never again am *I* gonna get involved in a job with *you*!' And he walked away to the cells.

That's exactly how I feel about *you*, thought MacHale.

But when he left the court building he felt miserable, disloyal, and guilty. An outcast.

PART THREE
Reprisals

16

The reprisals began that very afternoon, just before parade.

When he entered the locker room, Punchy, Vindscreen, Tasty, Snatch, Tubby, Filthy Phil and Hercules were already there, in the process of changing into their uniforms; they'd been talking amongst themselves, prior to MacHale's arrival, but now an uneasy silence fell over the room, as they became aware of his presence.

He opened his locker door, ignoring them, and hung up his anorak; then he took out a brush and duster and began buffing his boots.

'Y'know,' said Tubby, loudly, artificially, to no one in particular. 'This job's got its faults an its ups-'n'-downs, but there's strong loyalty. I mean, it's comfortin to know the back-up's always there whenever ya need it.' He shot a savage glance at MacHale, then continued buttoning his tunic.

'Yeah,' agreed Tasty Tom, settling his helmet on his head. 'There is loyalty among us . . . Ain't always too strong, though.'

'Ain't there at *all*, in some cases, dear boy,' offered Snatch, his tone soft and regretful.

'You're talkin about bottlers,' put in Vindscreen. 'Some blokes just ain't got the *bottle* to give ya back-up.'

'*Never* there when ya need em,' said Punchy Paterson.

'Better off *without* em,' came back Tubby.

'Drop ya *right* in it, that sort,' mumbled Filthy Phil, turning aside to spit on the floor.

MacHale felt his temperature soaring, the anger rising from his gut to his throat, making his arms and legs quiver. Vindscreen, as well, he thought; Vindscreen was supposed to be an affable, humorous character, easy to get along with, and yesterday, when they'd walked out together, MacHale had felt an affinity with him. But then, MacHale had been disloyal to him, as well, by refusing to go along with his suggestion that they should enter-up that tom for a caution she hadn't had and wasn't going to get.

What about Hercules, though? MacHale wondered. Which side of the fence was he standing on . . .? Neither side, he concluded. Hercules was sitting on *top* of the fence. He hadn't joined in the ribaldry because he was a listener and a watcher and a thinker, one who rarely if ever committed himself verbally when there was conflict among his colleagues. Anyway, his colleagues liked him about as much as he liked them, and that all added up to a mutual wariness. But there was Mathieson, too, of course; where was he? Not present, MacHale now realized. Even if he were present, though, he'd only have been banged-up in that private world of his, thinking solely about where and when he was going to get his next drink.

The room was silent again, and MacHale continued buffing his boots. He was determined not to allow them to get to him – or at least not to give them the satisfaction of knowing they *had* got to him. If he rose, physically and verbally, they'd never let him down; they'd prod and prick and pull and pinch and wind him up, until his head exploded; then, it'd be *him* who'd finish up on the dab, not them.

He stood, threw his brush and duster onto the floor of the locker, and put on his tunic, buttoning it. Why haven't they gone? he asked himself, suspicious of their lingering presence. They'd finished changing, yet they were *still* hanging around, making yet more unnecessary adjustments to their ties and head-gear; brushing and picking non-existent pieces of fluff and specks of dust from their tunics; checking the laces of their boots and shoes; killing time; watching him out of the corners of their eyes.

They're gonna grab me, he thought, and he became as jumpy as a flea on a hotplate. Quickly, he took his stick from the locker's shelf, stuck his thumb through its strap, twirled it, flipping the strap over and around his hand, and held it tight by his side, his fingers flexing on the handle's concaved grips; he'd give the bastards plenty of stick, and *then* some, if they physically threatened him. And to hell with the consequences. Now, his eyes darting from side-to-side, he took out his helmet and dropped it down on his head. *Then* he found out what they'd been waiting around for. A small pile of horse manure had fallen from inside thc helmet, down over his hair and the shoulders of his tunic; impregnated with urine, it stank, too.

The locker room reverberated with coarse laughter and cheers, as the other PCs fell about, pointing at him, taunting him, revelling in his predicament. All except Hercules, that was; he merely stood there, not knowing, it seemed, whether to look appalled or amused – whichever expression he chose to fit his face with, he'd be sure to have allied himself with someone; a commitment he'd be most uneasy with, in these circumstances.

Now they left the locker room, well satisfied, chuckling and congratulating themselves, while MacHale just stood there, bent forward, clawing straw and excrement from his hair.

Hercules, who'd remained, walked over to MacHale and put an arm around his shoulders – now, now the others were gone, it was relatively safe to show his true feelings over what had happened. 'I want you to know, Juan,' he softly said, 'that I didn't have anything to do with this. I'd have told you, if I'd known. Honest, I would.' He began flicking pieces of straw from MacHale's head.

'Yeah, okay,' MacHale said, shrugging away from Hercules' arm. 'I believe you . . . Just as well this stuff's a bit on the dry side, I s'pose.' *Would* he have told me? MacHale wondered. If he'd known.

'It smells terrible,' Hercules said, grimacing.

'Could've been worse,' MacHale philosophically muttered. 'It might've been *dog's* crap.'

'Look,' Hercules apprehensively said. 'I, er . . . I do know what this is all about. I heard them talking when I first came in. And, well, *I* respect your feelings. I do, really I do, Juan. You've got to do what you think's right . . . Only thing is . . .' He broke off, detaching his eyes from MacHale's eyes, not knowing how to go on.

At length, he found the words: 'What I mean is, I can't side with you, Juan. It's not that I'm *scared* of them, or that I agree with them, or anything like that. It's just that, well, I've – '

'I know,' MacHale interrupted. '*You've* gotta *work* with them.' And *stop* fuckin calling me *Juan*, he thought; it's getting on my thrupenny bits.

'That's it,' Hercules relievedly said. 'I've gotta work with them.'

'And so've *I*,' retorted MacHale. 'What about *me*? How d'you think *I* feel?'

'Don't worry,' Hercules soothed. 'Ignore them. They've had their bit of fun. That'll be an end to it, now.'

'Yeah, maybe you're right,' MacHale sighed. But he was afraid that this was only the beginning of it.

When he arrived on parade, in the Collator's office, and stood at the end of the line, next to Hercules, he was greeted with cold stares and a spiteful silence.

The Collator, an elderly, silver-haired PC who wore

Job-issue spectacles – white-metal frames with shatter-proof lenses – stopped writing, leaned back in his chair, and looked up, having noted the sudden cessation of parade small-talk, and having sensed the ensuing hostility; his head was motionless, but his eyes roved back and forth along the line of PCs who stood with their backs to him, trying to identify which of them was the pariah.

'Funny smell in here,' Tubby Tompkins suddenly said, turning up his nose.

'Yeah, I can smell it, an all,' agreed Snatch.

'Horse shit, ain't it?' said Punchy Paterson, laughing.

'Na,' disagreed Vindscreen. 'It's fear.'

'That's right,' said Filthy Phil. 'Must be a bottler in here, somewhere.'

'Wonder who it is?' asked Tasty Tom.

And the line began shuffling sideways, moving away from MacHale and Hercules. Then, Hercules, who'd been sandwiched between MacHale and the rest of his colleagues, also moved . . . slowly, awkwardly, trying not to be noticed . . . until he was in a position in no-man's land – two feet away from MacHale, and two feet away from the last man in the line.

Jesus Christ, this is childish, MacHale thought. And he shook his head and smiled – with frustration, not amusement.

The Collator, too, shook his head, then leaned forward over his desk and continued with his work.

Pat Coles then walked in. She smiled, at all members of the parade, then stood next to MacHale, casting him a concerned glance.

'What's the matter, John?' she whispered out of the corner of her mouth. 'You look very downcast.'

'I am,' he whispered back. 'Tell you later.'

Then, in walked Barker, carrying a clipboard, and stood several feet in front of the line, looking from left to right. He frowned, sniffed at the air, and, as he strolled along to the far end of the room, to slide open a window, said, 'Funny smell in here, ain't there?'

At that, each member of the Relief – save MacHale, Pat and Hercules – began giggling and sniggering and shifting his feet.

Barker looked even more puzzled as he walked back to the line-up. '*I* wasn't aware I'd said anything funny.' He paused, again looking from left to right along the line of officers, waiting for someone to enlighten him; and when no one did, he grunted his annoyance and began reading out the postings.

When Barker had almost finished the postings, in came a young whizkid of a DC, carrying a crime-report sheet. His hair, long, dark and shaggy, had flashes of blonde streaking through it, and he wore a grey-chalkstripe waistcoat and trousers – waistcoat unbuttoned – with a white-collared red shirt and cream-silk tie – shirt unbuttoned at the neck, tie loosened. As he lingered at Barker's side, he cast a superior eye over the Relief, although he outranked not even the most junior man who was present, MacHale.

'Who's that, dear boy?' whispered Snatch to Tubby Tompkins.

'A new DC,' Tubby whispered back. 'Thinks he's ace, don't he?'

'Thought the CID was s'posed to be in *plain*-clothes,' Snatch remarked.

'Yeah,' Tubby came back. 'Flash little scrote . . . been watchin too much telly, y'ask me.'

'Looks like a poufdah, to me, dear boy. Just look at that Barnet he's got: it's fuckin *dyed*, ain't it?' And Snatch glanced along the line, to Hercules, who seemed entranced by the DC's appearance, physical and sartorial. Jabbing Tubby in the ribs, Snatch tilted his head in Hercules' direction, indicating that Tubby, too, should take a peek.

Tubby did so. 'Two of a kind,' he disgustedly muttered, and slowly shook his head.

'Right,' said Barker, attending at last to the DC. 'What d'you want?' – his tone reflected his dislike of the Department.

'Heavy screwing, Skip,' said the DC. 'Last night, at Woolies, down the High Street. The villains had it off with ten grands'-worth of snout and spirits, and one of them left his jacket behind.'

Barker's expression said, *So?*

The DC turned to face the Relief. 'Now, this jacket – '

'Where is it?' snapped Punchy Paterson. 'I wanna *see* it.'

'It's gone to the lab, for forensic,' the DC told him, unruffled by the interruption.

'Huh!' grunted Punchy.

'As I was saying, this jacket tells us a lot about one of the team on the screwing,' the DC continued. 'First thing is, it's a very small jacket, which expert opinion tells me would fit someone who's no taller than five-three.'

'Expert? What expert?' demanded Tasty Tom.

'Morrie Lewis, next-door to Woolies . . . the tailor.' The DC's face was colouring, slightly.

'Some fuckin expert *he* is,' scoffed Vindscreen. 'Morrie Lewis don't know a sports jacket from a fuckin *strait* jacket, judgin by the tat he's got in his window.'

The DC went on, determinedly: 'In the right-hand pocket of this jacket, there was a packet of cigarettes – '

'So what?' cut in Filthy Phil.

The DC was beginning to perspire. 'I'm *coming* to that,' he said. 'Now, as I told you, the cigarettes were in the right pocket, and in the left pocket there was a lighter. Which indicates to me that the suspect is left *handed*.'

'Oh yeah?' challenged Snatch. 'How'd ya work that out, then, dear boy?'

'Yeah, that's what I'd like to know, an all,' Tasty Tom said.

'It's a loada crap, if y'ask me,' Punchy said.

And Tubby Tompkins, a wicked grin on his fat face, animatedly and with emphatic flourishes of his hands, took a lighter from the right pocket of his tunic, a packet of *cigarettes* from the right pocket, and began to smoke a filter-tip, all the while keeping his little piggy eyes on the DC. Tubby, of course, was right *handed*.

'Look,' Barker said to the bewildered DC. 'Just get to the friggin point, an tell us who we're s'posed to be lookin for, will ya?'

'We're *s'posed* to be lookin for a left-handed cigarette-smokin *midget* who's partial to a dropa Scotch,' shouted Tasty Tom. 'Any circuses in town?'

Everyone burst out laughing, and one or two stamped their feet on the floor. Even MacHale found it amusing. The DC, though, was destroyed. 'Call yourselves *police-officers*!' he yelled. 'You make me *sick*! The *lot* of you!'

'Sod off!' shouted Tubby.

'Couldn't arrest my *attention*,' sneered Punchy.

'Or investigate a knock at his own front-door,' Filthy Phil added.

And the DC stormed off out, slamming the door and making the windows rattle.

'Okay, okay, settle down,' Barker told the Relief – he'd heard Old Crikey's feet, thumping along the corridor, outside.

'Good afternoon,' Old Crikey tersely mumbled as he entered the room and stood by Barker's side, his eyes roving back and forth along the line . . . looking puzzled, and frowning more deeply when he returned his eyes to MacHale and Pat Coles. Clearly, he was wondering why they were so close together, but apart from the rest of their colleagues. However, he sniffed away his curiosity, clicked together his teeth, and looked to Barker.

'All correct, sir,' Barker routinely said. 'Blinky's back from UC-sick, but Mathieson's taken his place – gut trouble, or somethin. Anyway, Miss Coles's back on the streets, today.'

Old Crikey glanced fondly at Pat Coles, then frowned again, wiping the back of his hand across his mouth, removing the film of white powder that was lining the inner edges of his lips. 'Any special comittments, today, Sarge?'

'No, sir,' Barker told him. 'The CID've removed us from the hospital guard on the black kid who slashed his wrist, yesterday, and have got a crime-squad PC on it.'

'Good, good,' said Old Crikey. 'Let's try some more of this policing by objectives, then, shall we? We're going along to the Rat Farm, and we're going to stop everything that moves. *Everything!* Put the fear of God into some of those drug-pushers up there.' His face said, How d'you like *that* for an idea, then? But the line-up was unenthusiastic; past experiences suggested that they wouldn't be on the Rat Farm for five minutes before the blocks' occupants began stoning them from the upper floors, and obliged them to retreat.

'Now then,' Old Crikey went on, undeterred, looking in turn at each member of the Relief. 'How shall we divide up . . .?'

While he was deliberating, the phone rang . . . and was answered by Barker, who almost immediately handed the receiver to Old Crikey.

'For you, guv,' Barker said.

'Inspector Crawford,' snapped Old Crikey, annoyed by the interruption. 'Yes, yes . . . of course I remember . . . *What? . . . Now? . . .* Oh, *crikey*! . . .' He slammed down the receiver, making the set's bell jingle, and frowned deeply, sliding his lower jaw back and forth, grating his teeth.

'Whassup, guv?' Barker wanted to know.

'The balloon's gone up,' wailed Old Crikey, his face whitening. 'Downstairs, there's a CI and a Skipper from the District's Complaints Office. And they want to see several members of *this* Relief.'

The members of the parade began looking anxiously at one another, and the air began buzzing with speculative whisperings.

'*Which* of us do they want to see?' Barker asked.

'Don't interrupt me!' Old Crikey agitatedly said. His eyes had been empty, staring, and it was obvious that he'd been searching his own conscience, trying to worry out a piece of long-forgotten culpability.

MacHale, too, was lost in anxious thought. It was himself and Punchy Paterson they wanted to interview, he told himself. Harvey, having been released on bail from the court, had decided to complain that he'd been fitted-up and coerced into pleading.

'Well? What d'you want me to do, guv?' Barker impatiently asked.

Old Crikey tut-tutted. 'All right, Sarge, all right,' he whined. Then he pointed at MacHale, Tubby Tompkins, Snatch and Tasty Tom, saying, 'You, you, you, and you, wait here, and the rest of you, get out on the streets.'

Barker nodded his head, and fell in behind the dismissed members of the Relief as they filed out, while Old Crikey coughed meaningfully and stared hostilely at the Collator, so that he, too, left the room.

Old Crikey sniffed aggressively, and wiped the back of his right hand across the tip of his nose. 'Right,' he opened. 'You'll all remember that you nicked a prisoner called Schofield, a couple of night-duties ago . . .' He paused, allowing the four some time to make their recollections.

So *that's* it, thought MacHale. *Schofield* . . . The ringed Jag. What the hell's *he* complaining about, though?

'*I* didn't nick him, guv,' disclaimed Tubby Tompkins.

'Nor me,' said Snatch.

'I was just *there*, at the scene,' Tasty Tom protested. 'Respondin to a shout for assistance, which wasn't needed.'

''Course,' said Snatch, 'if Schofield had been *charged*, and sent to *court*, there wouldn'ta *been* any complaint.' He shot a frigid glance at MacHale.

The lying bastards, thought MacHale. It was Tasty Tom who'd dropped Schofield in the gutter, with a right-hander, and Snatch had then 'cuffed him. They were *all* involved.

'Typical!' snapped Old Crikey, his fingers springing in and out from his bunched fists. 'As soon as there's any trouble, you all start rowing for the shore. Well, let me tell you, you're not leaving *me* floundering with this one. *I'm* the one who wasn't even *there*, when Schofield was allegedly assaulted.'

'Schofield *wasn't* assaulted, guv,' Tasty Tom said.

'That's right, guv'nor,' Snatch assured.

'Not 'less MacHale did it,' Tubby added. 'Before we got there.'

'Just a *minute*,' MacHale said, pointing a finger at Tasty Tom. '*You* were the one who – '

'Shuddup, shuddup!' shouted Old Crikey. 'You're right, you're right . . .' He nodded at Tasty Tom. 'Schofield *wasn't* assaulted. And, don't forget, he didn't *complain* – to *me* that he'd been assaulted . . . when he was brought in, that is. This is the first we've heard of it.' He took out a digestif, and popped it in his mouth, lodging it at the left side of his cheek. '*I* – that is, we, I mean – don't know anything about *anything*.'

Not bloody much we don't, thought MacHale, and he was certain that if he were to lie to the CI, and say that Schofield hadn't been hit, the CI would spot a facial cue that was completely contradictory. On the other hand, if he were to drop the others in it, and admit he'd seen

Schofield hit in the gut, the CI would want to know why he hadn't forthwith notified a senior officer on arrival at the station. There was no clear way out, it seemed.

'MacHale!' shouted Old Crikey.

'Yessir?'

'Go downstairs, and wait in my office. I want to speak in private to these three.'

MacHale left the room and began making his way downstairs, now convinced that Old Crikey and the others were conspiring to ensure that he'd be the one to take back the can.

When he reached the foot of the stairs, Pat was waiting for him. She smiled. 'Come along to my office, John. I'm dying to know about this morning.'

'I can't, Pat,' he told her. 'I've got to wait in Old Crikey's office. I'm one of the PCs who the Complaints CI wants to see.'

She frowned. 'Harvey?'

'No. *Schofield.* The prisoner I brought in a couple of night-duties ago, in connection with a ringed Jag. Remember?'

'Oh yes, I remember.' She paused.

'Well, come on, anyway,' she said. 'It won't take a minute, John, really.'

He momentarily hesitated, then agreed.

In her tiny office-cum-changing-room, he took off his helmet and sat on the edge of the desk, facing her as she sat opposite, in a chair.

'Right,' she said. 'Tell me about this morning, first. How'd it go? Did you have to give evidence?'

'No. Punchy managed to screw a plea out of Harvey . . . Much to my relief, I might add.'

'And?'

'He got remanded on bail, with a surety, to seek legal advice. The Magistrate warned him that he'll probably be going away.'

'Well that's that, then, John. Nothing more to worry about.'

'*I* wouldn't say that,' he said.

She looked perplexed. He told her about the horse manure.

'So *that's* what it was I could smell, upstairs,' she said. Then she looked pained. 'I'm sorry, John. I really am. I . . . we, we should have realized this sort of reprisal was likely . . . if not inevitable.'

He shrugged. 'I can take it. Doesn't worry me. They'll get fed-up with it before I do.' He wasn't himself convinced, and didn't sound as if he were.

She opened the door of her locker and reached inside for a can of hair-spray that was on the top shelf. 'Here,' she said. 'This'll take away the smell until you can wash your hair.'

'What's that?' he wanted to know, wary.

'Hair-spray.' And she pointed the can's nozzle at his head, spraying him with a triangular-shaped mist of perfumed laquer.

'Stop it!' he told her. 'If the others smell that, they'll think I've gone the other way.' He brushed frantically at his head as he jumped off the desk-top.

'Want me to wash it for you . . . your hair? I'll do it this evening, if you like.'

'Hmmm.' He brightened. 'That'd be nice.'

'Okay, then. I'll see you at the back gate after the shift.'

'Can't wait,' he smiled. And he moved close to her, held her tightly in his arms, and kissed her.

It took an effort for them to part themselves, and when they did so they were flushed and breathless. 'I *must* go, now,' he whispered. 'Old Crikey'll probably be looking for me.' And he picked up his helmet and walked to the door.

'Wait a minute, John,' she said, tidying her hair and

straightening her tunic. 'You haven't told me about Schofield, yet. What's he complaining about?'

'That he was assaulted, before being nicked.'

'He was, too, wasn't he?'

MacHale nodded. 'Yeah. By Tasty Tom.'

'What're *you* going to say about it, John?'

His shoulders rose and fell. 'What *can* I say? I've decided I'll just have to play it by ear. If I put Tasty in the frame, the others'll really have a go at me. Alternatively, I could lie, and say Schofield wasn't assaulted. But then I'll give myself away . . . Go red in the face, or something.'

'But *if* you say there was an assault,' she pointed out, 'you'll also have to try and justify your not having reported it on arrival at the station.'

'Yeah, that's already occurred to me,' he told her. 'Can't win, can I?'

'You know, this is absolutely appalling, John,' she said, her hands on her hips, her face reflecting anger and defiance. 'Those . . . those *Cowboys* go around taking the law into their own hands, and then expect everyone else to cover for them. You'd think they'd have the sense, if they *must* take shortcuts, verbal and assault people, and do all of the other things they do against the book, to do a *thoroughly* bad job of it, so that all the doors would be closed after them.'

'They're incompetent at being incompetent,' MacHale suggested, half joking, half sighing.

'Ah well,' she resignedly said, her hands falling off her hips. 'As you said, John: just play it by ear.' She walked to the door. 'I'll keep my fingers crossed for you.'

'Thanks,' he said. 'See ya later. Maybe at grub-time.'

He waited for over an hour in Old Crikey's office, but no one came near him or sent for him, and he was wondering if they'd forgotten him. Unlikely, though. It was nerve-wracking, and he began nibbling at his fingernails. He'd heard it said that this was a deliberate ploy which investigating CIs used, especially with inexperienced or naïve officers, whose resilience was thought likely to crumble very easily: tell them they're being investigated, then leave them alone for an hour or so, to be slowly braised by their own guilt; and then they'd crack that much easier.

The phone rang, making him jump.

'Inspector Crawford's office. PC MacHale speaking.'

'CI Hilton, here,' a voice informed; it was flat, but forcible too, in a strange way. 'I'm ready to see you, now. Upstairs in the CID's interview room.'

'Yes sir, I'll be right up,' MacHale said, hoping like hell that he hadn't sounded too afraid.

He put down the phone, took several deep gulps of air, and went on upstairs, knocking at the interview room's door, entering, taking off his helmet and holding it at his left side – a habit implanted at TS: always hold anything you're carrying, in your left hand, leaving your right hand free to salute a senior officer, should you pass one.

He stood there, then, in the small, green-carpeted room, and announced himself, wondering which of the two, stony-faced, dark-suited men who sat at a desk, before him, was the CI: 'PC MacHale, sir.' The older one's the CI, he decided . . . the black-haired one; the other one must be the PS.

The older, black-haired man nodded. 'Siddown, MacHale.'

MacHale pulled out a chair and sat facing the CI, leaning over sideways to place his helmet on the floor.

'Now then, MacHale,' the CI opened, sorting through a sheaf of papers. 'As I think you know, I've been appointed by the Commander to investigate a complaint made by a man named Schofield, who alleges that, during the course of being arrested by you, some weeks ago, he was assaulted . . .' He found the particular piece of paper he was looking for, and handed it to MacHale. 'This is a Form One Six-three, which sets out, in writing, the complaint. Read it, please.'

MacHale read through the Form, his heart knocking against his ribcage. It was very brief, and concise, and merely stated that Schofield had been arrested on day, date, time and place, was alleging that he'd been punched in the stomach, by *a* police-officer, and that MacHale, as arresting officer, had been present. The bottom line of the Form reproduced the Rule Two Caution, which informed MacHale that he wasn't obliged to say anything in reply, but that whatever he did say would be put into writing and given in evidence.

He looked up, signifying he'd read the Form.

'Okay,' said the CI. 'I have a list of pre-prepared questions which I'm going to put to you. And the Sergeant, here . . .' He nodded aside, in the Sergeant's direction. '. . . will write down your answers.'

The Sergeant was seated there, pen poised over a piece of paper. Presumptious sods, thought MacHale. There might not *be* any answers. I've been cautioned, haven't I?

'First, though,' the CI went on, 'let me say that I've already spoken to Mister Crawford, and to your three colleagues who were also present at the time of the alleged assault, and they strenuously deny the allegation . . .

'There was a fourth PC present,' the CI continued, 'discounting yourself, but as he was merely completing some checks on a vehicle, and was, apparently, in a police-car while the alleged assault occurred, he isn't complained of . . . Paterson's his name, I think.'

MacHale nodded his agreement. 'Yes, sir. That's right.' Thinking again about that, though, it *wasn't* right: Paterson *had* returned from checking the Jag in time to see Tasty kick Schofield in the back of the neck, just before Snatch 'cuffed him.

'Of course,' the CI was now saying, 'Schofield is a recidivist who sees complaining against the police as an essential first step in the preparation of his defence, every time he's nicked. It's a pity, in this case, that he wasn't actually charged and convicted. Had he been, it would have been even more clear than it is now, that this . . .' He paused, flicking a dismissive hand at the One Six-Three MacHale was holding. '. . . This is nothing more than a bit of retaliatory poison.'

Retaliatory poison? thought MacHale. They've decided the complaint's a non-runner already.

'Let's get on with the Q-'n'-As,' said the CI. 'One: "Did you arrest Schofield on the night in question?"'

MacHale's lips had just formed the word, 'Yes,' and were about to deliver it, when the CI turned to the Sergeant and said that the answer to that question was, obviously, 'Yes,' and should be thus recorded.

The next question was: '"Did you assault Schofield, during the course of either the interrogation on the street or the ensuing arrest, or at *any* time during your dealings with him?"'

And then, to MacHale's astonishment, he again turned to the Sergeant and said, 'The answer to that lot is a prile of "Nos," Sarge.' Looking back at MacHale, he added: 'It must be, because your three colleagues have said so . . . Unless, that is, you want to be contradictory?'

'Well, I – '

'Good,' said the CI. 'Next question: "Did *any* police-officer who was present, assault Schofield?"' And, again, before MacHale could respond verbally, he informed the Sergeant that a negative answer should be recorded.

This is incredible, thought MacHale. But it *was* happening.

And so it went on, until the interview was at an end: the CI, asking the questions, *and* supplying MacHale's answers.

'And now, finally,' concluded the CI, 'I want you to sign the record of questions and answers.' The Sergeant handed the record to the CI, and the CI placed it before MacHale, on the table, offering his pen.

MacHale hesitated.

'Come *on*! I haven't got all bloody day, MacHale!' said the CI, raising his voice. 'I'm a busy man.'

At that, MacHale quickly took the pen and signed his name on the false document; he believed he'd have done almost anything to get out of that room.

'Right,' said the CI, taking back the record and standing up to pile his papers into a briefcase. 'You can go, now. This lot'll be either unsubstantiated or withdrawn, and you'll officially hear so in due course. Meanwhile, keep bringin em in.'

MacHale left the interview room and stood outside in the corridor, putting on and then adjusting his helmet. Through the closed door he was able to hear the CI and the PS, talking . . . chuckling. Is that how they deal with *all* complaints? he wondered, as he walked away to the head of the stairs. Probably, he decided. The Commissioner's Annual Reports invariably showed that only about three per cent of complaints were of any substance – *officially*, that was; the remainder were either withdrawn or unsubstantiated.

When MacHale reached the foot of the stairs, on the ground floor, Old Crikey was waiting for him. '*Well*, MacHale?' he asked, his face strained with anxiety. 'How did it go, what happened, what did *you* say?' And he began furiously chewing a digestif as he waited for MacHale's answers.

'*I* didn't say *anything*, sir,' MacHale told him.

But before he could explain why, Old Crikey came back with an effusive, 'Good, good. I'm – that is, *we* – we're in the clear, then.'

'Seems like it, sir,' agreed MacHale.

'Now then,' said Old Crikey, moving on to another subject. 'I want to see you tomorrow afternoon, MacHale. In my office. Your next progress-report is due.'

'Oh, yes, sir,' MacHale apprehensively said. 'I thought it must be.' And his eyes searched Old Crikey's face, for an intimation of what shape the report might take – adverse or commendatory, or maybe just a satisfactory average. But all he could identify was agitation and concern: Old Crikey's everyday expression, in fact.

'So, we'll say three o'clock, then, MacHale,' Old Crikey concluded. And he terminated the meeting by about-turning and walking away.

MacHale took out his record-of-work book and began flicking through its pages . . . Process, in abundance, but a paucity of arrests. He desperately needed a good body, he decided; but there were only about eight duty-hours left, before his meeting with Old Crikey, in which to try and claim one.

17

By six o'clock he'd done five Process – a defective tyre, an ATS, two for unnecessary obstruction, one insecure load – and had claimed a hot-doggie for footway. The hot-doggie, a sweaty and unshaven young Turkish kid with shoulderlength greasy hair and black fingernails, also went on the sheet for a host of hygiene offences – no overall, no hot water, no soap, no towel, smoking on the job, and so forth – but the arrest still didn't amount to Body of the Year, nor even of today.

What was more, the Station Officer, Harry Tanner, was annoyed: the hot doggie was wanted on warrant for non-payment of fines which had previously been imposed for footway offences, and therefore couldn't be bailed. Which, in turn, meant that Tanner was now landed with a steaming trolley, laden with Cokes and Pepsis and stale buns, which stank of stewed onions and burned sausages and hamburgers. And while he was trying to decide how they were best going to dispose of it, he'd had it placed in the furthermost corner of the yard, where the stables' cat was tentatively dipping a paw into one of its recessed cooking-pans, trying to hook out a hot sausage; if it succeeded, it'd probably be dead from food poisoning, come the morning; even the cops, who generally cherished anyone who was GTP, would *never* accept a free hot-dog or burger from a street vendor.

Eventually, Tanner managed to persuade the rental firm, which hired out trollies on a daily basis, to send down a truck and reclaim its property.

When the truck arrived, MacHale went to the yard to supervise the loading, and found the cat, having given up on the sausages – they were just *too* hot – half buried inside a plastic bag full of buns. He set it down on the ground, where it purred vibrantly and circled him, its tail, erect, brushing against his legs.

When the truck was loaded and had driven away, MacHale brushed and picked stray cat-hairs from his trouserlegs, then returned to the front office, where he saw Barker, who was looking after the shop, while Tanner was taking a break in the comms room.

'Sarge?' MacHale said. 'If a lorry, driving along a street, sheds a pile of scaffold poles, which then fall on a car, denting its bodywork, is it a damage-only or is just a Process?'

'Sounds like it's a loada fuckin *grief*, to me,' said Barker. 'Why? What d'you wanna know for?'

'Well, Sarge, I saw it happen in the High Street, this afternoon, and I wasn't sure whether to put it in a Process book or an Accident book.'

'Didn't they teach you fuck all at TS, MacHale?' Barker said. 'What does the RTA say about accidents?'

MacHale blanked off his eyes, momentarily recalling the relevant Section of the Act. '". . . If, owing to the presence of a motor vehicle on a road, an accident, causing damage – "'

'Right. Stop there,' cut in Barker. 'Did this incident occur because of the presence of a motor vehicle on a road?'

'Well . . . I . . .'

'*Did* it or *didn't* it?' persisted Barker.

'Well, yes, Sarge. The lorry and the car *were* on the road.'

'There's your answer, then.'

'Wha's that? What you on about?' asked Tanner; having returned to the front office, he'd overheard the tail end of the discussion and was always ready to offer his superior knowledge.

'Scaffold lorry, along the High Street,' explained Barker. 'Sheds some poles over a stationary motor, dentin its roof. No PI, but it is a DO or just a Process report? I say it's gotta go in a DO book. What d'you reckon?'

Harry Tanner grimaced, and thought about it. 'Just a Process, innit? No question of WDC, or reckless drivin, is there? No, a Process report for insecure load, or dangerous load, whichever ya like.'

'No, no, Harry,' Barker dogmatically retorted. 'That's wrong.' And, to reinforce his point, he began quoting the RTA.

'I agree,' said Tanner. 'The vehicles *were* present on a road. But *what's* the definition of *accident*, eh? How about that?' – he looked pretty smug now.

Neither MacHale nor Barker could offer an answer.

'Well, let's have a look in *Stone's*, then,' said Barker, reaching into the bookshelves and fetching out the three blue-covered hardback tomes of *Stone's Justices' Manual*. He flipped through the index in Volume Three. 'Accidents . . . accidents,' he abstractedly muttered as he searched the index. 'Here we are: page thirty-eight forty-eight . . .' After turning up the page, he went on: 'There's a footnote, here, that says, and I quote, "There must be a direct cause or connection between the motor vehicle and the occurrence of the accident." That's it, then. Scaffold lorry, car, fallin poles, *accident*. Enda story, all cars MP out.'

'Don't talk fuckin crap,' muttered Tanner, exasperation on his face. 'Gimme that. Let's have a butcher's hook.' And he perused the relevant entry. '*That's* not a definition of *accident*,' he said.

'Well what *more* d'you want?' demanded Barker. 'How could it talk about slight bumps or almighty crashes or broken headlamps, or even *attempt* to define nature or extent of damage?'

'An accident,' Tanner came back, 'is an unforeseen

incident . . . not preventable. Now, if a geezer shoots off down the road with a lorry loada poles that ain't securely tied, he oughta know he's likely to lose em over the side. What happened here *was* foreseeable . . . *could've* been prevented.'

'Where's it say that?' Barker indignantly asked. 'What's your source? Come on.'

'Common-sense,' snapped Tanner. 'That's what it is. No one's *ever* defined *accident*. It ain't *capable* of bein defined. You said as much yourself, a minute ago.'

'What *I* said,' shouted Barker, 'was that . . . Here, just a minute. *You* were the one who asked *us* what the definition was. *Now* you're tryin to say there *ain't* one!'

'Well what *shall* I do, Sarge?' pleaded MacHale.

'Put it in a damage-only book,' Barker told him.

'No, a Process book,' contradicted Tanner.

'Do as *I* say, MacHale,' warned Barker.

'It'll be wrong,' cautioned Tanner.

'He's *my* prob',' Barker informed Tanner.

'So what?' Tanner returned, unimpressed by Barker's ownership of MacHale.

'So he does what *I* tell him. *That's* what. How would you react if *you* had a prob', and I tried to . . .?'

MacHale discreetly walked out and left them to it, deciding that he was still none-the-wiser, but that as he'd initially reported the incident in a DO book – because it had boxes to be completed, under the headings, *Vehicles One and Two*, for recording damage *and* Process offences – , he'd leave it in a DO book. Anyway, it now occurred to him, if he did transfer his notes into a Process book, they'd be secondary notes, not original ones, and he'd be unable to refer to them in three or four months' time, when called to give evidence against the lorry driver whom he'd reported for having an insecure load.

Why couldn't Tanner or Barker have worked that out? he wondered. Whether or not the incident amounted, in law, to a road-traffic accident, was of no consequence, he now realized.

That settled, he looked at his wristwatch – six-thirty. Time for some grub.

When he reached the canteen, he found Pat there, sitting alone at a table, in a quiet corner, reading the evening newspaper.

She folded the paper and placed it aside. 'Well, John,' she smiled. 'You're still alive, I see.'

He returned the smile, and stroked her hands, which were now clasped loosely before her, resting on the table. 'Very much alive,' he softly replied, staring deep into her eyes. Spiritually, she was an oasis in a desert, he thought, providing mental refreshment, recuperation and strength. Is this *it*? he wondered . . . And his face moved inexorably closer to hers, while his hands moved up her forearms, to her upper arms, to her shoulders . . .

'Chicken salad!' The coarse voice of the evening cook, Dora Clarke, crashed through the air, making MacHale and Pat jump apart. Pat was flushed, embarrassed, and she quickly rose, picked up her shoulder-bag, and walked to the counter, taking out her purse.

MacHale followed her and wrote out his meal ticket – ham, egg and chips.

'Bad for you,' Pat told him, having glanced at his order.

'It'll fill an ole,' said Dora, and her greasy fingers picked up MacHale's ticket.

'So will concrete,' Pat said.

Dora shuffled back into the kitchen and MacHale and Pat returned to the table. 'So how'd it go, then?' she asked. 'The complaint. Did you play it by ear?'

'Yeah, *literally,*' he told her. 'I just sat there, listening, while the CI asked the questions *and* provided my answers . . . which were complete denials of the allegation. It's going to be written off, the CI said.'

'I bet Old Crikey was relieved.'

'Not much! He obviously got a One Six-Three, as well, because it was him who dealt with Schofield, at the station . . . He wants to see me in his office, tomorrow afternoon, too.'

'Oh? What for?'

'My progress report. I'm not looking forward to it, I can tell you.'

'Why not? Your record's not that bad, John. You've done a lot of Process over the last twelve weeks. And you've had a few bodies: drunks, beggars, one or two shoplifters. Harvey, as well; you can count him as a result, even though you were only a witness.'

'Yeah . . . the Process figures're quite good, Pat,' MacHale uneasily agreed. 'But let's face it, they're easy. Vagies're easy, too, like picking apples off a tree. And shoplifters're just handed over to you. I haven't achieved a lot on my own initiative, you see; at least, that's what Old Crikey'll tell me.'

'Well you can't manufacture bodies, John. If you don't come across them, you don't come across them.'

'Hmm, it's strange, y'know,' he thoughtfully remarked. 'You look in the crime-books and you see so many fresh entries, every day. Everywhere, villains are at it. Yet you rarely *catch* em at it. I mean, just for one instance, eighty-six thousand cars were nicked, last year, in the MPD. Eighty-six *thousand*. How many of them drove *past* me, out there? And why didn't I *spot* them and try and nick the drivers?'

Pat shrugged. 'As I said, luck plays a big part. But most villains are only caught *after* they've committed crime – if they're caught at all, that is – while they're making away with whatever it is they've thieved. They've got all of the advantages, though, haven't they? They know where and when and who and how.'

'Yeah, but it's still frustrating, though, Pat. D'you

know, several months ago, I decided to keep obbo on a block of flats in Morton Street, where cars were regularly being nicked from the park, outside, during the early hours.'

'Ham, egg and chips!' screamed Dora.

MacHale went to the counter, collected and paid for his greasy meal, and returned to the table.

'What happened?' asked Pat. 'Did you catch him?'

'Did I hell,' MacHale bitterly replied, dipping a chip into the yolk of his egg. 'The villain responsible had a Punch-'n'-Judy show with his missus, and she phoned the CID and said he'd got a load of nicked gear in the flat . . . car radios, spare wheels, that sort of stuff. The CID claimed him, and he then put his hands up to all the outstanding TDAs. After *I'd* spent hours trying to catch him at it.' He popped the yolk-tipped chip into his mouth.

'That was *bad* luck, John,' Pat sympathetically said.

'Yeah, I was sick,' MacHale said. 'I wondered, afterwards, though, if maybe we should be more objective about crime detection. I mean, *target* all of the real villains, and follow them around till they do something. Not just aimlessly patrolling, or waiting to be called to a shout.'

'We do target villains,' Pat told him. 'The Robbery Squad's been doing it for years. So've C-Eleven. And now there're Surveillance and Intelligence-Gathering Units in all four Areas. Mind you, though, it can be a dangerous policy. If you tell a copper to target a villain, he believes that that villain must be nicked at all costs. If the villain doesn't get nicked, the copper thinks he himself has failed.'

'Which he has, hasn't he?'

'Depends on whether or not the villain's committed crime. The danger comes when the copper gets so much evidence on his target, but no more, and then feels inclined to invent the rest. The prisons are full of professional robbers and burglars and the like, who're claiming to have been fitted-up by us.'

'Schofield's a target, you know,' MacHale said, recalling how he'd been told, on the night Schofield was nicked with the Jag, that the Robbery Squad and C-Eleven were interested.

'Won't be long, then, before *he's* behind bars,' Pat said.

Now, the canteen began filling up.

First, in came Old Crikey, clutching his daily *Observer*, a brown-paper bag containing four slices of bread, and an egg-crate containing three eggs – he'd stopped leaving his food in the fridge, ever since Vindscreen had played that practical joke on him. After casting a quizzical eye over MacHale and Pat, he bought a glass of milk, went to the cooker to fill a pan of water, then sat nearby while his eggs were boiled.

Next came the noisy crew of one of the District's DSUs: twelve officers, half in uniform, half in plainclothes, who ordered their refreshments, pulled two tables end-to-end, and began three separate games of solo. Last of all came Punchy Paterson, Tasty Tom, Snatch, and Tubby Tompkins, who also began a game of cards, after ordering their food.

'I've got an idea, John,' said Pat, finishing her salad and pushing away her plate. 'If you really want a crime arrest, why not go along to that building site in Jeffries Street, and keep obbo? They're losing stuff almost every night: scaffolding, bricks, cement, sand . . . Everything, practically.'

'Well, it is on my beat,' MacHale interestedly said. 'But who can I take with me? I can't do it alone.' He'd also finished his meal, and was leaning back, his hands clasped behind his head, his tunic unbuttoned, his stick hanging by its strap from the corner-post of his chair. 'What about you, Pat? Let's do it together.'

'I'd like to,' she apologetically told him. 'But I've got to go across to ZD, and pick up a female prisoner for our CID.' She looked around the canteen. 'Why not ask one of the DSU PCs? They're always looking for bodies.'

Briefly, he thought about it . . . and would have preferred working with an officer whom he personally knew. 'What about Hercules? He'd do it with me, wouldn't he? What d'you reckon?'

'I reckon he'd *like* to,' said Pat, smiling.

'Mmmm,' murmured MacHale, cancelling the idea in his mind. 'Be asking for it, wouldn't I, going onto a pitch-black building site with Hercules, and cuddling up with him in an empty shed?' He got up, and went over to speak with the crew of the DSU.

'Any joy?' asked Pat, when he returned.

'Yes,' he said, pleased. 'One of the plainclothes blokes said he'd come with me. In about half an hour, when the game's finished.'

No sooner had MacHale sat down, though, than Punchy Paterson, who'd closely watched his conversation with the DSU crew, went over to speak with the plainclothes PC. The plainclothes PC's expression then became serious, and he cast several quick glances at MacHale as he intently listened to what Punchy had to say.

When Punchy had returned to his own table, the plainclothes PC got up and approached MacHale. 'Look, I . . .' he hesitantly began. 'I'm sorry, but, well, I've just remembered that I've gotta see my guv'nor, later on . . . about an AQR. Sorry, mate.' And he walked back to his cards.

'That was so *obvious*!' MacHale angrily said.

'Don't let *them* put you off,' she defiantly said. 'Go and give Bill Goodman a ring. He'll definitely go with you.'

Goodman, a PC who was posted to an adjoining station, was one of the District's dog-handlers, and he'd recently taken charge – or was it the *other* way round? – of a new Alsatian, named Horace, whose training and existence he was required to justify in terms of arrests for crime. To date, though, while Goodman had made just under forty arrests, Horace had made none – because he was far more interested in scoffing food and biting *cops'* ankles, than he was in chasing and capturing bodies.

'Good idea,' MacHale told Pat. 'I'll go and phone him.'

'Okay, John . . . And don't forget your stick. You may be needing it.'

He picked it up and slipped it into the right-hand pocket of his trousers, letting it drop into the long pouch that hung down the outside of his thigh, thinking it more likely he'd have to use it against the unruly Horace, than against an unruly prisoner.

'How's it goin, then?' said Goodman, by way of a greeting, as he strolled, bandy-legged, his cap set at a jaunty angle on his head, along the pitch-black street, and halted before MacHale. He was a tall, sandy-haired, big-boned man with jug-ears, whose ill-fitting uniform had been a challenge which the clothing store was defeated by: it hung around him in folds and creases of hair-matted blue serge. 'Parked the van a couplea streets away, so's we won't get sussed.' Horace – Shouldn't he be on a lead? thought MacHale – was several feet behind Goodman, sniffing the kerb . . . moving around in tight circles before cocking his leg to mark and obliterate a rival's deposit of urine.

'Glad you could come, Bill,' MacHale smiled. 'The site's just over there.'

Goodman looked in the direction of MacHale's nod, across to the tall sheets of grey, corrugated tin, which lined the pavement's inner border for the entire length of the street; the side on which they were standing was lined with one-storey terraced houses, their interiors gutted, their windows and doorways filled-in with cemented breeze-blocks, many of which had been knocked out with iron bars, by totters and other opportunists who were seeking unlawful entry and an easy profit from scrap lead and copper. The street's lamps had been disconnected from the electricity supply, and there was scarcely any light from the clouded night sky. Mounds of bulging sacks of rubbish were strewn, at intervals, along the roadway, and at its far end, behind MacHale, a fly-tipper had shot a lorry-load of rubble and earth, in front of an abandoned and vandalized car whose wheels were missing and whose doors were hanging lopsidedly open. It was *still* a better place to live than that Rat Farm, though, MacHale thought.

'Those signs,' Goodman said, squinting his eyes and leaning forward to penetrate the wall of darkness that was before him. 'They genuine, are they, or what?'

MacHale looked across the street, to the white boards, with their bold, red-painted cautions of, '*Warning: Guard dogs on patrol*', which had been fixed, every twelve-or-so feet, to the corrugated-tin fencing. 'No,' he said. 'They're just frighteners, put up by the contractor. If there were guard dogs in there, they would have to be accompanied by handlers . . . *and*, the site wouldn't've been getting screwed, every other night.'

'That's okay, then,' said Goodman. 'Only, we'd come out a lot faster'n we went in, if there were dogs on the loose.'

'Shall we get started, then?' MacHale eagerly asked.

'Might as well,' said Goodman, looking around to see where Horace was. 'Horace, come ere,' he commanded. But Horace's snout was now rooted to a lamp-post, and he completely ignored Goodman.

Who's handling *who*? wondered MacHale, as he

watched Goodman walk to the dog and clip a short lead to the choke-chain around its neck, before dragging it away, its backside skidding and bumping along.

'*Sit!*' ordered Goodman, as he reached MacHale, the dog, now standing, attempting to drag him back to the lamp-post; and he patted . . . pressed . . . smacked the dog's rump. But Horace, as soon as Goodman's hand was removed, immediately raised his backside, and stood, wagging his tail.

With Horace under some sort of control, Goodman and the dog followed MacHale across the road, through a loose flap in the tin fence, and on to the site. After stumbling and tripping their way across a clearing, MacHale and Goodman sat on a patch of dry grass, resting their backs on a low stack of bricks, while Horace lay down in-between them.

For a while, they sat there in silence, listening to distant noises: car-doors, slamming, in nearby streets . . . a dog, barking . . . cats, wailing . . . the far-off noise of the RT-car's whip-tones, as it hurtled towards the source of an Emercall . . . And when the noises had subsided and faded away, the faint throb of inner-city traffic, *always* in the air, but so familiar, so congruous, it was inaudible on all but the most silent of nights, and in all but the most silent of places . . . like the ticking of a clock on a person's mantlepiece: always there, but so rarely heard.

Goodman released his grip on Horace's lead, took out a tobacco tin, and began rolling a cigarette.

Now there were high-pitched squeaks to be heard . . . from above? Or in the near distance, beyond Goodman and MacHale . . .? MacHale wasn't certain. *Is* it bats? he asked himself. Or were the squeaks too loud? He strained his ears and listened more intently, holding his breath. More like a door, he felt, on again hearing the noise . . . *yes*, a *door*, creaking open on dry hinges. Someone could be entering the foreman's hut . . . wherever that was, on the site.

Horace raised himself up, frowned, erected his huge ears, lowered his head, and sniffed the air; the fur on his neck began rising, and a low, deep growl broke from his throat.

MacHale leaned over Horace's back and prodded Goodman. 'Here we go, Bill,' he urgently whispered. 'Someone's out there. Horace has got him on radar.'

Goodman nodded his head and sniffed his concurrence.

And then a shower of pebbles and earth was flung into MacHale's face, as Horace started away, his back paws scrabbling for grip on the loose surface of the ground; as he found his feet, his body jolted aside, hitting Goodman's hands; in turn, Goodman's hands smacked him in the mouth, knocking the rolled cigarette halfway down his throat.

Goodman choked and spluttered, spitting strands of tobacco and shreds of paper, and as his palms moved flat onto the ground, behind him, his right leg shot forward, its heel making frantic stabs at the fast-disappearing lead that was attached to Horace's neck.

But Horace was gone, deep into the black site.

For several seconds the sound of falling bricks and growling and panting were to be heard from the near distance: Horace was angry, it seemed.

MacHale looked apprehensively at Goodman, who, not unduly concerned, was rolling himself another cigarette. 'Should we go and get him, Bill?'

'No,' said Goodman. 'You'd break a leg, out there. Horace'll be back with a body, in a minute; you'll see . . . Don't worry about it; he's *trained* for this sorta stuff.' The reassurance was offered with some pride, too.

If you say so, MacHale sceptically thought. And he waited and listened and strained his ears and his eyes.

Then, hurtling towards himself and Goodman came a

huge, round, black object . . . with fur on it . . . and a long tail . . . Horace, hot on its heels. MacHale and Goodman fell apart, as the cat and Horace whistled between them, up and over the stack of bricks they'd been leaning against, and away into the night.

MacHale and Goodman scrambled to their feet.

'Horace! . . . Horace! . . . Get *back* ere!' bellowed Goodman . . . on and on, until he was hoarse and MacHale was sick of hearing it.

But Horace was well gone, and he *wasn't* coming back.

MacHale and Goodman left the site, and for a long while they scoured the streets in Goodman's van, hoping to find Horace with his leg cocked against a lamp-post or car tyre. In the end, Goodman stopped the van, reluctantly picked up the RT-set's transmitter, and circulated Horace's description to All Cars One and Three. He was almost in tears, convinced he'd be the laughing stock of the MPD.

He was right, too.

The wits came back over the RT-set, almost non-stop: Some *police* dog, goin on the trot, like that . . . Yeah, some *handler*, an all, for *lettin* him . . . Better show him time-off, till he's captured . . . Who? The dog or the handler? . . . *Both* of em . . .

And so on. Until the RT-operator at IR, switched off the talk-through and put a stop to the backchat.

Later on, Old Crikey organized the Relief into separate search-parties, with instructions that they should implement the streetsearch plan; but still there was no sign of Horace, and by half-past ten there was nothing further to be done except recirculate the dog's description by way of an AS teleprinter-message, then hope for the best.

'How much longer?' he whined, pressing the wet flannel even tighter to his screwed-up eyes. 'It's *stinging* me!' He was kneeling over the bath, while Pat, bending close beside him, shampooed his hair. They were each wearing a long, white-cotton nightshirt, which she had bought at an indoor market along Kings Road, several months ago.

She tut-tutted as she began showering away the rich suds, the flat of her left hand pressing against his scalp, its skin squeaking over his wet hair as it followed the jets of warm water, from the nape of his neck to his forehead. 'You're worse than a baby, John, honestly you are.'

'Wha's that? What're you doing, *now*?' he demanded, reaching blindly up with his right hand as he felt a wet coldness envelop his scalp. 'It *feels* like a loada *slime*.'

'Conditioner,' she told him, and began massaging the thick, perfumed liquid into the roots of his hair.

'And what's *that* s'posed to do?' he asked.

'Gives your hair some body,' she explained. 'Makes it more manageable.'

'Manageable? . . . *Manageable*?' he muttered. 'All I wanna do is *comb* it, not . . . *sculpt* it or something . . . *Manageable*. Huh!'

'You'll see,' she said. 'You'll like it.'

'Oh, come on, Pat,' he moaned, gasping for air. 'My mouth's dry as a bone . . . I can't breathe through me nose.'

'There,' she said, turning off the shower taps and pressing the excess water from his hair. 'Finished.' She took a towel from the heated wall-rail and threw it over him.

He stood, red-faced, gripping the corners of the towel and bringing them to his saturated eyes. 'Ah . . . That's better.'

'Good.' She reached over the sink and drew aside the curtains, then opened the small, frosted-glass window and allowed the swirling clouds of grey steam, which filled the bathroom, to be sucked out into the chill night air. 'Now, into the kitchen, John, and I'll blow it dry for you.'

'Hang on a minute, I want to comb it, first.'

'Okay,' she said. 'I'll go and make a drink, then. What do you fancy? Beer, tea, coffee . . .?'

'Tea, I think, Pat.'

She went away to the kitchen, and for a while he amused himself by combing his wet hair into all sorts of weird styles: parted along the centre, with kiss-curls at his temples . . . then, Elvis-style, straight back, with a huge quiff hanging down his forehead . . . finally, Punk, the wet strands of hair sprouting vertically from his scalp.

'Here,' he said, as he entered the kitchen, a smile on his shiny red face. 'What d'you reckon Old Crikey'd say if I turned up on parade with my Barnet like this?'

After unplugging the boiling kettle, she turned . . . and burst out laughing, her hands covering her mouth. 'You look just like Gizzard Puke. Maybe you should let me dye it orange and stiffen it up with jelly water.'

'Yeah,' he said. 'Then I could join the Drug Squad.'

'More likely you'd be *nicked* by the Drug Squad,' she laughed.

He sat in the chair which she'd positioned in the centre of the floor, watching as she poured boiling water into the teapot. 'Pat,' he said. 'Are you going home on the next weekend leave? To your parents' place, I mean.'

'I was thinking of going this weekend, actually,' she said.

'*This* weekend? We're not *off* this weekend.'

She handed him his mug of tea, placing her own on the worktop opposite him while she plugged-in the blow-drier. 'No, I realize that, but I thought I'd take some time off, or annual leave, and go, anyway . . . How about coming with me?'

'Will that be okay?' he asked. 'Your parents won't mind, will they?'

'Don't be daft. Of course they won't mind. They want to meet you.'

'Oh, well . . . Yeah, I'd love to go, then . . . Here, hang on; what d'you mean, *they* want to meet *me*? Have you – ?'

She nodded, smiling, and moved behind him, combing the hot air through the top of his head. 'I phoned them, this morning. While you were at court. Told them about us.'

'Hmm,' he murmured, feeling uneasy. When a girl told her parents all about a new boyfriend, wasn't that supposed to be a sure sign she'd been planning well ahead in the relationship? Not that he minded; he was rather pleased that Pat seemed to think there was a future for them, together. No, it was the idea that he'd be on trial, under close scrutiny when he met her parents, which bothered him. 'What exactly did you tell them?' he wanted to know. 'About me, I mean.'

'Don't worry, John,' she said, inclining his head as she redirected the blower's air. 'Just be yourself. They'll like you.'

'Hmm,' he again murmured. 'But how about . . .? Well, where . . .? I mean, we can't . . . Not under their roof . . . *Can* we?'

She tossed back her head, and laughed. 'John, we're grown-ups. We can do what we like. But you needn't worry about that, anyway. They live in a cottage, in the grounds. *We'll* be staying in the staff quarters, above the restaurant.'

'Yes, but they'll *know*, won't they,' he said, really anxious, now.

'And what's wrong with that, anyway?' she said. '*We're* not Victorians, and neither are my parents.'

'Yeah, okay,' he agreed, smiling away his concern. The lure of the idea of spending a weekend in the country was finally overpowering. 'Actually, I can't wait.'

'That's the idea,' she told him, switching off the blower and reaching for her tea.

'C'mere,' he said, pulling her onto his knee.

'Careful,' she said, steadying her mug.

'Never mind that,' he said, taking the mug from her, and reaching out, sideways, to place it on the worktop. He smiled mischievously. 'Maybe we'd better get some practice in for this dirty weekend.'

He stood, picking her up with him, swaying from side-to-side as they kissed . . . then walked to the doorway . . . nudging off the lightswitch with his shoulder, as they passed from the kitchen to the hallway, making for the bedroom . . .

'Oh, John,' she whimpered.

'Shhh,' he gently breathed.

Words had become superfluous.

18

Each early-turn officer he passed – while making his way across the yard, passing through the station building, descending the stairs to the locker room – looked rivetingly at him, and with excited eyes asked, 'Have you heard, have you heard?'

He was hooked by the first officer, and halted his stride, saying, 'No. What?' Thereafter, he just smiled, slowed his pace to say, 'Yes, *I've* heard,' and continued on his way.

They'd found Horace, it seemed. This morning. In a small, riverside park near Fulham. Two PCs in a GP-car had been called to deal with a 'savage Alsatian' which was terrorizing kids and young mums as they strolled across the grass, enjoying the early-morning sunshine. The PCs, initially chased away by Horace, returned with a piece of canteen liver attached to a long length of string. Then, trailing the tit-bit across the grass, they lured the ravenous Horace into the GP, and slammed its doors.

When Horace had devoured the liver, they attempted to enter the car. But Horace turned nasty and refused to admit them, growling and barking, and jumping all over the seats until Bill Goodman arrived, pacified him, and took him away.

Not so funny, thought MacHale, was that yesterday evening, while he, Goodman and half the MPD were turning the manor upside-down for an AWOL police dog, a couple of villains entered the building site in Jeffries Street and went on the trot with a lorry-load of housebricks and a ton of cement.

As he reached the basement of the building, turned left, and began walking along the narrow corridor, past the entrance to the canteen, MacHale thought he saw Punchy Paterson and Vindscreen, pulling quickly away, in through the locker room's open doorway. What the hell're they up to, now? he apprehensively wondered.

As he reached the locker room, Punchy Paterson, Tasty Tom and Vindscreen came hurrying out past him, completely ignoring his presence. He shrugged, smiled wryly, and walked inside the changing room.

He hadn't proceeded far across the room before he was stopped dead in his tracks by what he saw before him: his locker, wide open, its door hanging lopsidedly from its hinges, its thin, grey metal, crumpled and dented as if it were no more than just a piece of stiff cardboard. And inside the locker, his tunic, which he'd left draped around a coat-hanger, was reduced to shreds and strips of blue serge, having been viciously slashed with a razor-sharp blade.

Do they really hate me that *much*? he asked himself, as he stood there, wide-eyed and bewildered, on the verge of breaking up . . .

He felt so sorry for himself . . . so vulnerable, so fragile: a tiny chick inside a shell which was being remorselessly tapped and tapped with the back of a heavy spoon, slowly and methodically, each blow producing a bigger crack, piling stress upon stress, until . . .

But then he stopped himself from inwardly crumbling, and breathed long and hard, banishing the choking emotion from his throat and eyes. Those were the reactions they wanted, he realized. Well, to *hell* with them. He'd force himself to endure whatever they threw at him, until the time came for him to strike back. The tunic was a personal belonging, true enough, and that made this a personal attack, but MacHale's title didn't extend to ownership: the tunic was the property of the Official

Receiver, and would be replaced, free of charge. The Official Receiver, therefore, was the *real* victim, not MacHale.

So here, MacHale now told himself, was an ideal opportunity to strike back. The damage to police property would have to be reported on a Seven Twenty-Eight, with a notation to the effect that MacHale wasn't willing to be assessed for the cost of a replacement garment. More than that: there'd have to be a crime-book entry, too; this wasn't merely damage, it was *criminal* damage.

He cleared out his locker and transferred the contents to another, unallocated one at the far side of the room. Then he hung up his anorak, went around to the back of the lockers, and took his spare tunic from the metal stand which he'd hung it on, several weeks ago; it really needed pressing, but compared with the tunics of some of the other PCs, it was immaculate.

He put it on, went to fasten the buttons – and found they were missing. 'The thieving bastards,' he muttered. The buttons must have been removed by one of the nick's many black-marketeers, he believed: most foreign-tourists, or private collectors, would pay well for items of police equipment, although it was more usual for such things as helmets or helmet badges to go missing, not small pieces, like coat or tunic buttons; an American tourist would give as much as fifty quid for a policeman's helmet, MacHale had heard.

What to do? he wondered, as he stood there, gazing out of the window. Up above, it was a bright and sunny afternoon, so he'd be no less conspicuous, on parade, if he were to wear a mac over the buttonless tunic. And then he saw the buttons, glinting at the edge of his vision, lying scattered on the floor, in a corner of the room. He walked over to the corner, squatted and picked up the buttons, deciding, now, that this piece of vandalism was also down to Punchy Paterson, Tasty Tom and Vindscreen.

He glanced at his wristwatch – two-seventeen – and wondered if Pat would have sufficient time to sew-on the four buttons, before parade; he knew she kept needles and thread in her office, because she'd once sewn-on a shirt-collar button for Barker, after a drunk had ripped away his clip-on tie, leaving the button hanging by a loose thread. MacHale hurried upstairs to see her.

She was furious, and threatened to rush up to the Collator's office and give them a double portion of her mind – which had got GBH on it, at this moment. But MacHale managed to dissuade her, convincing her that it would be far better to affect an oblivious posture for them. Besides, he went on, if there were to be a battle, then he'd have to wage it himself; he was grateful for her concern and her back-up, but felt it would only serve to weaken him, not reinforce him.

For a few seconds, she was silent, staring at the floor, her eyes ablaze. Then she looked up, inspired, her eyes now twinkling, an impish smile breaking open her mouth. '*I've* just had the most *brilliant* idea,' she said. '*Don't* report the damage to your tunic; the CID would only crash it, anyway . . . you know, write it off. No. Just follow me, John.'

And before he could attempt to wheedle any further explanation from her, she was gone, out of the office, down the stairs, and along to the locker room in the basement of the building.

Ten minutes later, they walked on parade, their expressions enigmatically triumphant, while the members of the Relief, save Hercules and Mathieson – Hercules was still in no-man's land, Mathieson was still UC-sick – , looked . . . stared . . . altered their expressions from peaks of expectancy to troughs of anxiety, and wondered just what the hell was going on, here. MacHale was wearing a buttoned tunic – Pat had sewn-on the buttons – and was carrying what looked like a bundle of slashed and shredded blue-serge. Pat momentarily savoured the scene, then walked to the end of the line and stood near to Hercules, while MacHale walked to Vindscreen, tossed him the slashed tunic, and said, 'Here ya go, mate, this is yours, I think. Found it lying on the locker-room floor.'

Vindscreen caught the tunic, looked at it in astonishment, and retorted, 'What're *you* on about? This ain't *mine*.'

'Take a look at the numerals, then,' MacHale advised him.

Vindscreen did so; and went into shock. The tunic did, indeed, belong to him – *now*.

Pat's 'brilliant' idea had been to take Vindscreen's spare tunic from his locker, removed the District letters and numerals from its shoulders, and replace them with the letters and numerals from MacHale's damaged tunic. Thus, MacHale now had an intact tunic – albeit one which didn't fit too well, because Vindscreen was taller and thinner – and Vindscreen had the damaged one, which now bore the letters and numerals from his own tunic. Later in the week, MacHale would attend the clothing van when it called at the nick, and exchange the tunic for one which properly fitted him; in the meantime, all of his belongings would remain in Pat's locker, out of harm's way.

'You . . . *bastard*!' spluttered Vindscreen.

'Up yours, an all, Vindscreen,' returned a jubilant MacHale, and he walked along the line to stand next to Pat, who was almost quivering with delight at the coup they'd together pulled off.

Three o'clock. MacHale paused before Old Crikey's office door, adjusted his tie, ran a hand over his hair, knocked, then entered. 'You wanted to see me, sir. About my progress report.'

Old Crikey was seated at his desk, bent over a wad of papers, a pen in his right hand. He extended his left hand, shaking it, not looking up, indicating that he was trying to concentrate on what he was reading, and was annoyed by the intrusion.

MacHale looked at Old Crikey's bald head; the plasters which had been stuck on top of it, were now removed; the skin looked sore and red – one or two scabs, as well, and a couple of potholes, as if someone had been practising banging four-inch nails into his nut; the idea of it made MacHale inwardly wince.

At length, Old Crikey sighed, appended his signature to one of the papers, picked up the wad, stacked it level, and placed it aside. 'What were you saying, MacHalc?'

'My report, sir. You said, yesterday, that you wanted to see me at three this afternoon.'

'Oh, *crikey*! I'd forgotten.' He turned aside, opened a desk drawer and brought out the confidential report, which had been prepared by Barker. 'Get me a glass of milk from the canteen, will you, MacHale?' he said, grimacing and rubbing his gut. 'I'm in agony, here.'

'Yes, sir,' MacHale dutifully said – the request had, in fact, been framed as an order. He lingered there, however, hoping to intimate that Old Crikey should provide him with some money.

Old Crikey looked squarely at him . . . frowned, then turned aside in his chair and dipped into the right pocket of his trousers, fetching out a fifty-P coin. 'Here,' he grudgingly muttered. 'Take that.'

Within three minutes, MacHale was back with a half-pint glass of milk, and some change, both of which he placed on the desk, by Old Crikey's right hand.

He was still studying the report, and, unusually, his face gave nothing away. He reached blindly for the milk, raised the glass to his lips, swallowed a mouthful, contorted his face as the cold liquid hit his gut, and set down the glass. Then he sniffed, averted his eyes, picked up his change, carefully checked it, and shoved it into his pocket. 'Now then, MacHale,' he began, wiping the back of his hand across his upper lip, removing the milk moustache. 'Overall, it's not good. The report consists of many boxes, of course, but the sum of it is, *Could do a lot better.*'

Mentally, MacHale cringed, and wished that Old Crikey would ask him to be seated. 'Can you explain, sir, please?'

'"Attitude to the public,"' said Old Crikey, reading from the report. '"Polite but not sufficiently firm when a display of authority is called for."' He peered up at MacHale, before going on: '"Process: numbers adequate, but insufficient variation of offences."'

'With respect, sir,' put in MacHale. 'I've done all *sorts* of Process: ATS, defective tyres, warning instruments and brakes; insecure loads, ped-X offences, dangerous conditions . . .'

'You're saying that Sergeant Barker is wrong, then, are you, MacHale?' challenged Old Crikey.

'Well . . . No, sir, I'm saying that I disagree with his opinion.'

'Hmm,' grunted Old Crikey, in-between another swallow of his milk. '"Arrests: beggars, drunks, obstructions of the footway, shoplifters, and so on, but little or nothing in the way of crime; lacks initiative."'

That *hurt*. 'But I *don't* lack initiative, sir,' protested MacHale. 'I do plenty of stops – good stops, with reasonable suspicion – I check the crime-books to see what's going on where and when, and I even study the One Three-Two, to see where all the stolen cars are being dumped. I'm *always trying*, sir.'

'That's as maybe,' retorted Old Crikey. 'But if The Job

was *full* of types like you – tryers who're non-producers – where would we be? *Results* are what count. You've got to *prove* yourself, MacHale.'

'Well I don't see what more I can do, sir,' MacHale said, his face pleading for some understanding. 'Maybe if you or Sergeant Barker were to take me out and *show* me how to do The Job, things'd improve.'

'Don't be impertinent, MacHale!' snapped Old Crikey, his teeth grating as he belted out the words. '*We* haven't got time to wet-nurse incompetent probationers. We want intelligent, resourceful, mature men who can go out there and give it *stick*. The *streets* are a sufficient guide and mentor for anyone who's got the wherewithal for a determined, gutsy approach.'

MacHale was now red in the face, annoyed, hostile; to hell with tact and diplomacy; they got you nowhere except trodden on, or pissed on from a great height. 'With *respect*, sir,' he tersely said. 'You and Sergeant Barker are supposed to be my supervising officers. How can either of you write a report about my performances on the street, when you're never *with* me to *witness* them? How does Sergeant Barker know *anything* about my attitude to the public, or my initiative, when he's never *patrolled* with me? All he does is occasionally read my *reports*.'

Old Crikey's face was draining of colour. He'd scarcely believed what he'd heard. His lower jaw was cracking violently back and forth. 'This is insubordination, MacHale!' he shouted, thumping his right fist, sideways down onto the desk-top, and making the glass of milk skitter across its polished surface. 'Sit *down*!' And when MacHale had sat, he jumped to his feet, to claim for himself the advantage of a superior, towering height over his adversary.

'I'm sorry, sir,' said MacHale; although it wasn't toned

as an apology, but as a prelude to justification of his stance: 'I had to say what I said, and I meant it, too.'

'Well let me tell you, MacHale,' seethed Old Crikey. 'If you don't pull your socks up, you'll be *out*! Overnight! We don't have to give reasons for dismissing probationers, you know. If we decide you're unlikely, for *whatever* reason, to become a good and efficient Constable, that's *it*!'

MacHale was silent. The prospect – of a fulfilment of Old Crikey's threat – was unthinkable. Okay, so The Job was a *pig*, sometimes, and things *were* rough at the moment, but you just *couldn't* do without it. It was a weird feeling, and MacHale couldn't fully analyse or understand it, but it was there, binding him tight. One thing was for sure, though, you only ever got *one* chance at The Job: if The Job unloaded you, you were *forever* finished as a cop, for no other force in the land would take you on, thereafter.

'And now,' Old Crikey was saying, 'you can get out of here, and go and wait in the canteen. The Chief Superintendent can deal with *you*!'

Suddenly, MacHale wanted to *hit* him; and put the biggest fuckin plaster that he was ever *likely* to have, on top of that incompetent, bottleless, *ugly*, hateful nut of his. But the feeling passed as quickly as it had materialized, leaving MacHale feeling hot and sticky and weak.

He left Old Crikey's office, went to the canteen, bought a Coke, and sat alone, feeling miserable, wondering how the Chief Superintendent would react to the reports of Old Crikey and Barker; he wouldn't side with MacHale, that was for sure. MacHale was dispensable, far *more* dispensable than an Inspector or Sergeant. But Barker's write-up – or what little MacHale heard of it – *was* unfairly adverse.

The phone rang. A traffic-warden got up to respond.

'It's okay,' MacHale called out to her, himself getting up. 'It'll be for me, I expect.'

It was: the Chief was ready to see him. He replaced the receiver, returned to the table, drained his glass of Coke, then made his way to the third floor of the building – the top floor, where all of the station's senior officers were located. You could judge a man's status in the force, just by asking him in which part of the station building he was housed. If he told you, 'In the basement,' then he was either a station mouse or a PC, the lowest of the low; if he replied, 'On the top floor,' then he was a senior officer, or a non-operational hanger-on, such as Collator, or Admin staff.

Out of breath, MacHale paused at the Chief's door, composing himself. The narrow, green-carpeted corridor was deserted and silent – unnervingly so.

MacHale knocked at the door, and waited, mentally genuflecting and crossing himself.

'Come.' – arrogantly intoned from within the Chief's office.

MacHale walked in, closed the door, and stood before the Chief's desk, body erect, feet slightly apart, hands clasped tightly behind his back. He could smell perfume in the air . . . after-shave, maybe cologne . . . sickly sweet.

The Chief placed aside this morning's copy of *The Sun*, which he'd been reading, and looked up at MacHale, his features horse-shoe shaped – eyebrows, mouth, his *whole* face – or so it seemed – trying to push upward from the centre. Supercilious, domineering bastard, with a piece of rotten cheese for a moustache. 'Ah, MacHale,' he said – dismissively, MacHale thought – , and reached into his In-tray to fetch out the report, which he began reading, thoughtfully and in silence.

He was a meretricious man, middle-aged, wearing a double-breasted grey suit, a blue-silk shirt, a blazing-red tie, and a pair of built-up black moccasins, which, if anything, accentuated his short stature – he was only *just* five-eight, MacHale believed. His collar-length grey hair was worn original Beatle-style, and while a chunky silver bracelet – cheap and nasty, thought MacHale – drooped from his limp, right wrist, his left wrist sported an enormous, stainless-steel watch that bore numerous buttons and displayed dials within dials – tell you everything except the time of day, mused MacHale.

The Chief's appearance said all about him, really; but while *he* sincerely believed he was *hot* shit, there was no one at the nick who *didn't* think he was anything other than a flashy, stuck-up ponce who'd have difficulty organizing misery in an earthquake. As a PC and a Sergeant, he was plain Frank Brown; but as soon as he reached senior-officer status, that is Inspector, he adopted his mother's maiden name and became *Francis Parker-Brown*, making official the change, by way of deed-poll.

First, MacHale *again* felt like hitting someone – the someone who was slouched before him in a chair, charting his stars. But then he found himself inwardly smiling. He was reminded of the time when he and a few other lads had been leaning out of the section-house's third-floor library window, one Sunday morning, looking down on the yard. Parker-Brown drove in at the wheel of his new car – a Triumph Stag – and seemed pleased that he had an audience, looking down from the library window. For a while, he chatted to the blonde piece who was in the car's passenger seat, then went inside the nick. When he re-emerged, checking to make sure he still had an audience at the library window, he climbed into the Triumph, started it, giving it plenty of his right toe, and shot back in a tight circle, wheels spinning and spitting plumes of black smoke . . .

'Who's he think he is? . . . Fangio?' asked one of the audience of young PCs.

Now, in second gear, Parker-Brown was streaking across the yard, intending to exit with a flourish, by taking the corner which led out onto the main road on two wheels . . . *Terrific* stuff . . .

Only thing was, the station van then came poodling around the corner and met the Triumph, head on . . . *Kee-rash!*

The lads in the library nearly fell out of the window, they laughed so hard and so uncontrollably.

Now, Parker-Brown emitted a long, nasal sigh, which peaked and died away, accompanied by a brief closing of his small grey eyes. He placed the report on his desk, and rested his right elbow on the arm of his chair, allowing the side of his face to fall into the upraised flat of his hand. 'Not good enough, MacHale,' he indignantly said. 'And what's this I hear about you being discourteous to your Inspector, Mister Crawford?'

'Well, sir,' he began. 'I only told Mister Crawford that I believed the report was not a fair reflection of me and my performance.'

'Your supervisors are very experienced police-officers, MacHale,' Parker-Brown said. 'I respect their judgements.' He paused, pulled down the cuff of his left shirtsleeve, and toyed with its gold-Sovereign link, his eyes quickly flicking sideways to ensure that MacHale had taken note. 'If *they* say you're not pulling your weight, you're *not* pulling your weight.' Now he opened a desk drawer, removed a huge cigar, clipped one of its ends, and lit it, filling the room with clouds of dense, sweet-smelling grey smoke.

The theatrics had given MacHale a moment or two in which to deliberate. Take the initiative, he decided, while there's a temporary lull in the proceedings: 'I'd like to point out, sir, that if – '

'Of course,' cut in Parker-Brown, waving aside his cigar. 'I take note of the fact that your CTC results are up to scratch, but this doesn't in any way excuse you . . .' He broke off, drawing on his cigar.

Try again, thought MacHale: 'I want to tell you, sir, how I feel that – '

'What we need in the force, you see, MacHale, are people who are capable of putting theory into practice,' Parker-Brown again interjected. He leaned over sideways and tapped cigar ash into a metal waste-paper basket that was beside him, on the floor.

For Christ's sake, thought MacHale; he's just not *listening*; it's as if he's wired-up to transmit but not to receive. '*Sir,*' he began again, his voice more forcible than before. 'I'm trying to – '

But, as before, Parker-Brown cut straight in: 'However, I'm prepared to be tolerant, MacHale. I shall recommend to the Commander that you be given a chance to improve yourself: show us that you *can* do it, that you *can* become a good all-rounder.' He leaned forward, placed his cigar on the edge of the desk, opened a drawer and removed a large, brown envelope, together with an orange sticker on which was printed, in black capitals, the words, *Staff In Confidence*. After scrawling, in brilliant turquoise ink, a few lines along the bottom of MacHale's report, he signed it with a flourish, placed it in the envelope, then licked the sticker's gummed back and pressed that flat across the envelope's flap. Finally, after throwing the envelope into his Out-tray, he picked up his cigar and *The Sun* newspaper, turned aside in his chair, said, 'I'll see you again in three months' time,' and thus dismissed MacHale.

MacHale about-turned and walked quickly out, resisting a powerful urge to slam the door. Instead, he paused outside in the corridor, muttered, '*Slimeball*,' and offered a vigorously-gesticulated series of V-signs to the closed door. 'Up *yours*, Parker-Brown!'

What am I gonna do? he thought, as he walked away,

feeling even more frustrated and miserable than he had after his bust-up with Old Crikey. But there was nothing *to* do. It was just . . . bad luck; and he cursed it.

Things *had* to get better, he told himself – if only because they couldn't get a lot worse. Something was bound to turn up and alter the course of his fortune.

Micawberism. But that state of mind made possible the perceived fulfilment of your greatest expectations. So, MacHale now strove to put this afternoon's events to the back of his mind. Approaching was an undeniable highlight: he and Pat were going away for the weekend, to breathe clean, fresh air; to relax; to forget . . . When he returned, invigorated and recharged, he could pick up the pieces and begin anew.

19

It was a little after eleven o'clock, Sunday evening.

He felt exhausted, depressed, and as he climbed into bed and lay back against the pillow, clasping his hands behind his head, he believed he knew how a junkie, suffering the effects of withdrawal, must feel. The week-end was over – almost before it had begun, it now seemed – and tomorrow, Monday morning, loomed black and cold and shiveringly miserable in his mind, because he knew that this was precisely how he would first encounter it, at five-thirty A.M., when Sid Broadbent, the night-duty warden, came crashing through the room's door to waken him for early-turn.

He closed his eyes, sighing, and began withdrawing from his mind's archives the weekend tapes, replaying them from beginning to end . . .

Saturday morning, ten-past eight, an enamelled blue sky. They were cruising along the near-deserted motor-way in the red Ford Fiesta they'd hired. He was at the wheel, she was reclined in the passenger seat, her eyes half-closed, carelessly humming in tune with the radio – Duran Duran: *The Reflex* . . .

He wiggled his head into the pillow, and smiled . . .

They'd turned off the motorway, and the sun was now to their right, steadily climbing, becoming stronger, casting shadows which grew steadily shorter . . . A narrow, two-lane road in the middle of – nowhere, he'd thought, although Pat knew exactly where they were, and was acting as navigator. There were tall trees, either side of the road, and through gaps in their rows of stout trunks, he was able to snatch glimpses of ploughed fields, and pasture, rising and falling, dotted with grazing cows and sheep. Occasionally, Pat would start forward in her seat, her eyes wide open, and point ahead to the grassy verge, excitedly shouting, 'Look, John, a squirrel! . . . A magpie! . . . A rabbit! . . .'

They hadn't been out more than three-quarters of an hour, and she was now pointing ahead, saying, 'Pull in there, John . . . into that lay-by. We'll have our picnic, now.'

At nine o'clock in the *morning*!

He'd laughed, but nevertheless complied with her instruction. And when they were halted in the lay-by, she'd jumped out of the car, hurried around to the back, raised the rear door, and pulled out a hamper and two fold-away chairs. And there they'd sat for the next hour, chatting, enjoying the thin, but warm, sunshine, eating and drinking – cold sausages, savoury pastries and flasks of tea and coffee; her diet was having a day off, it seemed. Before continuing on their way, they sat in silence, feeding crumbs to the birds . . . sparrows, blackbirds, thrushes, a solitary chaffinch – the boldest of them all – , and a robin. Then a squirrel ventured along, from behind a tree, squatting on its bushy grey tail and looking askance at them with shining, almond-shaped eyes, its whiskers trembling as it scented the air. The squirrel, too, received its share of the crumbs before scrurrying away and racing nimbly up the vertical trunk of a lofty silver birch.

It was so peaceful, there . . . a deep quietude, only occasionally stirred by the fluttering of a bird's wings, or by the warble of a thrush, or by the *chip-chip* call of a robin or the passage of a passing car. It became a vapid peace, though, for him, and he was soon on edge, pivoting his left leg on its toes and tapping his heel against the ground.

'Relax,' Pat told him.

He stopped the tap-tapping of his heel, and allowed tension to drain from him, but a minute later his fingers were drumming the arm of the fold-away chair. In the city, in The Job, you were ever alert, always on the look-out for predators, conditioned by a myriad, oppressive features of urban existence – pollution, crime, traffic noise, *always* movement and sound and danger and excitement – , so that stress became a way of life, and hypertension was, to some degree, dissipated by hyperactivity.

'Did you ever hear about those battery-farmed chickens, Pat?' he asked. 'They once tried to set some free in a run, but the poor little buggers were terrified of freedom. They'd never experienced or witnessed it, therefore never coveted it. They just kept running back inside the box, to the darkness and the confined space. *I'm* beginning to feel like one of them, out here in this lay-by. I want to run back to the city, use my senses, my instincts, rejoin the struggle for survival. I *like* it here, but I just can't uncoil.'

'Those chickens were institutionalized,' she told him. 'So are you, in a sense. The city's an institution of the worst kind. This is rehabilitation, out here. It just takes time to adapt, that's all. If you got used to it, you'd never go back, and you'd be better off for it, believe me.'

He believed her. And he became used to it by the time the weekend was over. And he didn't want to go back, to rewind, to live on his nerves, to apprehensively ponder the future.

Broad Cross: a tiny village – a hamlet, actually, so Pat had said – , about five miles north of Henley, buried deep in the Oxfordshire countryside, amid a vast, National Trust plantation, stocked with limes and birches and firs. They arrived just after noon.

For almost half an hour they'd driven slowly, between low, flint walls, along narrow, meandering lanes, passing through open country, never sighting a living soul, and only occasionally sighting the sinewously-smoking chimney of a thatched cottage, its broken-backed roof jutting from among a clump of densely-packed conifers, usually at the foot of a bank of tree-studded hills that dominated the far-off horizon.

And then they were there: the road had suddenly become wider . . . and wider . . . and they'd come upon a pub which had a thatched roof, whitewashed walls with black timbers – none of which seemed truly vertical – and small, lattice windows . . . then a large expanse of green grass, to their right, which was dead level and closely mown, occupied by two teams of out-of-season cricketers and a scattering of spectators, and bordered by a forest of towering deciduous trees which were thick with pregnant buds and the massive, ramshackle nests of huge, black rooks and crows.

Further on, the roadway was lined either side with little cottages, each with a thatched roof, leaded windows, and neat lawn, squared off with shrubs and privets . . . one or two shops, as well, along here . . . a post-office-cum-general-store – Mrs Martin's, according to Pat – , an ironmonger's – Mr Jones' – , and a greengrocer's – Mr Harris's. A blacksmith's shop, too – known simply as *Smithy's* – , whose white-painted boards were hung with old cartwheels, horseshoes, and pieces of black-painted wrought-iron . . . a gate, shelf brackets, candle holders, telephone shelves, and so on, all at '*Reasonable prices*', and '*Made to order, if required*', according to a painted sign that was fixed to the entrance.

At last, on their left, was the coffee shop: *Ye Olde Coffee Shoppe Restaurant*, so declared the gilt-scripted sign that hung on chains from a yardarm affixed to the shop's red-brick front wall.

'Here we are,' said Pat. 'Park out front.'

'Ye Oldey Coffee Shoppey?' MacHale mused aloud. 'Is that English or *Chinese*-English?'

'Just *old* English,' she said. 'Very old . . . Like most things around here.'

When they left the car, MacHale stood on the narrow pavement, admiring the building. Its roof, with a line of four eye-shaped dormers, was of the ubiquitous thatch, covered with fine-wire mesh, and its eaves overhung the wall by a good four feet; the first-floor windows, nestling beneath the eaves and the neat, stubbled cut-off of the thatch, were small and leaded, but the two ground-floor windows of the restaurant, were large, Georgian-style bows, with varnished-wood frames, many of whose squares contained bull's-eye panes of glass; between these bows was the entrance, a wide, studded-oak door, open on a catch, emitting the aroma of fresh, strong coffee and roast beef, together with the muted chatter of seated customers, the occasional clatter of cups and plates, and cutlery, ringing crystal clear, against fine bone china.

'Looks busy,' observed MacHale.

'Usually is, Saturday afternoon,' Pat told him. 'Come on in.'

He followed her inside, looking around as he passed through the warm, dimly lit, interior, whose broad, knarled-oak ceiling beams were hung with coloured lanterns and dotted with horse-brasses and picture postcards, the latter sent from grateful tourists who'd long since been and gone. The floor was of red stone, shiny clean, its centre aisle concaved by the passage of thousands of feet over hundreds of years; either side of this aisle, there were heavy-oak benches, and carved chairs with floral-patterned cushions taped to their seats and backs, arranged in neat, well-spaced rows; at the top end of the room was the counter, where the cash register was maintained, and, beyond that, a closed door – bearing a gold-lettered sign which said, *Staff Only* – that entranced the kitchens and bakery.

The room's focal point, however, was its fireplace, to MacHale's left as he passed through: tall, wide, made of soft, red brick, beneath a long, oak mantle which bore a colourful arrangement of cut flowers in a copper bucket; logs were aflame, hissing and crackling in the dog grate, and every so often the wafted scent of burning pine overpowered the aroma of coffee and beef; on the hearth there were burnished copper-and-brass ornaments, a huge trugful of cut logs, and a stout, brass poker with soot-blackened end; and in one corner, the ingle nook, with a deep-buttoned leather seat and low, carved-wood table, where a customer might sit, face aglow, cradling a cup of steaming coffee, or perhaps an aperitif, while gazing into the glowing embers, or perusing the pages of the menu.

'What a place,' whispered MacHale, most impressed by it all.

'Lovely, isn't it,' agreed Pat, pleased, turning to smile over her left shoulder.

As they reached the checkout counter, a portly, dark-skinned man emerged from the kitchens, carefully backing out through the swing door, a tray of freshly-baked loaves and rolls, loading his arms, his brow glistening with perspiration; he was about fifty, MacHale decided, with the face of a hedonist – sparkling brown eyes, wide mouth, crinkly black hair, laughter creases at the corners of his eyes and mouth, and on his cheeks. He wore a dark-serge suit, white shirt and black tie, with a fresh, red carnation in the lapel buttonhole of his jacket – a manager's attire, MacHale thought.

'Diego!' exclaimed Pat, as the man turned away from the door, and she moved towards him, arms outstretched.

Ah, thought MacHale. He must be a Spaniard.

The man looked quickly at her, on hearing his name, and then his mouth expanded into a huge, surprised smile, exposing brilliant-white teeth. Quickly, he tossed the loaves and rolls into a bin beneath the counter, put down the tray, and rushed the few paces to her, hugging her like a long-lost friend. 'Senorita Pat!' he loudly laughed, his thickly-accented voice echoing around the room. 'What a surprise!' He released her, and stood back, looking her up and down, appraising her as he took out a pure-white handkerchief, flapped it open, and dabbed it at his damp brow. '*Como esta Vd?*'

MacHale frowned, trying to make the translation . . . *How . . . how are you?* Yes, that was it. Then he turned and cast an anxious glance over his shoulder: many of the customers were observing the reunion of Pat and Diego, amused by the effusiveness of it. MacHale, though, felt embarrassed.

'I'm fine,' Pat told him, in answer to his query, which had been framed in his native tongue.

'*Bueno, bueno*,' Diego now gushed. 'You are looking emarvellous!' He slowly shook his head, affecting wonder at her appearance, although she was very casually attired, in tight, faded denims, a chunky, white-wool sweater, and a pair of white plimsolls; MacHale was similarly dressed, and although he, too, thought Pat looked okay, he also thought they looked out of place in such a classy establishment as this one undoubtedly was.

'Now,' said Pat, turning aside and drawing MacHale close to her. 'I want you to meet a very good friend: John.' Then, to MacHale: 'This is Diego, John; our manager.'

MacHale stepped forward, smiling, his right hand on offer. He hoped this was correct: '*Buenas tardes*, Diego.'

Diego grabbed MacHale's hand, and began pumping it up and down, laughing gustily. 'Emeesta John!' Then he looked at Pat, excitedly shouting, 'He ees *ESpanish*. Whaddaya know about it, eh?'

MacHale took another anxious glance over his

shoulder; they were still drawing amused glances from the diners; he felt a hot flush, seeping upward from his neck. 'Third generation Spanish-English,' he apologetically informed Diego. 'On my mother's side. Fourth generation Irish-English, on my father's side.' – a potpourri of wogs, he thought, is what I *really* am.

Diego laughed, shrugging away the explanation, gesticulating with his arms, whose absence would probably have rendered him mute; each word was constructed out of air, by his fingers and hands, as it emerged from his mouth. 'You *look* ESpanish, you *are* ESpanish. *Sabe Vd. hablar Espanol?'* – Can you *speak* Spanish?

MacHale grimaced, and frowned, and found himself aping Diego's manual gesticulations. '*Lo* . . . er . . . *Lo* . . . *siento* . . . *Lo siento mucho* – I'm sorry. No, I'm sorry. Just bits and pieces I picked up from my mother. But she can't speak the language too well, either.' – another anxious glance over his shoulder.

'Ah, well,' beamed Diego, shrugging, grimacing, nodding his head and spreading his hands. 'Eeesa just as well *I* can espeak the bloody English, then.' And he laughed like hell.

'Very good it is, too,' Pat told him.

He shrugged again, inclined his head and gripped the lapels of his jacket. 'Room for improvement, as I tell the estaff.' Again he loudly laughed. 'And a now . . .' His right index-finger was pointing to the ceiling, and he glanced past Pat and MacHale, into the interior of the room, where a diner was politely beckoning him. '. . . You must excuse a me. The duty, she calls.' He bowed expansively, his head almost touching his knees, first at Pat, then at MacHale. '*Senorita* . . . *Senor*.'

'Okay, Diego,' said Pat. 'See you again, later on.'

'Yes,' agreed MacHale. 'Nice to meet you.'

'Come on,' said Pat, taking MacHale's hand. 'Let's go over to the cottage.'

She led him out through the busy kitchens and bakery – hot as a sauna, clean as a new pin – , and onto the patio at the rear of the restaurant, where they stood among white-plastic-coated wrought-iron tables and chairs, looking across a long, wide expanse of springy lawn, towards a tall berberis hedge that had a gap in its centre, beyond which were more gardens.

'This is the first garden,' Pat told him. 'Used by the customers, when the weather's warm enough.' She cast an eye over the empty tables and chairs, which in the summer would be shaded by huge, gaily-coloured parasols, fixed to the tables' centres. 'Not today, though, it seems.'

MacHale looked up at the blue sky, at the shimmering sun, squinting. 'They don't know what they're missing.'

Now she led him across the lawn and through the gap in the berberis, to the second garden, enclosed by tall, box-shaped privet; another springy lawn, bordered with pruned roses and hardy fuchsias, with a sun-dial on a concrete spindle as its centrepiece, and a revolving summerhouse in one corner. Crossing this lawn, they walked through an arch which had been sculpted from the wall of privet, and found themselves gazing across the third lawn, towards a thatched cottage with white-stone walls, dormer windows, and leaded lights; either side of its black-oak-panelled front door, there rested a wooden-spoked cartwheel, leaning decoratively against the wall, and at intervals along the stone patio that ran parallel to the cottage, there were small, cut-down water-butts that had been painted black and filled with planted geraniums.

MacHale shook his head in wonder. 'It's beautiful. Everything bursting into life. In summer, it must be a firework display of colour, here.'

Pat smiled, pleased by the compliment. 'Come on. Let's go and meet my parents. It's lunchtime, I think.'

MacHale walked with her over the lawn, towards the

cottage, feeling uneasy, as if he were about to be placed in the dock of some social court, wondering how her parents would react to him; they were obviously quite wealthy people, judging by this place . . . a class above him, he feared.

But he found them to be very genial people, indeed, and ones who had perfected a naturally-based art of making a guest feel perfectly at ease in their company.

Pat's father – 'Call me George, old boy' – was a slim, wiry man of about fifty-five, with a thick head of steel-grey hair which he lightly oiled and combed straight back from his high forehead; he wore black-rimmed spectacles, baggy, blue-corduroy trousers, a blue-check shirt, and a grey-wool cardigan that had seen some action in the garden, judging from the number of snagged threads which were on it. He was a most unpretentious man, full of smiles and set-you-at-ease looks and nods when he was listening to conversation. Within fifteen minutes, MacHale was ensconced in a well-upholstered chair in the living-room, sipping iced gin-and-tonic, while telling George about the vagaries of police duty – an expurgated account, of course.

Pat's elderly mum was equally hospitable and easy to get along with: permed grey hair, a well-proportioned, kindly face with pale, unblemished skin, and those risible, hazel eyes, which her daughter had inherited. The way she stole those sparkling, smiling, affirmative glances at MacHale, while she and Pat laid the table for lunch, denoted her approval of him; and maybe, too, there was a hint of wistful regret in those looks: that she wasn't herself twenty-five years younger and in the place of her daughter.

'He's a very handsome young man,' she whispered to Pat. 'Nice manners, too.' – yet another, sparkling, smiling, affirmative glance across the room, to where MacHale was seated.

Pat just looked at her mother, and smiled excitedly.

After lunch, Pat's mother and father said their farewells, and, after changing, departed – they, also, were going away for what remained of the weekend, it seemed; to a friend's riverside mansion at Henley – while Pat and MacHale spent the afternoon, sitting in the centre garden's sunhouse, drinking iced wine, and watching garden birds as they fed on a scattering of lawn seed which George had laid down, only that morning. Now, MacHale was relaxed, and not so much as a fragment of thought about the city or The Job drifted into his mind; he could have stayed forever, here, rippling in oblivion, soaking up the early-spring sunshine as he lay outstretched in a deckchair, expiring his breaths with contented, nasal groans.

In the early evening, they walked, their feet encased in slowly-drifting mist, across rolling fields, through forests of pine and lime, spotting birds and squirrels, before coming upon an isolated, country pub, where they lodged themselves in a quiet, fireside corner for the remainder of licensing hours.

Real ale, and country, home-made food. The ale did funny things to you, too, if you weren't accustomed to it: it made your eyes go all queer, and when you got up to visit the toilet, you felt like keeling over to lie on the floor, shouting and laughing and gurgling, how you didn't care, not about *anything*.

At closing time, they walked back over the moonlit hills and through the dark forest, smelling woodsmoke and damp grass on the chill air . . . often pausing to listen to the bark of a fox . . . the scratchings of a badger . . . the hoot of an owl . . .

After supper, they sat in the darkened living-room, by the french windows, their flushed faces reflecting the writhing, orange and red and yellow flames of the sibilant log-fire. Pat had set down, on the lawn, a dish of milk-soaked bread, and now they were observing a hedgehog, which had been lured by it; the noise, as the hedgehog sucked-up the milk and ate the bread, was amusing, and they smothered their giggles, fearful that even the slightest distraction would unnerve the hedgehog and send it scurrying away.

'Sounded just like the nick's canteen, at grub-time,' said MacHale, when the hedgehog had eaten its fill, and departed.

'No,' disagreed Pat. 'The hedgehog's a relatively *refined* diner, I reckon.'

Now, they openly laughed.

And suddenly there were two badgers at the dish, making similar, but much louder, noises to those which the hedgehog had produced while eating; they were a handsome pair, too, with long, broad snouts – the ends of which were glistening wet and black in the light of the moon – , short, flat ears, and wide, black flashes through the sides of their grey-white faces.

'You'd think they'd be frightened,' whispered MacHale. 'They're so close to the window.'

'They can't see us,' Pat told him, her voice hushed. 'They're practically blind.'

As the badgers departed, a fox approached; but, and to MacHale's surprise, the two species were obviously not enemies, because the badgers ignored the fox and the fox ignored the badgers. When he mentioned this to Pat, she told him that this was usual, and how, some time ago, while watching, late at night, from this same window, she'd seen a fox-cub lay down at a badger's heel, and just wait its turn to eat from the tin dish on the lawn.

When the fox had licked clean the dish and trotted away into the darkest recesses of the garden, MacHale and Pat prepared for bed. He was relieved, now, that her parents were away for the rest of the weekend: they wouldn't see that guilty, averted look upon his face and in his eyes, when he came down for breakfast, in the morning; there wouldn't be a need for such a look, not now.

On Sunday afternoon, after lunching in the restaurant, they were contentedly dozing in the centre garden's summerhouse, when Pat suddenly opened her eyes, leaned forward and aside in her deck-chair, and said, 'I've just had a great idea, John.'

'Whassat?' he mumbled, stirring.

'Why don't we finish off the weekend with a trip to Southend? I'd like to meet your parents . . . if you agree.'

Now he was wide awake. There were several reasons he could think of for *not* going: he was liking it here; he was too tired; it was too far; it was too late, therefore . . . But deep down he felt a twinge of shame, of inferiority; his parents were plain, simple people, who lived from week-to-week in a two-bedroomed semi, set in urban, working-class Southend. What would she think of them? How might she react? . . .

And then he felt a deeper shame for having thought of his parents as second-class citizens. They were proud, honest people, with integrity, and what little they possessed, they'd worked long and hard for; they'd given him everything they could, and it didn't matter that, materially, it hadn't been a lot; it had been *sufficient*. Pat wasn't a snob, anyway, he told himself; she was an affable girl . . . kind, generous and understanding . . . strong, decisive – *very* decisive, usually, as a matter of fact – , but consultative, too. Christ, how he hoped that some of those qualities would rub-off on himself. He was trying to . . . learn from? . . . emulate her? . . . Something like that.

'Well?' she asked. 'What do you think, John?'

'Okay,' he told her. 'Let's do it. But I'd better phone

them before we leave . . . Give them some warning . . . And you'll have to drive, by the way; that Diego poured so much wine down my throat, at lunch, I'm bound to be over the top if I get stopped and breathalysed.'

'Leave it to me,' she said, and she was up and away into the cottage, collecting their weekend bags and the car keys.

They arrived at teatime, a little after five o'clock.

His mother, an olive-skinned, black-haired, slim woman, who wore with ease, outwardly, her forty-five years, had put on her best dress – bottle-green polyester and cotton, printed with bunches of white, rust and blue daisy heads, long-sleeved, loosely fitted at the waist, very slightly flared at the hem. She'd put on her best smile, too, when she'd greeted Pat, although this was a feature of her that was worn naturally and often, not just for special occasions, and despite her large brown eyes intimating that she might be a secretly-timorous woman who'd never had, and would probably not now receive, all which she'd anticipated in life. The same eyes secretly looked at her son, long and hard and penetratingly, and with a desperate affection; she'd invested her future entirely in him.

His father, a sluggish, dark-haired man with soft-blue eyes and a relaxed face, had also made an effort. He had on a white shirt – collar points curling upwards – , a dark-blue knitted-wool tie – loose at the neck – , a navy cardigan, a pair of navy trousers, and *brown* shoes. Will he *ever* have any dress sense? wondered MacHale. He was a motor-mechanic, by trade – his thick, stubby-ended fingers with their perma-black creases and blunt-edged, chipped fingernails, testified to it – , a hard-working but totally unambitious man whose idea of a *cracking* Sunday was a long lie-in, an opening-time visit to the local pub – to charge his pot belly – , roast lamb and mint jelly for lunch, *The Big Match*, and a half-dozen bottles of beer, followed by a snooze in the armchair, before a night in front of the goggle-box. His eyes, immobile and deeply contented, said, What's the *rush*? Why *worry*? Take it *easy*, why don't you? Life's too short.

The tangible proof of his philosophy abounded within and without the house: the bathroom cabinet's door was hanging on one hinge, just as it had for the last three months; the hover-mower was inoperable because a wire had worked loose inside the plug; the kitchen taps were drip-dripping because they required new washers; and the electric kettle wasn't working because the new element had gone, a week after MacHale's *mother* had, in desperation, fitted it herself – *wrongly*; outside, the garden looked as if it had been faithfully modelled on a section of Amazon jungle, and the TV-aerial was promising to come loose from its rusty bolts and mountings, and crash down into the yard, next time there was a strong south-westerly.

When you looked at him, though, or talked to him, or just *thought* about him, you couldn't help smiling. He was . . . well, he was too *nice*, and humorous, and totally harmless, to be angry with – no sharp edges, at all, and very easy to work on, if you had patience.

Tea was light and cold – meat salad and fruit salad; probably because MacHale had whispered to his mum that Pat was trying to diet – , but the conversation was natural and warm. MacHale was relieved and pleased. His parents had quickly taken to Pat, and she to them.

All too soon, though, MacHale and Pat had to leave, to make the return trip to London, but not before delivering an exacted promise to call again in the near future. As they drove away, his mother had that vague cast in her large brown eyes. He'd grimaced and sighed and told her not to be silly and given her exasperated reassurances when she'd said he should be careful, and should eat proper food, and should try and restore that invigorated, seaside complexion to his pale, thinning face – women's stuff, again; irrational.

And then he and Pat were fast putting behind themselves the weekend, as they approached the suburbs of the metropolis. She seemed highly contented, pleased by how pleasant it had all been and how well it had all proceeded; but he felt as if they were driving from sunshine into smog; he was becoming depressed by thoughts of early-turn, shiftwork, noise, pollution, uncertainty; yet he was curiously anxious to go on, too; to succeed; he was ambivalent, and hopeful, and when he glanced at Pat, or snatched and held-on to a passing thought of what they'd shared, a golden ingot of light pierced the blackness and touched his heart; hope *was* justified.

All the way back, his thoughts see-sawed as his moods rose and fell: a glance at Pat, as she dozed, recumbent in the passenger seat, her rosy face, cushioned by her shroud of plangent hair, and he felt inspired . . . wanted, needed; but then, once more he felt downhearted as he drove through the inner city; tediously threading his way along narrow, congested streets, past towering blocks of black-windowed concrete and stone . . . like creeping nervously through a never-ending, deep, winding canyon whose sides were crumbling away; at any moment, the whole lot might come crashing down on top of him, burying him alive.

When they reached the section-house, he drew into the kerb, cut the engine and snapped off the headlights. For a moment or two he just sat there in the darkness, looking at her, a surge of emotion swelling in his chest and throat; it was touched off by not only a feeling of fondness but also by a desire to protect and cherish . . . Why *couldn't* they still be sitting, at midnight, in the darkened living-room of the cottage, the log fire hissing and crackling? Why couldn't they *still* be there, tomorrow?

Tomorrow. God, the thought of it. His stomach felt sick, and his eyes closed as he took in a long, shallow breath, which was expired as an equally long groan.

He leaned over her, gently shaking her arm, wakening her. 'Pat,' he whispered. 'Come on, wake up . . . We're here.'

She stirred, opened her eyes, blinked furiously, then looked about herself, yawning, bringing the back of her right hand to cover her mouth. 'Oh, we're here,' she murmured, and eased herself upright, shaking her head, swirling strands of hair around her face and neck. 'I was having a lovely sleep.'

He looked at his watch – ten thirty-five. 'I'd better get in, Pat. And you'd better get home, too. We're due to work in about seven hours.'

She shivered, and her eyes rolled upward. 'Oh, don't remind me,' she groaned.

He kissed her goodnight, left the car, and stood on the pavement, watching, as she slid across to the driver's seat, switched on the headlamps, started the engine, and pulled smoothly away from the kerb. He waved after her, then turned and walked into the side entrance of the section-house. The car-rental firm was located just around the corner from her flat, no more than a couple of miles away from here; she'd drop the car on the forecourt, lock it, shove the keys through the showroom's letterbox, then walk home; she'd be there within twenty minutes, he believed.

And now he opened his eyes and saw the cracked, grimy-white ceiling of his small room; in one corner, a fluffy cobweb, floating up and around on a single, gossamer-fine stay; in another corner, a huge spider, motionless; a ring of brown-black dirt, scorched into the plaster around the rose above the dangling shade. It just about summed-up, visually, what he'd returned to. Dirt, traps, and predators.

Now his eyes were tilting upward, his heavy lids were falling down, a hand had slid from beneath his head, and lay lightly open on the pillow . . . his head lolled sideways, and his jaw began slackening as his breathing took on an adenoidal pitch . . .

But suddenly he bolted wide awake, his head rising from the pillow, his confused eyes staring, his ears bristling.

Another knock at the door, followed by, 'Juan?'

Oh, *hell*! he exasperatedly thought, recognizing the voice. What does *he* want at this time of night?

Before he could say anything, though, the door opened and in came Hercules, preceded by a mist of beer and Scotch. He closed the door and moved into the room, slowly, unsteadily, an idiotic, slanting smile on his anaesthetized face. His eyes were half closed and his sharp features were blistered with perspiration; tight, blue denims drew attention to the unnatural length and frailty of his legs, while a fitted, plaid shirt made MacHale realize just *how* hollow and bony was Hercules' bowed torso.

MacHale sat up in bed, rubbing his eyes, blinking, now frowning. 'You're flying three sheets to the wind, Herc. Where the hell've you been?'

Hercules grinned lopsidedly, clasped together his hands, began washing them, and hovered over MacHale's bed, like a bird predator. 'Oh, just out . . . drinking,' he slurred, and he swayed backwards as he brushed a strand of loose hair from over his left eye. 'Took some time-off and did the clubs.' He lurched forward, staggered sideways, then fell down obliquely to sit on the edge of the mattress.

MacHale quickly drew-up his legs, and sat there with his arms folded around the top of his sheet-and-blanket-covered knees. 'Had a good time, then?' he said, not really caring, one way or the other.

Hercules shrugged, and leaned back, supporting himself on the palms of his hands. 'Not really . . .' He sniffed, and his head jarred forward and down, his chin resting on his chest. 'I . . .' He broke off, swallowing heavily and again sniffing. Then he turned his head and looked upward at MacHale, his eyes bleary and red and watery, leaning forward to interlock, in his lap, the bony fingers of his hands, which now began wriggling and writhing. 'I can't *help* it,' he quickly mumbled, a hopeless, pleading look on his gaunt face. 'Every time I *see* you, I . . .' He leaned over sideways and placed a hand on MacHale's knee, gently massaging it.

'Get off!' snapped MacHale, alarmed, and he wriggled further away from Hercules, wedging his body between the edge of the bed, and the wall. 'You're *drunk*. You're outa your *mind*. You don't *know* what you're *on* about.'

'I do, I do, Juan,' Hercules thickly mumbled. A tear was now slithering down his left cheek, and he moved closer to MacHale, his left arm outstretched. 'Why d'you think I'm always coming along here to *see* you? Why can't I stop *thinking* about you, about how I *want* you, Juan? Oh, God, *how*.' His voice was now broken up with emotion; tears were trickling down his face; his play had made him totally vulnerable, and he knew it; but he was inflamed with drink, and utterly desperate. '*Please*, Juan.' He fell forward against MacHale's legs, wildly groping, moaning, crying, pleading, scrambling to raise his own legs onto the bed and draw himself on top of MacHale.

MacHale's eyes were wild with fear and bewilderment, his face was drawn tight with panic, and sweat was breaking out all over his body. 'Get off me, ya slimy fruit!' he shouted, kicking and pushing and shoving and writhing, until Hercules fell, with a flat, nauseating thud, onto the floor at the side of the bed. 'And get *outa* here! *Now!*'

Hercules drew himself up onto his hands and knees . . . to his feet, swaying and staggering, looking disbelievingly at MacHale, terror imprinted on his sickly-looking, wet-streaked face; his mouth fell open, and his eyes popped, blinking him back to reality, it seemed. Then he gasped. 'Oh! . . . Oh, my God, what . . .?' A huge cloud of emotion burst in his throat, and his face fell into his hands as he whimpered like a maltreated child in the throes of an horrific nightmare. Now he reeled forward, clutched at the handle of the door, pulled open the door, and fell out into the corridor, choking and crying.

MacHale just sat there in the top corner of the bed, his face the colour of caramel, his chest rising high and falling heavily, his expression asking, *Did that really happen just now*? But his parched throat, his pounding heart and his shaking legs confirmed that it had.

What *now*? he wondered . . . What'll he *say* to me, tomorrow? . . . What'll *I* say to *him*? . . . How can we continue to *work* together, after *that*? Christ, *that* was an indecent assault! What would the *others* say or do, if they were to find out? . . . What an unholy *mess*!

And then he felt a sharp pain of pity for Hercules, as he glimpsed a vision of the pathetic man, lying prone on his bed inside his dark room, his thin body racked with convulsions as the shame, the panic, the fear and the spectre of his rejection and total exposure slammed into him in spasmodic bursts.

Next, he felt shame, as he recalled what he'd hurled out in his wild, unthinking effort to detach himself from Hercules' clutches. '. . . ya slimy fruit!' The noun might be considered contemptible enough, but the adjective which had preceded and modified it, made it even more so . . . *ya slimy fruit!* . . . It *wasn't* Hercules' fault, MacHale now realized. Whatever he was, he couldn't *help* it. Poor bastard. There but for the grace of God . . .

He threw back the bedclothes and went over to the sink, running the cold tap and gulping mouthfuls of icy water down his burning throat. Then he stood upright, wiping the back of his hand over his wet lips, looking in the wall-mirror, not quite knowing what he *expected* to see, reflected before himself, but *seeing* only a pulsating vein as it rhythmically throbbed against the glistening skin of his left temple.

Go and see him, urged a voice from within his aching head. *Apologize for what you've said. Let him know he's forgiven – although make it clear there must never be a repetition. Assure him that his secret's safe. Promise him you won't tell anyone . . .*

Yes, do it, he decided, and, having wrapped a bath towel around his waist, walked out of the room. Straight away, though, he came back. It might've been tempting providence, he'd thought, walking into Hercules' room, wearing nothing but a wrap-around towel, so now he changed into a T-shirt and jeans.

The door was closed, and there was no strip of light showing through the gap between its bottom and the floor. He began breathing through his mouth, listening for sounds from within the room . . . Nothing, though. He knocked lightly, and waited . . . No response. He shrugged, opened the door and walked in. But the bed was empty. Further into the unlit room, he could see the bare table, and the unoccupied chair that stood before it . . . to the right, the easy chair, also unoccupied.

He left the room and closed the door, walking back along the corridor, to the washroom – no one in there, either. Now he resignedly sighed and returned to his own room. Maybe it would all work out better, anyway, if slept on?

But sleep was a long time coming, and when it finally visited him, it brought with it a terrifying nightmare.

20

He was aware of himself falling rapidly through a narrow, black hole, the wind, rushing upward, tearing into his mouth, his nostrils, his eyes, the G-forces contorting his face into a widely-stretched inverted U-shape, so that the corners of his mouth were drawn grotesquely down to touch the lower, back bones of his jaw . . .

There was no time to think, to comprehend, to analyse, to apprehend. Just an overwhelmingly acute certainty that this was *Death*.

He was half awake, sitting up in bed in the dark room, his knees drawn into his chest, his arms wrapped around his shins, only vaguely certain that the scream *had* been surreal, a figment of the unconscious hallucination. He uncoiled his shiny wet body and lay back on the pillow, taking a deep breath of relief, restricting its outward flow, shaping it through funnelled lips, so that it was expired as a long groan which inflated his cheeks and took with it the tension that had locked and rippled his muscles. But his heart was still doing a drumroll, and his head was still throbbing, marking time with the flurry of bass beats in his chest, so he began to deep-breathe, flexing his fingers and toes, then allowing them to spring back into a natural, relaxed state, repeating the exercise with his jaw – opening it wide, taut, letting it close autonomously, so that his lips were slightly apart, his teeth were unclenched, the muscles in his cheeks had stopped bunching and pulsating . . .

Finally, he was as relaxed as he could be, and now he began delving into the deepest recesses of his mind, probing its subconscious, lightly concentrating . . . wanting – no, *needing* – to hook out and land as many of those wriggling, slippery, silver-black slivers of nightmare, as he was able to. They were horrible and they were venomous, extremely dangerous if not properly handled. But they had to be uncovered and dealt with. Their elusive configurations had symbolic meanings which were capable of interpretation and analysis, providing clues and hints and insights, not only for, and into, the future, but, for, and into, the past, as well.

Now he had a mist-shrouded snatch of something – a bite . . . *He was climbing a ladder up the side of a tall, brick building, struggling futilely against a preternatural gravity which bore down as a hot, leaden wind, scorching his body, forcing him relentlessly back . . .*

Frustration, anger, determination . . . Something which he badly desired could not be achieved . . .

Now he was falling into the black hole . . . spinning, suffocating . . .

Suddenly, the line went slack . . . But there was now a fresh bite:

He was lying supine on the ground, paralysed . . . nowhere, anywhere, it didn't matter where . . . A feculent vagrant, in ragged clothing; his features . . . horribly . . . deformed, mutilated? . . . A leper? Not a vagrant. A leper; yellow-green pus-flesh, rotting, dropping away from his face and hands . . . a lecherous grin on the remains of his face . . . reaching for MacHale, exposing himself . . . masturbating . . . Not frightening, not now; just painfully intriguing . . .

Not *possible* in the waking state; but what *did* it symbolize? . . .

Gone . . . Fighting, now . . . MacHale and . . . and . . . someone he didn't know; a man . . . more, just aware of his presence, than actually seeing and looking at him; could be anyone, punching and kicking and grabbing fistfuls of MacHale's hair, smashing his head onto the pavement . . . MacHale, driving his fist into his opponent's testicles . . . a scream of agony, and the face, shrieking defeat . . . retreating . . .

Different bites: *riding a bicycle, but getting nowhere . . . Now, in a prison cell, forever locked away . . . shame, disgrace, for a police-officer; worse than death . . .* Nothing more; *just blackness, spangled with a mass of electric sparks, white and yellow and red.*

He opened his eyes, and sighed heavily. What *did* it all mean? The submerged images were suffusing, vanishing . . . were gone . . .

And now he began to feel hot and uncomfortable as his thoughts, inevitably, remembered last night's happenings. He had to do *something* about Hercules, but he was no longer sure what it should be, beyond trying to apologize for what he'd said, and making it clear it shouldn't recur. *Maybe Pat would be able to suggest something further*, an inner voice then told him; *ask her what she thinks*. But he immediately decided against it. He'd *tell* her, all right, and swear her to secrecy, but not before he'd fronted Hercules, taken him aside, and said . . . yes, this would do; something like – and MacHale now began rehearsing it – , *Look, I'm annoyed and embarrassed by what you did, last night, and I want to apologize for having called you that name, but it's all over and I'm willing to forget it, if you are. Do what you like, off-duty, but be in no doubt that you and me are switched on by different currents. Okay? . . . Right. We'll leave it at that, then.* Hmm, that sounded all right, MacHale decided.

Now he reached up and switched on the wall-lamp above the head of his bed, then squinted his paining eyes and glanced at his wristwatch – almost five A.M. He switched off the light, lay on his side, curling up, settled his head, deep into the pillow, and tried to snatch a little more sleep.

But just as he was on the brink of sleep, the door swung inward and the room was flooded with bright yellow light. He was stirring, in the act of turning over onto his back, frowning, blinking, bringing his fingers up to soothe his tired eyes, but the hand still reached out for his shoulder, and vigorously shook him, its owner shouting, 'Wake up, wake up, it's twenny to six.'

He pulled himself up into a sitting-forward position, glanced up at the uniformed PC who was standing beside the bed, and mumbled, 'Where's Sid? . . . Thought *he* was on nights.'

'That's right. He *was*,' said the PC, a grave edge to his voice. 'But he was carted off to hospital, at two o'clock this morning . . .' The PC paused, for effect, building tension, then added: 'After he found Hercules, hanging from a pipe in the weightlifting room, down in the basement.'

The words were like icy fingers, gripping MacHale's vital parts, squeezing the breath from his lungs, the beats from his heart. '*What!*' he shouted, now fully awake and sitting bolt upright, disbelief on his face and in his bulging eyes.

The PC solemnly nodded. 'It's true. He slung a rope over the boiler pipe that runs along the centre of the ceiling, stood on a chair, knotted the rope around his neck, and took off. Sid went down to turn off the lights, and almost had a heart attack. Poor ol sod's in hospital, with shock.'

'Is he *dead*?' demanded MacHale. 'Hercules, I mean. Is he *really* dead?'

'As can be,' said the PC. He shrugged. 'Don't ask me why, though. *Nobody* seems to know.'

I do, *I* do! MacHale inwardly screamed. And it's *my* . . . No, *no*! That's *ridiculous* . . . *Fate*. How could *anybody* have . . .? The poor bastard. *Dead! Hanged!* . . . Oh, Christ! God rest his soul . . . *please*.

'Okay. I've got the rest of Sid's calls to do, now,' said the PC. 'Mind you don't go back to sleep. See ya.' And he walked out, shutting the door.

'Yeah . . . yeah, thanks,' mumbled MacHale, abstractedly and belatedly. He was deeply shocked, and began to shiver. The same words kept thundering into his mind, toned with vast incredulity: *Dead! . . . Hanged!* I only *saw* him, last *night . . . Here*, in this room, *alive*, and drunk and sweating and speaking and . . . But the rest of it was too painful, now, to be pored over; it was surely the *cause*, the final straw – the ultimate rejection. Christ, why did he have to go and do *that*? *I* wouldn't've told anybody. *I* was gonna square it up with him, later on.

And then an even more horrific thought struck out at MacHale's brain: supposing Hercules had left a letter for the Coroner, setting out his reason for . . .? Oh, God, no, please God don't let there be a letter, for . . . *yes*, for *my* sake.

He sprang out of bed and began running the cold tap, sluicing his face . . . brushing his hair . . . his teeth . . . shaving; but his hands were so shaky he had to stop for fear of cutting himself with the new razor; he tossed it into the wall-cabinet, brought out an old, blunted one, and continued the shave with that, all the while incredulously thinking, *Dead! . . . Hanged!* I just *can't* take it in. And then the alarm-clock, inside his wardrobe, began clanging, and he jumped like hell, nicking his cheek, anyway, with the blunt razor.

Something – he didn't know what; disbelief, maybe – impelled him, and he found himself creeping down the back stairs to the darkened basement . . . along to the gymnasium, his boots squealing on the polished parquet floor as he walked, hesitantly, breathless, tense, towards the open double doors of the windowless, concrete-walled weightlifting room. He still was unable to comprehend it . . . *Dead! . . . Hanged! . . .*

He moved in through the doorway and fumbled around for the lightswitch . . . snapping it on and flooding the large, square room with cold light. It was . . . shiveringly weird, atmospherically, and he felt sick, tremulous, ready to turn about and run. Weights were scattered over the floor . . . a vaulting horse, tufts of stuffing spilling out through a split in its rough-hide flanks, stood in one corner . . . a skipping rope, like a coiled serpent, was in the centre of the floor area . . . benches, chairs, rubber mats . . . the white-stone floor, marbled with black shadow. He cast upward with his eyes, saw the thick, insulated pipe that ran across the centre of the ceiling . . . no dangling rope, but a V-shaped indentation on top of the pipe, at its centre, where the rope had bitten deep into the lagging, pulled tight by the weight of a dangling, kicking, foaming-mouthed, scarlet-faced body . . . MacHale could *smell* it, and *hear* it, and felt turbulence in the cold air . . .

He turned, and ran fast away across the gymnasium floor, sensing a gaining presence behind him, but too terrified to look back over his shoulder . . .

Now, he believed it.

He knocked at her office door and called out her name: 'Pat? Okay if I come in?'

'Yes, John,' she called out, her voice cheery and bright.

He walked in and moved to sit on the edge of her desk, pushing aside the telephone and correspondence tray, watching as she stood before the wall-mirror by her wardrobe, adjusting her uniform hat.

'John,' she said, patting the sides of the hat's brim, and panning her head, left, then right, to study the profiles of her smooth, pink-fleshed face. 'There's something I want to discuss with you. You see, I've decided, after the weekend we've spent together, that – ' Abruptly, she stopped speaking, having caught sight of his reflection in the mirror. She turned, a concerned look on her face. 'What's the matter with you? You look as if you've seen a ghost.'

He huffed out a hollow laugh. 'You could say that,' he dryly commented. 'At least, you could say I've just been in the *presence* of a ghost . . . You obviously don't know what's happened, then?'

'No. What? I haven't heard anything. You're the first person I've seen, this morning.' She was frowning, her head cocked aside. 'Tell me.'

So he told her, beginning with last night's events, and ending with this morning's impulsive visit to the section-house weightlifting room.

'My God,' she murmured, shocked, her eyes blank, her head moving slowly from side-to-side. Then her eyes came alive and she was her usual, practical self. 'You must say nothing, John. *Forget* you saw Hercules, last night. It'll be the best thing. I mean, there are his parents, his family, to consider. Bad enough they should have to cope with his suicide. Why burden them additionally with the motive . . . that their son, their brother, their cousin . . . was gay? Better that they should just be left in ignorance.'

'Which'll be equally burdensome, if you ask me,' MacHale said. 'They'll forever be wondering, *Why?*'

'And if they knew, *Why?* – his parents – , they might irrationally blame themselves. It's a possibility. No, let them wonder. Eventually, they'll decide it was pressure of work . . . depression . . . something like that.'

'Hmm, maybe you're right, Pat,' he said. He wanted to believe she was; if the truth came out, the facts would be almost wholly distorted; new, more scandalously-attractive facets would be cut into them . . . Like MacHale and Hercules were secret lovers who'd had a tiff . . . something like that, anyway. And then, MacHale would be ridiculed to distraction by his own colleagues, who were *already* gunning him down. 'Okay, I'll do what you suggest, Pat,' he told her. 'But if it turns out there's a letter, the truth'll be out, anyway. And then they'll want to know why I didn't come forward, right from the off. They'll think I was trying to hide something shameful, like me and – '

'Have a look at the Sixty-Sixes at the rear of the charge-book,' she said. 'After parade. If there is a letter, it'll be logged in there.'

'Yeah, okay,' he wearily said. 'I'll do that.'

'Now, we'd better get upstairs,' she said, glancing at the wall-clock, and noting that it was two minutes to six-thirty A.M.

He took his helmet and tunic from her locker, dressed, and followed her out of the door.

There wasn't a letter, and the whole nick was jumping with speculation.

'He done it because he was a poufdah,' said Tasty Tom. 'Had a bull-'n'-cow with his boyfriend, and topped himself.'

'Yeah . . .'bout right,' was Punchy Paterson's considered reply.

'Be a bloody wreath-collection, *now*, I s'pose,' moaned Tubby Tompkins.

'D'you reckon we'll get a toura duty out the funeral?' Vindscreen wanted to know.

'Overtime'd be a better prospect, dear boy,' said Snatch.

'Yeah,' agreed Filthy Phil. 'Especially if it's gonna be on a weekly-leave.'

You filthy, dirty, disrespectful, cynical bunch of slags, thought MacHale, as he sat alone, listening to them. It were as if an unloved dog had died, at an inconvenient time.

They were in the canteen, having their grub. Two card-schools were in progress – the refreshment schedules were shot to shit, as usual – , and the streets were empty of cops; anyone could take his chance out there, right now, and be clean away before the first puff of blue smoke had been punched from the RT-car's exhaust.

MacHale drained his tea-cup and walked to the counter to order a refill. While he was there, he decided he'd *have* to eat something; his guts were still turning over, but they needed food to grind their linings against. He settled for a bacon sandwich and gave his order ticket to the cook, a Negress, name of Clarissa. After placing his tea on the table by the door, he went out to visit the toilet, to splash cold water against his face and look again at his drawn features.

When he returned, his bacon sandwich was on the table. He sat down, turning to look towards the counter, intending to thank Clarissa – not many of the cooks or counterhands would bring your food to the table; in fact, most of them went out of their way to let you know that waiting on table *wasn't* a part of their duties. Clarissa wasn't there, though, having returned to the kitchen, MacHale supposed, to snatch a sit down, while things were quiet.

He bit disinterestedly into the first half of sandwich, and began mechanically chewing it . . . finding it difficult to swallow. As he progressed, however, it began to taste better, to go down more easily, and now he ate with something resembling enthusiasm.

Until, that was, he tasted something unnatural, indigestible, on his tongue and against his cheek . . . something like . . . *rubber?* . . . all wet and slimy and stretchy. His intestines bolted upward with a broad, sharp pain as he leaned forward and spat onto the plate, completely unaware that his card-playing colleagues were sniggering, taking sneaky, sideways glances at him. He was horrified:

it was a used, knotted condom that was lying coiled before him on the plate. He half stood, falling forward over the table, retching, choking, gasping, pressing his hands tight against his belly; but only white fury came flooding up through his mouth, his nostrils and his eyes . . . out of control, hell bent on retribution.

For a moment, he was paralysed by it, and was rooted where he stood, half crouching, his chest heaving in and out, his eyes blank and crazy. Then he exploded, violently, uncontrollably, snatching up the plate and hurling it through the air; it shattered against the wall, high above the heads of the diving, ducking members of the card-schools, showering them in shards of white-glazed clay . . .

'*Bastards!*' he bellowed, and now he was rushing towards them, his arms flailing, his teeth clenched, his eyes completely wild, his expression murderous. They threw aside their chairs and scrambled to their feet, panicking, their alarmed faces becoming paler, unbelieving; and then MacHale was on them, knocking and shoving them aside, grabbing the ends of the two tables, heaving, pushing, throwing, upending them and scattering cups and plates and saucers and cutlery and cards and coins, all over the floor . . .

Now he grabbed a chair and swung it ferociously at Punchy Paterson's head, making terrifying, enraged-bull-like noises as he sought the smell of blood . . . Paterson turned sharply aside and ducked down, his hands moving up fast to protect his head, as the chair crashed down in a blur of an arc onto his wide, bowed back, and splintered into sticks of wood. Paterson roared with pain and thudded, face down, onto the floor, rolling from side-to-side, his hands moving up behind him, clawing blindly, hopelessly, at his shoulder-blades . . .

MacHale was bending, reaching down for a piece of chair-leg . . . Tasty Tom, moving in on him, from behind, grabbing his shoulder, spinning him around, snarling, lining up his right fist with the left side of MacHale's head. MacHale swivelled away, ducked, twisted out of Tasty Tom's grip, and hurled himself forward, burying the top of his head in Tasty's gut. The big man looked a whole lot smaller, now, lying ten feet away on the floor, air gushing in and out of his twisted, gaping mouth . . .

And then Clarissa was at the counter, her fingers digging into the inside of her lower lip, her face destroyed by fear and panic, her wide-open mouth emitting staccato bursts of shrill, screaming, gasping noises . . .

Vindscreen was now springing at MacHale. MacHale sidestepped him, picked up another chair, and swung down and around onto Vindscreen's right shoulder, dropping him on his knees . . .

Then, wheeling around and dropping what remained of the broken chair, he advanced on Snatch, intent on grabbing him by the throat and squeezing and ripping the life from him. But the old PC was backing off, his hands held up before himself, as if MacHale were pointing a gun at his chest. 'No, no, no, dear boy,' he mumbled. 'Not *me*! I had *nothing* to do with it.'

MacHale just grabbed him by the lapels of his tunic, swung him around, and . . . threw him away across the floor . . .

And now he began looking for Filthy Phil and Tubby Tompkins. But they'd done a runner, right from the off, and were nowhere to be seen . . . they were well gone.

It was over, then, and had lasted for no more than a minute and a half.

Stark realization then broke against and washed over MacHale, and for a moment he stood there, immobile, blinking, shaking his head, as if he were emerging from a powerful, narcotic stupor, drained of energy, sweating and breathing hard, quivering and aching from head to toes, trying to remember . . . scarcely believing what he'd done . . . He wasn't *capable* of it . . .

Quickly, he glanced over his shoulder. The canteen floor was a hell of a mess: broken tables and chairs and crockery; scattered cutlery and cards and coins . . . and pools of spilt tea and coffee, floating slivers and splinters of wood . . . Jesus *Christ*! . . . Vindscreen, groaning and muttering, pulling Punchy Paterson to his feet; Snatch, shaking like a jelly, assisting Tasty Tom, whose screwed-up face said he thought he'd got a hole in his gut . . . Clarissa – no longer a Negress, but a pretty white lady with frizzy black hair – moving from behind the counter, a dustpan and brush in her hands, wide-eyed, shaking her head, saying exactly what she'd said at the conclusion of Brixton '81: 'Tank de Lard it all ovah an I breathin *sweet* air . . .'

'Sorry . . . Clarissa,' mumbled MacHale. 'Sorry, but I . . .' He couldn't finish, though, and turned away, walking out, wanting to break up and cry.

It took him half-an-hour to recover.

After leaving the canteen, he went to the washroom and spent a long time just splashing water over his hot, sticky face. What the hell would Old Crikey say? he wondered. What would Parker-Brown have to say? More to the point, though, what would they *do*? To *him*.

Whatever the hell they like, he eventually told himself. He was still angry enough not to care. Anyway, the others, if they'd got any sense, would see to it that the hierarchy never *did* find out what had happened; chairs and crockery had been broken many times before in the canteen, and just stacked in a corner, awaiting collection and replacement by a van from the stores. No one had ever been interested or concerned enough to ask how such damage was occasioned; and, okay, so a couple of PCs *had* been assaulted by one of their own, and that *was* a disciplinary offence, but they hadn't been hospitalized – more through sheer luck, than good intent or judgement, as it happened – , and they'd get over it, maybe learn a lesson, once and for all: don't mess around with MacHale, not any more.

Yeah . . . maybe he'd just earned himself a reputation? He nodded defiantly. He liked it: *Don't mess around with MacHale*. So now he completely denied himself those remorseful feelings which had been striving to dominate his conscience, for the last half-hour. Why *should* he feel sorry, or guilty? Those bastards had put a used French-letter in his sandwich, hadn't they?

He grimaced, feeling sick at the thought of it. He could've *swallowed* that thing.

As he left the washroom, he felt at ease with himself. Whatever he'd done could be justified. He was now certain of it.

A few minutes later, though, he was no longer so sure. As he passed-by the front office, Barker came hurrying out and told him that Old Crikey wanted to see him – *immediately*.

Now, he began crumbling at the edges.

27

As he turned the corner and began making his way along the corridor, he saw that Pat was standing outside the closed door of Old Crikey's office.

'What're you doing here?' he asked, as he reached her.

She nodded at the door. 'He wants to see me, so I've been told.'

'Me, too,' said MacHale, puzzled. 'Any idea what for?'

Her shoulders lightly rose and fell. 'I haven't got a clue, John. How about you?'

'No. Beats me.' – it couldn't be in connection with what had earlier happened in the canteen, because Pat wasn't present or involved when that went off.

For a while, they stood in silence, leaning back against the wall of the corridor, their arms folded across their chests, their heads downcast, their thoughts the same: why had they been called for?

The sound of Old Crikey's telephone receiver being dropped into its cradle broke up their thoughts, and they straightened themselves up in anticipation of his appearance.

The office door opened and he looked out at them, his taut lips out of alignment, several of his back teeth clicking against one another, his jaw muscles popping in and out. 'Come in,' he said, and an arm, with upturned palm, cleared a way for them through the air.

MacHale and Pat stepped inside the office and halted, side-by-side, in front of Old Crikey's desk; their bodies were standing easy but their minds were at rigid attention.

Old Crikey closed the door and walked to sit behind his desk. 'Sit down, please,' he said, and when they'd thanked him and pulled up a couple of chairs, he forthwith rose, clasped his hands behind his back, and began walking up and down . . . to the window, back to the centre of his desk . . . pause . . . about-turn, back to the window . . .

MacHale and Pat exchanged glances; Old Crikey's antics evoked many an inner feeling – despair, amusement, annoyance, puzzlement, bewilderment . . . *pity*? Yeah, *pity*, thought MacHale. Pity the silly ol' sod wouldn't request a transfer out to the sticks, and give us *all* some respite.

This time, Old Crikey halted when he returned to the centre of his desk. He looked as if he were on the threshhold of pain, MacHale considered, and the way in which his narrowed eyes were examining Pat's features – making her uncomfortable, and forcing her to avert from his face, her own eyes – suggested that he was scanning her for a physical manifestation, a denouncement of some unpalatable truth he'd learned; as if he'd uncovered something about her which he *hoped* wasn't substantial, or could scarcely *believe* was substantial.

'It's come to my notice,' he began, glancing alternately at Pat and MacHale, 'that *you* two are having an . . . are . . . well, are seeing a lot of each other when you're off-duty.' His indignant tone of voice and his severe expression had added a large measure of condemnation to the . . . yes, the *allegation*; he *had* made it sound as if they'd each conspired to commit a crime.

Again, MacHale and Pat exchanged looks, their wide-eyed faces reflecting the astonishment which they were experiencing.

'Oh, there's no point in your denying it,' Old Crikey went on, now sounding triumphant. '*I've* checked the nights-out book at the section-house, you see, and that tells me that *you* . . .' He pointed an accusing finger at

MacHale. '. . . *you* have spent several nights away with Miss Coles.'

'We have no *reason* to deny it,' Pat told him, her face flushed with annoyance.

'That's right,' agreed MacHale, feeling equally angry; they were, he considered, being treated like a couple of pre-pubescent kids who'd been caught with their drawers around their ankles, behind the school bicycle-shed. 'We're both grown-up people, and, yes, you're right, we *do* have a relationship.' His tone of voice and indignant countenance had tacitly added, *And what of it? What the hell's it got to do with you, anyway?*

Now, Old Crikey sat down, popping a digestif into his mouth; he felt easier, it appeared, because the prospect of a trial by cross-examination, with him acting as prosecutor, had receded. 'Don't think . . . don't think I'm . . . making any . . . judgements,' he told them, in-between sucking, crunching, and, finally, hurriedly swallowing the digestif. 'I'm not. It's just that such a relationship poses problems. The main one being that it could disrupt your professional obligations, with each of you being posted to the same Relief.'

'With respect, that is nonsense, sir,' Pat curtly informed him.

'And I agree, sir,' MacHale said. 'We're responsible people. We wouldn't allow the relationship to interfere with our duties, It hasn't, so far, has it?'

'No, no,' Old Crikey assured. 'Not that I *know* of, anyway. But the point is, it *might*. Experience tells me so. Therefore I have but one option, which I'm sure you'll understand. To wit: one of you must be transferred.

'I've consulted the Chief Superintendent, and he agrees. So, from next Monday, MacHale, you will be working at an adjoining station.'

The news stunned MacHale. It was what he'd feared, from the outset of his relationship with Pat; that was why they'd always met at the back gate, after finishing work. Now he just wished that he'd taken a chance and *not* complied with the standing order which required that nights spent away from a registered address must be logged in an official book.

Pat stood, her hands on her hips. 'I think this is . . . *Victorian*, petty, spiteful . . .' Her right hand moved off her right hip and flicked at the air. '. . . and vindictive. But it's also *pointless*. You may just as well let PC MacHale *remain* here, because *I'm* the one who'll be going. As from this Friday, in fact. You see, I've decided to put-in my papers.'

'*What!*' exclaimed Old Crikey.

'*What!*' echoed MacHale.

Pat turned to MacHale. 'Yes, I mean it, John. That's what I was beginning to tell you, this morning, when you called at my office, before parade. Only, you . . . Well, we discussed something which was more . . . pressing.'

'Why? What's the reason, Miss Coles?' Old Crikey wanted to know. 'I mean, you're . . . we *need* . . .' But, for the time being, he could find no more words with which to express his dismay.

'I've been considering it for a long time, now,' Pat told him. 'You see, my parents are retiring to Spain, in the near future, and I shall be taking over their business . . . keeping it in the family.'

MacHale was dumbfounded. Sure, she'd *mentioned* the possibility of her returning to the country, to manage her parents' business when they retired; but in view of the depth of his relationship with her, he felt offended that she hadn't thought it necessary to talk it over with him before finalizing her plans. This wasn't at all like her. It was so sudden. A shock. And what *did* it mean, exactly? Was she *ditching* him? . . . That was something that would have to be privately discussed.

'Are you *sure*?' asked Old Crikey. 'Is it *really* what you want? After all, you've got a career, here. With good prospects for the future, too.'

Pat doubted that, very much. To her, The Job had been little more than an exploratory excursion, adventurous, when she'd joined; and the further she'd ventured along its pitted path, the more she'd thought about backtracking or diverting. 'My mind's made up,' she told Old Crikey. 'I know where I'll be most happy, and it isn't here.'

'That's it. There's nothing more to be discussed, then?' said Old Crikey – veins of hope, resignation, disappointment, all mixed up in his voice; he really was fond of her; that was why he'd intended retaining her on his Relief, and offloading MacHale.

'No, sir,' she finally told him. 'There's nothing more to be discussed.'

Not bloody *much* there isn't, thought MacHale.

'Jesus Christ, that was a bolt from the blue,' said MacHale. 'Why couldn't you have talked it over with *me*? . . . Given me some warning?' They were in her office, now, having made their way there, immediately after Old Crikey had dismissed them.

'I *intended* to, John,' she pleadingly assured him. 'I started to tell you, just before parade.'

'Your mind was already made *up*, though,' he snapped. 'You were just going to . . . yes, *dismiss* me.'

'*John!*' she intoned, shocked and offended. 'That's not *true*! It's not *fair*! In fact, I was *hoping* I'd be able to persuade *you* to come *with* me. I *want* you with me.'

'Oh, *now* I get it,' he said, feeling disgust for what he'd perceived her motive to be. '*You* thought it'd be a *fait accompli* or whatever they call it, didn't you? That if you finalized *your* plans, I'd be *forced* into submission.'

'No, no, John!' she cried, reaching into her shoulder-bag to pull out a white, frill-edged handkerchief, which she unfolded and began dabbing at her eyes and nose. 'That's a terrible thing to say. I decided all this at the end of the weekend. I saw how much you liked everything – the house, the gardens, the countryside and things – , and I was convinced you'd be *eager* to come with me. I *want* you, I *need* you, I . . .' But she burst into tears.

He just couldn't take any *more*. All of the seething, cumulative pressures, of late, began gnawing at his already frayed nerve-endings, drilling into his inflamed head, making him wince, his eyes flicker, mentally cowering him. 'It's blackmail!' he shouted. 'But it's not going to work, because *I'm* not paying up.' And he strode out of her office, slamming the door.

For over an hour, MacHale aimlessly wandered the busy streets, unaware of the throb of noise and movement, his hands clasped behind his back, his head erect, his eyes vacuous, cocooned in his own, private thoughts.

At first, he was convinced he'd been right: she had attempted what he'd often heard referred to as *emotional blackmail* . . . maybe, for all he knew, had been emulating her parents', who'd given her a similar ultimatum – come back and claim the business, or forever lose it . . . something like that. Christ, he was annoyed; he wasn't *ready* to go, perhaps wouldn't be for another twenty-odd years, when he'd be nearing retirement. Okay, so things *had* been a right bastard, lately, what with the way the others had treated him . . . and then there was the adverse report by Barker and Old Crikey, not to mention what had happened, last night, with poor old Hercules. But he was getting on top of all that; this morning, in the canteen, he'd been acquainted with a dormant aspect of himself which he hadn't known existed until it was aroused and given life, and after he'd converted the fear of it into a new plan for self-confident advancement, he'd been convinced that he *could* go on to succeed. He knew, now, just what he was *capable* of. So he despised the idea of chucking it all away, so quickly, so easily; he was much more tenacious a person than that; he didn't want to find himself, in, say, three or four years' time, regretful and depressed, wishing he'd given it just that little bit longer, in case things *had* improved and become bearable . . . *enjoyable*.

He'd been becalmed on a surfboard, a shark, circling; but rolling in towards him was a huge breaker that would carry him on forever. And *that* wasn't Micawberism; he could *sense* it . . . *knew* it.

Trouble was, he couldn't kill the growing feeling that none of it would mean so much unless Pat were there to share it with him. And as the feeling grew more potent, so did his remorse for having accused her and shouted at her and walked out on her. She wanted him; she'd said so. She'd said she needed him, too. And she was about to say how she . . . *loved* him? He dared to believe it . . . because that, perhaps, was how, in the deepest, most sensitive parts of him, he felt about her. *Hell*, he thought, what a mess. But there was time to reorder it. He wouldn't be able to dissuade her from going, and he still didn't feel ready to accompany her, but they could maintain their commitment to each other, all the same; they wouldn't be *that* far apart, and could see each other on his days off and during weekend leaves, and, who knew, maybe it *wouldn't* be all that long before he was ready to permanently join her?

His Final Exam was due in a few months' time, and a pass would signal the end of his probationary period of service; perhaps, also, it would signal to him that he'd made it as much as he needed to in order to prove – primarily, to himself – that he *could* do it; that he *could* be a good cop; that he *was* a good cop.

He'd go straight on back to the nick and apologize to her, he decided. Right now. And he'd take her out to dinner, as well. Tonight. Come Friday, her last day, there'd be one hell of a party, too. Something would sort itself out, he just knew it. They'd both feel so bad at being apart for more than a day, they'd *make* the thing work itself out.

He began walking back along Martin Lane, intending to call in at the High Street branch of the National Consolidated Bank, before he reached the nick. You needed money to take a lady out to dinner, and the weekend had practically cleaned him out of green ones.

As he entered the bank, he inwardly cursed. In every bank he'd ever set foot inside at this time of day – the tail end of the lunch-hour – the same scene was reenacted. Three of the four service-hatches were unattended – why *couldn't* the clerks stagger their mealtimes? – , and at the counter in front of the fourth was the owner of a small business, who was paying-in yesterday's takings – why couldn't *he* choose a less busy time of day? And, come to think of it, *why* couldn't that middle-aged man, behind a desk on the staff side of the counter, or that younger, ginger-haired bloke who'd just come out of an internal office to speak to him, stir *them*selves into action and man the unattended hatches? Indolent buggers.

Behind the businessman who was paying-in, there was, of course, a ten-deep line of exasperated office-workers, cheques in hands, who were wondering exactly what MacHale was wondering about bankworkers and small businessmen, and whether they'd make it out of here in time to grab a bite of food, or maybe a pint of beer, before their breaks were over and it was time to recommence work.

MacHale went to a desk and wrote out his cheque, then stood on the end of the line, waiting his turn, becoming infected by the sighing and foot-shifting that was taking place in front of him, as well as the cheque-fluttering and, occasionally, sniffing and tut-tutting. He began wondering if the countertop-to-ceiling, clear-perspex wall, which separated the cashiers from the public, were shatterproof . . . and supposed it must be. But why were there squares cut out of it, in front of each of the four service-areas? Weak points, he decided. They permitted speech and hand-to-hand transactions between customers and staff, but they also permitted a would-be blagger to stick a shooter through and demand the contents of the cash drawers. Why couldn't they fill-in the squares and set sonic discs into them . . . like he'd seen at cinemas' cashier cubicles? There, you spoke through the perforated disc, put your ticket money in a metal cup that was recessed into the countertop, and the cashier swivelled it round to her side, took your money, replaced it with your ticket and your change, and then swivelled the cup back to you, to enable you to collect them. No one could stick a shooter up a cinema cashier's nose and have it off with the day's take – well, not while she was banged-up inside that cubicle, anyway.

Now, MacHale suddenly felt *watched*. Because he was *being* watched. He knew that, somewhere above him, a video camera was recording everything that went on inside the bank's public area. He began looking up and around, trying to spot the concealed lens . . . and concluded that, although he couldn't locate it, it undoubtedly was somewhere over at the far wall, on the staff side of the counter, high up, panning down and around, recording full frontals and profiles of each one of the bank's customers, as they arrived, stood at the counter, then departed with their money.

And now another customer entered the bank . . . hesitated at the door, put off, it appeared, by the length of the queue, but then continued on into the public area. MacHale was momentarily distracted by the approach of this new customer – a stocky man, dressed in a navy-blue mac and black-wool bobble hat, his head bowed, a blue-canvas sports bag hooked by its carrying strap into the crook of his left arm, his hands holding a cheque-book . . . opening it as he walked towards the queue of customers and leaned over a desk at the back of where MacHale was standing . . .

MacHale took no more notice of the man, but had unconsciously stored the memory of the man's tattooed hands – swallows on the webs of skin between forefingers and thumbs, and single letters, forming the words, L-O-V-E and H-A-T-E, on the fingers above the knuckles of each hand.

Again, MacHale raised his head and sought out the concealed camera, shuffling forward a couple of feet as the businessman was dealt with and the line moved up.

Now the cash transactions were quick and smooth, and as MacHale drew nearer to his turn at the counter, he gave up looking for the camera. In a couple of weeks' time, though, when he came to see a replay of the camera's recording, he'd learn, to his amazement, that he'd looked it straight in the lens and yet *still* not spotted it.

But, for now, he was at the counter, handing over his cheque to the young, female clerk. He offered her a smile, thinking she looked attractive: long, naturally-blonde hair, smooth, pale skin – no make-up – , and a white blouse, open two buttons at the neck, affording him a tiny glimpse of her cleavage.

She returned his smile. 'How would you like the money?'

'Twelve fives, please,' he said, laughing – the cheque was made out for only *fifty* pounds.

She smiled again, and looked reprovingly at him; but it was only affected displeasure.

'No,' he said. 'I'm only kidding. I'll take ten fives, please.'

She turned over the cheque, placed it on the counter in front of herself, and wrote on its reverse side, 'Ten X five'.

As she opened the cash drawer and reached inside to the wads of five-pound notes, a movement behind MacHale distracted her, and she glanced up . . . looked back to the drawer, did a quick double-take, froze, and screamed shrilly through her fingers.

MacHale was in the act of whirling around when he was knocked sideways onto his stomach. He coiled himself up onto his hands and knees, seeing his helmet roll away across the blue-carpeted floor, hearing a voice from behind, shouting at him, '*Stay* there, copper, or you'll *die*!'

His breaths began coming in short, gasping bursts, his limbs were quaking with the surge of adrenaline that had ripped through his body; and there were many other physical manifestations of his bewilderment and fear, which together added up to an intense feeling of nausea in his head and gut. He turned . . .very slowly, still on his hands and knees, looking up, seeing a tall, stocky man, towering above him. It's *him*! he thought. The bloke who came in a couple of minutes ago, wearing a navy-blue mac and black-wool bobble hat; only, now, the bobble hat was rolled down over his face, slits having been cut out of it, to permit vision; it didn't quite reach his upper lip, though, and was loose fitting; and those large, tattooed hands were now holding a sawn-off shotgun, pointing it downward at MacHale. Through the slits in the woollen mask, he could see the intense, shiny pupils of black eyes, piercing him . . . the mouth, tight and drawn, the right index-finger pressuring the sawn-off's trigger.

'You try anythin, an y'll be a sieve for the resta ya life,' the man told MacHale. 'Get on ya belly, an *stay* there.'

The eyes, the voice, the mouth, the stance . . . the *gun*, all convinced MacHale that he'd be dead if he didn't comply. He took one last, fleeting glance, upwards, inside the man's loose-fitting mask, then lowered himself onto his belly, his arms at his sides, his head resting sideways on the carpet, his eyes now on the man's footwear and ankles – black lace-ups and navy-blue socks, nothing distinctive or identifiable.

He heard the girl cashier's whimpering from above . . . the man's heavy, but controlled, breathing, his shouted demand, 'Fill it!' . . . had a mental flash of the girl cashier just sitting there, motionless in her seat, paralysed by fear, her hands still covering the lower half of her face, the shotgun pointing at her chest, threatening to blow a hole the size of a dustbin lid, right through her, and leave most of the upper half of her torso sliding in flecks of blood-soaked bone and flesh, down the bank's far wall . . .

'I *said, fill* it!' repeated the man's voice, more loudly, more desperately, more threateningly, and now MacHale heard her scream and sob . . . *God*, let her *do* it, he silently pleaded. If she doesn't, we're *both* as good as dead. The shaking in his body intensified; his throat was burning dry; his heart was *crashing* around inside his ribcage.

And then there was a *terrific* explosion, followed by wild screaming; MacHale's body jolted, as if shocked by high voltage; his eyes screwed-up tight, he shuddered, his fists bunched, his teeth clenched and grated . . . and when it had subsided, and he'd opened his eyes, he saw flakes of white ceiling-plaster, falling down, like brittle snow, onto the blue carpet beside his head . . . felt them settling into his hair, on his neck, on the side of his face and on his hands. '*Do it!*' he shouted. '*Give* him what he wants!' He paused, spitting out dust and plaster. 'He'll *kill* you if you don't!'

It was the girl he was thinking of. The explosion had violently angered him; afterwards he'd wonder why. Now he began asking himself if the man had loosed-off *both* barrels . . .? Because if he *had* . . . MacHale began slowly, surreptitiously reaching for the strap of his stick, which protruded from his right trousers pocket . . .

'That's better,' the man was saying. 'Fill it *up*! *Right* up!'

And MacHale could hear her sobbing, whimpering, could hear the cash drawers, sliding open . . . the sounds of rustling paper . . . a zip being drawn shut . . . a bag? . . . yes, that canvas bag he was carrying when he came in, holding the cheque-book, and walked by MacHale . . . it was being placed down on top of the counter . . .

Do it! Do it *now*! an inner voice yelled at MacHale. Before it's too *late*! . . . It *was* both barrels! . . .

In one, continuous flow of movement, his thumb pulled out the stick's strap, his hand and fingers wrapping themselves around the grip, and his arm swung round in a wide, blurred arc as he rolled onto his side, drew his knees into his stomach, and smashed the stick into the man's right leg, just above the ankle . . .

The man roared with pain, and his right leg kneed the air as he swivelled and hopped on his left foot, and bent over, clutching, with his right hand, at the lower side of his injured calf . . .

MacHale was rising to his feet, his right arm blurring backwards, as he prepared to deliver another, braining, blow to the side of the man's lowered head . . . *That leg of his!* . . . What *was* that? . . .

The man hobbled backwards, almost off balance, grunting, spitting air, steadying himself, before moving quickly forward on his left foot, his right foot swinging back, his left arm moving out sideways to deflect MacHale's blow, with the barrel of the sawn-off; his right foot now flashing forward and up, its shoe crunching into the left side of MacHale's face. '*Bastard!*'

MacHale felt shockwaves of pain rush up from his jaw to his brain . . . his vision, becoming hazy . . . his back, hitting the floor . . . no feeling in his legs. He rolled over, gasping for air, grabbing wildly for his stick, which had fallen from his hand . . . finding it, getting up . . . falling sideways, steadying himself, seeing only a swirl of light and colour . . . a dark shape, moving fast away from him . . .

He threw the stick, as hard as he could, at the fuzzy dark shape that was disappearing before him . . . following on with the momentum . . . colliding with the side of the counter, bouncing off it, snatching at the air, for support . . . crashing over, backwards . . .

The man's voice, bellowing, out of control, 'I fuckin *warned* you!' – demented with fury . . .

Bursts of screaming . . . '*No, no-no . . . No!*' . . . *demoniac* screaming . . .

An orange tongue of flame, licking out at MacHale, accompanied by white-and-black smoke and a deafening explosion; simultaneously, a thousand, burning splinters being driven into his right side . . . lightning, streaking across his eyes . . . his body, spinning away across the floor . . . the blue carpet, spattered wet and red . . .

Then, an intense silence, bringing with it a dark void of helplessness. No pain. Just a hot, thick wetness, seeping all over his body . . . Disbelief, futility . . . peace . . . acceptance . . . falling through a black hole, the wind tearing at his mouth, his nostrils, his eyes . . .

A blinding flash . . . *Deja Vu!* . . . Followed, now, by a shower of brilliant, multi-coloured sparks . . . bursting . . . cascading . . . Gone.

Finally, nothing.

PART FOUR
Acceptance

21

What remained of Monday was forever lost to him.

Tuesday – if it *were* Tuesday – could be summed-up as a vague awareness . . . of half-opening his eyes and wondering if he were still who he was . . . frantically blinking and looking around the small, private room, seeing shiny, cream-gloss walls . . . drawn blinds . . . bright lights . . . A drip! Alarming! In his left arm. A blanket-covered cage over his torso . . . putting his right arm – *why is it bandaged, like this?* – under the bedclothes, holding his breath, cautiously feeling around, with mounting apprehension . . . a painful jolt, as he touched his right side and ignited a myriad, burning flares. Then, desperate relief, as he knew he was *alive*, wasn't *dying*, and wasn't *going* to die; followed by a heavy, splitting throb behind his eyes as the pain came flooding into his head, making him moan and begin to wish that he *were*, in fact, dead.

Finally, tiny footsteps, padding across the floor . . . a soft, gentle, encouraging voice . . . soothing . . . a hand, behind his splitting head, absorbing some of the pain, raising him up, bringing a small, plastic cup to his parched lips . . . making him swallow every last drop of the viscous, bitter-sweet analgesic . . .

Wednesday – he'd asked, and was told, *Yes, it is Wednesday* – had a little more shape to it. His parents were there. He couldn't believe that they'd also been there, yesterday, because he hadn't seen them by his bedside, hadn't heard them whispering to him; they didn't tell him that they'd also been on Monday evening, as well. His mother, looking thin and pale, and heavy-lidded in her eyes, had cried, and had told him how proud they were . . . of what he'd done, of what he'd attempted to do. His father didn't cry, but agreed they were proud; then he ate the grapes and the two peaches he'd brought for his son, and wondered, out loud, if it were opening time yet, because the warm, dry atmosphere in these places made you thirsty. MacHale had inwardly smiled, at that, and had bet himself that the ol' man would have had the bollocking of his life, from MacHale's mum, before he was out of the hospital gate. The day closed early, with the same, heavy, splitting throb behind MacHale's eyes. He was unable to prevent himself crying.

Thursday. Again, he cried. Because Pat had cried. He couldn't recall her having been there, yesterday, and the day before, and the day before that. She promised to come again, tomorrow, before leaving for home. And when she'd gone, he felt desolate, and cried once more.

Friday. He was thinking and seeing and talking and sitting up. He was now completely aware. The dressings came off his wounds, and he was astounded when he saw his right side and arm: from waist to shoulder, he was tattooed with Christ knew how many holes, most of them sutured, *all* of them with crusty, red and black rims around their healing craters; they stung like hell, too, whenever he coughed or sneezed or suddenly moved, or accidentally brushed over them with the inner side of his right arm. He was curiously proud of those wounds, though, and of how he'd achieved them – *achieved* being the most apposite choice of word, he felt. The doctor, or whoever he was – he might have been a surgeon, actually – , had said he was lucky to be alive: at *close* range, that sawn-off would've punched a huge, ragged hole, almost right through him, with its twenty-three-hundred-odd pieces of burning shot.

Lucky? MacHale had thought. Well, relatively, maybe.

There was an enormous bump on the side of his head,

too, around a deep gash which had taken ten sutures. That accounted for the concussion, the giddy spells, and the blinding headaches, and had been sustained when he'd fallen against the bank's counter, after having hurled his stick at the departing gunman.

Christ, how I hope they capture that bastard, he thought.

The day ended on a depressing note, with more piercing white flashes and sharp stabs of pain behind his eyes. Pat came and went, and wouldn't be returning. She'd been too upset to stay very long, and had softly cried for most of the time she was there, especially when he'd mentioned that the reason he'd been in the bank, on Monday, withdrawing money, was to enable him to take her out to dinner, that night, as an apology. She'd squeezed his hand and gazed into his eyes – they'd seemed just to melt into each other – , and he'd wanted to jump out of bed and run away with her, but she'd left alone, with his promise that he'd soon send her a letter. When she'd gone, he couldn't stop looking at the get-well-soon card she'd left behind, reading the poem she'd written on the inside leaf, and which she'd forbade him to look at until she was away:

It grieves to go;
Pain, to depart.
The tears flow;
But there's fire in my heart!

I love you, John.

As he absorbed the words, over and over, he felt a swelling in his throat and lower jaw . . . a moistness in his eyes, his lips begin to tremble. And with the darkness came rushes of hot wet tears, which shamed him, he felt; they soothed mental scars, but they somehow devalued the others, his physical scars.

On Saturday, he was up and about, wandering the corridors, visiting the out-patients' cafeteria and shop, dodging doctors and nurses, but finally getting himself captured by Hitler in drag – she did *have* a tuft of wispy black hair beneath her nose, too – , and chased back to his room. The sutures were to be removed on Monday morning, he was told, as the healing wounds were now well-closed. Monday afternoon, he'd be discharged.

But then what? A week in the police nursing-home, at Hendon? A week off, still sick, after that? Maybe another couple of weeks on light duties, when he did resume, and then a return to normal Relief-duties? Something along those lines, he supposed . . . *And*, talking of the Relief, where *were* those uncaring bastards? None of them had visited him, or even phoned to inquire about his state of health – as far as he was aware. Miserable loada snotgob-blin . . . *bastards*! He'd never forget this, he told himself.

But, on Saturday afternoon, an hour after early-turn had ended, they arrived, in high spirits and smelling of beer . . . even Old Crikey had come along with them.

'Hello, dear boy,' smiled Snatch, shaking MacHale's hand and making his side twinge with pain. 'We're all here, cept Mathieson, who's still Tom-'n'-Dick, and Harry Tanner, who's up-town on a demo. Thank God you're alive.'

'Yeah,' agreed Vindscreen. 'That was some belt in the side you took there.' He was gazing in awe at MacHale's torso.

They *all* were.

'Hope you're not in any pain, Mac . . . John,' mumbled Old Crikey – who was clearly embarrassed.

He called me *John*, thought MacHale. Inwardly, he giggled like hell. I've *arrived*! He laughed. 'No, sir. No pain . . . Only where it hurts.'

Old Crikey laughed, too; unnaturally loudly, relievedly, and looked at the others, expecting them to follow suit.

They all smiled and nodded and began sitting on the edges of the bed, pulling-up chairs . . . a table, making MacHale suspect that they were about to ignore him and begin a game of three-card brag or something; he wouldn't have put it past them.

'Here's a card for ya, son,' said Punchy Paterson, and he handed MacHale an enormous, white envelope, which could never have been fed into a letterbox, for posting – at least not without having been bent in four, beforehand, and thereby ruined.

'Oh . . . Thanks,' said MacHale, surprised, and he opened the envelope and pulled out a huge, get-well-soon card – a portrait of a spray of red roses and green ferns, arranged in a fluted, white urn – , which was signed, on the inside, with good wishes from each member of the Relief who'd been on duty this morning. Whose choice of card *was* this? he wondered. He'd've thought that if it were down to any one of those who were *present*, including Old Crikey, the choice would have been for one of those humorous cards, probably one which had some sort of a cartoon on its front, with a message inside that alluded to sex. Maybe they'd asked one of the female members of the canteen staff to go out and purchase it? Whatever, it was nice, MacHale thought, and he was quite moved by it.

'Thanks,' he repeated. 'Thanks a lot.' And he placed thc card on his bedside locker, next to Pat's.

'And there's this, an all,' said Tasty Tom, bringing his hands from behind his back, and handing MacHale a white-plastic carrier-bag. 'We had a whip-round, ya see, an . . . well, it ain't much, but . . .' He shrugged embarrassedly.

'Hope you like it,' said Barker.

MacHale opened the bag and pulled out a small teddy-bear, gold and fluffy and cuddly, with enormous brown-button eyes and tweaky little ears; it had a red-tin badge pinned to its chest, which bore the white-painted words, *My Hero*. MacHale kissed the bear's cheek. 'It's terrific,' he said, beaming, and cradled it in his left arm.

'Ain't it just,' said Barker, pleased as MacHale.

'Had the badge made special,' said Tubby Tompkins, equally pleased by it all.

'Cute little fucker, ain't he?' put in Filthy Phil.

'Who?' asked Vindscreen. '*Him?*' And he pointed at MacHale.

Everyone burst out laughing.

'And now,' Punchy Paterson conspiratorially whispered, looking furtively about himself as he pulled a bottle of Scotch out of his trousers pocket. 'Where's the glasses?'

'Oh, I dunno about that,' said MacHale, looking with concern at the bottle. 'We're not s'posed to drink in here.' If Hitler in drag caught them, she'd be looking for her castrating scissors.

'We're celebrating – your good health,' said Old Crikey, dismissing MacHale's concern. '*I'll* square-up the matron, if we get caught at it.'

He's *already* drunk, thought MacHale. He *must* be. This was unheard of, totally uncharacteristic. Old Crikey? Conniving at a breach of rules?

'Yeah, come on,' urged Tasty Tom. 'I wanna see the stuff spurtin outa them holes in ya side, when ya swallow a shot.'

'Yeah!' chorused the others. 'Come on!'

So, off went MacHale, on a tour of the bathrooms and adjacent rooms and wards, returning with nine tumblers and a jug of water.

He could scarcely believe this was happening. But it was. And by the time they left, at about four-thirty that afternoon, MacHale was undefeated heavyweight-champion of the world, seeing one-and-a-half of everything he tried to focus his bleary eyes on.

He lay back, exhausted, on the bed, looking at the one-and-a-half teddies he'd been presented, and the get-well cards, and found it all even *harder* to believe. A week ago, he was a pariah. Today, though, he was a hero. Then an idea that they were a bunch of . . . hypocrites? . . . implanted itself in his mind; they still owed him an apology for the way they'd treated him, these past weeks . . . But he soon uprooted the notion, and destroyed it. Christ, *they'd* moved towards *him*, hadn't they? So let *him* now move towards *them*. No use harbouring grudges. Here was a chance to start all over again, on a different footing.

But *still* he felt sad. There'd been something missing. Some*one* missing. Not so much Pat; she'd been here, all week. Not Mathieson, either, or Tanner. No, it was Hercules who was missing. And the reason for Hercules' absence made MacHale feel even sadder. Hercules would've been here at MacHale's side, on *Monday* afternoon, had he been alive; his motives were really of no relevance; he would've brought himself *over* here; straight away. But now . . . well, for MacHale's part, it was all regret and futile wishing.

He fell asleep as darkness closed in, cuddling the teddy.

On Sunday afternoon, MacHale was visited by two members of the Central Robbery-Squad – or The Heavy Mob.

He was lying on his bed, dressed in a white towelling-robe, thinking that tomorrow the stitches were coming out, and wondering how much it would hurt.

He glanced up as he heard the door opening, and saw the two men coming through and walking towards him. One was dressed in a navy, chalkstripe suit, crisp-white shirt, and dark-blue, knitted-silk tie; he was tall, and wide-shouldered, with a dark complexion, broad nose and straight, black hair that was neatly trimmed; in his left hand, he held a black briefcase, while his right hand was buried deep in the pocket of his trousers. The other man, curly-blonde hair, hard face and flinty-blue eyes that gave nothing away, except, *Watch out*, I'm *about*, was slightly younger than his colleague, MacHale guessed – about thirty-five, thirty-six – , and wore a tan-leather bomber-jacket, grey slacks and open-necked red shirt; both of his hands were in his trousers pockets.

And, suddenly, MacHale had the crazy notion that this slightly older man would open his briefcase, whip out a shooter, and kill him. He began rising from the bed, looking expectantly at the two men.

The older man reached the side of the bed, and put on offer his right hand – a huge implement, with hairy-knuckled fingers. 'No, no. Stay put, son.' He was smiling reassuringly. 'I'm DCI Bruno, C-Eight, and this is DS Bell. We're investigatin the one across the pavement that you got stuck into, last Monday.'

MacHale shook the hands of both men. 'One across the pavement, sir?'

'The blag . . . The robbery,' explained Bruno.

'Oh,' said MacHale, and thought that Bruno must be of Italian extraction . . . the name, the dark complexion. He also thought that both of his visitors must just have come from the pub; they each smelled strongly of drink.

They pulled-up chairs, and sat, one either side of the bed. Then, Bruno opened his briefcase, reached inside it, and took out a fistful of five-pound notes, handing them to MacHale. 'For you,' he said.

'For *me*?' said MacHale, puzzled. In all, there were ten notes: fives; fifty pounds. Are they trying to *bribe* me?

'Your kite . . . your cheque,' explained Bruno.

'Tha's right,' said Bell. 'Remember? You handed it over the jump, but never received your dough. So, we collected for you.'

'*Ahh!*' intoned MacHale. 'I'd forgotten. Thanks, thanks a lot.' And he placed the money in the drawer of his bedside locker. 'By the way,' he added. 'How much did the *robber* get out of it?'

'Handfula monkeys,' Bruno told him.

'Twenny-five hundred,' interpreted Bell. 'Hardly worth all the aggravation, if y'ask me . . .' He shrugged. 'Still, murders might be done for a whole lot less than that.'

And almost *were*, thought MacHale.

'Anyway, down to business,' said Bruno, in a very businesslike fashion. 'First off, we wanna go over with you, in detail, exactly what happened, Monday lunch-time.' His dark-brown eyes were penetrating, analysing, all-pervasive, but in a covert way.

'Okay, sir,' said MacHale. 'It's all a bit hazy, but . . . well, where d'you want me to start?' Unconsciously, he'd moved his right hand up to finger the bump on the side of his head.

'Why were you in the bank?' Bell wanted to know.

'To withdraw some money. I was going to take a girlfriend out to dinner, that night, and I was short of cash.'

'So you entered the bank,' said Bruno. 'Then what? . . . Describe the scene. Who was there, what you did . . .'

MacHale looked, blank-eyed, at the ceiling, and cast back his mind; until now, he'd thought only superficially about what happened. 'It was the tail-end of lunch-time . . . about one-thirty . . . a queue at the one service-area that was manned . . . Or should I say, *womanned*? . . .'

'What?' said Bell.

'It was a woman, a young girl behind the screen . . . by herself. A man, a businessman, I s'pose, was first in line, paying-in a lot of coins and notes. Behind him there was a queue . . . maybe ten, twelve people, I didn't count, just felt annoyed because it's always the same at lunch-time, when it's busy . . . They let all but one of the staff go to lunch, and it causes a build-up of customers.'

'There were staff on the far side of the counter, though,' said Bruno. 'Behind the cashier, I mean.'

MacHale frowned, and thought about it. 'Yes, yes there were, now I think of it. A middle-aged man in a suit – he was at a desk – , and a younger bloke, who came out of an office to speak to him. That's right, because I remember thinking, Why can't *they* help out to clear the queue?'

'So you stood in line and waited your turn?' Bell asked.

'Yes.'

'Then what?'

'I was just standing there, idly wondering where the camera was. The security camera. Daydreaming, I s'pose, waiting for the line to move on up.' Immediately, MacHale regretted the confession: cops were not *supposed* to be hanging around in banks, daydreaming, were they?

Bruno glanced at Bell, and smiled. Then he said, to MacHale, 'We've taken possession of the camera's videotape, and we've played it back. At one stage, you looked right *at* the lens.'

'Really?' said MacHale, amazed.

'Yeah,' confirmed Bell. 'Right at it.'

'We'll play it for you,' Bruno told MacHale. 'Next week, sometime. You'll need to see it, anyway, before you make a written statement . . . make sure what you say on paper, corresponds with what we *know* took place. But go on with what you were telling us. You were in the line . . . daydreaming, wasn't it?' – just a *tiny* hint of sarcasm in his voice.

MacHale flushed, and coughed. 'The line moved up. The businessman had completed his transaction, and left. From then on, the line began moving fairly quickly . . .' But they must already *know* this, thought MacHale. They said they've seen the video. Mentally, he shrugged, and went on, anyway. 'I remember seeing a man walk in. His head was held forward . . . looking down . . . so I couldn't see his features. He was . . .' MacHale broke off, pleating his brow, having difficulty with the recollection.

'Just lean back on the pillow,' Bruno told him, 'and close your eyes. Relax. *Think* about it . . . *see* it . . . take yourself *back* there. It'll come.'

MacHale did as he'd been advised, and began relaxing, closing his eyes . . . seeing back . . . Now it became easier. 'He was holding a cheque-book . . . flipping its pages . . . looking down at it . . . wearing a woolly hat . . . with a fluffy bobble on top of it, black in colour . . . the sides of the hat, furled up, forming a sort of . . . brim . . . black hair at the sides of the brim, or roll of wool. A navy mac, too . . . He went to a desk behind where I was, and that's all I remember seeing of him . . . until . . .'

'Until what?' prompted Bruno.

'I'd handed over my cheque . . . it was my turn. I remember asking for twelve fives . . .' He smiled to himself. 'A joke, she was an attractive girl . . . She smiled at what I'd said,' MacHale went on, 'and then, after I'd said I'd have *ten* fives, she wrote a ten, an X, and a five on the back of my cheque. And then it happened. There was her, screaming, and I was knocked flat on my back, or it might've been my side, I can't remember exactly . . . just went crashing over, with the air rushing out of me, and he said – shouted – something like, "Don't move, copper, or you're dead". *Shouted* it, yes, and pointed a sawn-off shotgun at my head, and . . .' MacHale was breathing heavily, now, frowning, fidgeting, beginning to sweat.

'Okay, relax,' Bruno told him. 'Take your time. Who was this man?'

'The man who'd walked in, holding the cheque-book. I'd forgotten about him. I was, well, I was thinking about things. No other customer had come in, I'm sure. I'd've noticed. It *was* the same man, but now, *now* he . . .'

'Had his *appearance* altered?' tried Bell.

'Yes. Yes. The mac was the same, but he'd . . . unfurled, unrolled the brim of the bobble hat, and now it was pulled down over his face, with eye-holes in it . . .'

'So it became a mask?' said Bruno.

'Yes, that's right, a mask, out of an ordinary hat . . . like the sort of thing a skier would wear. But, pulled down like that, not quite to his upper lip, it was all . . . sort of loose, so's he could breathe up through it, I s'pose. I remember *noticing* that . . . that I could see *up* it, a little way, while I was on the floor. It was *definitely* that same man. He *had* those tattooes.'

'What tattooes?' asked Bell.

'Swallows . . . blue swallows. On each hand, by his thumbs. And letters on his fingers . . . *LOVE* and *HATE*. I'd noticed them on the hands of the man who'd come in holding the cheque-book, and I saw them on *this* man's hands, while he stood over me with the shotgun. And oh, yes! He had a blue sports-bag, too, hooked over his arm . . . to hide the sawn-off and to put the money in, I s'pose.'

'Any rings on the fingers?' asked Bell.

'Or a watch or bracelet . . . maybe an earring? Anything at all like that?' Bruno added.

'No . . . No, definitely not – well, I dunno about a watch, because I didn't see enough of his wrists – , but definitely no jewellery. He was a slag.'

'What d'you mean?' said Bruno.

'Those tattooes. I've never seen a respectable person with stuff like that on his hands . . . Only ex-cons, people like that.'

'Yeah, 'bout right,' conceded Bell.

'*Respectable* people don't go about blagging banks an

shootin young Wall – young coppers, either,' Bruno pointed out.

He was *gonna* call me a *Wally*, MacHale indignantly thought.

'Carry on,' said Bell. 'What happened after that, after he knocked you on the floor and told you not to move?'

'I rolled onto my belly, like he told me, and then I saw his socks and shoes . . . black lace-ups – not fancy or anything – , which might've been Tufs, like a lot of coppers wear, and navy-blue socks . . . He was shouting at the girl, telling her to fill-up the bag. And then he shouted again, told her *again* to fill it up. She must've been too frightened to move, though . . .'

'She was,' confirmed Bruno.

'And then there was this terrific bang, and plaster started coming down all around me . . . just like it was snowing . . . I must've jumped a foot off the floor when I heard that bang . . .'

'Yeah, he put one into the ceiling,' said Bell.

'Well, it annoyed me,' MacHale went on. He was gritting his teeth, now. 'I felt *furious*, because of what he'd done to that girl. I told her to do what he wanted, otherwise we'd both be killed. I really believed he'd *do* it. But . . . funny . . . *I* thought he'd let go with *both* barrels, it was such an almighty bang, and I thought I'd have a chance, then, to jump up and give him some stick . . . *I* could've killed *him* . . .'

'Hmm, that's what your face said, an all,' Bruno told him. 'The camera got it all – it's over at the entrance, by the way . . . just above the door, as you come in.'

'Oh,' said MacHale. 'I'd thought it must be on the far wall, behind the counter.'

'No, over the door,' said Bell. 'Takes everythin that happens on the public side, an most of what happens on the staff side, too.'

'Oh,' MacHale again said. 'Anyway, I managed to get

my stick out, and I smashed it into his ankle . . . just above his ankle, I think . . . the right one . . . trying to get up at the same time, to give him another one, on his nut . . . knock him out or something.'

'So what'd *he* do, then?' asked Bruno. 'After you'd belted him.'

'He sort of . . . yelped, shouted . . . made a noise that said it'd hurt. And he grabbed at his calf and rubbed it, hopping about a bit. But, I mean, this only took a couple of seconds, like. It all happened *very* quick. And then, while he was parrying my stick, with the sawn-off, he kicked me, with the leg that was hurt . . . the same leg I'd hit, I mean, and I remember . . . yeah, that's right, I remember saying to myself . . . well, it sort of registered with me that he'd *got* something *unusual* – while he was rubbing his leg and then kicking me. His trouser-leg rode up, and I was kind of unconsciously struck by . . . with . . .' He broke off, shaking his head and drawing the back of his right hand across his damp forehead.

'What?' said Bruno, very interested. 'You saw something . . . or noticed something. What was it?'

'A weapon? A knife, maybe? Tucked in his sock?' suggested Bell.

'No, no,' said MacHale. 'I don't *know*. There *was* something about that leg, but – '

'A limp?' tried Bruno. 'A caliper on his leg, perhaps?'

'No, no,' repeated MacHale, his eyes blank, his face creased with concentration and frustration. 'He'd've been limping when he first came in, if he had a gammy leg. There *was* something, but the memory's out of focus, now . . .

'He kicked me, and my brain was jolted, and I must've fallen over, and I couldn't see straight, and I grabbed at my stick, which had fallen on the floor, and I chucked it at him, and I was gasping and choking and there was like hot red sticky stuff, sliding slowly down across my eyes –

funny, that – , . . . and . . . just crashing over, again . . . backwards, sideways . . .' He shot bolt-upright on the bed, his eyes wide in shock, his mouth gaping, his chest heaving up and down. The memory seemed by far more frightening than the reality of it had been. Because, perhaps, there was now time to *think*, to dwell, to ponder just *how* bad it was, and just how much worse it *might* have been.

'Okay, okay,' said Bruno. 'Take it easy.' And he placed a hand on MacHale's shoulder, gently forcing him back down onto the pillow. 'Lie back and close your eyes again . . . get your breath back.'

'I'll have to keep my eyes open,' MacHale said, sighing an enormous sigh. 'It'll be okay if I keep my eyes open.'

'You sure?' asked Bell. 'We could leave it, for now, if you want.'

'Yeah, sure.'

'Okay,' said Bruno. 'Finish off.'

MacHale shrugged. 'He *shot* me.' There was a note of incredulity, mixed up with indignation, in his voice. 'The bastard *shot* me. He'd only emptied *one* barrel into the ceiling.'

'And then?' Bruno said.

Again, MacHale shrugged, spreading his hands. 'I woke up in here.' He pulled a hand around his jaw. 'Funny thing is, the side of my face doesn't hurt. Where he kicked me. The pain from that must've been completely relegated by the pain I got when my head hit the counter as I fell over. Strange, that. It's just a little bit tender in a difficult-to-find spot, but it doesn't *hurt*.'

'Bet ya nut does, though,' said Bell.

'Yeah . . . like hell,' confirmed MacHale, gingerly putting the flat of his hand over the duck-egg that was on the side of his head. 'Not as much as it *did*, though, when I first woke-up in here.'

'Be worth a nice few quid, that,' said Bruno, either

enviously or reassuringly, MacHale wasn't certain which it was. 'The bump, I mean. And that moonscape down your right side.'

'How come?' MacHale wanted to know. 'I don't follow.'

'Criminal injuries compensation,' explained Bell. 'We'll prepare a claim on your behalf, to put up to the Board.'

'*Can* I apply for that?' asked MacHale. 'I thought that was only for civvies who were victims of crime. I'd've thought my stuff'd be put down to . . . well, an occupational hazard.'

'No,' said Bruno. 'The scheme is open to anyone who's criminally injured.'

'Well, that's good news, anyway,' smiled MacHale. What a wonderful analgesic was money. 'But won't it all depend on whether he's caught?'

Bruno negatively shook his head. 'No. That's a side issue, as it happens. Which leads me to a point: d'you reckon you'd be able to ID this blagger, if we stuck him up on a parade?'

'Think about it,' said Bell. 'Before you answer. Remember what you saw of him, and think carefully.'

MacHale sighed, and grimaced. 'It's difficult. If you put him in front of me, with a shotgun, wearing the same clothes and the bobble hat, I'm pretty sure I'd know him. But if there were *twelve* of them, *all* looking like that . . .' He blew out his cheeks. 'Trouble was, I hardly saw *anything* of his face. I remember the black hair, at the sides of the bobble hat, when he first walked in, head down; and when I was lying on the floor, looking up, seeing a little way past the hat, which was down over his face, loosely fitted . . . I dunno . . . The eyes, what I saw of them . . . just . . . well, just black, or very dark brown . . . A broad, straight nose, I think, and a heavy jawline, uncompromising, . . . and tight lips, not thin, not full. But, of course, he was adopting an aggressive stance, so his lips would be like that, I s'pose, and his jaw would be jutting, sort've stubborn, like . . .'

'Anythin else?' asked Bruno.

'His jaw, again,' said MacHale. 'It had a kind of heavy, nine o'clock shadow, y'know, blue-black – not stubble or anything; he'd had a *shave*, but you could still see . . . what d'you call it . . .?'

'The black roots of the follicles?' suggested Bell.

'Yeah, that's it,' agreed MacHale. 'I'd say he was a bloke who needed to shave a couple of times a day, maybe . . . a dark complexioned bloke . . . not as dark as me, or you, sir, but – '

'Not half-chat, was he?' asked Bruno.

'No,' said MacHale. 'Definitely not. Just . . . a *bit* dark-skinned.'

Bell and Bruno exchanged glances, but their expressions gave away nothing of their feelings.

'How about the voice?' said Bruno.

MacHale hunched his shoulders, then winced as he felt the action inflame a part of his right side. 'Cockney. Fairly deep. But that, too, might've been distorted by his aggression.'

'Anything else, you can think of?' said Bell. 'Anything at all?'

'Only the tattooes I've mentioned. But, then, every slag in the country – in the *world*, for all I know – has got those sort of pictures on his hands.'

'Yeah, true enough,' agreed Bell. 'The tattooes are more useful for elimination purposes than identification, in this case.'

MacHale slowly shook his head, and his eyes became glassy. 'There must've been something about that *leg*. I can *see* it, now. It was pale – in relation to his face, anyway – and hairy and the calf was thick . . . and he rubbed at it and his trouserleg rode up, and . . . nothing, when there should be *something* . . . I dunno. My brain, at the time it all happened, soaked-up something about that leg; I got a mental imprint from it. Trouble is, my eyes were taking in so *many* things, I s'pose.'

'Must've been something quite unusual, whatever it was,' said Bruno.

'So *why* don't I remember it?' MacHale frustratedly returned. 'It couldn't've been *that* unusual, or I *would* remember it.'

'Forget it,' advised Bell. 'Maybe it'll come to you outa the blue.'

The *blue*! *Blue*! It was *blue*! *Now*, MacHale got a foggy, mental flashback of it: a blue . . . *blot*! Blot? No . . . A *bruise*! That's what it must've been . . . not where the stick hit him – it'd've been too soon for that to have shown up. An *old* bruise, maybe. Useless, though – if that's *really* what it was – , because by now it'll probably have disappeared – and the one my stick made, too.

MacHale gave-up on the problem of the leg. For the time being, anyway. 'How about the video, though?' he suddenly said, immediately resurrecting the problem, as he was struck by the possibility of the camera's recording having highlighted any distinguishing mark which the blagger's leg had had, or still had, if it *were* something other than a bruise. 'Whatever it was about the leg, might be on the film.'

Bruno shook his head. 'No chance. All we saw, when we re-ran it, was a blurred portion of ankle and calf muscle, when he lifted his foot off the floor, reached down, and rubbed at where you'd clobbered him.'

'Yeah, it was a poor angle, an all,' said Bell. 'We *could* have the relevant frames blown-up as stills, but I don't think it'll help, because, at the stage we're talkin about, he wasn't fully sideways-on to the camera.'

'Oh, well,' said MacHale. 'That's that, then, I s'pose.'

Bell glanced at his wristwatch, then stood. 'Time we shot off, guv, innit?' he said to Bruno.

Bruno nodded, slapped his knees, lifted his briefcase off the bed, and walked around to join Bell. 'Yep,' he said, glancing at the wall-clock. Then, looking at MacHale: 'I've got a briefing at the Big House, in half an hour. We're gonna spin a few out the Method Index; see if we can't get a result outa that.'

'How about my written statement, then?' MacHale wanted to know. He didn't want any of what he *could* recall, slipping away from his memory.

'Next week,' Bruno told him. 'Like I said, earlier, after you've seen the video. Meanwhile, just keep thinkin about this geezer. Maybe somethin else'll come to you.'

'Okay, sir,' said MacHale. 'I'll see you next week, then.'

'Right.'

'Be lucky,' said Bell, and followed Bruno out of the door.

'You, too,' MacHale called after them.

And then he felt a trickle of excitement, and wished he were going along with them. He could just see it: all over the MPD, villains who were in the frame for this one, sitting indoors, having tea or dinner, or whatever, and suddenly the front-door comes flying along the hallway, closely followed by the Heavy Mob, waving shooters and knocking people out the way.

Okay, it *wasn't* right, but the only thing MacHale wanted, at this moment, was for the villain who'd shot him to be laid to rest in the cells.

23

It was six-thirteen A.M., Monday morning.

The narrow street was dark and empty of people: its one-storey, red-brick terraced houses, with their shiny-black windows and deep-shadowed doorways and gardens, were heavily silent, still merged with night. Overhead, the sky was a midnight blue, but a crack of deep turquoise, against which the ridges of rooftops on the street's eastern side were silhouetted, was lengthening and growing steadily thicker. The air was pure, and calm, prickled by early-morning chill.

It was going to be a fine day. For most people. But not for all. And especially not for one person, who resided in this street.

A maroon Rover Two-Six turned into the northern end of the street, somehow menacing and shiny wet in the poor light; its headlamps and sidelights were unlit, and as it simmered gently along in a low gear, its disc-brakes emitting an intermittent, revolving squeak, the driver and three passengers turned their heads and strained their eyes; one of the men was counting chimney-stacks on rooftops, while the others were looking for numbers on front-doors.

In the street which ran parallel to this one, there was parked an unlit, yellow Cortina Two-Litre, whose four heavily-built occupants were casually dressed and rigid with apprehension.

None had spoken a word for the past five minutes. Three of them were fighting severe hangovers, and one was smoking cigarette after cigarette. *All* of them were nervous, however, as they awaited the RT-message which would inform them that it *was* going off, and which would then send them on their way over a back wall and into a dark garden, armed with floods of adrenaline and .38 Smith & Wesson revolvers.

A streetwise passer-by would have marked the occupants of this car as a team of villains; then he'd immediately have questioned his judgement, and suspected that they were coppers; ultimately, he probably wouldn't have been sure. In fact, they were a team from the Heavy Mob, on an early-morning spin, and in a couple of minutes' time, all hell would break loose as they steamed into a well-practised plan of action. Nervous, they might have been, but afraid they certainly were not, and when it went off, they'd make it bang.

The maroon Rover braked to a halt, its rear lamps glowing red in the half light, and double-parked alongside a white MGB-GT. The driver cut the engine and the rear lamps died. A Unigate milk-float then whined, rattled and chinked its way along the street, passing the Rover and turning right at the street's northern end. There were no lights showing in any of the houses' windows: the occupants of the street, almost all unemployed, the remainder either in prison or on the trot, were in bed. And now, suddenly, it seemed, the air was alive with the tangled sounds of warbling birds . . . then a cockerel, crowing from a nearby garden . . . once, twice . . . a third time.

'When the cock crows thrice . . .,' said DCI Bruno, slowly, quietly, meaningfully. He was leaning back in the Rover's front passenger-seat, and the Biblical significance of the bird's crowing had not escaped him; it was uncanny that it should have occurred, he felt, in view of what was about to go off, here at any moment.

'What d'you say, guv?' asked Bell, from the seat behind Bruno. He'd heard both the crowing and Bruno's remark, but couldn't connect the two.

'Nothing,' Bruno dismissively said. He leaned forward in his seat and looked out through the car's screen, along the street. 'He in, d'you reckon?' he asked of no one in particular.

Bell leaned aside in the back, nearside seat, peering through the gap between Bruno and the driver-PC who was at the Rover's wheel. 'Can't see his motor anywhere.'

'It's there,' said DC Hoskins, pointing along the line of Bell's vision. 'That blue BMW . . . in front of the orange Granada . . . opposite chummy's drum.'

'Yeah, got it,' said Bruno.

Bell leaned further forward, squinting his eyes at the BMW's plates . . . 'That's it, all right; it is Frankie James's motor . . . although it looks more like black than dark blue, in this light.'

Bruno's wide shoulders rose and fell. 'Let's do it, then.' He bent forward again, and pulled at the volume-and-tuning knobs of the car's Motorola radio, unclipping its false front and allowing it to jar down on its hinges, revealing a small cubby-hole which contained the RT-set. After switching on the set, he opened the car's glove-compartment and pulled out the hand-set, depressing its *Send*-button. 'Central Nine-Nine from Four-Five, 'ceivin over?'

'R-five,' crackled back the response.

'Nine-Nine from Four-five, it's *on*. I repeat, it's *on*. Over.'

'Yeah, 'ceived. How many stacks along, over?'

Bruno turned aside in his seat and looked back at Hoskins. 'How many was it, Terry?'

'Eleven, guv.'

Bruno returned the hand-set to the side of his mouth. '*E-leven,* over.'

'Yeah, re-ceived. On way. Over-'n'-out.'

'Give em a couplea minutes to get over the wall,' said Bruno, looking at his wristwatch. 'Then we'll steam in.'

In the Rover's back seat, Hoskins tightened his grip on the pick-axe handle that was lying across his lap, while Bell leaned sideways down and picked up off the floor a pair of heavy bolt-cutters and a weighty crow-bar.

Now, a palpitating silence filled the car, as they awaited the off . . .

'That's it,' said Bruno, as the second hand of his wristwatch swept around and up to hit twelve. 'Let's go an give that Frankie James some stick. Wicked bastard.'

When they reached the target's front-door – squares of frosted glass forming its upper half, green-painted wood forming its lower half – , Hoskins stepped forward with the pick-axe handle, while Bruno, Bell and the driver, stood aside, tensely watching, impatiently waiting. First, Hoskins placed the thickest end of the pick-axe handle at the top of the door's frame, on the lock side, and leaned forcefully into it; the top corner of the door gave way; just a little; sufficient to indicate that there was no bolt which had been shot-home there on the inside. Next, he repeated the action at the door's bottom corner; again, on the lock side; no bolt was shot-home there, either. Now, he studied the lock itself: just the one . . . a simple Yale.

He stepped back, both hands gripping the thin end of the pick-axe handle, and stabbed sharply forward with it, striking it forcefully against the square of frosted glass that was adjacent to the lock. The glass shattered inward, and now he quickly began knocking out the jagged slivers that remained set in the puttied frame, before discarding the pick-axe handle and reaching in to twist open the knob of the lock. The door swung inward, but immediately banged to a stop, held by a secured night-chain, which was fixed to the middle, lower half of the inside of the frame, and couldn't be reached through the broken pane above it. Hoskins moved away, therefore, and made room for Bell, who now went to work with the bolt-cutters and easily snapped in half the thick chain.

They were in; it had taken no more than a minute and a half, and the crow-bar hadn't even been required. Officially, of course, if anyone later wanted to know, they'd banged seven kinds of crap out of that door's knocker, and had verbally demanded admission, but without good result, so had *then* been obliged to force an entry. And whatever anyone thought about that, what was the *use* in kicking around on a doorstep, stabbing bell-pushes and rattling knockers, and shouting, 'Please let me in, I've got a warrant to search,' while the geezer whose collar you wanted to claim was feeding smack down the khazi or doing a runner across the rooftops?

Bell dashed along the hallway, which was carpeted in dark-blue Wilton . . . then up the stairs, closely followed by Hoskins; both men had drawn their revolvers, and, if necessary, wouldn't hesitate to use them – none of this shoot-to-wound crap, though, which the anti-police brigade and their banner-carriers – who knew next to fuck all about *anything*, never mind policework – were forever on about, every time the law *killed* a villain who was either armed or believed to be armed; no, anyone who pointed a shooter at these three cops, would end up supine with a neat hole in his ten ring.

Now, Bruno followed on along the hallway, his right hand reaching inside the jacket of his suit, to his left shoulder; he was softly singing, and humming: *Humpty Dumpty sat on a wall, Humpty Dumpty had a great fall; all the King's soldiers and all the King's men, couldn't put Humpty together again . . . RIP, Humpty, my son . . .*

Outside, the driver stood guard at the front-door, holding the pick-axe handle over his left shoulder – a baseball player, posing for a strike, it seemed – , and in the unlikely event of anyone getting past the three armed detectives who were inside, he'd be wiped-up by that wooden pole, before his feet so much as touched the garden path.

At the head of the stairs there was a small, square landing, beyond which was an open door that led into a darkened bathroom and toilet. To the left, there was a closed door; to the right, an open door. Bell peeled away to the left, threw open the closed door, and fell to a half-crouch stance, fanning the gun, squinting his eyes in the room's black interior, his senses bristling. Hoskins had moved to the right, in through the open door, crouching forward, feet spread, holding his gun before himself in a two-fisted grip; it was a bedroom . . . foggy, half light, soaking in through the closed curtains of a window that was opposite him. At his left, a sudden movement . . . a white hand, a leg, two faces, bedclothes being flung back, a penetrating, high-pitched, female scream; a man's voice, thick with sleep, but nonetheless alarmed, saying, '*What? . . . What the fuck . . .?*' . . . his tattooed right hand instinctively reaching out towards a bedside, whitewood locker . . .

'Armed police!' shouted Hoskins, moving quickly, now, to the far side of the room, just as Bruno came in, pointing his own gun at the head of the bed. 'Stay put, and don't even blink,' ordered Hoskins, every living piece of him concentrating on the occupants of the bed, their movements and vibes . . .

Bruno's left hand fumbled for the lightswitch by the jamb of the door, while his eyes and his gun-hand remained trained on the head of the bed; finding the switch, he snapped it down, flooding the bedroom with bright yellow light.

Still, the man's hand was sneaking towards the bedside locker . . . while his right foot was still moving slowly down in search of the red-carpeted floor . . . his deep-brown eyes, flickering, calculating the chances . . .

'Go on, Frankie. Go on, son,' taunted Bruno, tight-lipped and slit-eyed. 'Do it . . . An I'll put one straight through ya.'

'No, Frankie! *No!*' screamed the woman next to him. 'He'll *kill* you!' She was kicking herself up into a sitting position in the bed, her hands pulling up the floral-patterned white duvet, to cover her naked breasts; her eyes were crazy with fear and bewilderment, and her complexion was fast matching the colour of her straggly, bleached hair.

James's tongue flicked out to wet his lips, and his Adam's apple rose and fell as he swallowed hard, his movements now frozen. Then he slowly retracted his hand and his foot, eased out a controlled sigh, relaxed, and sat up in bed, leaning back against the brown-draylon-padded headboard, his hands clasped behind his neck.

'Tha's better, son,' Bruno told him, and slowly moved along the side of the bed, until he'd reached the white-wood locker. He slid open the locker's drawer; and there, lying handy on top of some correspondence, was a flick-knife, blade sprung open. Bruno took out the knife, briefly looked at it, then folded away the blade and pocketed it. 'Nice little tool, that, Frankie,' he said. 'I wish, now, I'd let you pull it on me.'

James made no answer, just looked hard at Bruno, then jerked back his head, the movement flicking some loose strands of straight, black hair from his eyes and forehead; he still looked feral, though; the shiny black stubble around his throat and chin was like rough emery-cloth.

'Who *are* they?' the woman demanded of James, her whole body quivering.

James' eyes rolled ceilingward. 'Well it ain't Christmas fuckin *mornin*, is it?' he said.

'We're from the Robbery Squad, babe,' Bruno told

her. 'Stay with Frankie a bit longer, an you'll get used to these early-mornin spins.' He looked at James. 'Won't she, Frankie?'

James continued to stare hard at Bruno, and half-snarled.

'Didn't he tell you, babe?' Bruno went on, addressing the woman. 'Before you moved in, I mean. That's why his ol donkey moved *out:* she'd had a gutful of getting turned over every other week.'

'*I* gave *her* the fuckin elbow,' James put in, indignant at the suggestion that it was his wife who'd dumped *him* – which was actually the case, as it happened. 'Anyway, what is this? A fuckin wind-up, or what? Gettin a pull on the strength of me form, I s'pose – *as* usual. This time, I'm clean, though, so you may as well fuck off back where you crawled out from.'

'*You're* about as clean as a cow's arse,' Bruno told him.

'An twice as fuckin shitty, an all,' added Hoskins.

DS Bell then entered the room, preceded by the raucous screams of a child whom he'd woken in the bedroom opposite this one. He stood before Bruno, thumbing back over his right shoulder. 'Just a little kiddy in a cot, guv. Woke it up, I'm afraid.'

'*You* fuckin *slags*! *Filth*!' shrieked the woman. 'If you've harmed an air on my baby's head, I'll fuckin *swing* for ya, so help me *God* I will . . . You *cunts*!' She was seething rage and spittle, and her fists were clenched and brandished at the three detectives.

'Lady,' Bruno told her. 'When God put a tongue in your gob, he ruined a perfectly good arsehole . . .' He broke off, wincing, as the child's screams became more piercing, more insistent. 'Now,' he went on, his voice irritable, 'get ya drawers on, an go stick ya tit in that sprog's gob . . . It's giving my brain fuckin *stick*, it is!'

'Don't you talk to her like that,' James hissed, moving

his hands from behind his neck and clenching his fists as he began moving forward from the waist.

'Shhhuddup!' Bruno told him, again wincing as the child's screams reached a new peak. He pointed his gun at James' duvet-covered loins. 'An lean back, less ya wanna be pissin out a plastic tube for the resta your life.'

James leaned back, his face reddening, his lips tightly compressed, and reclasped his hands behind his neck.

Now, the woman swung her feet out from beneath the duvet, leaned forward, and picked up a pink, frill-edged slip from the carpet; she eased it down over her head, wriggled her arms through its straps, bounced her backside off the bed, and tugged it down over her thighs; then she stood, folded her arms defiantly across her chest, and, glowering, strode off out to the child's room, across the landing.

'Go with her,' Bruno told Bell, resisting an urge to smack the woman's arse as she passed-by him. 'That room hasn't been turned over, yet.'

Bell followed the woman, who now turned on him, shouting, 'Fuck off!' And then there was the sound of the child's bedroom door being slammed . . . the door being reopened, Bell insisting, 'I've gotta come in with you, darlin . . .' . . . The child, still screaming . . . 'Fuck *off*, I said!' . . . The door, once again being slammed . . . the muted sounds of raised voices from within the child's room . . . the woman, cursing Bell, in-between soothing the child; Bell, attempting to pacify her . . .

Bruno nodded at Hoskins. 'Go downstairs, Terry, an let the others in through the kitchen. Tell em to start spinnin the back garden.' He quickly glanced at James, and noticed the almost imperceptible twitch at the corner of James' right eye; that back garden could yield a nice result, Bruno felt.

Hoskins left the bedroom, and Bruno now closed the door, shutting out the noises from beyond the closed door of the child's room. Then, turning, he looked searchingly at James, before moving to sit on the edge of the bed. 'Frankie,' he said. 'It's bad news, I'm afraid, son. You're well in the frame for that one across the pavement, last Monday . . . When that Wally got weighed down with the barrel of a sawn-off.'

James, outwardly, was unmoved by the news.

'He can ID you, Frankie,' Bruno went on. 'Swallows on your hands; *LOVE* and *HATE* on your fingers . . . Black hair, stubborn jaw . . . stocky build . . . It all fits, son. Be a nice bitta forensic, an all, I shouldn't wonder, when we've turned over that garden an found the shooter an mask . . . maybe a bitta ceilin plaster, too, stuck on the soles of your shoes. An then there's the wedge: handfula monkeys, wasn't it? That's gotta be somewhere. Can't all've gone up against the wall, can it? Not in a week. I know you *like* a drink, Frankie, but you can't have done it *all* in a week.'

'Look, just nick me an get me a brief,' said James, showing signs of agitation, now. 'Never mind all this fuckin wind-up. We'll see who comes out on top, when we get up the steps.'

Bruno stood, shrugging. 'Suit yourself, son. You can have it on your head or your toes. Makes no difference to me.' He moved to the foot of the bed, bent down, picked up a pair of pyjama trousers, and slung them at James. 'Here. Get em on.'

'*I'm* not goin out of *here* in me fuckin pyjamas,' shouted James. 'I wanna be wearin a *suit* when I leave here.'

Bruno shook his head. 'We'll be sendin your civvies for forensic, Frankie. Besides, it's the factory we're goin to, not a dinner-'n'-fuckin-dance.'

'Shitbag!' muttered James.

'Just keep it up, son,' said Bruno, 'an I'll put you in line for a visit from the tooth fairy.' He moved to the window, and opened the curtains, while James climbed into the pyjamas.

The sky was now a clear, pale blue, and the street was filled with deep shadow and strong sunlight. For the unemployed, it *was* a day for gardening and car-washing, before a trip out into the country or to the seaside. But not *this* early. Every other garden contained a hoe-wielding man or woman, and every other car was being sluiced with frothy water; but only one of each pair of eyes was attending to the job in hand.

'Nosy bastards,' mumbled Bruno, and turned away from the window.

By lunch-time, James was banged-up alone in a cell, sweating it out, both physically and mentally, as he paced back and forth – six steps to the far wall, a glance up at the glass-brick window, high above . . . about turn, six steps back to the steel-lined door, *etched* with graffiti by previous bodies who were *supposed* to have been thoroughly searched by arresting officers . . .

There was little prospect, now, of James' getting a result, either here or up the steps, but he still couldn't stomach the idea of ducking his nut and going for a plea. Whichever way he studied his predicament, it added up to a ten stretch; maybe more.

There were heavy charges, and Bruno had promised James he was going on the sheet for each and every one of them: robbery, for starters; then, the attempted murder of that Wally, followed by the prohibited possession – because James had previously done a five stretch for robbery – of a shotgun; finally, unlawfully shortening the shotgun's barrel and converting it to a sawn-off.

If there were only the filth's verbals to contend with, he'd consider himself on a promise; but they had tangible evidence, too, and that was priceless. Christ, they'd been thorough when they'd turned over his drum. *Nothing* was left undisturbed or unprobed or uninspected, not even the inside plates of the lightswitches. It was a wonder they hadn't looked up the *baby's* arse, as well; they'd made a right mess of its cot, its nappy and its stuffed-animal toys, the evil bastards.

But that's the way they always were; they knew *every* hiding place. He'd known that they knew, too. Or at least he'd *thought* he'd known. Until today. Last week, he'd been certain that the garden was a safe bet: they'd *never* go to the trouble of excavating the flowerbeds. Only, they *had*.

And their forks had soon struck the hard wooden board beneath the surface soil; and after the board was lifted, the pit was uncovered, and in the bottom of it was the sawn-off, six cartridges – wrapped in oil-soaked rags – , and the woollen hat with eye-slits . . .

It was all on top, after that; in every sense. James shivered, despite the cloying atmosphere of the small cell, and the sticky hotness of his body. The money he'd got stashed away – from the blag he was about to go up on, as well as three earlier ones for which he hadn't come to notice – would be of no comfort to him, not where he was going; and by the time he came out, inflation would've eaten it away to little more than the crumbs of a round of cheese sandwiches . . .

In which case, he now reluctantly considered, he might just as well try and minimize his losses, by going into Bruno, with a piece of the wedge. A *big* piece. The whole *team* would probably want straightening, but if James got his outer it'd be more than worth it, and he could at least start earning again.

He stood, slapped the sides of his thighs, resignedly sighed, walked to the cell door, and began stabbing at the bell-push that was set into the white-ceramic-brick wall.

24

MacHale was standing in a small rest-room on the first floor of the nursing home, at Hendon, north-west London, looking out over the training-school grounds: away to his left, the grey, concrete-and-glass tower-blocks – *A*, *B* and *C* – which accommodated recruits and external-courses' students; before him, the fawn-brick classroom-and-staff block; beyond that, a wide expanse of flat, bright green turf – for recreation and sports, otherwise *Keep off it!* – , the gymnasium-and-swimming-pool complex, the driving-school buildings, and the Cadet-training school, known to TS-instructors as *Disneyland*, because it knocked-out immature, closeted and cosseted young boys and girls who knew as much about the real world as did *Mickey Mouse*, and were more difficult to train as cops.

He'd been here in the nursing home since Monday afternoon, when he was discharged from hospital, and on Monday evening he'd written to Pat, telling her how he was progressing and how much he'd been missing her. Now, it was Wednesday afternoon, and tomorrow morning he was expecting her reply, telling him how much she was missing him, and wanting to know when he'd be coming to join her.

He'd been constantly wondering himself about that. When *would* he get to see her? He felt his body tensing, now, and his brow furrowing, because there were strong pulls in opposing directions, here: one towards Pat, the other towards The Job – especially now that he'd made a name for himself over that bank robbery, a week ago last Monday. Up till then, the wrench away might have been easier – might not have been a wrench, at all, in fact – , but now . . . There was no easy solution. *Why* couldn't he have both . . .? And then he couldn't help himself feeling annoyed at Pat, as he'd felt annoyed when she'd first sprung on him the news of her departure. She *ought* to have given him advance warning . . . discussed it with him. Maybe he could've persuaded *her* to stay, at least until something definite was worked out for their relationship.

Then, again; maybe it *was* an attempt, on her part, at emotional blackmail. That idea still hurt him, too; not so much because it might just be true, but more because he'd dared think it of her. She really *wasn't* capable of such a thing. It was just that she'd had such a gutful of The Job, lately, there had seemed no other way forward. That had to be it.

The door then opened, and his thoughts were blown away by the draught that cooled his face, as Neil Coleman appeared, wearing a blue towelling-robe and carrying a black-plastic bin liner. Coleman was a young PC, as well – maybe twenty-two, twenty-three – , with pale skin and crew-cut blonde hair, who'd fallen off a wall, several weeks ago, while chasing three villains, after having responded to a Suspects-on shout at a burgled factory, over in the East End; his right ankle – which was fractured in the fall – had been encased in plaster – in fact, the plaster went right up to almost mid-thigh – , and now he was hobbling around on crutches.

'Hello, Neil,' said MacHale, rising to pull up a chair for the disabled PC. 'How's it going?'

Coleman eased himself down into the low chair, and laid aside his crutches. 'Oh, not three bad, John,' he yawned. 'I was just dozing off, along in the ward, when I was woken by a loud-mouthed drill-pig out there. Whoever decided that this place should be built right next to the school, *and* a railway line, oughta be stuck *in* here himself for a week, next time he gets flu . . . See how *he'd* like it.' He began easing the bin liner up over his plaster-encased leg; when it was tied around the top of his thigh, it would keep the leg dry while he took a shower.

'Yeah,' agreed MacHale. 'It does seem thoughtless, now you mention it, building the place here. When you're ill, you really want to be away from the environment of The Job, not stuck right on top of it. I mean, you wouldn't send an ailing dray-horse down a mine, to convalesce, would you?'

'The Job would,' said Coleman, with all the cynicism of a twenty-five-year officer. 'Still, we'll survive. It's those blokes who're goin barmy, I feel sorry for. This is the *last* place they should be. Let's face it, it was The Job that *made* em barmy, in the first place.'

'D'you think so?' said MacHale. 'I mean, they're all under threat of disciplinary proceedings, aren't they? Couldn't it be that factor that's made them ill?' – there were five of them, down in the wards: all suffering from depression and acute anxiety, and all suspended from duty.

'No,' insisted Coleman, now tying a piece of white tape around the top of the plastic sack, just below his groin. 'I've had a word with em, see; and each one was receivin treatment for depression, *before* he came unstuck on discipline. It's the fuckin Job's fault. The guv'nors just won't admit freely that stress-related illnesses are a problem. Coppers aren't s'posed to *have* stress-related problems. So, when they do get em, they try to hide em, and sooner or later they go over the top.'

'How d'you mean?'

'Well, would *you* feel happy about reportin sick with somethin like anxiety? These blokes just start shovellin prescribed pills – tranquillizers, sleepers, anti-depressants – down their throats, and next thing is they're walkin around in a fuckin trance, hardly knowin what day it is.

Their judgements're *severely* impaired. Then, sooner or later, they do somethin wrong.' He shrugged. 'It's inevitable. But *then*, stead of ensurin that they go sick and get proper rest an all that, the fuckin Job *suspends* em, and brings out the hammer, the nails an the fuckin *cross* . . . I really feel sorry for these blokes, havin seen em for meself, up here.'

'But the CMO once said,' MacHale pointed out, 'that coppers're no more prone to stress-related illnesses than ordinary people.'

'Bullshit!' snapped Coleman, leaning back in his chair, and, with a grimace, raising his bad leg up onto a low table. 'Coppers're *more* prone to such illnesses . . . like trick-cyclists an doctors. But The Job still won't fully accept it. And the *real* reason is that no one wants to take the trouble to do anythin about it. See, if you openly admit to the existence of a problem, you've also gotta present your plans, your strategy, to counter it an treat it. But the guv'nors don't wanna know.'

'But . . . *Why*?'

''Cause they're fuckin useless, that's why. They don't know their men or their own jobs,' Coleman bitterly responded. 'When I came out of hospital, with me leg like this . . .' He leaned forward in his chair and jabbed a forefinger at his bin-liner-covered leg. '. . . I phones my Chief, right?, an asks him if he'll arrange for a GP to run me up here; an *he* turns round an says, "No"; the bastard. Tha's fuckin guv'nors for ya. Says he couldn't spare one for an unofficial journey. How's *that* for looking after your own?'

He stood, picking up his crutches and sliding their padded tops under his armpits. 'Time for my shower, See ya later, John.'

'Yeah, okay,' said MacHale, moving to open the door for Coleman.

He'd just sat down again when the door reopened, and

in walked one of the nurses. She smiled. 'John, there're two visitors for you. Two detectives. Shall I bring them along?'

He stood. 'Oh . . . well, yes, bring them along, then, please.'

The nurse left the room, and returned with DCI Bruno and DS Bell, the latter pushing a trolley which bore a TV and a video-recorder – borrowed from the training school's visual-aids department, MacHale supposed.

'All right, son?' said Bruno, then turned and thanked the nurse, who now left, closing the door.

'Not too bad, sir,' replied MacHale.

'Told you I'd show you the bank's video,' said Bruno. 'And here it is.' He spread a hand in the direction of the trolley that Bell had wheeled into the room.

'Oh, great,' said MacHale. He'd been looking forward to seeing the replay. He moved to the windows, and closed the curtains.

Bell was placing three of the easy chairs in a line abreast, while Bruno was plugging-in and activating the machinery on the trolley, and when this was done, the three of them sat back to watch.

The black screen erupted into a fuzzy whiteness that was speckled with pulsating grey dots . . . horizontal black bands began rolling over, from top to bottom, and the darkened room was filled with flickering light. Then the picture popped into vision, and the playback began: in monochrome, no sound . . .

It was harder to relive than MacHale had imagined it would be, and he felt himself tensing . . . his hands gripping the wooden arms of his chair, his eyes dilating, wanting to avert themselves, his heart-rate increasing . . . He'd just been knocked over sideways by the gunman, who was now levelling the sawn-off at his head . . . Christ, the damage that would've done if the gunman *had* pulled the trigger, at that stage . . . The young-girl cashier was trying to *eat* her hands! . . . Terror was imprinted on her twisted features, which must now be forcing that series of screams through her nostrils, mouth, and claw-like fingers . . . her face was swelling . . . bloated with fear . . . The gunman was now extremely agitated, pointing the sawn-off at the ceiling . . . a discharge of smoke was punched from a single barrel . . . it was snowing plaster, all over MacHale and the gunman and the cashier . . . The cashier had taken hold of the bag which the gunman had thrust through the service hatch, and was filling it from the drawer, stuffing it with notes, spilling many of them onto the counter, in her frightened haste . . .

MacHale, suddenly swinging his stick, hard at the gunman's right leg, the gunman jumping back, his free hand instinctively moving down to clutch at his calf muscle as his right knee jerked up to almost waist-high . . .

Again, that leg! MacHale had the same rush to his brain. *Something* . . . hazy, blue . . . *black*? . . . an *old* bruise? . . . Gone . . . *Frustration*!

The gunman, kicking out, hard, with the injured leg, parrying, with the sawn-off, MacHale's intended blow to the side of his head; the gunman's right foot, hitting the edge of MacHale's jaw . . . MacHale, crashing over, backwards, rolling sideways, grabbing wildly, mostly blindly, for the stick, which was knocked from his hand as he fell . . . pulling himself up, hurling the stick at the gunman's departing back . . . the stick, glancing off the gunman's right shoulder . . . rage on the lower, exposed portion of his face – the mouth, in particular . . . twisted, snarling – as he turned, levelled the sawn-off, and let go with the remaining barrel . . .

MacHale, flying backwards through the air, the momentum he'd entered, having reeled forward and struck the side of his head on the counter, being completely reversed . . . spinning away across the carpeted floor . . . which was now spotted with dark patches that caught the light . . . All over. Finished.

The screen, a dotted whiteness once more; black, horizontal bars, rolling up, bottom to top . . .

Bruno got up, switched off the recorder and TV, then walked to the windows and opened the curtains, moving back to lean his buttocks on the top of the trolley. 'Well, that was it, son. Didn't last long, either, did it?'

'Long *enough*,' said MacHale, relaxing and leaning back in his chair. 'I can't believe it *was* so quick, actually. When it was happening, it seemed to go on all afternoon.'

'Yeah, I can imagine,' said Bell, a sympathetic look on his face.

MacHale frowned, and slowly shook his head. *That leg*. He looked in turn at Bruno and Bell. 'I *still* can't get that leg out of my mind . . . that there *is* something about that leg, which I took in, at the time, and yet *can't* remember . . .' He looked, now, at the floor, his eyes vacuous.

Bruno and Bell exchanged quick glances.

'Understandable,' Bell told MacHale.

'Yeah,' agreed Bruno. 'It's like if you were out on the street, bustin for a crap: you'd only have eyes for the nearest khazi, an wouldn't see anythin else.'

'Or if you were hungry,' tried Bell, coming up with another analogy, 'you'd unconsciously blot-out all of your senses, cept smell an taste.'

'That's right,' said Bruno. 'You see, you were so busy tryin to stay alive, you saw without seein, heard without hearin . . . Like that.' He looked very self-satisfied with his amateur, shrink's thesis. '*If* there was anythin about that leg,' he sceptically went on, 'it went in one eyeball an straight out the other.'

'Yeah,' agreed Bell.

'There *was* something,' insisted MacHale. He just *knew*

there was; and yet, at the same time, *didn't* know; the frustration of it was both painful and confusing, too.

'No, I don't think so, son,' Bruno confidently said. Moving to the chair he'd been sitting in while the video was replayed, he picked up his briefcase. After unzipping the case, he pulled out a sheaf of A-four size, black-and-white photographs, and then handed them to MacHale. 'Here, take a butcher's hook at these.'

MacHale studied them: six blow-ups of the gunman's right leg, the frozen actions showing the stages when he'd clutched at his injured calf, hobbled back, almost lost his balance, moved forward, brought the right leg up behind himself, then kicked out at MacHale's jaw; the shots clearly showed that his right trouserleg had ridden up, when he'd massaged his injured calf, but he was either facing *away* from the camera, or wasn't quite sideways-on to it; and, really, there were no more than blurred backshots and profiles of his right calf-muscle, sock-covered ankle, and black, lace-up shoe. Useless. No distinguishing marks, at all, on the leg; or, if there were, none that the film or photographic stills were able to capture and highlight.

A further fifteen photographs were equally useless – for identification purposes, anyway – blow-ups of the gunman's part-masked face, from every conceivable angle, while the final half-dozen were blow-ups of the back of his head – when he'd entered the bank, wearing the bobble hat, and when he'd stood at the desk behind where MacHale had waited in the queue – again, back to camera – , pulled down the hat's furled rim, and whipped out the sawn-off, from inside the sports bag.

'You can't *tell* from these,' said MacHale. 'They're either too blurred or at the wrong angle.'

'We can tell from the villain's body, though,' said Bruno.

'An we've had a look at it, an all,' put in Bell. 'In the flesh.'

'What d'you mean?' MacHale wanted to know, puzzled, looking from Bell, to Bruno; back to Bell; finally, settling his eyes on Bruno. 'D'you mean you've – ?'

Bruno nodded. 'Yep. Nicked him yesterday – Tuesday – , early in the mornin.'

'Well, that's great,' said MacHale. 'Terrific!'

'Thought you'd be pleased,' said Bell.

'Too true,' smiled MacHale. 'But who *was* it? . . . Who *is* he?'

'Schofield,' said Bell.

'*Freddie* Schofield,' added Bruno. 'A right vicious slag who's never done a day's honest work in his life.'

'*Schofield?*' shouted MacHale. 'I *know* him! We nicked him with a ringed Jag, but had to let him go. I can't *believe* it!'

'It's true, son,' assured Bruno.

'Got him bang to rights, an all,' said Bell.

'He's put his hands up, then, has he?' asked MacHale.

Bruno huffed out a laugh, and almost choked on it, while his expression said, *Are you kidding?* 'Schofield never pleads to *anythin. He* wouldn't even admit to havin been *born*.'

'Hmm, yeah, that figures,' said MacHale, remembering how, when Schofield was nicked with the Jag, he'd just sat in the chargeroom and remained obstinately silent. 'How did you manage to get him, then?'

'A snout,' explained Bruno. 'Another right villain by the name of Frankie James. We gave him a spin on his form, but drew a blank on it. While he was at the factory, though, binned-up, wonderin how much we knew about some of the other strokes he's been pullin, he decided to work his way out . . . lay-off the blame.'

'Yeah,' smiled Bell. 'Sweet, it was. He stuck Schofield

up for your blag, in exchange for us not stickin *him* up for it. Little did he know, though, we had no evidence to stick him up with, anyway.'

'Because it wasn't him who did it,' Bruno went on. 'It *was* Schofield. The evidence is that Schofield put the blag up to James, three weeks before it went off. Asked James to ride shotgun with him. James didn't want any, so Schofield weighed in by himself. James has made a written statement to that effect, *and* has picked Schofield out on a line-up.'

'Will they *believe* James, when it gets to court?' asked MacHale. 'I mean, he might just be settling an old score or something. That *is* what they'll say, isn't it, to try and discredit his evidence? You did say *he* was a right villain, as well.'

'Yeah, that's true enough,' agreed Bruno. 'But there's other evidence, apart from James's statement. When we gave Schofield a turnin over, yesterday, we found a sawn-off, half-a-dozen cartridges, *and* a black-wool bobble hat with eye-slits cut out of it, all tucked-up in his loft.'

'There'll be a nice bitta forensic, an all,' added Bell. 'Plaster that we took from the bank's ceiling will no doubt match the flakes that're in the weave of the woolly hat, and samples we took from the floor will no doubt match those that were embedded in the soles of Schofield's shoes. It's practically a stone bonker.'

'*Practically?*' intoned MacHale. 'Sounds to me as if Houdini would've had trouble getting out of it, with all that evidence. Schofield's *well* stitched-up, isn't he?'

'*Would* be,' Bruno ruefully said, 'if there was any such thing as justice in this world of ours. But we're up against the naïvety of juries, an bent briefs, an villains' complaints an allegations, so that *real* issues become *side* issues, an fact is diluted by unsubstantiated fiction; like, *The law beat me up*, or, *The law fitted me an planted me an verballed me . . .*'

'Or, *The law's been out to get me for years, now,'* added Bell.

'In short,' explained Bruno, 'we've got a credibility problem, these days. One time, *whatever* we said, on Oath, was considered Gospel. But not any more it isn't. Now, we've gotta really work at it to get a villain down.'

'What the guv'nor's sayin,' enlarged Bell, 'is that by the time Schofield's brief has gone through the jury with how evil a liar James is, *and* how many previous he's got, they won't know what to believe. Then he'll pile on how evil *we* are: how we fitted Schofield, an planted him. All bollocks, of course, but at the enda the day, the jury'll be so fuckin confused, they'll've forgotten there *was* a blag in which you got blown off your feet an a few grand got liberated, an *we'll* be on fuckin trial. In the end, they'll acquit Schofield, *and*, by implication, convict *us*. Because that'll be the *safest* thing for em to do.'

MacHale's expression was a mixture of concern and disbelief, mutating to the agitated query, Well what the hell're we gonna *do* about it, then?

'So what we need,' said Bruno, responding to MacHale's expression, 'is for *you* to ID Schofield. We need you to walk up the line an pick him out as the slag who gave you all them potholes in your side. Then we'll have a proper chance of gettin him some bird.'

That startled MacHale. It had never so much as occurred to him, before he'd received today's news from Bruno and Bell, that Schofield was even a remote possibility for the blag. 'But how *can* I ID him, sir?' he asked Bruno. 'I hardly *saw* the villain's face, when the robbery was happening . . . just got a glimpse of his mouth and chin, a little piece of his nose . . . the colour of his hair and eyes. It *could've* been Schofield, what with the tattooes – Schofield has *got* swallows on his hands, and *LOVE* and *HATE* on his fingers – , but, well, I dunno. I just don't *know*.'

Yet another of those quick glances was passed between Bruno and Bell.

'Look,' said Bruno. 'You *do* know. We *all* know, *now*, that it *was* Schofield who pulled it off. James says it was him. The sawn-off an the bobble hat say it was him, an the forensic'll say it was him, too. Now, if *you* can say it was him, as well, we'll get our result.'

MacHale, frowning and thinking deeply, was slowly shaking his head . . . reflecting, lying on his belly, on the bank's floor . . . looking upward, seeing the part-masked face, the heavy jaw, the glistening, blue-black stubble around the cheeks and chin . . . the tight-drawn lips . . . the minatory, black-brown eyes, piercing him through the slits in the mask . . . casting further back, retrieving the previously-implanted vision of Schofield's face, bringing it forward, trying to match its features with the features of the part-masked face in the bank . . . Now he vigorously scratched the crown of his head, sucking in air . . . shook his head, and the recollections parted, began spinning . . . and fading. 'I just don't *know*, sir,' he finally said. 'It *might've* been him . . .' He looked helplessly at Bruno.

'It *was* him,' insisted Bell.

'Look, son,' Bruno agitatedly said. 'I don't like to remind you of this, but when you nicked Schofield with that Jag, an then let him go, you gave him a fuckin *licence* to pull this blag. If you'd put him away, then, when you had the chance, we wouldn't *be* here, today, havin this chat. Don't let him off the hook again, for fuck's sake, or somebody'll be murdered . . . eventually.'

'Wouldn't like that on *my* conscience,' said Bell, leaning forward in his chair and staring at the carpet as he rested his forearms on his knees and clasped together his hands.

Pressure. Like a tightening vice, gripping MacHale's conscience. And he remembered a similar taunt: *Don't worry about it*, Hales had said, after MacHale had insisted he couldn't ID Schofield as the Jag's driver; but then Hales had quickly added, *Unless, that is, chummy goes out on a blag, next week, when he ought by rights to be banged-up over the wall, on a ringing charge, and murders some poor fuckin security guard or bank clerk . . .*

And now, MacHale felt himself feeling *grateful:* that it was *he* who'd been shot; it so easily *could* have been a security guard or bank clerk; *he'd* got what he *deserved* . . . for having allowed Schofield to be set free . . .

At length, Bruno broke into the silence: he walked over to MacHale, patted his right shoulder, and said, 'Just keep thinkin about it, son. It'll come. We'll see you again on Friday, an maybe by then you'll've made your mind up about all of this.'

And with that, Bruno and Bell walked out, the latter pushing the trolley that was laden with the TV and the video equipment.

For a *long* time, MacHale just sat there alone in the small room, his eyes opening and closing; his body and his mind, restless. He had a decision to make, and whichever way he jumped he'd be beset by feelings of uncertainty and guilt . . .

In the end, though, it would be easier than he'd imagined, because it could be rationalized, and the guilt, shot out and shut out – not publicly, but privately, in the deepest shafts of his mind. It was like staring, long and hard, at an amorphous shadow on a dark night: eventually, it *must* take on form and shape, and become whatever you wished or believed it to be, or whatever you'd been assured it was . . .

The features, recalled, were matched, side-by-side, time and again, over many hours . . . then superimposed, one over the other . . . slid apart . . . back together . . . apart

. . . together . . . until they soaked, indistinguishably, into one, inseparable vision . . .

The next morning, after a long, restless night, MacHale phoned Bruno and gave him the news: it *was* Schofield. There no longer could be any doubt.

On Friday morning, Bruno and Bell returned. First they took down a written statement from MacHale, in which he recounted the bank robbery and positively identified Schofield as the perpetrator. Then, early in the afternoon, after lunching at the nursing home, they drove MacHale to the nick, put Schofield in a line-up, and asked MacHale to walk along and see if he could pick him out.

Ridiculous, MacHale had thought. And unnecessary, too. He *knew* Schofield, so there was absolutely no chance of his *not* making the identification. Still, he'd decided, Bruno must know what he's doing; this is just another nail in Schofield's coffin.

The parade took place in the station yard, and was conducted by a uniformed Inspector from C-Relief. Bruno and Bell were present, as was Schofield's brief, but they would merely observe the proceedings, taking no active part and having no influence on the witness or the parade's participants. Having been collected from his anxious wait in the canteen, MacHale was taken out into the yard, where he was met by the Inspector, who told him that he should slowly walk the line of twelve 'suspects', from whichever end he so chose, take his time, and see if he were able to identify the man who was responsible for shooting him, a week ago last Monday.

MacHale was surprised to see that all twelve 'suspects' in the line were wearing nothing but dark grey cell-blankets, draped around their bodies; this because Schofield's clothes had been seized for forensic tests, and, in protest, he'd refused to don the replacements which

Bruno had obtained from Brixton Prison – just as well it was a dry, reasonably warm day.

Beginning at the first man on the left, MacHale, accompanied by the Inspector, began slowly walking the line. All of the participants in the line-up were stocky men of roughly the same age and height; all were dark-skinned, and all had dark-brown eyes and black hair, too; but their facial features were easily distinguishable. Schofield was seventh along, his body erect, his blunt jaw, protruding, his eyes reflecting a rock-hard challenge. MacHale looked him over and then passed him by. He felt it was important that he should assess *all* of the 'suspects'. Having reached the twelfth man, therefore, he turned around and walked quickly back to Schofield, spending several seconds, just staring at his bare, right leg, intently studying it, plumbing the depths of his memory, for the . . . Christ knew *how* many times it was, now . . . at least a thousand; frustratedly asking himself what it was he'd seen and yet not seen on the calf of . . . no, not of the *man* who'd pulled the robbery, but of *Schofield* . . .

Nothing, though. Just an impenetrable blank, painfully tantalizing, because it held forth the promise of revelation if only he could *somehow* break through it . . .

He gave up dredging his memory; it was too late; it was like waking from a light dream, trying to mentally snatch at puzzling, vaguely formed images which were fast draining away; or like trying to make a whole out of a shredded photograph, the pieces of which a hand had just released to flutter down before your eyes, into an inaccessible black recess. No chance; once the pieces were gone, they were irretrievable. It *may* have been a bruise, a scratch; a pattern of hairs, maybe; or some other, non-permanent feature that was visible on Schofield's calf at the time of the robbery. But *whatever* it was, it wasn't there now. There wasn't even a mark where MacHale had belted him with the stick.

MacHale looked up, stared Schofield in the face, deflecting that hard, defiant stare; then he reached out with his right hand, tapped Schofield's left shoulder, turned to the Inspector, and unequivocally said, 'This is the man who shot me and robbed the bank.'

Then, all hell plus one broke loose. Schofield roared like an enraged bull, lunged at MacHale, making a grab for his throat, and knocked him to the ground, while the other members of the parade broke out of the line-up and fled in the direction of the charge-room door, their blankets fluttering behind them in the air.

Bruno, Bell, the Inspector, and a handful of eager PCs who'd been watching the proceedings from the window of the stables, fell on top of Schofield, pulled him off MacHale, and pinned him, face down, on the ground, before 'cuffing him and dragging him back to the cells, screaming, shouting and kicking his legs.

MacHale, gasping for breath, struggled to his feet, his right hand soothing the skin of his neck and throat. As he watched Schofield's departure . . . his head opening the charge-room door, he felt not pity but satisfaction. Schofield was a wild *animal*, a danger to the public – not to mention the police – , and *deserved* to be banged-up for the remainder of his useless life.

On Saturday morning, he received a letter from Pat, informing him that she was *aching* for him to be with her once again. Her words bit deep into the tenderest, most sensitive parts of him, and he was sick with longing as his memory replayed the tapes of her smile, her laughter, her warmth and softness, and their most intimate moments of togetherness. He continued reading . . . The business was going well, and Diego sent his regards; the locals, though, were constantly complaining about the seasonal influx of foreigners – an alien, apparently, was anyone who didn't reside within a stone's throw of the village pond . . . on which, incidentally, flotillas of ducklings were now sailing up and down . . . Sparrows were nesting in the eaves of the cottage, and the badgers, hedgehog and fox were still regularly arriving for their nightly suppers . . . It was a *dream*, there, at this time of year . . . everything bursting with renewed life and vigour and erupting colour . . . When *was* he going to join her? She wanted him there, and needed him there, but not on a part-time basis; he shouldn't feel pressurized, but if he did come he must be certain that he wanted to set their relationship on a permanent basis, as she herself did . . .

The rest of it was now irrelevant. He folded the letter and concernedly thought about what she'd written . . . It was . . . yes, it *was*, he decided; it was an ultimatum: *If you're not prepared to join me for good, then don't bother coming*. It was crazy, too; not like her. Surely, a little of what you loved was by far better than none at all?

He decided to phone her, right now, and try and get to the bottom of it. He began placing the folded letter back in its envelope, and now noticed that there was a Polaroid photograph in there; he took it out and studied it: Pat, in the centre garden, with Diego; she was standing behind him – *hiding* behind him? – , her chin on his right shoulder, her arms slung around his neck, her long hair, frozen in a swirl around her left shoulder; she looked vibrant . . . smiling, her cheeks having regained their inherent, rustic flush, which several years of shiftwork, and exposure to the city's polluted air, had deprived them of.

He tucked the photograph back inside the envelope, and then went on a tour of the wards, asking fellow patients if they could help him out with some change for the telephone; when he'd broken down two pounds, he collected the telephone trolley from the corridor, wheeled it into the rest room, plugged-in the set's cable, using the socket which was set into one of the room's walls, and dialled Pat's private number . . .

After a lengthy series of far-off, down-the-line whirrings and clickings, he heard the ringing tone, and almost immediately it was responded to at the other end: 'Hello?' – Pat's voice, a pleasant, lilting timbre.

He quickly fed some coins into the mechanism, and the rapid beep-beep noises, ceased. 'Pat? It's John, here.'

'*John!* What a surprise. How are you, now? Did you get my letter? I got yours on Wednesday. How's the nursing home? When are you – ?'

'Yes, I got your letter this morning,' he cut in. 'That's why I'm phoning.'

'Oh?' – she'd detected the ill-concealed unease in his voice.

'Yeah, well . . . I don't understand it, that's all, you saying you want me there with you, but *only* if I'm prepared to come for good. What's that s'posed to mean, that's what I'd like to know?'

She was silent for a while.

'It's an ultimatum, if you ask me,' he continued. 'And, quite honestly, I don't like it. I don't know what to make of it.'

'No, John,' she protested. 'It's not . . .' She sighed. 'It's just that I want you to do what's best for *you. I* don't want you to uproot yourself and replant yourself here, not unless you're *absolutely* sure it's what you want. I'm not trying to *force* you.'

'It seems that way to me,' he told her. 'First, you just up and away, without any warning, without even telling me, and now you're saying you want all of me or none at all. Let me come down there, Pat. Next week-end. And we'll talk it over.'

'No, John,' she quickly said. 'I don't want that. I've

told you. There's something . . . *things* . . . which we should discuss, but not till I know your intentions.'

'This is crazy!' he shouted. 'I just don't understand it. You're trying to *force* me into something.'

'I'm not, John,' she pleaded, her voice quivering. 'It's just the *opposite*, in fact . . .' She burst into tears. 'I'm doing this because I *love* you!'

'If you love me, then let me *see* you,' he shouted. 'We can't have a relationship over the bloody telephone, or on pieces of paper, for Christ's sake. *I* love *you*, too!'

'Oh, John,' she moaned, and spent several seconds, sniffling and gasping, before going on: 'Believe me, John, it's for the best. If you *really* love me – '

'I do!' he shouted. 'I just *said* so, didn't I?'

'Then you'll – '

'What?'

'I don't know . . .' She sighed a deep, despairing sigh. 'You'll try and understand, and you'll come to a decision. Whatever it is, though, my feelings for you won't change.'

'This *is* crazy,' he mumbled, almost totally confused, now. 'I can't make head nor tail of what's going on, here. Maybe it's your time of the month or something. Maybe you're intoxicated with all that fresh air, up there. I dunno. But for the time being, okay . . . we'll leave things as they are. See what happens.'

'All right, John,' she softly said. 'Take your time, and *don't* feel pressed. It's up to you. Entirely.'

'I'll be a while,' he warned. 'There's this trial, over the bank robbery – they got the villain, by the way – , and then there's my Final Exam; and, well, I feel as if I'm starting to get a grip on things around here. Things're looking up. D'you know, Old Crikey actually *called* me by my first *name* when he came to see me in the hospital.'

'I'm pleased,' she said, although she sounded disappointed.

'So,' he went on, 'I might just have a future in The

Job, after all . . .' He paused. 'I want *you*, too, though, Pat . . . I'm being split right down the middle by all this.'

'It'll work out,' she assured him. 'You'll see. And in the meantime, we'll wait for you, and hope. I'll still write, of course.'

'Me, too . . .' He hesitated, not wanting to sever the connection, but not knowing what more there was to be said. 'Bye, then, Pat.'

'Bye, John.'

He replaced the receiver, and sat there and thought and thought about her. Desperate thoughts. One moment he wanted to get up and run like hell, all the way to that remote part of the country, to be with her; the next, he wanted to stay on just that little bit longer, to see how things progressed, here.

Finally, he settled on thoughts of the impending trial of Freddie Schofield. Nothing could change before then.

PART FIVE

Trial and Error

25

MacHale took a seat at the rear of the cool, brightly lit court-room, among the tiered benches that were reserved for police witnesses and the Press. It was very still and quiet. He glanced at his wristwatch – ten-fifteen A.M. Within the next fifteen minutes, the room would begin to fill with bodies: police-officers, counsel, solicitors, members of the Press . . . the public gallery, too, would be packed to capacity, with relatives of the accused, one or two tourists, perhaps, and the just plain curious who'd dropped in off the street to observe at first hand the workings of what was reputed to be the finest system in the world of justice.

But, and as so many accused and police-officers were only too well aware, justice rarely entered into the spirit of the proceedings in such places as this. Trials were never an objective search for the truth of the matter, because each side had its axe to grind; the already elusive truth was buried, obscured, overlooked or manipulated.

MacHale had only once before set foot inside a Crown Court – during the final stages of his initial training, when the whole class had been taken on a flying visit to Southwark Crown Court – , but *never* before had he been called upon to give evidence at such a court; and he was feeling anxious about it.

Supposing Schofield's brief caught him out on a fine point . . .? *What* fine point? Who knew? They were slippery bastards, those defence briefs, so Bruno had said. Supposing the judge *was* a cantankerous ol' shitbag – like Bell had said they *all* were – , and didn't much care for callow-faced cops who didn't know if they were punched, bored or countersunk when it came to giving evidence at the higher courts? *Supposing* . . .? And what if his nervousness were mistakenly to be interpreted as the manifestation of his *own* guilt? Christ, it *was* nerve-wracking. Right *now*. And the whistle hadn't even gone for the off, yet.

If only Schofield would *plead*; duck his nut; in which case, no one would be called upon to give evidence. But such a hope was totally unfounded, and MacHale was quickly forced to concede it to logic: Schofield would never plead to anything; not even to having been born, so Bruno said.

No, it was futile, hoping for a last-minute outer. And, anyway, what had *he* got to be afraid of? It was Schofield who'd robbed a bank, terrorized a young-girl cashier and shot a cop, not MacHale. MacHale was a hero, and was in line for a commendation, both from the court *and* the Commissioner of Police – whoever *he* was.

Provided . . . Provided that Schofield went down. Provided Schofield was not acquitted. But the very *idea* that Schofield might get a result made MacHale feel angry, and resolute, too. Not only was he, MacHale, a witness, here, he was a *victim*, as well, and he wanted . . . revenge? . . . retribution? . . . He cast away those words, not liking them, and settled for *satisfaction; that* was what he wanted: the satisfaction of knowing that justice *had* been done.

Now MacHale had a goal in sight, he felt better, stronger, and began to believe he could get on top of his lack of confidence. It was *easier*, giving evidence at these higher courts: you had a brief to lead you through all of your evidence *and* conduct the prosecution and cross-examination of the accused; not like at the lower courts, where the whole job was, usually, yours. This was going to be a doddle, then.

A vision of Pat flashed suddenly across his mind. It was

just over four months, now, since he'd had that telephone conversation with her when he was at the nursing home. Since then, he'd phoned her many times, and they'd talked for hours and hours, but had always skirted around the subject of his moving to join her. There'd been letters, too; both ways; sufficient to fill a sack, MacHale believed; but, again, there'd been no discussion of his future plans.

He *still* felt the pull towards her; absence really did make the heart grow fonder. Which made her refusal to allow him down for a weekend visit all the more difficult to comprehend; she'd assured him, in so many ways, and on so many different occasions, that she desperately wanted him there. If she'd lived across the other side of London, he'd long ago have been around to her place, to confront her, to try for a face-to-face explanation of her refusal – and it *was* a refusal, not a mere reluctance – to allow him to see her.

She lived too far away, though, for a speculative visit by public transport, and he couldn't really afford to hire a car.

Christ, it was frustrating. But then, he had to remind himself, he'd never really intended doing anything positive about their relationship until this trial was over. And when it was . . . He didn't know. *Still* didn't know. There was his Final Exam, too; and his Probationer's Final Course; both were imminent. They were further . . . *excuses* for remaining indecisive.

He'd tried, many times, to make a resolution, but had always put it off, telling himself that there was plenty of time, yet.

Since the bank job, his relationship with the other PCs on his Relief had dramatically improved. Also, lately, he'd been enjoying The Job, and suspected he actually was becoming dependent upon it. Almost any other job would kill him with boredom, before a week had passed.

Eventually, *all* cops became dependent upon their jobs; The Job became their reason for living.

But Christ it took its toll.

The shiftwork was beginning to deplete MacHale's physical resources; he'd never felt so unfit in his life, but was far too drained to knock himself into shape, with exercise. His face had thinned out, and was even paler; his eyes were flat, and very easily became tired and sore, as did his brain, so that at the end of a shift, all he wanted to do was fall down in a heap, and try to unwind. Which wasn't possible without some help from a bottle. Now, he never ended a late or early tour, without making a visit to Mulligan's back bar, and at the end of a night-duty, he'd be unable to resist a visit to New Covent-Garden Market for an early-morning drink.

He knew he was drinking too much, and for the wrong reasons. He wanted a drink, *now*, as he sat alone in the empty court-room; just to build himself up. But then a flashed image of Mathieson immediately killed the need. MacHale was terrified of the idea that *he* might end up like Mathieson. Mathieson was burned out, finished. Last month, after recurring bouts of sickness – stomach complaints, headaches . . . everything save what actually *was* wrong with him, physically and mentally – , he'd made a final return to duty, and had got himself arrested in Woolworths, down the High Street, for shoplifting. On duty, if you *don't* mind!

He'd wandered around the store, pocketing silly things, like pencils and erasers and loose sweets, and had got his body claimed by the store detective, when he'd left without paying; had it been the first occasion on which he'd been caught pilfering in the store, the store detective might've let him go; but this, it later turned out, was the *third* time.

Now, Mathieson was banged-up in the nursing home, suffering from alcoholism and depression, while the papers in his case were being considered by the DPP. Just in *case* the DPP slung it, though, the CIB had stuck-on Mathieson for having been absent from his beat, and for failing to account for property – they'd found a civvy's driving licence in his locker which he'd forgotten to hand in as lost property.

So, if Mathieson did get a result from the DPP, he'd then be hit with the Discipline Code, and sacked – the bullet in the back. They'd persecute the poor bastard for having been ill.

Which reminded MacHale. Poor old Hercules, too. He was almost forgotten, now, by his ex-colleagues. A couple of months ago, at the Inquest, the jury had returned an *Open* verdict, having concluded that there was insufficient evidence with which to infer that he'd intended taking his own life. In the euphemistic words of the Coroner, 'This might just have been an experiment which went dreadfully wrong.' – in other words, Hercules *might* have been some sort of a masochist who'd been trying to get his jelly while his throat was constricted; lots of such people *did* pop-off that way, as all cops were aware. In this particular case, however, MacHale knew different; but he'd never confided to anybody the truth of the matter of Hercules' death. There was no point. Hercules' body was collected by his relatives, and taken to his home town – somewhere near Luton, in Bedfordshire – for burial. MacHale would never forget him. And would never forget *why* . . .

MacHale looked at the members of the jury – four women, four blacks, and four . . . *nondescripts* – and considered that more than a few of them were about as bright as soot and would never be convinced that today was the day after the day after the day before yesterday.

It'd be far easier to doubt that fact than to accept it or try and work it out. Which was exactly why Schofield's brief, Mister Julian Beecher, QC, MP, had not raised any objections, on his client's behalf, when the jurors were empanelled and swore the Oath. Had any one of them looked halfway intelligent or respectable – and looks were all which Beecher could be guided by, because no questioning or background research into jurors was permitted – , then he'd have unloaded that member and took his chance on being fed an inferior replacement.

He *did* look a slippery bastard, too, that Beecher. Tall and thin, with razor-sharp features, a gaunt, pasty face, and round metal-framed spectacles – like a preying mantis with defective eyesight. It was difficult to tell his age because of the uniform silver wig he wore. He had an arrogant posture, too, MacHale thought: the way he stood there, behind his table, his head tilted back, his eyes peering down his nose, his small, white hands gripping the lapels of his black robe.

The prosecution's brief – Mister Ivan Croft, QC – , seated at his table, slowly turning the pages of a voluminous file, occasionally looking back over his shoulder to confer with his instructing solicitor, looked much more amiable; wigged and robed, of course, and somewhat portly, he had a flaccid face with naturally-rouged cheeks, large blue eyes, and, overall, a placid countenance. MacHale hoped that Croft would be up to the task which was before him.

But the judge, Mister Justice Gilbert-Shaw, looked a *real* wicked old basket. He must have been at least seventy-five, thought MacHale, and had a thin, shrivelled face, a tight, lipless mouth, and tiny grey eyes that were decorated with gold-framed pince-nez, which perched on a beak-like nose.

MacHale stood, made a slight bow from the waist, in the judge's direction, and began walking from the court. He would wait outside to be called.

Meanwhile the court settled, and silence reigned.

The proceedings opened with the clerk, who occupied a

table and chair immediately beneath the judge's position, rising to put the indictments to Schofield, who'd been placed in the dock, where he stood erect, hands clasped behind his back, sandwiched between two screws from Brixton Prison, who were wearing air-force-blue uniforms. Schofield looked terminally ill: he'd lost none of his defiance, but he'd lost a lot of weight; his cheeks had concaved, and his haggard face was the colour of cigarette ash. He knew only too well that if he went down, here, at the end of this trial, he'd be staring at a minimum of twenty years over the wall. By the time he came out, he'd be a broken old man, fit for little else but the graveyard.

In all, there were three indictments: attempted murder, robbery, and possessing a shotgun whose barrel had been shortened to a length of less than twenty-four inches; the prosecution hadn't proceeded with the charge that alleged Schofield, being a prohibited person – by virtue of having previously been sentenced to a term of more than three years' imprisonment – had possessed a firearm; this, because it might have been considered prejudicial to a fair trial, the wording of the indictment in such a case, intimating to the jurors that Schofield had got previous. So, the three indictments were put. And, needless to say, Schofield, in a loud, resolute voice which reverberated around the court, denied each one of them.

Now, silence again, as the clerk took his seat and the court awaited the next stage of the proceedings.

The judge, having poured himself a glass of water from the decanter that was on his desk, sniffed, made an unnecessary adjustment to his starched wing collar, and, nodding in the direction of the prosecuting counsel's table, croaked, 'Yes, Mister Croft.'

Croft, already on his feet, his left hand gripping the lapel of his robe, his right hand holding his brief, returned the judge's nod, bowed respectfully, said, 'Your Honour,' then turned aside and began his opening address to the jury.

Croft outlined the detail of the evidence in the case, which took some fifteen minutes, and then the prosecution witnesses began to be called, in the chronological order in which they'd become involved in the events leading up to Schofield's arrest and arraignment before the court.

First on, then, was the young-girl bank clerk, whose name was Jeanette Asher – Miss. She took the Bible in a tremulous right hand, and swore the Oath, her voice hushed and barely audible. When she'd finished, her whole body was trembling and her face was plum-coloured.

The judge leaned over sideways across his desk, in the direction of the witness box, and peered over the top of his pince-nez. 'Miss Asher,' he croaked, as gently as he knew how. 'You *must* speak up, so that we may all hear you. Do you understand?' – he'd been entirely unable to conceal his irritability.

She nodded her head, and her long, naturally-blonde hair did a jig on the narrow shoulders of her grey-velvet jacket.

The judge grunted, sat back, pen poised, and gave a ponderous nod in the direction of Croft, who began leading Miss Asher through her evidence.

Eventually she was through her ordeal, and no one in the court-room was in the slightest doubtful that she had, indeed, witnessed a bank robbery, and that this had been the most terrifying experience of her life. It was then Beecher's turn to cross-examine.

Beecher couldn't dispute that a robbery was committed, and didn't attempt to do so. He was merely concerned, here, with the matter of identification of the perpetrator. *How was he dressed?* She couldn't remember. *How did he speak?* She didn't know. *You were not able to tell the police that you would recognize him if you saw him again, were you, Miss Asher?* She couldn't say. *You can't swear that the man in question is the defendant, can you, Miss Asher?* No, she couldn't . . . And so on.

Beecher sat down with a supercilious expression on his face, while Schofield looked well satisfied; throughout, Schofield had sat in the dock, leaning forward, attempting to intimidate her, with his glowering eyes and sneering mouth; but to no avail, simply because she'd been too terrified to even glance at him.

Next on was MacHale. Until now, he'd been in the corridor outside the court-room, pacing up and down, rehearsing his evidence, and being reassured by Bruno and Bell.

'Good luck, son,' said Bruno, as MacHale was called in by the usher.

'It'll be a walkover,' added Bell, smiling. 'You'll see.'

And so it was. Croft led him through his evidence – during which, Schofield rushed to the rails of the dock, shouted, 'You lyin bastard!' and had to be restrained by the screws – , and everything seemed sweet.

Until, that was, Beecher rose to cross-examine. Then the pressure was applied.

'Officer,' began Beecher, studying the high, sculptured-plaster ceiling, and chandelier, his hands gripping both lapels of his robe. 'Will you look again at the blow-ups of the bank's video film, please.' – it wasn't a question.

MacHale, his heart beginning to beat faster than was good for it, picked up the album of photographs which he'd earlier placed on the broad rail of the witness box. 'Yes, sir.' – the inside of his mouth seemed suddenly to have dried up, and his voice was sticky and thick.

'Now, officer,' Beecher continued, after MacHale had looked at the photographs. 'Are you *seriously* saying that you can positively identify the man in those blow-ups as being the defendant, Mister Schofield?'

'Yes, sir. There's no doubt in my mind.' His tone of voice was flat, unemotional, worked at that way; he hoped it was also convincing.

'Liar!' shouted Schofield, his voice making MacHale jump.

'Silence!' croaked the judge. 'Or I shall have you removed to the cells.'

'Oh, come, come, officer,' retorted Beecher, his head swivelling slowly sideways to afford the jury a profile of his sickly-cynical smile. 'In these photographs, all which we are able to see is *a man;* a man with a bobble hat pulled down over most of his face. How can you *possibly* say with any credibility that *this* man is the defendant?' He glanced aside to ensure that the jurors were also studying the photographs, they having earlier been supplied with albums which contained copies of the original blow-ups.

'Well, sir,' responded MacHale. 'I'm not basing my identification *solely* on these photographs. I was *lying* on the floor of the *bank,* when the robbery was committed, looking up in the direction of the accused's face, which wasn't fully masked by the bobble hat. It was only part-masked; his mouth and chin were visible, as well as a portion of his nose; the mask was loose-fitting, you see.' He glanced at Schofield, who sneered threateningly at him, forcing away his eyes.

'And for how long were you afforded a view of the robber's features, officer?'

MacHale paused for thought. 'I'm not sure, sir. It all happened very quickly.' – sod it, he immediately thought; he hadn't wanted to commit himself, but, in effect, had done just that.

'It would only have been the briefest of glimpses, then?'

'Well . . . no, sir. I had a good look at the robber's features, so that – '

'Officer!' Beecher rudely and obstinately cut in. 'On your *own* admission, it all happened *very quickly*. Therefore, how *could* it have been, as you put it, a *good* look?'

'It was sufficient, sir,' said MacHale, and felt his face and body becoming hot.

'Well, we shall see for ourselves how good a look it was,' Beecher dryly retorted, bending forward to study his papers. '. . . We shall, in fact, be seeing the video, in due course. Now . . .' He glanced up from his paperwork. 'Is it not a fact that some months before this robbery was committed, you arrested the defendant?'

'Yes, sir,' admitted MacHale, thinking, *Here we go: sidetracking.*

'On suspicion of having stolen a Jaguar motor car?'

'Yes, sir.'

'And were obliged to release him, for want of a shred of evidence to substantiate your unwarranted suspicion?'

'Yes, sir, but – '

'He *wasn't* charged, officer, was he?' interrupted Beecher.

'Well . . . no, he wasn't, sir.'

'If there'd *been* any credible evidence, he would have been charged. Is that not right?'

'Well . . .'

'Is it or is it not right, officer?' demanded Beecher.

'Yes, sir. It is right,' conceded MacHale; he wasn't allowed to say that he was now convinced Schofield was *guilty* of ringing the Jag.

At this point, Croft rose, Beecher sat, and the judge awaited a submission: 'Your Honour,' Croft opened. 'I don't see that my learned friend's line is at all relevant, here, to the matter at issue. What has gone before – '

'Mister Croft,' croaked the judge. 'If *you* will permit Mister Beecher to *pursue* his line, we shall no doubt *learn* whether or not it is of relevance.'

'Your Honour,' Croft graciously said, bowing; and then sat down.

'Your Honour,' nodded Beecher, rising, also bowing, and smiling obsequiously. Then, to MacHale: 'Is it also not a fact that, subsequent to your arrest of the defendant, and your having had to release him for want of evidence, he complained of your conduct towards him?'

'Yes, sir.' – anything to mislead the jury, thought MacHale; *anything*. He believed, as Bruno and Bell had once prophesied, that the jurors must *already* have forgotten that a bank was robbed and he was shot at.

'He complained,' went on Beecher, 'that you assaulted him. Did he not, officer?'

'Not me specifically, sir,' said MacHale. 'There were several officers involved in the arrest, and the complaint merely alleged that the defendant had been assaulted, *during arrest* . . .' He paused, then added, 'However, that complaint was unsubstantiated . . . for want of evidence, sir.' – *terrific*! he thought; I've just fed the prat his own words. *Touché*!

Beecher looked nettled, and immediately changed-up a gear, becoming more hostile:

'Officer, you bear a grudge against the defendant. Is that not so?'

'No, sir, I – '

'You arrested him, were obliged to release him, and he later complained of your conduct. You held that against him.'

'No, sir. That's not true. I'd forgotten about those things.'

'Until it was suggested to you that the defendant was responsible for the robbery in which you were shot.'

'*No*, sir,' MacHale protested – *why the hell did he ever let Schofield off the hook, that night, when he nicked him with the Jag?*

'And then,' Beecher relentlessly pressed on, 'you seized

the opportunity for revenge, and were – *are* – prepared to perjure yourself and have him committed to imprisonment for a crime he is totally innocent of.'

MacHale glanced at the judge, hoping he'd sling out a lifeline. But the judge merely deflected the glance, and then awaited MacHale's response. Defiantly, MacHale said, 'All of your suggestions and insinuations are completely without foundation, sir. And I resent them.'

The cross-examination went on for almost an hour, with Beecher persistently attempting to excavate holes in MacHale's evidence-in-chief. *Why did it take you over a week to decide that it was Schofield who'd committed the robbery? You made that written statement, identifying Schofield, eleven days* after *the event.* That was Bruno's decision, MacHale had said. Bruno had probably wanted to afford him as much time as possible to think over what had happened, and who was responsible . . . to be absolutely certain, before committing himself. *Why, then, officer, being, as you put it, certain, did you not walk right on up to Schofield, at the identity parade, and pick him out, there and then? Why did you think it necessary to look at all of the parade's participants, if you were so sure he was responsible? You weren't sure, were you? But, after realizing that Schofield was who he was – the man whom you'd earlier lost on a car-stealing charge, the man who'd complained about your conduct –, you then decided that Schofield would do nicely for the bank robbery . . .*

And so forth, *ad nauseam:* accusations, denials . . . always circumventing the *real* issue . . .

MacHale left the witness box, feeling as if he'd just run a marathon. But Beecher hadn't succeeded in scoring many points off him – he hoped.

He walked to the back of the court and sat among the police benches, keen to hear the rest of the evidence. The usher, and two PCs who were attached to the court staff, were now wheeling in two trollies that bore a TV-set and a video-recorder . . . setting up the equipment at the front of the court . . . Croft, having scribbled a note which his instructing solicitor had taken possession of, was looking over his shoulder, towards the rear of the court, offering MacHale an encouraging smile. The solicitor, having made his way over to the police benches, now delivered the note to MacHale. MacHale unfolded and read it . . . *Well done! Round One has gone to us, I believe.*

MacHale refolded the note and placed it in the left, breast pocket of his tunic, glancing over at the jurors. Now he felt some sympathy for them. *He* was no longer sure that today was the day after the day after the day before yesterday . . .

26

The jury had watched with avid interest the replay of the bank's security video, although they must have been more than a little disappointed by the poor quality of the film – hazy, snowy – , the lack of sound and the absence of colour. However, they'd donated expressions of horror, then sympathy, when they'd seen MacHale shot, and blown halfway across the bank's public area; that could do him, and the prosecution's case, nothing but good.

At the same time, though, the jurors must have been left in no doubt that it *was* impossible to match the masked face of the gunman with the face of the defendant in the dock; MacHale saw them all make for themselves the comparison, each man and woman taking several quick glances in the direction of Schofield, as the relevant frames of the tape were replayed.

It could only be hoped, then, that they would give credence to MacHale's insistence that he, having been there for real, on the bank's floor, looking up at the part-masked face above him, had indeed seen as much as he'd sworn in his evidence, and was able to make the identification, having seen that face – Schofield's face – on a previous occasion. It was an imperative point: one which the judge would emphasize in his closing address to the jury.

After lunch, Bruno was called to give evidence from the witness box. He swore the Oath, gave his name, rank, and branch of attachment, and awaited the attention of prosecuting counsel.

Croft took him slowly, carefully and minutely through

what he had to say, while Schofield, leaning forward on his bench in the dock, listened attentively, his expression hostile; it was clear that he could hardly contain his emotions and was fighting a raging battle within himself.

Having arrived at the point where Bruno and Bell had allegedly searched Schofield's loft and found a sawn-off shotgun, six cartridges and a woollen bobble-hat with eye-slits cut out of it, Croft continued by saying, 'And after you'd confronted the defendant with these articles, Chief Inspector, what was his reply?'

Without consulting his official note-book, Bruno answered, 'He replied, "It's your birthday, innit? What can I say? I'm bang to rights, now, I s'pose".'

A load of verbals, if ever MacHale had heard any.

Schofield could now contain himself no longer. He rushed forward to the rail of the dock, his face wild with frustrated anger, and bellowed, 'You *liar*! You fuckin liar! It was a *plant*, an you fuckin *know* it, you filth!'

Bruno remained completely detached, neither surprised nor offended; it was, perhaps, *less* than he was used to or expected in such circumstances. That apart, he was an extremely professional witness. The best.

As the two screws who'd flanked Schofield sprang forward to grab his arms and drag him back to the rear of the dock, the judge, his shrivelled old face quaking, leaned forward and croaked as loudly as he could, 'Take that man down! At once! There will be no further outbursts in this court!'

And Schofield, screaming dementedly and struggling wildly, was bundled backwards down the stairs, and banged-up in the cells.

When the echoes had died away, and the air had settled, Croft went on: 'And did you then proceed to search the defendant's bedroom, Chief Inspector?'

'I did, sir.'

'And, in particular, the wardrobe?'

'Yes, sir.'

'And will you now disclose to the jury what you there discovered?'

'Yes, sir. In particular, I discovered a pair of black, lace-up shoes with ridged soles . . .' He paused, watching the usher walk to a table at the centre of the court, where the official exhibits were on display. The usher picked up a sealed, clear-plastic bag containing a pair of black, lace-up shoes, walked to the witness box, and handed them to Bruno, still sealed in the bag. Bruno gave them a cursory examination, paying more attention to his exhibit label, signed by him, which was attached to the bag's neck.

'These were the shoes I found, sir,' he said. 'Exhibit RB-Six.' – the shotgun, the cartridges and the bobble hat were Exhibits RB-Three to Five, while plaster samples from the bank's ceiling and floor were Exhibits RB-One and Two; further exhibits – Seven and Eight – consisted of shotgun pellets, extracted from the bank's walls and from MacHale's body.

Bruno went on: 'I said to the defendant, "Are these your shoes?" He replied, "Well they ain't my old woman's, are they, you cunt?" I took that to be an admission of ownership, sir. Then, I examined the shoes and saw that there were what appeared to be small flakes of white plaster, lodged in the ridges of the soles.'

'And did you put this to the defendant?'

'Yes, sir. I said, "What looks like white plaster is lodged in the soles of these shoes. Where might that plaster have originated?" The defendant replied, "I dunno, do I . . .?" He paused, apparently thinking, after that. Then he said, "Must've come from that house I helped a mate to plaster, a day or two ago. He's a self-employed builder. Does all sorts of sitework. I just gave him a hand 'cause he was short of labour".'

'And was the defendant able to assist you with the identity of that, as *he* put it, "mate"? Or, indeed, with the location of the property which he claimed he had worked at on that "mate's" behalf?'

'No, sir. He persistently refused to assist, in any way, with those matters, saying, "I can't put him up, because he's only a casual mate who I met in a boozer, one evening last week. I don't even know his name, do I?"'

'Well, was he able to assist with the location of the public house in which he claimed he'd met this man?'

'He was unable to remember either the name of the pub or where it was located.'

Briefly, Croft consulted his papers. Then, looking up: 'Now, Chief Inspector, return with me, if you will, to this bobble hat: Exhibit RB-Five, which was found in the defendant's loft. After examining the shoes which you'd located in the defendant's wardrobe, did you then feel it prudent to make a close examination of the woollen weave of the hat?'

'Yes, sir, I did, and I was able to see that the black wool which the hat was constructed from, appeared to have minute flakes of white plaster adhering to it.'

'And, of course,' said Croft, 'we shall, in due course, hear evidence from an expert witness in such matters, as to whether or not your assessment of the nature of the white substances which were visible in the hat and on the shoes, was accurate. But, for now, will you tell the jury what the defendant had to say when you pointed out to him that the flakes in the hat appeared identical with the flakes lodged in the soles of his shoes?'

'Yes, sir. The defendant replied, "So what? I wore the hat, too, didn't I, when I was helping out with the spreading?"'

And so it went on, for the remainder of the afternoon. Croft, inching forward, eliciting everything, sometimes darting backwards to contrast one fact with another, earlier one which reinforced it, but all the while building the case against Schofield, and, finally, pointing up the joints and the angles and the corners, and topping it out.

Bruno was like ice-cream, MacHale thought; very smooth and palatable; very impressive and convincing a witness; never the slightest hesitation when responding to a question, never the smallest intimation that he'd permitted himself to become personally involved, on an emotional basis, by either the nature of the case or the character of the defendant.

Funny, though, thought MacHale, how Bruno's accent had been valeted for this occasion: from rough Cockney, to highly respectable sub-urban London. Last night, he'd probably been three-parts shackled in a boozer or a club, effing and blinding with the rest of his team, recounting lewd jokes and pinching barmaids' arses.

The following morning, Bruno was back in the box, awaiting his cross-examination by Beecher, while Schofield, unrepentant for his outburst of yesterday afternoon, was still banged-up in the cells, down below.

Bruno wasn't in the least daunted by the prospect of Beecher's cross-examination, either. He anticipated nothing, therefore nothing could take him unawares.

'Inspector,' Beecher began, with an alluring smile – which was counterfeit, of course, and which Bruno was far too cute to be ensnared by. 'I want to take you back to your evidence-in-chief, yesterday afternoon, to the stage where you recounted your search of the defendant's loft and allegedly discovered a sawn-off shotgun, six cartridges and a woollen hat, concealed behind the cold-water tank.'

'Yes, sir.'

Beecher coughed, sniffed, and went on: 'Now, Inspector, my instructions are that these incriminating articles were, in fact, carried into the defendant's property by the police-officers who searched there, as were the samples of plaster which it is claimed were *found* in the hat and in the defendant's shoes.'

'Most certainly not,' replied Bruno, maintaining his emotional detachment, despite the serious nature of the allegations which Beecher had just laid.

'And I further, suggest, Inspector,' continued Beecher, 'that when you planted these articles in the defendant's possession, you said, "We've just had a raffle down the factory, Freddie, and you've drawn first prize. Have this little lot with me, it'll go nicely with that bank blag you're in the frame for."'

'Most certainly not,' reiterated Bruno. 'The articles were discovered in the defendant's loft.'

Beecher ignored the reply, and carried on as if there'd been no denial: 'And when the defendant demanded to know why he, an innocent man, had been singled out for this wicked piece of victimization, you said to him, "It's your turn, son. You're well overdue for a nicking, all the strokes you've been pulling, lately."'

'Nonsense, sir,' Bruno respectfully and flatly said. 'The defendant was targeted by the word of an extremely reliable informant, and was arrested with the clearest possible evidence.'

'Well, it will be for the jury to decide just how reliable a man that informant is,' Beecher dryly retorted, 'when he is called upon to give his evidence. But, for now, I want to turn to a quite different matter. Is it not right, Inspector, that the defendant has lodged an official complaint with the Complaints Bureau, concerning the circumstances of his arrest on the matters before this court?'

'Yes, sir, he has.'

'Alleging that yourself and Detective Sergeant Bell conspired together to pervert the course of justice, in making a case against him . . . in as much as you planted a sawn-off shotgun and other incriminating articles in his possession?'

'That sums-up the nature of the defendant's complaint,' agreed Bruno. 'And, of course, the matters are being officially investigated.' He glanced towards the police benches at the back of the court.

MacHale followed Bruno's line of vision, and his eyes settled on a pair of well-dressed men who were sitting two rows in front of him, listening carefully to the proceedings; they'd been in attendance since the opening of the trial, but until now MacHale hadn't realized they were from the CIB. He also hadn't realized, until now, that Schofield *had* complained about the conduct of Bruno and Bell, and was surprised that he himself hadn't been complained of; after all, it was he who'd picked out Schofield, on the line-up.

'On how many previous occasions have arrested persons had cause to complain of your conduct, Inspector?' Beecher now wanted to know; he placed a forefinger on a paragraph of his brief, looked quickly down at it, then looked back at Bruno, his expression saying, *And, just in case you're thinking of being less than open in this matter, I've got it all down here, in black and white, to throw in your face.*

Bruno looked fleetingly to the ceiling as he considered the question. Then, returning his eyes to Beecher, he said, 'I can't be certain, sir, but I believe a figure of about twenty-five complaints, throughout my service, is near enough accurate.'

'*Twenty . . . five!*' Beecher slowly exclaimed, echoing the figure, just for the benefit of the jurors. 'And what were the nature of those complaints?'

'Assault, corruption, conspiracy, planting evidence, perjury – practically every criminal offence, save murder, I should think, sir.'

Jesus Christ! thought MacHale, and glanced at the jurors, all of whom seemed openly taken aback by Bruno's unashamed admission.

'Some very serious allegations, indeed,' observed Beecher.

'They certainly were,' conceded Bruno. 'But each and every one, I'm bound to say, was levelled by a professional criminal under arrest, and each and every one was found to be entirely without substance, after a thorough investigation.'

'After a *police* investigation,' Beecher sarcastically put in, intimating that no such inquiry could ever be impartial or objective.

'Chief Inspector,' croaked the judge, turning aside in the direction of the witness box and peering over the top of his pince-nez. 'Is it your experience that, since the inception of A-Ten – now named the Complaints Investigation Bureau, I understand – , many professional criminals view the lodging of a complaint against an arresting officer, as a necessary first-step in the preparation of their defences?'

'Indeed, that is my experience,' agreed Bruno. 'In fact, Your Honour, I'd say it was exceptional if a professional criminal I'd arrested, *didn't* complain of my conduct.'

Nice one, thought MacHale. The judge had obviously taken a shine to Bruno, and the jury was now reassured.

'Please continue, Mister Beecher,' croaked the judge. 'And let us, from now on, adhere ourselves to more relevant matters.' He'd obviously decided that Schofield's complaint was already unsubstantiated. But then, the judge had not only a list of the witnesses' statements of evidence before him, but a list of the defendant's previous, as well; and that latter form, as long as an ape's arm, was a shocking indictment of Schofield's criminal past.

By mid-morning, Beecher had done with Bruno. Bruno's evidence had been clear, concise and credible, and just couldn't be vitiated.

* * *

When the court reconvened, after lunch, Bell was called to the witness box, and was as impressive and convincing a witness – with *his* valeted accent, and smart, pinstripe suit – as Bruno had been. He closely corroborated Bruno's evidence, but without giving rise to the suspicion that he and Bruno had conspired with each other to the prejudice of Schofield; he did, however, admit, when cross-examined by Beecher, that he and Bruno had *consulted* each other when making their original notes of evidence, some hours after the searching of Schofield's house; it was a natural enough thing to do, and a denial that it had occurred would righly have been viewed with suspicion by the jury. Both detectives' original notes were a distillation of their separate recollections of conversations they'd had with the defendant, and, when all was said and done, were – if *honestly* constructed – far more likely to be an accurate record of what passed between them, than Schofield's memory.

So, when it came to choosing between the defendant's version of events on the morning when his house was raided, and the version offered by Bruno and Bell, the jury would have little difficulty in deciding, MacHale believed.

At the end of the second day, then, the prosecution was well ahead on points.

27

Day three began with Frankie James being called to give evidence; and he was as nervous as hell. This was the first time MacHale had set eyes on James – who'd been under police guard at an undisclosed address, since picking out Schofield on a line-up – , and he was immediately struck by the man's physical resemblance to Schofield. Both were well-built men, and both had dark complexions, brown-black eyes, black hair, and, of course, those swallow-and-LOVE-HATE tattooes on their hands.

MacHale now believed that if Bruno and Bell hadn't told him that the bank job *was* down to Schofield, and had instead just fed him into a line-up which contained both men, he wouldn't have known *which* of the two to pick out. For a moment, therefore, MacHale found himself engulfed by serious, doubt-inspired guilt, suspecting that Schofield might, indeed, be innocent . . .

But then he remembered how it was that Bruno and Bell had found the sawn-off, the cartridges and the mask at Schofield's house, not to mention the plaster samples in the mask and on the shoes, so that now his doubts and guilt began quickly to recede and wash away. It *was* Schofield. There *couldn't* be any doubt.

After James had identified himself, he was permitted to write down his address; ordinarily, he would have been obliged to openly declare it, but as the court's gallery contained friends and relatives of the defendant, and the witness was stated to be in real fear for his life, due to his presence here, today, and the nature of his forthcoming testimony, the court readily acquiesced in the prosecution's request for secrecy.

Now, Croft began eliciting James' evidence.

'Mister James, are you a man with a lengthy criminal background?'

'Yes.' – his eyes, highly mobile, moving quickly from jury to Croft, to Beecher, to the police benches, to the wall at the back of the court . . . back to Croft . . . back to the jury, not knowing *where* to settle; his hands, tightly gripping the rails of the witness box, a film of perspiration on his upper lip, his voice, dry as dust.

'What type of offence is it,' Croft went on, 'that you have convictions for?'

'Everything,' replied James, his eyes still flitting around the court. 'Burglary, theft, goin equipped, TDA, deception, robbery, possessin shooters . . . You name it.'

'Yes, but what I'm driving at, Mister James, is that you have a specialization, as it were, do you not?'

'Well, yeah . . . Blagg . . . Robbery's me game, these days, as it happens.'

'You are a professional, armed robber?'

'Tha's right, sir. But I've never harmed a fly. I wouldn't, would I? I carry shooters as a frightener, but I'd never actually use one.'

'Mister James,' continued Croft. 'Have you *ever* had a regular, honest job?'

James thought about it, and his right hand left the rail of the witness box, to draw its back across his upper lip. 'No. Never. I'm a professional criminal. Me form goes back to when I was about ten . . . before that, as it happens, only it never *counted* till I was ten.'

'Form?' croaked the judge, peering hostilely at James.

'Previous convictions.'

'I'm obliged,' croaked the judge.

'Thus far,' resumed Croft, 'we have established your background. Will you now tell the court how you came to be acquainted with the defendant in this case, Frederick Schofield?'

'Yessir,' agreed James. 'He's a pro – '

'Without mentioning any details of his antecedent history . . . his type of *work*,' cautioned Croft.

'Oh,' mumbled James. 'Well, I've known Freddie for a lotta years, now. I see him around a lot. We used to use the same clubs, boozers, that sorta thing. He's a face I know very well.'

'Now, can I take you back to one evening, some six months ago, when I believe you met Frederick Schofield in a public house in the West End? In the *Goat and Boots*, in Grant Street, to be exact.'

'Yeah, we had a meet there. I remember it quite well, as it happens.'

'Why? Why do you remember the occasion? Why this night, in particular, Mister James?'

'Because Freddie put one up to me, didn't he?'

The judge exasperatedly sighed, and loudly tapped his pen on top of his desk, glaring at Croft.

'He put one up to you?' said Croft. 'Now what, precisely, does that mean?'

'He put a blag up to me . . . a robbery. Asked if I wanted a taste. Wanted me to go on it with him, like. He knew I was a good worker, and he trusted me. Wanted me to supply a shooter . . . a sawn-off. Only, I couldn't, at that time, because I wasn't interested, was I? Had a bitta me own business to attend to.'

'But did Schofield reveal to you the location of the proposed robbery, and the target?'

'Oh yeah, course he did. It was the National Consolidated Bank. The branch at High Street, near the junction with Martin Lane . . . north of the river.'

'And did he specify a day, date and time for this proposed robbery?'

'Yeah. He said it was on for the Monday, a couplea weeks ahead, at the lunch-time . . . at the tail end of it.'

'Can you be specific about the date, Mister James?'

James shook his head. 'Na. But you *know* when it was, don't you? I mean, it went *off*, didn't it? All I know is, it was a couplea weeks after Freddie Schofield put it up to me, and it was the same bank he'd had in mind.' He shrugged. 'Two-'n'-two makes four, dunnit?'

Croft thanked James, asked him to remain where he was, and then addressed the judge: 'Your Honour, I find myself in some difficulty. While the witness has *verbally* identified the defendant, and while I – '

'Yes, yes, Mister Croft,' croaked the judge, getting Croft's drift. 'Very well, bring up the defendant.'

At length, Schofield, sandwiched between a pair of screws, appeared at the head of the stairs which rose up from beneath the dock; he wasn't permitted to sit, and his wrists were held tight by each of the screws, as well as being 'cuffed behind his back; he stood there, then, his lips curled and snarling defiance, his jaw stubbornly jutting, his wild eyes burning James with an excoriating glare.

Croft, half-turning, pointed in the direction of Schofield. 'Is this the man who attempted to recruit you for a robbery at the National Consolidated Bank, at High Street, junction with Martin Lane, on a morning, some six months ago?'

James looked across at Schofield, swallowed hard, then said, 'That's him, all right. No doubt. I picked him out on an ID parade, an all, don't forget.' Then he quickly looked at his own feet.

'You stinkin fuckin grass!' screamed Schofield, lunging forward towards the front of the dock, dragging with him the two screws. 'Why don't ya tell em how much of a drink ya put into the Robbery Squad to row ya fuckin *self* outa this one! Ya slag!'

James, his face draining of colour, backed away from the front of the witness box, his right hand moving involuntarily to his neck, to massage his throat. But he was in no immediate danger, and was able to watch in safety as the screws dragged Schofield back down the stairs, his shouts and screams echoing all the way up from the cell area, beneath the court. Then, a stunned silence pressed down on the room.

Now, Beecher rose to cross-examine.

'You, James,' he aggressively opened, 'are a man with an appalling record of crime. On your own admission, you have convictions for almost every criminal offence which it is possible to commit. You have stopped short only of murder in order to pursue greed and indolence.' And then he proceeded, at great length, to recount James' long criminal past.

Next, Beecher went on to suggest that Bruno had some sort of hold over James . . . had knowledge of a crime which James had committed, yet had suppressed the evidence in exchange for James' agreeing to incriminate Schofield. Why else would James *be* here, putting himself in great, personal danger, by informing on a fellow criminal?

Yeah, *why*? MacHale, for the first time, wondered. Beecher had a real point, there.

'I considered it my public duty,' James weakly tried.

The judge raised incredulous eyes, and peered over the top of his pince-nez . . . first at James, then at Beecher; finally, at the jury.

James shuffled his feet, wiped the back of his right hand across his lips, then embarrassedly coughed. 'I mean, after I read about how that young Wall . . . that young copper had got shot, I decided to put meself on offer like this. I mean, Freddie was right out of order, on that score, wasn't he?' – still unconvincing.

'And *what* is in it for *you*?' insisted Beecher. 'By presenting yourself here, today, and giving the evidence which you have, and are, giving, you are jeopardizing the lives of yourself and your family. You will have to move to another house, probably in another part of the country. Even your removed relatives may be in danger . . . Not, I hasten to add, through any action which my client might order or endorse; but the underworld is a close-knit community, and informers are generally despised by all.'

James just stared in shocked silence at Beecher. It appeared that Beecher's statement had for the first time brought fully home to James the implications of informing. At length, he mumbled, 'There's nothing in it for me. Nothing at all, except a new life.'

Beecher pressed him, though: 'Are you denying that you have gained, financially, from informing on the defendant?'

'That's a joke,' answered James – but he wasn't smiling; no one was. 'Hundred-an-fifty quid from the Informants' Fund? How could *that* be an incentive. There won't even be ten per cent of the bank-raid money, because none of that was recovered, was it?'

So, *why*? MacHale again wondered. *Something* must've induced – no, *forced* – James to put himself on offer, like this. But Beecher was unable to elicit it, so that at the end of the afternoon, everyone – except, maybe, Bruno and Bell – was *still* wondering.

And there it rested, to be finally decided by the jury.

Next morning, day four of the trial, Croft introduced the written statements of evidence of the prosecution's expert witnesses.

The first statement to be read, then, was that of the police SOCO – pronounced SOCKO – who'd attended the bank on the afternoon of the robbery. He'd obtained samples of the bank's ceiling plaster, had hoovered the bank's floor, and had recovered three jars of pellets, obtained from the bank's walls and ceiling, together with two, separate samples of shotgun-cartridge wadding, which were discharged, along with the pellets, when the sawn-off was fired.

The second statement was that of a Senior Scientific Officer from the police laboratory, who had received the SOCO's samples of plaster, and had matched them with the samples removed from Schofield's shoes and the bobble hat which allegedly was found in his loft. A further laboratory witness was the ballistics expert who'd received the sawn-off shotgun, also allegedly found in Schofield's loft, together with the pellets and wadding located by the SOCO, at the bank; he'd also received a jar of pellets that were removed from MacHale's side and arm, at the hospital.

According to the ballistics expert, it wasn't possible to attribute the wadding and pellets to the sawn-off he'd examined, although he could say that the pellets – measuring 0.05 inches in diameter – and the wadding, *were* attributable to a twelve-bore cartridge – two, actually – of a type which the sawn-off was constructed to accommodate and discharge; further, an examination of the sawn-off had disclosed that it had recently *been* discharged, and test firings, contrasted with measurements of the spread of MacHale's wounds – supplied by the hospital's casualty officer – indicated that, if the sawn-off examined was, indeed, the one used in the bank robbery, it was fired at MacHale from a range of not less than sixteen yards.

The following two statements to be read were those of the casualty officer who had treated MacHale on his arrival at the hospital, and the specialist – a consultant surgeon – in whose care MacHale had been, prior to discharge from the hospital. The conclusion was that MacHale's injuries had not endangered his life, in the circumstances. But this fact was irrelevant to a charge of attempted murder, because the *mens rea* didn't require it to be established that a life *must* be endangered, and the jury would be reminded of that.

Finally, the written statement of a police photographer was read aloud; he merely described how he'd attended the venue of the robbery, and produced, as an exhibit, an album of black-and-white pictures, which had been reviewed by the jury and the defence.

And, thus, the prosecution's case was closed.

After lunch, it was the turn of the defence.

Schofield swore the Oath and announced his name and address; he was no stranger to the witness box. He spoke loudly and clearly, and never took his eyes off the jury, many of whose members must have felt intimidated by that hot, unflickering glare – and maybe that was Schofield's intent.

'Mister Schofield,' began Beecher, going for an open, nothing-to-hide approach. 'You do not deny that you are, and have been for most of your adult life, a criminal?'

'No, I don't,' admitted Schofield. 'But don't get me wrong . . . I mean, I ain't proud of it.' – he hadn't sounded ashamed, either.

'Quite,' Beecher sympathetically nodded.

'In fact,' continued Schofield, 'I'm tryin to reform meself . . . Or was, till the fil . . . the law fitted me up on this one.' He looked away from the jury and settled his eyes on the police benches, where Bruno, Bell and MacHale were seated.

'Your speciality was robbery, was it not?' asked Beecher, reclaiming his client's attention. '*Armed* robbery.'

Schofield nodded. 'Yeah. That's right.'

'But not the type of armed robbery which it is alleged you committed at the National Consolidated Bank.'

'Tha's right. There's just no way that *that's* my form. If *I* was gonna knock that one over, I'd be team-handed and I'd go for the delivery; from the security van; not a poxy two-an-half grand, over the jump.'

The judge tut-tutted and shook his head. 'The *jump*?'

Schofield looked obliquely at the judge. 'Yeah, the jump . . . The *counter*.'

'I'm obliged,' croaked the judge.

'Now,' continued Beecher, 'I want to come to the morning on which this robbery was committed, the morning on which you claim you were elsewhere than at the National Consolidated Bank. Where, in fact, were you on that morning?'

'At home. In bed.'

'*All* morning?'

'Yeah,' said Schofield. '*All* mornin. The night before, I felt a dose of flu comin on, didn't I? So, I took one of the wife's sleepers, had a couplea glasses of Scotch, and turned-in early. I was out for hours: till about one, two in the afternoon.'

'And who can corroborate that?'

'Me missus. She was home all day, looking after the kid . . . I gotta small kid, comin up for three.'

'Anyone else?'

'No. Tha's it.'

Not much of an alibi, thought MacHale. Surely he could've done better than that?

'Therefore, you were not anywhere near the venue of this bank robbery, on the morning in question?'

'Definitely not. Like I said, it just ain't my form, goin it alone, for peanuts.'

Beecher paused, studying his brief. 'Let me take you, now,' he continued, looking up, 'to the early hours of the morning when you were visited by the police-officers who searched your house. Give the court *your* version of the events of that morning.'

'Right,' Schofield aggressively said. 'We was in bed,

asleep – me an the missus, like – , when the front-door comes in off its hinges, an that slag, Bruno – '

'Mister Schofield,' interrupted the judge. 'You will refer to the police-officer as "Mister" or as "Inspector".'

Schofield didn't apologize, or even acknowledge the judge's rebuke; he just glowered, resentfully.

'Go on,' prompted Beecher.

'*Mister* Bruno,' Schofield contemptuously proceeded, 'came steamin into the bedroom, followed by Bell – *Mister* Bell – , stuck a shooter – a gun, that is – in me boat-race – me face – , and said somethin like, "How'd'ya like another mouth where your eyes are, Freddie?" Then they started turnin me over, good-'n'-proper. A right spinnin, it was.' He glanced at the judge, and added, 'I mean, they made a right mess of my house, searchin it.'

'And did they announce themselves, or produce a warrant, or state the purpose of their visit?'

'No,' said Schofield. 'But then I never s'posed they was from anywhere else *but* the Heavy Mob – the Robbery Squad. Tha's their *style*, innit, the fff – '

But Beecher, holding up his right hand, cut-off Schofield, before he could further irritate the judge, by denegrating, in classic East End terms, the methods of the Robbery Squad and its members. 'When Inspector Bruno searched your loft, and produced a sawn-off shotgun, six cartridges and a woollen bobble-hat, what was your reaction?'

'Well, it was a *right* body-blow, wannit? . . . I was knocked *out*.'

'Had you ever seen, or had prior knowledge of, those articles, before that morning?'

'No. When he put the shotgun up, it was just like he'd pulled a rabbit out of a hat. It was a plant, wannit? He brought all that stuff *in* with him. Just like the plaster, which *he* says was in me shoes. He *put* it there, didn't he?' Again, Schofield glowered across at the police benches.

'Well, I was coming to that,' said Beecher. 'But, for the moment, can we dwell on the Inspector's production of the articles he says were in your loft? *Did* you, in fact, tell the Inspector that it was his birthday? That he'd got you clean? Or words to that effect?'

'Did I *hell*?' said Schofield. 'That was a loada verbals, and he *knows* it . . . a loada lies. I've been around too long to throw me hands in the air, straight away like that. I'd've thought about it, and, eventually, maybe I'd've pleaded; *if* I was bang to rights; but not straight off, like he says I did. It *was* a plant.'

'And when the Inspector found your shoes in the wardrobe, pointing out that the soles appeared to contain flakes of ceiling plaster, what was your reaction to that?'

'That's just *it*!' Schofield indignantly retorted. 'He never *did* point out anythin like that, did he? Sure, he took me shoes to the nick, when he claimed me, but the first I know of any plaster bein in the soles is when he comes down the cells, three hours later, shows me the shoes, an says, "This is the nail in your coffin, Freddie." He *planted* the stuff in me shoes.'

Bruno and Bell appeared totally unmoved by the allegations; they just sat there, impassive, in their seats, intently watching and listening.

When Beecher had given way, Croft began his cross-examination.

'Mister Schofield. You have made some very serious allegations against the detective police-officers in this case; claiming that they planted in your possession – among other items – a sawn-off shotgun.'

'Yeah, because they *did*,' Schofield tersely replied.

'Now where do you suppose they got possession of that shotgun?' said Croft. 'Neither officer is the holder of a shotgun licence, and one doesn't just walk into a firearm dealer's premises and purchase a weapon for the purpose of incriminating an innocent man. One *can't*.'

'It's obvious, innit?' Schofield said. 'They *nicked* it – off some other villain; *then* they gave it to *me*.'

'Come, come,' said Croft, almost smiling, definitely taunting. 'To what end? Why on earth should they permit one criminal to go free, and – ?'

'Ask that slag Frankie James!' shouted Schofield. 'He's the cunt who put a drink into that filth, Bruno, to row *himself* out! Fuckin ask *him*, not *me*!'

'Schofield!' rasped the judge, his face reddening, his jowls trembling.

But Schofield now turned on him, bellowing, 'An as for *you*, ya shrivelled ol *cunt*! What fuckin chance do I *stand*, with you up the *law's* arse? *You're* as bent as the fuckin *rest* of em!' And then he began picking up the Bibles which were stacked on a ledge inside the witness box, unloading them at everyone within range.

'Take him down!' shrieked the judge. 'Take him down!'

'Don't, Freddie! Don't!' screamed a female voice from the public gallery. 'You'll only make it worse!'

And while the female screamed, and Schofield unloaded the stack of Bibles, and the judge croaked and shrieked – barely audible above the screams – and the occupants of counsels' tables ducked and weaved, and the jurors were preparing to have it on their toes, lest Schofield should next vent his anger and frustration upon them, and while MacHale, Bruno and Bell, simultaneously considered that this was the best piece of work which Croft had done throughout the trial – winding-up Schofield, like he had – , the two burly screws who'd been near Schofield's side while he'd given evidence, overpowered him and dragged him away, spitting and struggling and screaming obscenities.

That's the nail in your coffin, Freddie Schofield, thought MacHale; not the plaster in your shoes.

* * *

After a short adjournment, Schofield's wife was called to give evidence on his behalf.

She was a small, thin woman, about forty-five, with bleached, collarlength hair that had been permed and lacquered, full, wet red lips, and huge blue eyes that sported over-long black lashes and traffic-light-green eye-shadow; she looked completely washed-out, her features lined and weighted by stress, and, appropriately, thought MacHale, wore black – a two-piece, single-breasted silk suit, with black-silk blouse, open at the neck. Funereal.

In a hesitant whisper she repeated the Oath and announced her name, her address, and her relationship to the defendant.

Beecher took her slowly through her evidence, often reminding her to raise her voice, frequently asking her to repeat an answer when she lapsed into a nervous, halting murmur.

When Croft dismantled her evidence, though, it no longer sounded so plausible. She could have been right about her old man being in bed with flu on the morning of the robbery, but she didn't know on what date the robbery was committed. Nothing else of note had occurred on that day: the doctor hadn't been called, the baby hadn't broken its leg, and the budgie hadn't fallen dead off its perch; she didn't even know, now, what the weather was like, or what was showing on TV. So why *should* she have remembered, a couple of weeks later, that the day of the robbery *was* the day of her old man's illness? All she could say was, 'And why *shouldn't* I remember?'

Croft then moved on.

How could Mrs Schofield know what was or wasn't in her loft? She wasn't handcuffed to her husband when they were together in the house, and didn't always observe his coming and going. Why *couldn't* he have come in, after the robbery, and placed the sawn-off, the cartridges and the woolly hat, in the loft, while she was, say, washing-up in the kitchen?

He could have, and she was obliged to admit it.

That apart, why should the jury believe *her*, anyway? She was, after all, the wife of a self-confessed, professional criminal, and, as such, had shared in the proceeds of his violent crimes.

'I never knew anything about his crimes,' she tried, weeping into her handkerchief. 'I thought he was a bookmaker or . . . or something. Something honest and respectable.'

At which, Croft, his mouth gaping, his eyebrows raised, turned aside and glanced at the jury, his expression saying, *If you believe* that *load of unadulterated* bullshit, *you'll believe anything*.

'Mrs Schofield,' Croft then went on. 'My learned friend, here . . .' He paused, and spread his left hand in Beecher's direction. '. . . elicited from your husband that for practically all of his adult life he had been a professional criminal, specializing, latterly, in armed robbery. He has been arrested almost as many times as he has had birthdays. How could you *not* be aware of his true occupation?'

The jurors' eyes, trained unflickeringly on the witness, echoed Croft's question. But the witness didn't answer; or perhaps she did, in a way: she just stood there, shaking, her lower lip trembling. And then she broke-up, falling forward over the rail of the witness box, her chest heaving as she gave way to her tears.

Croft thanked her, indicating to the judge that his examination was over, and the usher then went to the witness, placed his arms around her shoulders, and led her, her body shuddering, from the court.

MacHale's eyes followed her to the door, and he found himself infected by her anguish; but cops weren't supposed to have pity, especially not for anyone else.

He wondered just how much longer he'd be able to repress the feelings he shouldn't even be experiencing if he wanted to succeed in The Job . . . And suddenly he craved a drink, to settle his nerves, his twanging brain. *Needed?* No. Because that was something else he shouldn't admit; least of all to himself.

So now he decided there'd be no drinking for him until the last day of this trial. Then there'd be a *real* excuse for having an almighty piss-up. There'd really *be* something to celebrate: Schofield, going over the wall for a quarter century.

There, now. *That* was the way for a cop to be thinking.

28

MacHale sat on the bench, next to Bruno and Bell, and waited for the closing stages of the trial to start.

Schofield was still banged-up in the cells, but MacHale was surprised to see that James was in court, sitting in the front row of benches, flanked by the two detectives who'd been assigned the duty of protecting him until he'd moved out of the MPD.

'Why's he still here?' MacHale whispered to Bruno, nodding at James' back.

Bruno's eyes followed the direction of the nod. 'My idea,' he said, his voice hushed. 'Thought it'd impress the jury if he was here at the kill, when he doesn't have to be. Apart from that, it'll remind em of what he had to say in the box, day before yesterday. Good evidence, that was.'

'Could they have *forgotten* it, then?' asked MacHale.

'What's been the most outstandin aspect of this trial, so far as you're concerned?' said Bruno.

Briefly, MacHale thought about it. 'Well, Schofield, I s'pose; his disorderly behaviour. I've never seen anything like that before in a court of law.'

Bruno put on a wry smile. 'See. Even you've forgotten there was a blag. An you were the one who got *shot*.'

MacHale sat up straight and looked to his front, thinking about what Bruno had said. Yesterday, after Schofield's final outburst, he'd believed the jury would be eager to convict; but now he had to wonder if the jury might not go right the other way, and interpret Schofield's vehement protests, allegations and denials as markers of his innocence. Bruno was both right and wrong; MacHale wasn't convinced that the jury had forgotten there was a robbery and a shooting, but Schofield's conduct in court must be, at this moment, anyway, *uppermost* in its members' minds.

To the left of the judge's dais, a door opened, and the usher then appeared, calling out, 'Please be upstanding!'

The hubbub of sniffing and coughing, and muted voices in conversation, abruptly died, and the court rose in total silence, watching as the judge appeared, walked to his desk, bowed, and sat at his throne, saying, 'Yes, Mister Croft.'

First, then, Croft addressed the jury with his closing speech for the prosecution, taking, in order of appearance before the court, each one of the witnesses and the nature of his or her evidence, contrasting that with Schofield's defence to the indictments.

Of course, certain facts had gone unchallenged by the defence: there *was* a robbery and a shooting; all which was really at issue, here, was who had been responsible for them. A police-officer – MacHale – had actually witnessed the robbery; further, that officer had been able to identify Schofield, a man with whom he had had an earlier encounter. By far the most damning indictment of Schofield's guilt, however, was the fact that, only a matter of weeks prior to the robbery, he propositioned a fellow criminal – the witness, James – with an offer to participate, naming the target and the day, the time, *and* the specific branch of bank to be involved.

It was right and proper that the jurors should treat with caution the testimony of James, who had a bad character and a lengthy record. However, to buttress his evidence, there were the incriminating articles – in the form of a shotgun, six cartridges and a woolly hat – which the police had recovered from the defendant's loft. The defendant had alleged that these articles were planted upon him by the officers. But where would these officers have got possession of such items? It could only be that they had got them from another criminal; the man who *was* responsible for the robbery and shooting.

'But *why*, members of the jury, should two police-officers of lengthy experience and wholly unblemished characters, choose to risk their careers and their liberty by setting free one criminal in an endeavour to convict another, innocent one?'

There would be no sense whatever to it. These wicked allegations by the defendant could be seen for what they truly were: the last gasps of a drowning man, desperate to save his skin. Similarly, the suggestion that those same long-suffering officers had planted samples of the bank's plaster in the defendant's shoes, was yet another gasp for air, equally desperate, and, Croft felt bound to say, '. . . equally wicked . . .'

The defence had been unable to cast so much as a mote of dust on the solid, highly-polished table of evidence that had been constructed by the prosecution and its witnesses, and, with the conclusion of his address, Croft left the jury no alternative but to return a verdict of *Guilty*, on each and every count.

Beecher, though, who next addressed the jury, hopped up on that solid, highly-polished table of evidence, and began jumping all over it, doing his best to scratch and gouge its flat, smooth surface.

MacHale was a thoroughly unreliable witness who bore a grudge against the defendant. Further, he was largely inexperienced and almost wholly incompetent, and, what was more – if what had already passed wasn't sufficient – , should never even have been *inside* that bank on the day of the robbery, because police-officers were not *entitled* to enter private premises, unless in the course of their *official* duties . . .

MacHale, Beecher went on, had not immediately identified the defendant as the man who had shot him, because he had *no idea* who had shot him . . .

The jury, claimed Beecher, had no alternative, unpalatable though it might be, but to conclude that Bruno and Bell, having negotiated some kind of sordid deal with the *real* perpetrator of the robbery, had then informed MacHale that the *defendant* was the man who had shot him; *that* was why it had taken MacHale a week to identify, in writing, the defendant, prior to picking him out on a parade at the police station.

And, speaking of Bruno and Bell . . . Well, a pair of more thoroughly untrustworthy witnesses would be virtually impossible to isolate . . . although the court had seen and heard from *one* who was at least their equal, in the form of the witness, Francis James.

Bruno's past conduct had, on his own admission, been complained of on no less than twenty-five separate occasions. Of course, Bruno had blithely shrugged away these matters, claiming that they had been vigorously investigated and found unsubstantiated. Investigated by *whom*, though? By a *fellow police-officer*.

'Likewise, Bruno's confederate, Bell, is similarly wanting in so far as credibility is concerned. You may think – and I entertain you to do so – that Bell would willingly corroborate *anything* which his superior had put to him, in an effort to further his own career.'

James, too, was utterly untrustworthy as a prosecution witness; he had profited financially by informing on the defendant, having received a sum of money from the Police-Informers' Fund. He was a Judas, but, worse still, his betrayal was false, for the defendant was entirely innocent. Bruno had a hold over this witness, and was blackmailing him – threatening to arrest and imprison him if he retracted his false evidence . . .

Of course, the defendant, too, had a lengthy criminal-record; but here was a man who was saying, 'Look here, I openly admit I've erred, in the past, but if I had committed *these* crimes, I would confess my guilt. I deny them because I'm wholly innocent . . .' By the way, he sent his apologies, from below in the cells, and sincerely trusted that his admittedly bad behaviour would not prejudice the jury's deliberations . . .

As for the defendant's wife . . . One could feel nothing but admiration for her loyalty and courage in coming here to her husband's aid, at his most dismal hour.

Croft was entirely wrong: it was the jury's clear duty to *acquit* Schofield.

But now it was the turn of the judge. His would be the final word, and in *his* own way he'd put matters straight. 'Members of the jury,' the judge began, adjusting his pince-nez as he turned aside in his throne to face the twelve men and women. 'You may think that the issues in question, here, are simple enough. And you would be right in so thinking; although, I'm bound to say, they may at times have seemed convoluted . . .' He broke off, shooting Beecher a contemptuous glance, which the jury tracked and took note of.

'However, I shall attempt to make matters even plainer as I assist you in the preparation of your verdicts. Let me say, first of all, that certain facts are immutable: a robbery *was* committed, and a young police-officer *was* shot. These matters cannot, then, be disputed, and, indeed, have been reinforced by the most lucid and striking of evidence . . . the evidence of Police Constable MacHale, the evidence of Miss Asher, the young bank-clerk, the corroborating evidence of the video film, and, lastly, the evidence of the shotgun pellets which were removed from the officer's body and from the bank's ceiling and walls.

'There it is, then: a young-girl clerk was terrorized, twenty-five hundred pounds was stolen, and a courageous police-officer was most grievously wounded when attempting to uphold the law and apprehend the offender. But now we are posed the question, "Who *was* the man carrying out this robbery and shooting?" The prosecution says it was the defendant, Frederick Schofield. The defence says it was some other man. This, therefore, is the premier issue to be determined.

'First, let us consider the evidence of Constable MacHale. He was there, *in* the bank, *witnessing* the crimes, and stated, under Oath, that he was afforded a good opportunity of looking upwards towards the *part*-masked face of the perpetrator, who was standing above him, brandishing a sawn-off shotgun. Later, he identified that face as belonging to the defendant; was in *no doubt* about it having been him, and went on to walk an identification parade and select the defendant from among eleven other men of similar age, height, build and physical appearance. The defence, of course, challenges this identification, alleging that MacHale could not possibly have seen sufficient of the robber's face, at the time when the crime was committed, to permit him to conclude that he *was* looking at the defendant.

'I'm bound to point out, however, that MacHale was familiar with the defendant's physical appearance, having *lawfully* arrested him on an earlier date, in connection with another matter, which, quite fairly and properly, was not pursued.

'There it is, then, members of the jury: if you accept Constable MacHale's evidence, you *will* be satisfied that the defendant was the man who entered that bank, with intent to steal and to discharge a firearm.

'Next we come to the evidence of the detective officers in this case: Chief Inspector Bruno and Sergeant Bell. Their testimony was clear, and supported by written notes which they made shortly after their search of the defendant's house. They claim that they found in the defendant's loft, a sawn-off shotgun, six cartridges, and a woollen bobble-hat of the type which the part-masked bank robber was wearing. The defendant claims that they planted this evidence upon him, and that they went even further and impregnated the soles of his shoes with samples of plaster from the bank's ceiling and floor. There it is, then: a straight conflict of evidence, you may think.

'But let me return you to Mister Croft's closing address, when he invited you to ask yourselves where the two detectives could have got possession of the shotgun, the cartridges and the woollen hat. The invitation is still open, members of the jury. The implication is that the detectives stole these articles from a criminal, planted them upon the defendant, and accused him of crimes he did not commit. But to what end? What *point* would there be in the police setting *free* one criminal – a guilty one – , and setting *up* an innocent one? It is for you to decide. But bear in mind that you are to take account of the characters here involved: Mister Bruno and Mister Bell, two officers who, unblemished, stood before you, and offered clear, concise accounts of their conduct; and Schofield, who made the allegations but failed to offer evidence – other than his *uncorroborated* word – in support of them, and who, what is more, resorted to violence and the most *foul* of outbursts when under cross-examination in the witness box . . .'

'Make these assessments of the witnesses' characters, then,' continued the judge, 'and decide for yourselves which evidence to prefer and which to reject.'

Next, the judge examined the evidence of James, and the question of his reliability.

'The defence has suggested, members of the jury, that Mister Bruno, having an unspecified hold over James, was able to coerce him and compel his testimony. But did Mister Bruno strike *you* as the type of man who would consort with blackmail, or as the sort of man who would have *no* truck with dishonesty, or even corner-cutting, in an effort to do his job?'

The judge went on: 'It is my duty to warn you that

James's testimony must be treated with the utmost caution. Were it not corroborated, it undoubtedly wouldn't stand. Therefore, you must ask yourselves what there is to support it, and look to the evidence of Constable MacHale, as well as the detective officers, Mister Bruno and Mister Bell, slotting it all together to see if it makes a picture out of a puzzle.

The judge proceeded to examine Schofield's alibi, contrasting the evidence of Schofield's wife with the prosecution's near-destruction of it, so that, in effect, the jury would no doubt find her lacking in credibility. At the conclusion of his summing-up, he'd laid out every piece of evidence there was and the pile on Croft's side was by far taller and more solidly founded than the pile on Beecher's side.

In his final words to the jury, the judge said, 'There it is, then. Now go away, appoint a foreman from amongst yourselves, and consider your verdicts, attempting to arrive at a unanimous decision in respect of each indictment.'

It was two o'clock – the judge having extended the morning session to accommodate his summing-up – , and the next few . . . hours? . . . minutes? . . . *days*? – MacHale hadn't a clue *how* long it would take for the jury to deliberate – would be a tense, drawn-out period of time.

'How long d'you reckon it'll take, sir?' MacHale asked Bruno, when the jury was gone and the court had recessed.

Bruno shrugged as if he didn't really care. 'Who knows? Might be two minutes, two hours, or two *weeks*.'

'*Weeks*?' intoned MacHale, incredulous.

'Well, maybe not *weeks*,' conceded Bruno. 'But it could be a couplea days. I had a fraud case, once, where the jury was out for *four* days.'

'Four *days*?' said MacHale. 'Christ, what were they doing for four *days*?'

'Fuck knows,' said Bruno. 'On the mornin of the fifth day – a Friday, like today – they came back an told us they'd slung it. Got homesick, I should think. They couldn't make head nor tail of the evidence, anyway.' He rose from his seat, stacking his papers and placing them in his briefcase. 'Come on. Let's go an get a cuppa tea an a bite to eat.' He walked towards the exit.

MacHale followed him, not feeling hungry, thinking about what Bruno had just said. The jury had got *homesick*, and hadn't *understood* the evidence, anyway. So they'd *slung* it, just to get *away*.

So, there really *wasn't* any such thing as justice.

Two hours later, the court reassembled, and the jury was sent for, the judge wanting to know if a verdict was near to being reached.

The foreman, a middle-aged black man with shiny, oily skin, told the judge that they were almost ready to deliver their verdicts, but needed just a little longer. Accordingly, the judge returned the jurors to their room, and the court went back into recess. Had there been no likelihood of a verdict, today, the judge would undoubtedly have adjourned the proceedings until tomorrow morning, and the jurors would have been taken away for the night, to a hotel.

'What d'you reckon, sir?' MacHale asked Bruno, when they were back in the corridor outside the court.

Bruno sat on a padded bench and stretched out his legs. 'Who knows? But with a fork-'n'-spoon as foreman, *anythin* can happen.'

'An probably *will*,' put in Bell.

MacHale shrugged, and yawned. *Fork-'n'-spoon?* . . . Ah, got it: *Coon*. It was just to be hoped that he didn't have teenaged kids who were forever being pulled by the law and asked to turn-out their pockets. If he *did* have, then here was his chance to avenge them.

At five o'clock, the court PC came along the corridor and informed Bruno that the jury was returning to deliver its verdicts.

'Keep your fingers crossed,' said Bruno, leading the way into court.

And MacHale began hoping like hell. It wasn't *supposed* to concern you, a jury's or a Magistrate's verdict, but . . .

When the court was assembled and waiting, the jury was led back to its enclosure in the hushed, expectant room, each of its members taking a quick glance at Schofield, who at last was back in the dock, having been finally warned, by the judge, against any further outbursts.

MacHale, noting the jurors' oblique glances towards the dock, felt disheartened. He'd once heard someone at the nick say that if jurors looked at the defendant when they were returning to deliver their verdict, it didn't bode well for the prosecution: jurors would *never* look at a man whom they were about to convict and have put away. So, MacHale began hoping even harder.

The clerk walked to the jurors' enclosure and stood before it, asking the foreman to stand. 'Have you reached a verdict in respect of the defendant? Answer *Yes* or *No*.'

'Yes,' said the shiny-faced middle-aged black man.

MacHale held his breath, and heard his heart, thumping in his inner ear. Schofield pushed back his shoulders, heaved out his chest, and braced himself, physically and mentally, for what was about to come.

'Count One,' the clerk was now saying, 'charges Frederick Schofield with attempted murder. How do you find him? Guilty, or not guilty?'

'Guilty,' the foreman unhesitantly said.

'Count Two charges Frederick Schofield with robbery. How do you find him? Guilty or not guilty?'

'Guilty.'

'Count Three charges Frederick Schofield with possessing a shotgun whose barrel had been shortened to a length of less than twenty-four inches. How do you find him? Guilty or not guilty?'

'Guilty.'

'And are these the verdicts of you all?'

'Yes.'

'Be seated, please.'

MacHale expelled his breath, and the banging ceased inside his ear. He glanced at Schofield, noting that his shoulders had sagged, his chest had concaved, and his head, moving slowly from side-to-side, was hanging forward over his chest; the verdicts had all but knocked the life out of him, and for the moment he was merely existing, totally bewildered. The sound of weeping from the public gallery drifted down and settled over the hushed court; MacHale glanced up and saw Schofield's wife, crying into a handkerchief, being comforted by a brassy-looking girl who resembled a tom; maybe she was Schofield's daughter.

Bruno, looking unmoved by the verdicts, was making his way to the witness box, taking a sheaf of papers from his briefcase. When he reached the box, Croft began taking him through the list of Schofield's previous – thirty, in all, for offences ranging from petty theft to aggravated burglary. When that was done, Croft then led Bruno through Schofield's antecedent history; usual stuff: left school at fifteen, had a score of odd-jobs – an unverifiable record – , and didn't appear or claim to have done anything decent, honest or worthwhile, ever since; married, with a three-year-old son, and a fifteen-year-old daughter from an earlier, dissolved relationship, he owned his own house, in Brixton, which property was worth some fifty thousand pounds, and was unmortgaged . . . Now where the hell did Schofield get the money to buy, outright, a place like that? It was a question which everyone present in the court must have tacitly asked himself. And it didn't take the brains of a lawyer to work out the answer, either.

When Bruno had left the box and returned to his seat on the police benches, Beecher rose and attempted to mitigate Schofield's past and present crimes; more, *usual* stuff: he was underprivileged, now, and as a child, and had fallen into bad company; until now, he hadn't used violence on innocent persons, only on fellow criminals; he knew no other way of life; he was a uxorious man, though, devoted to his children, and was set to turn over a new leaf, if given one last chance. But Beecher's pleas for leniency and mercy were not at all well received by the judge.

When Beecher had finished, the judge took over. 'Frederick Schofield,' he gravely croaked. 'You have been convicted, on the clearest evidence I have *ever* heard, of three despicable crimes, the execution of which made plainer still the already plain truth that you are an evil man, an unrepentant creature, who will stop at nothing in an endeavour to bring to fruition the base ambition which you appear to have formed and nurtured from the very day when you were able to distinguish right from wrong; to wit: to profit at the physical, mental and financial expense of decent, honest citizens.

'Throughout this trial, you have persistently made the most serious of allegations against those police-officers who were involved – one at great, personal cost, in the physical sense – in placing you before this court. However, by its verdicts, the jury has completely exonerated those officers.

'Now, Schofield, you must pay the price of your crimes. It will be heavy, but is designed both to deter you from committing further crimes, upon your release, and to give notice to those who may be of a like mind, that society will not tolerate such wicked, lawless conduct.

'On the first Count, of attempted murder, you will go to prison for Life. On the second Count, of robbery, you will go to prison for fifteen years. On the final Count, of possessing a sawn-off shotgun, you will go to prison for two years; the sentences imposed in respect of Counts Two and Three, to be served concurrent with that imposed for Count One. And I make the recommendation that the Home Secretary should not consider your release until a period of at least twenty-five years has elapsed . . . Take down the prisoner.'

Schofield was gutted. He stood his ground, numbed, motionless, his eyes popping, his mouth hanging open, his body quaking. *Twenty-five years!* He'd be knocking-on for *seventy*, when he came out. The screws at his side turned him around to face the descending stairs at the back of the dock, and led him down.

Above, Schofield's wife began screaming and shrieking from the public gallery, none of it intelligible; the brassy young blonde helped her to her feet and took her out of the gallery.

The judge thanked the jurors for their patience and attention throughout the trial, and then called before him the police-officers involved in the case.

When Bruno, Bell and MacHale were abreast beneath his dais, the judge spoke, his croak saturated with emotion: 'How can the law-abiding public even begin to commend or honour such officers as have been before this court during the trial of Frederick Schofield? It is nigh on impossible . . . but I shall make a best attempt . . . The courage and determination displayed by the young Constable, MacHale, was far above and beyond that demanded or expected of *any* police-officer. Society has been bankrupted by the debt which it owes him.

'The detective officers, too, did not shirk their duties in embarking upon the most perilous of missions, in that they entered the house of an armed and infamously dangerous criminal, who had already attempted to murder a colleague, in order to implement the law.

'These, then, are men we must admire and be eternally grateful to. They have upheld the finest traditions of the finest police-force the world knows.'

The judge rose from his throne. For a moment, MacHale just stood there, watching the judge's departure, his face burning with a mixture of pride and embarrassment, emotion choking him.

'Come on, my son,' Bruno told him, smiling, and led him out of court.

'*That* was a result-an-a-half,' said Bell, lighting a cigarette when they'd reached the corridor.

'Hmm,' agreed MacHale. 'He wasn't a bad judge, after all, was he?'

'The jurors weren't bad judges, either,' said Bruno. Then, to Bell: 'Shoot across the road, my son, and line the drinks up. *We* got some celebratin to do.' He reached into the outside breast pocket of his suit, fished out a five-pound note, and gave it to Bell.

'Just leave it to me, guv,' Bell eagerly said, and was on his way, leading MacHale by the right arm, to pick up his civvy jacket from the police-room.

Bruno watched them depart, then walked back into the court, to have a word with Frankie James.

MacHale and Bell walked across the road from the court buildings and entered the saloon bar of *The Ship*, looking casually about as they made their way up to the counter; the first thing on any cop's mind when he entered a pub, was to know what sort of place it was and who of any note was in there. Here, though, at five forty-five, fifteen minutes after opening time, there was just a handful of lone office workers, who'd dropped in on their way home.

'Wha's it gonna be, then?' asked Bell, as they reached the bar. 'A dropa shampoo? A large gold-watch? . . . A *bottlea* gold-watch? It's the guv'nor's dough.'

MacHale laughed. 'Just a pint of lager, please, Sarge.'

'Pinta Forsyth Saga, an a paira large Scotches,' Bell told the young Australian barman, who had shoulderlength greasy hair and dirty clothes. 'Oh, an a packeta peanuts, an all.'

The barman delivered the drinks and poured the nuts into a clean, glass ashtray.

MacHale raised his pint. 'Cheers.' And took a long, gulping swallow of the lager, feeling the gas-bubbles burn his throat, gasping for air when he'd downed half the contents of the dimpled mug. Then he shook his head, in wonder. He was still on a high from that result across the road. 'We came away from that, really sweet, didn't we, Sarge?' he said to Bell. 'I can scarcely believe what the judge said, at the end of it. About us, I mean.'

Bell shifted a mouthful of nuts to the right side of his face, swelling out his cheek, and paused in his chewing and crunching of them. 'About *you*, son, ya mean. If it hadn't've been for you, we'd never've got Schofield down.' Now he took a sip of his Scotch, before sucking up another handful of nuts.

MacHale picked out one nut from the ashtray, and thoughtfully chewed it, coming down several stages, as he wondered how Schofield, and Schofield's wife, must be feeling, right now.

Then Bruno, James, and James' two guards came into the pub, Bruno now looking as pleased as James had always looked depressed.

'Here ya go, guv,' Bell said to Bruno, handing him his large Scotch and his change from the fiver he'd donated for the round of drinks.

'Good luck,' said Bruno, and took a swallow of his drink. Then, after handing his change to one of the two detectives who were minding James, telling him to get himself, his companion, and James, a drink, he turned to MacHale, patted his right shoulder, and said, 'T'riffic stuff, my son. That wicked bastard, Schofield, won't be givin *us* any more aggravation for a long while.'

MacHale just smiled, rather weakly, and didn't know why he was starting to feel so low. It was probably the idea of what his evidence had done to Schofield, and to Schofield's family, that had depressed him. Maybe it was the sight of James, too . . .? And what was James doing in *here*, anyway, drinking with them . . .?

'I'm just gonna have a chat with Frankie,' Bruno told Bell. 'See y'in a minute.' And he moved away, down to the end of the bar, where the other men had settled with their drinks.

Bell looked at MacHale. 'Cheer *up*,' he insisted. 'This is a celebration, not a fuckin *wake*. Anyone'd think it was *you* who'd just drawn a pony, over the road.'

MacHale's eyes came back into focus, and he smiled again, more strongly this time. Yeah, kick the gloom, he told himself. *Stop* thinking like a bloody social-worker. This *is* a celebration, and after we've left here, and I've been back to the section-house, washed, changed and phoned the good news to Pat, the celebration'll go on all night. He picked up his glass and swallowed some more lager.

'. . .'Course,' Bell was saying. 'If y'ever wanna join the Department, this little lot'll stand y'in a treat. Y'know . . . give ya somethin to talk about, on a Board.'

'Never really thought about that,' said MacHale, but now began to. The CID? . . . No. He shrugged. 'Dunno if I'd like it.' What he actually meant was that he didn't think he could live with all the strokes he'd heard say they pulled in the CID.

'Oh, you'd like it,' assured Bell. 'Once you got settled into it. T'riffic life, it is. 'Specially on the Squad, where you've still got your autonomy, and can actually *do* the job you're s'posed to be doin.' He finished his Scotch, and turned around, catching the barman's eye. 'Same again?' he asked MacHale, when the barman was standing before them, ready to take the order.

'Oh, cheers,' said MacHale, and finished his pint.

Then, while the barman was pouring the drinks, and while Bell was watching the barman, money at the ready, MacHale's eyes wandered along to the far end of the room, where Bruno, the two minders, and James, were in conversation. James still looked miserable . . . And why not? thought MacHale. In a way, James was no better off than Schofield; on the outside, each of them was finished . . . And now Bruno and James were leaving the two minders at the bar; moving away, to sit at a table in the centre of the room . . .

Maybe Bruno was about to try and reassure James, try and justify his actions for him? But MacHale was in no doubt that if any of Freddie Schofield's firm got hold of James, the grass was as good as dead . . . Bruno, talking earnestly, a full glass of Scotch in his right hand, was sitting at the far side of the table . . . James, a pint of bitter in his right hand, was sitting opposite, setting down his pint, drawing-in his chair, leaning back, pulling up, from the knees, the legs of his trousers . . . settling his feet, hooking the toes of his shoes around the front legs of the chair . . . now, leaning forward, resting his elbows on the top of the table as his hands moved up to support the black-shadowed chin of his sagging head . . .

And suddenly a flash of horror streaked in, as a gasp for air through MacHale's mouth, settling as a cold, thunderous bang of terrible realization in his chest; he was mesmerized by the shock of what he was seeing and experiencing . . . It came all at once . . .

Deja vu!

His brain went hurtling back to the day of the bank robbery . . . slowed . . . deposited him on the bank's floor, then speeded-up again, rushing him through the frames which portrayed him lying face-down, reaching for his stick . . . viciously swinging it at the gunman's right leg, *showing* him that leg, blotting out everything else except the rising trouserleg, the white calf, the ankle . . . *the tattoo! . . . just above the ankle . . . a small, faded-blue rose!* . . . Now, the flashback stopping, pulsating before his eyes, freezing the frame, zooming it back and forth . . . *a hazy, round, blue-coloured orb; the rose; the orb . . . the-rose-the-orb-the-rose . . . THE ROSE!* . . . the vision, stark, now fully merged with the vision which was here before his eyes . . .

It was James!

That same *leg*, that same *tattoo*, just above the right ankle . . .

'Oh, Jesus Christ,' mumbled MacHale, and he felt himself stagger sideways as he turned away, unable any longer to look at what he'd seen.

'Here ya go,' said Bell, handing him a fresh pint of lager. 'Give that a seein to.'

MacHale's left hand made a grab for the glass, sloshing its contents onto the carpet as he swung it up to his mouth and gulped down, in one go, what was left of the lager. Then, gasping, his head spinning, he ran for the street, clutching his belly, not knowing where he was making for or what he'd be doing, after he'd thrown-up in the gutter.

Bell frowned, then shrugged, then swallowed a mouthful of Scotch, then shook his head in disgust. 'Fuckin amateur drinkers,' he muttered, and walked along the bar, to join Bruno and James.

29

A DC had tackled and detained a robber who was armed with an imitation firearm; a young PC had sustained serious, personal injury while disarming a mentally-deranged man who was threatening passers-by with a meat-cleaver; a DS had exposed himself to great physical danger by successfully infiltrating a team of drug smugglers, and obtaining the evidence which had later led to that team's conviction and imprisonment; an off-duty PC had suffered a hairline fracture of the skull, when arresting a professional burglar whom he'd stopped in possession of stolen antiques; the three-man crew of an RT-car had shown complete disregard for their own personal safety, by pursuing to arrest, in their vehicle and, subsequently, on foot, a team of armed robbers who had discharged firearms at them; and, finally, a PC had been shot and wounded when attempting to apprehend a robber in possession of a sawn-off shotgun.

Each of these officers had displayed great initiative, courage, determination, and devotion to duty, and each was here, today, in the front row of tiered seats which occupied most of the space in the large, CO briefing-room, to be highly commended by the Commissioner of Police. All, save one, were accompanied by wives, girlfriends and mothers and fathers, and three had brought along their teenaged sons and daughters. All, save one, were proud to be here, and would savour every moment of the impending ceremony.

MacHale sat there, alone, feeling worthless, and fraudulent, and depressed, his innards ripped apart by the undeniable knowledge of what he'd done. Schofield was serving a quarter of a century for three crimes he hadn't committed, and had recently been refused leave to appeal.

So what? some might have said. Schofield was a pro' blagger who'd only have gone on, anyway, to *commit* what he'd wrongfully been convicted of, had MacHale's evidence not put him away; he *deserved* to be where he now was; why worry? And there was more than a vestige of truth in that, too. But . . . It still wasn't *right;* that was the thing; it contravened a principle which MacHale had tried hard to honour ever since he'd joined his nick.

There was little consolation for him, either, in the knowledge that he'd only played an unwitting part in the conspiracy that had been scripted and cast by Bruno and Bell, who must have been aware, right from the off, that the National Consolidated job wasn't down to Schofield, but down to James, who, undoubtedly, had provided them with the evidence which they'd later awarded to Schofield. There could be no doubt, either, that Bruno and Bell had been solely motivated by the prospect of financial gain. MacHale wondered just *how* much of a drink James had had to put into them, in exchange for his liberty. A few grand, probably . . . at least. Jesus, it was sickening.

What most nauseated MacHale, though, was how they'd used *him*. They'd been so convincing, had seemed so straight, so professional. But there wasn't a thing MacHale could do by way of retaliatory action, and he wondered just how much longer the nights would deprive him of restful sleep, while the days besieged his mind with worry and guilt.

On more than one occasion in the past weeks, a determined resolve had started him on his way to the CIB, to confess all he knew about the Schofield job. But each time, he'd surrendered to the fear of what might happen when he got there. He'd made an honest mistake in wrongfully identifying Schofield; he'd been *told* it was Schofield who'd pulled the blag, and after he'd begun matching the mental picture of the part-masked face of the robber, with the recollection of Schofield's features, it had all seemed to melt into one, so that he'd become *certain*.

But would *they* see it that way? Then there'd be Bell and Bruno, not to mention the exhibital and forensic evidence, to deny it.

There was nothing to be done, then; except toss and turn at night, and worry like hell during the day; and, now, be present, here, to be highly commended for having aided and abetted a criminal conspiracy.

A side door opened, and the assembled company stood and watched as the Commissioner entered and made his way to a raised platform at the front of the room, followed by the AC(C), five District Commanders, and a reporter and photographer from the force's internal newspaper, *The Job*. While the AC(C) and Commanders sat at a long, polished-wood table, the Commissioner – a diminutive, bespectacled, balding figure, who looked more like an Archbishop than a cop – , stood before a lectern and began delivering his address.

'Ladies and gentlemen, we are here, today, to pay tribute to eight officers who, by their outstanding acts of gallantry when confronted by armed and dangerous criminals, have enhanced the very finest traditions of this service.'

And he went on at great length to commend not only the officers before him but the police-force in general.

Each officer was called in turn to receive his Certificate of Commendation, the Commissioner eulogizing each man before he came forward.

And so it went on, MacHale sitting there, listening but not hearing, wishing that he were *anywhere* but here, dreading the moment when he would be called out to receive his Certificate . . . wishing like hell that he could summon-up the courage to jump to his feet and run away . . . where, didn't matter . . .

He was last on the list, and the Commissioner was announcing his name: 'Police Constable MacHale . . . This young officer, not yet out of his probationary period of service, displayed remarkable courage and determination in tackling a man armed with a sawn-off shotgun. The man had robbed a bank of several thousands of pounds, and had discharged one barrel of his weapon into the ceiling of the premises, yet the officer, knowing full well what lay before him, and armed only with a truncheon, made a gallant and resourceful effort to disarm and detain him.

'The officer was shot in the side, and sustained serious harm, but, happily, made a full recovery and was able to provide officers of the Central Robbery-Squad with information that led to the offender's arrest, conviction and imprisonment. The officer was also commended at the Crown Court . . .'

The Commissioner collected the Certificate of High Commendation, and waited for MacHale to join him at his lectern on the raised platform.

MacHale stood, and walked forward, his heart beating fast, his face glowing, his legs unsteady; onlookers probably believed him to be affected by an inner coalescence of pride, embarrassment and nervousness; but, in truth, he was affected by a guilt-and-shame-inspired sickness that threatened, at any moment, to drop him on his knees.

He made it, though, and fed the Commissioner his right hand, while his left hand took hold of the proffered Certificate.

The Commissioner grinned, benignly, and pumped MacHale's right hand, saying, in a low voice, 'Very well done, MacHale. I hear you're sitting your Final, next week. Best of luck.'

MacHale just swallowed hard, and nodded, unable to manage even a weak smile, the applause from the audience thundering painfully in his ears and head. He turned to depart, but the Commissioner wouldn't release his hand, and wouldn't give-up the Certificate, not until *The Job's* photographer had taken a picture of the presentation.

Then, MacHale about-turned and walked back to his seat, breathing heavily, disturbed by the approving eyes and congratulatory faces which he knew were trained upon him. He just stared at his feet, and craved dismissal.

'And now,' said the Commissioner, 'let us depart from here, and partake of a little refreshment.' He smiled, turned away, and led his senior officers from the room, the audience taking up the rear.

MacHale made sure he'd be last out of the door, and when he was, he turned right – in the direction opposite that which the others had taken – and walked quickly away along the wide corridor, past the portraits of former Commissioners of Police, tearing to shreds the Certificate of High Commendation, as he made for the lifts . . . allowing the pieces to fall from his hands and flutter down onto the carpeted floor.

He felt like crying, and wished he were . . . *dead*.

It wasn't until the next morning that he felt he really did have the guts to go through with it; and it *would* take guts, ending it all, like that. When he'd arrived back from CO, early yesterday afternoon, he'd gone straight to bed, exhausted and depressed, all the while thinking that he *had* to do it because there was just no way he could go on. And yet he wasn't sure. There was one last challenge for him; his Final Exam. He wanted to sit it, and pass. *Then* he could do it, and no one would be able to say that he'd *only* done it because he was afraid of failure.

Next week, then, he'd do it . . . But today was only Wednesday. He'd never make it till next week; the stress would drive him crazy, well before then.

For most of the *night*, he'd lain awake, wondering whether to do it.

It was Sid Broadbent, the warden, who finally decided him.

Sid came crashing through the door of MacHale's room, at nine-thirty A.M., shouting, 'Wakey-Wakey! . . . Come on, up an at it!'

'Sid!' exclaimed MacHale, fully awake and starting to rise. 'Hang on a minute. What d'you do when you've gotta make an important decision in your life, and you just can't make your mind up?'

'Like when you're at a crossroads?' asked Sid.

'Yeah . . . I s'pose.'

Sid tilted aside his head, grimaced, and thought about it. 'You look at all the signposts, study your map, and *make* a decision. Then, you go one of four ways: left, right, straight on, or back the way you came – although sometimes you *can't* go back, 'cause the road's blocked off. That's what life's all about. What you *never* do, though, is stay put. That's fatal, that is.' He stared hopefully at MacHale. 'Look at me. I stayed put, and got lashed around by the elements.'

MacHale's eyes were far-off, introspective. 'Thanks,' he abstractedly muttered. 'Thanks, Sid.'

And Sid walked out, closing the door.

Now it seemed clear, very easy to discern. *He* couldn't go back; and neither could he go forward; but there was only *one* other signpost at this juncture of his route, and that directed him to the right. He jumped out of bed and began climbing into his clothes.

He'd *do* it. *Now*. Right this minute.

30

The phone rang for what seemed like an age, before it was answered.

He fed-in a pile of ten-pence pieces, the rapid pip-pipping noises ceased, and he spoke: 'Pat?'

'*John!*' she shouted. 'I was beginning to think I'd never again *hear* from you.'

'Yeah, well . . . What can I say? I'm sorry, for a start, I s'pose. But . . . well, my head's been going round, with all that's happened, of late.'

'Like what?' – she sounded concerned.

He hesitated, and sighed. 'I'll tell you when I see you.'

'*What* did you say?' she demanded. 'Do you mean . . .?'

'Mm-hm.' Now he was smiling a huge smile. 'I'm coming to join you . . . If you still want me, that is.'

She shrieked with delight. 'Oh, John! I can't *believe* it. Do you *really* mean it?'

'Yes,' he said, and found himself nodding, then laughing. 'It's taken me a long time to decide, but now that I have, I just want to get there as quickly as I can.'

'Where are you now?' she asked.

'In the section-house . . . the residents' phone-booth. I've put my papers in . . . this morning . . . and I'm using-up all my time-off and annual leave, so's I won't have to work-out a month's notice. I can be down there with you tomorrow morning.'

'Hang on, hang on,' she said, her voice losing its excited timbre. 'Are you sure, I mean *absolutely* sure, that you really want to commit yourself to this?'

'Yes. Certain,' he unhesitantly told her; he no longer had to consider it.

'Well . . . I hope you *are* sure, John, because – '

'What?' he said. 'I've told you, haven't I? I've got no doubts *at all,* Pat. Not now. I *want* you, *need* you . . . *love* you . . .' He paused, then quickly said, 'Marry me. Please? I'll beg you, let you pull me around the house on a collar and lead . . . live in a *tent* with you . . . *anything*, so long as I'm with you.'

'Oh, John . . .' She was crying. 'I'm so *happy*. I thought I'd *never* hear you say it – propose to me, I mean.'

'Well, maybe I was frightened to commit myself, before. But this morning . . . I dunno, it was all so clear. I just knew I wanted to do it. Anyway, Pat, you were saying, a moment ago, you hoped I was sure, *because*. Because *what*?'

She hesitated. 'Because it won't just be me you're committing yourself to.'

'I know *that*,' he said. 'There's the business and everything, and I'm looking forward to learning about – '

'No,' she cut in. 'It's not just *that*. There'll be three of us.'

For a moment, he was silent, thinking . . . And then it hit him. 'You *don't* mean . . .?'

'Yes,' she confirmed. 'I'm – *we're* – having a baby, John.'

'That's wonderful,' he shouted. 'I'm over the moon, thrilled . . . *everything*. Oh, Christ, I'm happy, Pat . . . But, here . . . Why didn't you tell me this before? I take it you've known for a while, now.'

'Yes,' she said. 'That was why I left The Job, so abruptly. I didn't tell you because I was afraid you might have considered that my pregnancy *obliged* you to come and support me. And I didn't want you here unless you'd made a carefully thought-out decision, unaffected by any suggestion that it was your *duty*, regardless of your *true* feelings. That's why I've all along been insisting that if you came you should come for good. And I'd decided that if you *did* make up your mind to come for good, I'd tell you, then – like I'm doing now – , and you'd still have a chance to reconsider.'

'Oh, Pat,' he mumbled, and felt his eyes becoming wet. 'And I was accusing you of an attempt at emotional blackmail, while all along you've been trying to practise the exact *opposite* . . . I'm sorry, I really am sorry.'

'There's nothing to regret, or apologize for, John,' she told him. 'Everything's come okay.'

The pips began sounding, and MacHale fed-in his last two coins.

'Look, Pat, I'll be down, first thing tomorrow. On the train, the bus, a taxi, I dunno, I'll get there somehow. I can't *wait* to get there.'

'I'll send Diego,' she said. 'In the car. It'll be quicker and more comfortable. What time?'

'Ten?'

'Okay. See you, John.' And she blew him a kiss, down the line.

After replacing the receiver, he just stood there in the booth, his eyes glazed. He could scarcely believe it; *him*, a father.

A surge of energy ripped through him, and he felt a strength of vitality he'd never before experienced. He didn't know *what* to do . . . Shriek, scream, laugh . . . Christ, was he euphoric . . .

In the end, he just settled for going along to Sid Broadbent's office, a huge grin on his face, and kissing the old boy on the forehead. '*I'm* getting *married*,' he announced, chuckling. 'I'm going upstairs, I'm gonna pack my bags, and I'm gonna *get* myself *married*.' And off he went, leaving a bemused Sid to stand there, scratching his head.

* * *

When he spotted Diego, turning the red XJ6 into the yard, manoeuvring it into a parking space, he collected his bags and dashed along the corridor, making for the stairs.

As he reached the bottom of the section-house steps, Diego climbed out of the Jaguar, saw him, and walked towards him, arms outstretched, a smile splitting his face. 'Senor *John!*' he enthused, hugging MacHale, and lightly kissing each of his cheeks. 'How good to esee you again. Welcome to home.'

'Thanks, Diego,' MacHale warmly said, smiling, but feeling a little embarrassed by the cheek-kissing. 'I can't wait to get there.'

He loaded his bags into the car's boot, took a lingering, backward glance at the section-house, and felt a twinge of sadness. He'd be taking a lot of memories along with him . . . some good, some bad . . . *mostly* bad, maybe. But everything else, everything tangible, he was leaving, discarding, shedding. And he wouldn't miss *any* of it. He was sure.

As he turned away, opening the car's door, an old PC from D-Relief came out of the nick's charge-room door, way across the yard; he paused, waiting for a new, probationary PC to fall into step with him. MacHale watched them walk off, out onto the streets, thinking that the new cop stood little or no chance of having fulfilled expectations of The Job; he was with a Cowboy; it was, as it invariably was, a case of the partially sighted leading the blind.

MacHale sat beside Diego, closed the door, and fastened his seat-belt. 'Let's go, Diego,' he said. 'And don't stop till we're there.'

Epilogue

He stood before the window in the front room of the cottage, and looked out over the three gardens, towards the snow-covered thatch of the restaurant, squinting his eyes against the translucent white glare.

It began the day before yesterday, late in the evening, and had stopped only this morning, having buried everything beneath a deep, fluffy duvet of crystallized ice.

Earlier today, he'd cleared the patio, and he and Pat had built a snowman: just a tall, plump torso of packed snow, with a large, round head, a carrot for a nose, an over-ripe banana for a smiling mouth, and two black-buttons for twinkling eyes; when they'd finished laughing at their creation, they'd gone rummaging in the garage, and had come up with an old cloth cap, a briar, and a red-wool scarf, adjusting these accessories until an inanimate block of snow had become an ebullient, grinning, pipe-smoking winter-grandfather.

Before him, the lawns were alive with birds, squabbling over the scatterings of breadcrumbs and maize-flakes which MacHale had spread over the snow. Tonight, he'd crumble two loaves of bread in some tin dishes, splash milk onto them, and leave them on the patio; and then, as they did on most nights, he and Pat would sit before the french windows, waiting in the firelit darkness to see what arrived for its supper; just the foxes and badgers, probably – the hedgehogs were long since in hibernation.

It would be Christmas in six days. The anticipation of it would never fail to thrill him. That magic which his parents had created for him when he was a kid – which all parents create for all kids – would never entirely be lost to him. Okay, so they lied, like *all* parents lied: there was *no* Father Christmas, and *no* fairies, and *no* Rudolph or Toyland. Christ, it was heartbreaking, too . . . all those images destroyed. But the magic was somehow *in*destructible. Everyone had his excuse – and plenty of people *needed* one – for being happy, carefree and sociable . . .

For the moment, though, MacHale felt . . . He wasn't sure *how* he felt; a little sad, maybe, and a little remorseful; helpless, and . . . just bad, really. He'd been thinking how happy he now was, and how this was going to be the best Christmas he'd ever had. The restaurant was closed until New Year, the staff having been sent away on a fortnight's holiday, and he and Pat had got a whole week to prepare for the forthcoming celebration; both their families were coming to stay with them – Pat's mother and father, his own mother and father – , so there was a lot of preparatory work to be done, before Christmas Eve. It was going to be a real, family Christmas, with laughter and warmth and happiness and peace, and snapping crackers and paper hats and pleasant surprises, replete in every sense, wishing that time would stand still . . .

And then, thinking of how much it meant to him, he'd wondered what it meant to Schofield, for whom time *had* stood still.

What *was* Christmas like, in prison? – if they *had* Christmas, in prison, that was. MacHale could only guess, of course, and supposed that what little joy there was, was completely vitiated by the gloomy environment and absence of family. Just *imagine* it: slopping-out, Christmas morning, and a screw standing guard over you while you ate your Christmas pudding . . . *every* year, for the next *twenty-four* years!

Pat had said he should forget Schofield. Forget The Job. He'd tried hard enough, too, but just couldn't put either out of his mind. He didn't *miss* The Job, and would never consider returning to it, but his *dreams* kept returning him to it, to uniformed duty on the streets.

As for Schofield . . . well, in a way, MacHale had forced himself to accept what had happened, there. Pat had spent hours, on and off, trying to rationalize it with him. If he were to be released he'd only go on to *commit* what he'd been wrongfully imprisoned for. Maybe kill someone . . . That sort of stuff . . . anything to make MacHale feel more at ease with his conscience.

But then, maybe *James* would go out and rob a bank . . . kill someone? There was no answer to that – or perhaps there was, and MacHale couldn't tenant it.

An involuntary sigh parted his lips. He was a believer in Fate, had always believed that *most* things were preordained; and if only he could keep that belief uppermost in his mind, he'd feel a whole lot easier, because what had happened was inevitable, uncontrollable. It was no use saying, *If only*. Somehow, somewhere, sometime, Fate would throw-up a resolution. If a belief was ingrained in you as opposed to instilled in you, there could be no room for doubting its integrity; and if you acted honestly and to the best of your ability, you *couldn't* be all that bad a person . . .

Pat's voice suddenly permeated his thoughts: 'John! Can you help?'

Dressed in blue denims and a chunky, dark-blue sweater, she was standing on a low foot-stool, on the tips of her toes, her right hand extended, trying to hook a silver ball onto one of the uppermost branches of the Christmas tree, in real danger of losing her balance. 'Can you do this, John?' she frustratedly asked, glancing at him. 'You're taller than me.'

He smiled, and moved across the room, to the corner where the tree was planted in a red-crepe-wrapped pot.

After helping her down, he took the ball, reached up, hooked it into place, and said, 'There. How's that?'

She nodded her satisfaction. 'Just right. Now . . . The *final* touch . . .' Pat handed a fairy with lace wings and gold wand to MacHale. 'There we are.'

He took the fairy from Pat, hopped up on the foot-stool, and placed the fairy on the tip of the trunk. 'Okay?' he asked.

'Beautiful,' Pat softly said, and her eyes twinkled.

Arms wrapped around each other's waist, they backed away to the fireplace, and stood there, the flames warming their backs, assessing the day's work: the tree, dripping with glittering, silver balls, twinkling, multi-coloured lights diffusing through its thick green foliage; gaily-coloured paperchains decorating the blackened-oak ceiling beams; looped strings of Christmas cards adorning two of the room's white walls; and gold and silver tinsel glistening along the mantlepiece and the tops of picture-frames.

Now the baby cried, claiming their attention, and they both looked to the settee, where they'd earlier placed the carry-cot.

'He's awake,' said Pat, looking at the carriage clock on the mantlepiece. 'Time for his feed.' And she began moving towards the settee.

'I'll get him,' offered MacHale, and he left Pat's side and plucked John Junior from the cot, raising him up and wrapping a blanket around his tiny body. Junior blinked his eyes, and yawned, and began chewing, with toothless gums, the fingers of his right hand. MacHale jigged him up and down, then held him at arms' length and very gently shook him. 'Hello. Who's awake, then?' At which, Junior began chortling and gurgling and kicking his chubby little legs.

Pat moved to take the baby from MacHale's arms, lying him gently down on the carpet while she began unfastening his plastic pants and nappy. 'He's beautiful, aren't you, John?' And she began tickling the baby's ribs, producing fits of giggles and thrashings of his arms and legs.

MacHale knelt down beside them, assisting with the undressing of the baby.

'What would you like for Christmas, John?' Pat asked MacHale. 'I know it *should* be a surprise, but . . .'

'Well . . .' MacHale considered it, looking at Pat, the baby, his surroundings, thinking of what he'd already got, what he was destined to have, and said, 'Nothing, Pat. I've got everything I want, here, I think.' – he sincerely meant it, too.

They exchanged a lingering kiss, but capped their rising emotions, wanting to get the baby changed and fed. 'Well,' Pat now said, 'what shall we buy the baby, then?'

'No idea,' said MacHale. 'He's too young for most baby-things, isn't he?'

'How about a cowboy outfit?' Pat thoughtfully asked. 'When he's older, I mean.'

MacHale affected a serious countenance, and shook his head. 'The police-force is *not* for *sale*, Pat.' Now he loudly laughed.

'Hmm, I don't know so much about *that*,' said Pat, wrapping the baby's soiled nappy in the plastic pants.

For a moment, MacHale looked deeply disturbed, and intense thoughts spiralled through his head; he felt agitated, and stood, walking to the window, his hands thrust deep into the pockets of his trousers . . . about-turning and walking back to Pat. 'It's no *good*,' he told her. 'I just can't go *on* feeling guilty for the rest of my life. I've *got* to do *something* . . . *see* somebody, tell them *everything*. I'm sick and tired of trying to rationalize what's happened. I *can't* rationalize it.' – *Fate*, perhaps.

Pat rose to her feet, hugging the baby to her chest. She

smiled relievedly, and nodded. 'It had to come from you, John,' she told him. 'Tomorrow, then?'

'Yes,' he agreed. 'Tomorrow.' And as he sighed deeply, the tension drained from his mind and body. He wrapped his arms around Pat and the baby, drawing them close to him, and felt nearer to them and to himself than ever he had before.

Outside, darkness was closing in; the deep layers of snow were alive with minute, sparkling crystals, white and fiery blue; the winter grandfather was serenely smiling as he smoked his pipe; the birds were no longer squabbling over the scattered food; the air was still, and crunchy and biting; feathery white flakes began fluttering gently down from the grey-black skies.

Inside, it was warm and cosy, secure; yellow-black shadows licking up the walls and along the ceiling; gaily-bouncing light from the fire, glancing off the spangling Christmas-tree and the decorations . . .

A large part of MacHale felt that now should never end. But a bigger portion of him longed for tomorrow.